GREGG HURWITZ
We Know

sphere

SPHERE

First published in Great Britain in 2009 by Sphere
This reissue published in 2017 by Sphere

1 3 5 7 9 10 8 6 4 2

A CIP catalogue record for this book
is available from the British Library.

ISBN 978-0-7515-4772-6

Typeset in Minion by M Rules
Printed and bound in Great Britain by Clays Ltd, St Ives plc

Papers used by Sphere are from well-managed forests
and other responsible sources.

MIX
Paper from
responsible sources
FSC® C104740

Sphere
An imprint of
Little, Brown Book Group
Carmelite House
50 Victoria Embankment
London EC4Y 0DZ

An Hachette UK Company
www.hachette.co.uk

www.littlebrown.co.uk

For Robert Crais
Thick and thin

I snapped awake at 2:18 am, the bloodshot numerals staring at me from the nightstand. For years on end, I woke up at this exact time every night, regardless of what time zone I was in. But after seventeen years, I had just started sleeping through the night. I had finally outrun the old fears. Or so I had convinced myself.

Remote sirens warbled in the night. At first I figured they were in my head, the soundtrack to the dream. But the distant wail got louder instead of fading. I hadn't awakened on my own.

I ran through what I remembered from the previous evening – the presidential debate had closed out prime time, and after the commentariat finished yammering, I'd fallen asleep watching a high-speed chase on the news. A guy in a beat-to-shit Jeep Cherokee, hauling ass down the 405, a legion of black-and-whites drawn behind him like a parachute.

I blinked hard, inhaled, and looked around. Same Lemon-Pledge scent of my third-floor condo. My sweat imprint on the sheets and pillow. Breeze rattling palm fronds against my balcony one thin wall over.

And a watery blue light undulating across the bedroom ceiling.

I sat up.

The TV, across the room on the steamer trunk, was off. But the distant sirens continued.

And then, along with the light on the ceiling, the sirens abruptly stopped.

I threw off the sheets and padded across the carpet, stepping over a discarded *Sports Illustrated* and sloughed-off dress shirts from the job I'd left a week ago. In my plaid pajama bottoms, I ventured into the all-purpose living room, heading for the balcony. The police lights had flickered through the locked sliding glass door. Halfway to it, I froze. At first I thought it was a trick of the mind.

A thick black nylon rope was dangling from the lip of the roof, its end coiled on my balcony. Motionless.

No longer groggy, I opened the sliding glass door and stepped silently out onto the balcony, rolling the screen shut behind me. My balcony with its Brady-Bunch-orange tiles overlooked a narrow Santa Monica street populated by other generic apartment buildings. Streetlights were sporadic. I confronted the rope for a quiet moment, then looked around, expecting who knows what.

Bulky shadows of cars lined the gutters. An SUV was double-parked, blocking the street. No headlights, no dome light. Tinted windows. But a huff of smoke from the exhaust pipe. A sedan, dark and silent, wheeled around the turn and halted, idling behind the SUV.

Terror reached through seventeen years and set my nerves tingling.

I squinted to see if I could make out a police light bar mounted on either roof. In my peripheral vision, the tail of the rope twitched. Before I had a chance to think, the roof creaked. A spotlight blazed up from the SUV, blinding me. A zippering sound came from above, so piercing my teeth vibrated. Then a dark form pendulumed down at me, two boots striking me in the chest. I left my feet, flying back through the screen, which ripped free almost soundlessly. I landed on my shoulder blades, hard, the wind knocked out of me. The black-clad figure, outfitted with a SWAT-like jumpsuit and an assault rifle, filled the screen frame with its bits of torn mesh. Even through the balaclava, the guy looked somehow sheepish – he hadn't seen me beneath the overhang before he'd jumped.

'Shit,' he said. 'Sorry.'

He'd made an expert landing, despite the collision, and was aiming the rifle at my face.

I guppied silently, a knot of cramped muscles still holding my lungs captive, and rolled to my side. He stepped astride me as I curled around the hot pain in my chest.

A hammering of boots in the hall matched my heartbeat, so forceful it jarred my vision, and then the front door flew directly at me, knocked from the hinges and deadbolt as if a hurricane had hit the other side. It skipped on end, landed flat on the carpet with a whump, and slid to within an inch of my nose.

As I writhed between the assailant's boots, fear gave way to panic. Three men flipped me hard and proned me out, my face mashing carpet, my front tooth driving into my bottom lip. Gloved hands ran up my sides, checking my ankles, my crotch. More black-clad forms hurtled through the doorway, aiming assault rifles in all directions, a few men streaking off to the bedroom. I heard my folding closet doors slam back on their tracks, the shower curtain raked aside.

'Nick Horrigan? Are you Nick Horrigan?!'

My chest released and I drew in a screeching breath. And another. I rolled onto my back, stared up at the one face not covered by a hood and goggles. Lean, serious features, a slender nose bent left from a break, gray hair shoved back from a side parting. The salt-and-pepper stubble darkening the jaw matched neither the neat knot of the standard-issue-red tie nor the high-and-tight haircut.

'*Are you Nick Horrigan?*'

I nodded, still fighting to draw in a proper breath. A warm, salty trickle ran from my split lip down my chin. The other men – fifteen of them? – had spread through the condo, dumping drawers, knifing open the couch cushions, overturning chairs. I heard cutlery tumble onto the linoleum. My clock radio blared on – a jingle for antifungal ointment – then I heard someone curse and it abruptly cut off.

The gray-haired man frowned at me, then surveyed the others, radiating authority. 'The hell's the matter with him, Sever?'

'I hit him in the chest when I rappelled from the roof.' A faint Southern accent – Maryland or Virginia, maybe. The guy tugged off his hood, revealing a square face further accented by a military-looking flattop. He was much wider than the boss-man crouching over me. Younger

4

too – probably in his mid-forties, though his creased tan aged him up a bit. His bearing suggested he was the alpha dog among the jumpsuits.

The boss returned his gaze to me. 'Nick Horrigan, born six twelve seventy-three? Son of Agent Frank Durant?'

'Stepson,' I managed.

He shoved a photograph in my face. A man shown from the chest up, wearing a blue blazer and the scowl of the unphotogenic. A wide mouth and slack lips lent him a slightly wild quality. His blond hair was slicked back, the camera catching furrows left by the comb.

'What's the last contact you had with this man?'

I said, 'I don't know this guy.'

'Then you've been in phone or email contact with him.'

I caught a worm's eye view of a man with tactical goggles peering into the empty Cup o' Noodles I'd left on the kitchen counter. The photo moved abruptly in front of my nose again. 'I told you,' I said. 'I don't know who the hell he is.'

The boss grabbed my arms and tugged me to a sitting position. Over his shoulder, I could see my framed Warner Bros still, sitting shattered at the base of the wall. Yosemite Sam was looking back at me with an expression of matching bewilderment. Glancing down, I stared numbly at the boot-sized red marks on my bare chest. 'Who are you?' the man asked, pulling my focus back to him.

My voice still sounded tight. 'You already know. I'm Nick Horrigan.'

5

'No, I mean what do you do?'

'I just left a job at a charity group,' I said.

One of the guys behind me guffawed.

Another appeared in the doorway of my bedroom, holding my now empty nightstand drawer by the handle. 'I got nothing.'

The boss swiveled to face a guy wanding the kitchen with a magnetometer. The guy shook his head. 'Sorry, Mr Wydell.'

'Okay.' Wydell ran a hand through his gray hair. It fell back precisely into the side parting. His exacting demeanor fit his professional bearing – the sole suit among rugged operators. 'Okay. Get him a shirt.'

A T-shirt flew from the vicinity of my bedroom, hitting me in the head.

'Put this on. Let's go.'

My Pacman shirt. Great. I tugged it on and two guys hoisted me to my feet. Figuring I'd want ID wherever I was going, I grabbed my money clip from the kitchen counter and stuffed it into the floppy pocket of my drawstring pajama pants.

'Let's go, let's go,' Wydell said. 'You got sneakers, something?'

I stopped moving and the two men commanding me to the door stumbled into me. 'Can you please show me a badge?' I said, though I pretty much figured.

Wydell's lips pinched. His hand darted behind his lapel, withdrew his commission book with its recessed badge. Hunched eagle and flag, rendered in gold. *US Secret Service.* His commission was behind plastic inside the leather book. *Joseph Wydell, Special Agent in Charge.*

6

He was from the Los Angeles Regional Office, which meant he wasn't on the protection detail of a particular politician, but oversaw general intelligence in Southern California. Why was the head of the Secret Service LA office on-site at a raid instead of waiting back in his air-conditioned office?

'What do you think I did?' I asked.

Someone handed him my sneakers and he thumped them against my chest. I took them. He hustled me out into the hall, Sever in front of us, another agent behind, one at each side. They held the diamond formation as we barreled toward the stairs.

Mrs Plotkin stood in her doorway in a white spa bathrobe, her copper hair heaped high, showing off white roots. She looked worried – one of her favorite expressions.

'Get back in your apartment, ma'am,' Sever said, the accent more pronounced now.

We were approaching fast, but she held her ground. 'Where are you taking him?'

'I'm okay, Evelyn,' I said, wiping blood from my chin.

'What did he do?'

'Out of the way, *now*.'

We reached her and Sever straight-armed her back into her apartment. Her head snapped forward and the glasses she wore around her neck on a beaded chain flew up, trailing her fall like the tail of a kite. As we whisked past I caught a flash of her, lying shocked on her fuzzy rug, glasses tangled in her hair, the door pressing against her side. It was just a shove, nothing drastic, but even a portion of a man's strength applied brusquely to a woman in her sixties had a certain grotesqueness to it.

I tried to stop, but the agents propelled me forward.

'*Hey,*' I said to Sever's broad back, 'let me at least make sure she's okay.'

The agents all kept moving me along. No time for retorts or even threats. That scared me even more.

I stumbled down the stairs, trying to keep pace, nearly dropping my sneakers. The lobby was empty save the vinyl couches and smoky mirrors, and beyond, the street was lit up like day. Police cars, spotlights, men in dark suits talking into their wrists. A few spectators, hastily dressed, stood on the opposite sidewalk, straining on tiptoes, waiting to see who would emerge.

We burst through the doors and stopped. I hopped on one foot, then the other, pulling on my Pumas.

'Cut the goddamned spotlights,' Wydell said. 'This isn't a fashion shoot.' The spotlights clicked off with a bass echo and suddenly the night was darker than it should have been. Wydell grabbed the arm of another agent. 'Where is it?'

'Almost here.'

'It needs to be here *now*.'

I said, loudly, 'Are you gonna tell me what the hell is going on?'

All of a sudden, a bass thrumming filled the night, as much a vibration as a sound, and then a Steven Spielberg glow came over the rooftops, turning the palms a fiery yellow. On the sidewalk, a little girl white-knuckled her father's hand, her mouth open in sleepy disbelief.

A Black Hawk loomed into view, massive and somehow futuristic in this context, on my street. The wind from the rotors buffeted the crowd, snapped at the

8

bushes, pasted my clothes to me. Wydell's tie pulled clear of his jacket and stood on end. The helicopter banked and set down magisterially on the asphalt. The spectators stared at me expectantly.

Wydell grabbed my arm in a vise grip and started moving me toward the helicopter. The sight of that waiting Black Hawk finally broke me out of shock, or at least helped me catch up to myself, to what was happening. I jerked free. 'Wait a minute. You can't just *take* me. What's happening here?'

I had to follow him closely to hear his words over the noise of the rotors.

He was shouting. 'A terrorist has penetrated the nuclear power plant at San Onofre and is threatening to blow it up.'

I felt a sudden hollowness at my core, that rushing emptiness I'd felt only twice before: clutching stupidly at Frank while he died; and watching live footage as that second plane hit the tower.

'Okay,' I said. 'Jesus. But what's that got to do with me?'

Wydell stopped, poised, one leg up on the skid of the chopper. 'He says he'll only talk to you.'

2

The Black Hawk banked and I felt my stomach go through my throat. I bounced on a seat opposite Wydell and Sever, one hand wound in the cargo netting to keep me from tumbling onto the deck. I'd blown out the heel air pocket of my left sneaker and the plastic window on the outsole clicked every time I leaned hard on that foot to keep my balance. As well as the pilot, copilot, and two flight-suited crewmen, there were three other agents, all talking into radio headsets. Pelican cases were strapped to the floor, a few lids laid open to reveal all order of weaponry nestled in the black foam – sniper rifles, machine guns, grenades, even a torn silly-putty block of what I assumed was C4.

The night air was crisp in my lungs and the smell inside the helicopter was oiled steel and canvas. The bleeding from my lower lip continued, the taste lingering at the back of my throat. We bounced again, the wind fighting back, and a wave of nausea rolled through me. With scant comfort, I recalled hearing that a helicopter was the only machine that tried to tear itself apart every time it powered on.

Even in the midst of an emergency, Wydell had the

assurance of a veteran agent. Square posture. An elongated face, the forehead made prominent by a sharp widow's peak. No emotion in the dark brown eyes. The kind of man with a built-in confidence I resented and grudgingly admired, who could torpedo a stock price or send men to war and still doze off the instant his head hit the pillow. His lank gray hair, battered by the wind, had settled back into place except for a few wayward locks that looked incongruous. His radio headset dangled around his neck.

I waited until he looked over at me, then I said, 'We're facing a nightmare and you need me. I get that. But you couldn't just knock?'

'Listen carefully.' Wydell talked loudly to be heard over the constant rush of noise, his voice hoarse. 'This isn't about propriety. We've been scrambling since this guy started beelining down the 405.'

I asked, 'Why is the Secret Service even involved with a terrorist threat?'

'When the terrorist asked for you, LAPD ran your name,' Sever said. 'They found out your stepfather worked Caruthers's detail when Caruthers was Vice President and they pulled us in. They figured we keep tabs on agents' families.'

'Have you? Been keeping tabs on me?'

Wydell said, 'Let me make this clear – until we're one hundred percent certain that you're not this terrorist's confederate, you are.'

'And there's no way to make you certain,' I said. 'At least not right now.'

'That's right. We don't have time to question you more

thoroughly. In fact, we don't have any time at all.' He leaned forward, elbows on his knees, bringing those impassive brown eyes within a few feet of my face. 'He wants *you*, Nick. We need to know why.'

We swooped back over the freeway, rocketing forward on a tilt. Sever put out his foot to stop a sliding Pelican case. Stress and adrenaline had left me lightheaded, and the lurching helicopter wasn't helping settle me down.

'I'm completely in the dark,' I said. 'I have no idea who he is.'

Wydell shot a glance over at Sever, who looked skeptical. 'Then we're gonna act like we believe you so we can move forward.'

Wydell pulled a handkerchief from his pocket, fluffed it with a sharp snap, and offered it to me. I pressed it to my lip to staunch the bleeding.

He continued, 'LAPD tracked the terrorist to a house in Culver City. Shots were exchanged. He managed to escape in his vehicle and was pursued southbound on the 405 until he reached the San Onofre nuclear plant. He wrapped a note asking for you around a rock and threw it toward the barricade.'

The taste of blood was sharp at the back of my mouth. 'Tell me how to help.'

The copilot shouted something back to Wydell and he pulled his headset up, pausing to catch my eye and then nod at Sever. 'This is Special Agent Reid Sever. Squad leader for Protective Intelligence here in LA. He'll fill you in.'

Wydell then grimaced and let the earphones close over his head. He gripped the bud of the microphone, angling it to his chin and speaking to whomever was on the other end: 'I'm aware of that, sir, but no one was expecting the pursuit to veer off into the nuclear plant. It's just a hundred yards off the freeway. LAPD managed to give a few minutes' warning to the guards, and they immediately set up a perimeter around the containment domes.'

Meanwhile, Sever unfurled a large scroll across his lap, tilting it so I could see. His thumb pinched a tiny LED light against the paper, illuminating a throw of blueprint. His voice was gruffer than Wydell's, lacking the polished edges that came with promotion.

'This is the blueprint of the power plant,' Sever said. 'The containment domes that hold the reactors are here.' A sturdy finger tapped paper. 'To the right. The reactors are housed inside these steel-and-concrete domes that could withstand a tank assault. Only problem is . . .' His lips twitched, a pinched smile that said nothing was funny. 'Only problem is, our boy veered *left*.'

'What's over there?' I asked.

Beside Sever, Wydell leaned back in his seat, still gripping the floating mike. He maintained the respectful tone for addressing a superior, but his face looked strained, the skin tight across his cheeks. I could see a pulse fluttering at his temple. 'The spent-fuel pool.' He paused, then said, 'A different building, that's correct, sir. Concrete blocks and regular sheet-metal siding. It's got negative pressure maintained by fans, but it's not even airtight, let alone rated for containment.'

He shoved the headset back down around his neck and sat for a moment, thoughtful. A band of sweat sparkled on his prominent forehead. He did not strike me as a man who sweated easily. The Black Hawk veered sharply, but he just turned calmly and stared out the window, his canted nose catching shadows. The 405 was flying past outside, a white-and-red-spotted ribbon. Traffic was moving normally. That no one had bothered to order an evacuation only highlighted the range of the potential blast. All those headlights down below, even at three in the morning. All those people, oblivious that their lives were in the balance.

The Black Hawk straightened up again, the ground righting itself beneath us where it belonged. Wydell folded his hands, leaned forward. His tongue poked at the corner of his mouth. 'Let me lay out the facts,' he said. 'The pool is rectangular, about forty feet deep, built with five-foot concrete walls and lined with stainless steel. Under the high-density water are spent-fuel rods making up one of the greatest concentrations of radioactivity on the planet.' His voice remained steady, but he armed moisture off his brow. 'The pool houses ten times more long-lived high-penetrating radioactivity than the reactor core. It holds more cesium 137 than has been deposited by every atmospheric nuclear test ever conducted in this hemisphere. There under the water, it's relatively stable and harmless. If that water goes away, bringing the spent fuel to within a few feet of the surface—'

'Like from an explosion.' Despite the night air, my T-shirt was damp where it pressed against the nylon seat.

'Like from an explosion. Then the scenario changes dramatically. That pool would catch fire at north of a thousand degrees Celsius. A fire like that' – he shook his head – 'a fire like that cannot be extinguished until the

14

burning's done and the radioactivity released. It would render Southern California uninhabitable for half a million years.'

Sever lifted a cell phone from inside one of the Pelican cases and extended it to me.

'So,' I said, 'you need me to call and talk to him.'

Wydell said, 'We need you to go in there and deliver this cell phone to him.'

At first, I thought I'd misheard. 'I'll *talk* to him over the phone, bullhorn, whatever, but I'm not a trained agent. Someone who knows what they're doing should go in. What if I make a mistake? Five hundred thousand years is a long time.'

'He made it clear he'll see only you, and it has to be face to face. We're out of options here.'

When I swallowed, my throat clicked dryly. Why would the terrorist want to see me in person? Would he recognize my face but not my voice? Sever held the phone out to me again and shook it impatiently, but I kept my hands where they were. Wydell took it instead, put it in his lap.

I said, 'I thought we don't negotiate with terrorists.'

Sever said, quietly, 'We negotiate with terrorists every day.'

Wydell didn't seem to hear him. 'Facing this level of destruction? What would you do?'

'I don't know,' I said. 'I'm not the one with the policy.'

'Listen,' Wydell said, 'this guy's holding the cards. You claim you're not with him. That means you're with us. And your part of the mission is to get this phone in his hand. Just give it to him when we call. We've got the top crisis negotiator in the state on scene already. Once we have comms, we'll take it from there.'

'What if I can't convince him to take it? What if he blows us all up first?'

Wydell nodded solemnly, pulling at the loose skin below his chin. 'I knew your old man. I bet we have a fighting chance, as long as you got a few of his genes.'

'He was my stepdad,' I said, 'so it's a safe bet I didn't.'

Wydell's dark brown eyes fixed on me. 'Frank Durant was a great man. Stepson or not, that gives you something to live up to.'

Instead of taking the phone, I released a shaky sigh and leaned back in my seat. A decision was inevitable. In the relative quiet, reality finally began to sink in, and with it, a bone-deep chill. What had I woken into? The dark flew by as we whipped along toward a nuclear plant and the terrorist inside.

I thought about what my stepfather would do. Frank Durant. Seventeen years dead. My hero, if such a word can be used anymore with a straight face.

3

Seven years to the day after my father died, I met Frank. He was sitting in our yellow kitchen and had his hand on my mom's knee and I thought, Fuck him.

My real dad ran his truck into a canyon when I was four, barely old enough to store some hazy recollections. I never had to experience his shortcomings, which were considerable, right down to his .2 blood alcohol level when they pried the steering wheel out of his rib cage. I could just idealize him, plain and simple. I kept a photo of him framed on my bookshelf. In the picture, he's wearing a white T-shirt with a pack of cigarettes cuffed in, his hair's short, and he's smiling. Down at the bottom, almost lost behind the frame, a Camel sticks out from the fork of his fingers.

When I came into the kitchen that morning, Frank took his hand off my mom's knee and stood, a weirdly formal gesture. I tapped the tail of my skateboard, jumping it up so I could grab the top truck. He was tall, maybe 6′ 2″, with a tapered waist and a tattoo in what looked like Chinese down his forearm.

My mom hopped up, clearing their cups of coffee, her

17

jangly bracelets making a nervous clatter. 'Nicky, this is my new friend Frank. He works in the Secret Service, protecting our new Vice President. Isn't that neat?'

I thought, *My new friend? Neat?* Where did adults get this shit?

'Doesn't sound so neat to me,' I said.

My mom's mouth got thin, but Frank just looked at me evenly and said, 'It's not.'

He was working out of the Los Angeles Regional Office, the liaison to the protection detail guarding Jasper Caruthers. Caruthers was from Hancock Park, spent a lot of time in LA pressing flesh and fundraising from Hollywood, and when he was in town, Frank helped coordinate protective movements.

As the weeks passed, he was around more and more. I watched him with my mom on the couch, her bare feet in his lap, or in his truck out front laughing together at the end of a date. I watched with that odd blend of jealousy and envy. I couldn't remember my mom smiling like that before.

My mom was an elementary school art teacher – pretty, casual, a touch of hippie. She was what old people would call a character. Callie Horrigan with her bushy ponytail, her paint-spattered men's shirts, her band of freckles across the nose. Her students called her Ms Callie and since I'd spent most of my pre-school years tagging along, fingerpainting and pasting glitter onto pine cones, I'd developed a habit of calling her by her first name too.

One morning Callie left early for work and I caught Frank at the table, hair damp from the shower, suit jacket on the chair back, shirt sleeves pushed back. The first concrete evidence that he'd spent the night. He was drinking from my mom's coffee cup, steam curling up. I poured myself some cornflakes, sat across from him, and ate in silence. My eyes kept drifting to those weird ideograms on his muscular forearm, faded blue beneath the faint blond hair. He watched me for a while, watched my eyes. And then he said, 'You're curious what that says?'

'"I'm a dumb round-eye?"'

He sort of smirked – Frank never laughed, from what I'd seen – and then he sipped his coffee. I slurped my cornflakes. The Garfield clock over the sink ticked away, pivoting eyes and pendulum tail.

Finally, defeated, I asked, 'Okay, what's it say?'

He looked down at it, as if reading it for the first time. '"Trust No One."'

I ate some more, my face burning. 'My mom know that?'

He nodded. 'After Vietnam, I was stationed in Okinawa. A couple of us went out and got these. Thought we were real hot shit. Had it all figured out. Idiots.' He shook his head. 'I learned a lot of lessons the hard way. And this?' He tapped the tattoo. 'As a life philosophy? It doesn't serve. Now it's just a reminder of how stupid I am most of the time.'

'Still?'

'You tell me.'

I cleared my bowl, reserving judgment.

A few months later, Callie and I moved to Frank's house, a two-bedroom bungalow in Glendale. It was tiny, but impeccably finished. Frank had laid down the hardwood floors himself. The crown molding he'd put up was razor straight. The books on the floating shelves above the TV were arranged by size. My mom rushed around, adjusting furniture and holding her framed charcoals against the wall, and Frank grimaced but held his tongue.

I liked him for that.

While she reorganized the refrigerator, I went out back. A porch, a swing, and a small square of grass, summer-brown, not big enough to kick a soccer ball on. My boxes of stuff were in the other bedroom, but I held one in my lap. Baseball cards, a trophy that had broken at the base, the Punisher's first appearance in *Spiderman*, and the photo of my dad. I stared at that loose, happy grin, the cigarette my mom had tried to hide with the thick frame. I heard the creak of the screen door beside me and there Frank was, looking down at me.

'There will always be a place for your father in this house,' he said.

My mom called him and he withdrew inside.

The rest of the night, I stayed in my room, getting used to the space, the furniture, the view from the high rectangular window. I unpacked a little, but kept rearranging my stuff among the drawers, like a dog circling before bedding down. I didn't like the brown carpet or where the desk was or the new smell of a new house.

There was a knock, which I assumed was my mom since it was Frank's house.

I was slouched on a bean bag she'd bought for me at a garage sale and re-covered in corduroy. 'Yeah?'

Frank came in, looked around. I was expecting him to be mad that I'd put the desk at a slant in the corner, but instead, he said, 'What are you scared of?'

I looked at him blankly. He smelled like aftershave.

He pulled his mouth to the side, then rephrased: 'What do you want me to not do?'

So I told him. Room off limits when I'm not here. Don't act dad-ish. Don't mess with my comic books.

When I was done, he nodded. 'I can manage that.'

He closed the door behind him and I thought I'd probably live my whole life and never be that goddamned wise.

Not that Frank was a saint. He was a little jumpy, a touch paranoid. He had double dead bolts on all the doors and an alarm wired to the windows that gave off a low tone from a monitor by his side of the bed. You could only disarm it using the touchpad in the master or a circular key he kept in a waterproof magnetic box adhered inside the garbage disposal, on the metal roof where the blades couldn't get it. And nights he'd make me sleep with the window closed, even when my room was baking. 'But it's so uncomfortable,' I'd say, and he'd say, 'Comfort matters. But security matters more.'

He kept his service weapon, a Glock, in a gun safe in his closet, the loaded magazine in a hidden location. You'd think an intruder could kill us all before he could unlock and load, but my mom and I'd hear the wind rattle the screen door during *Carson* and a half second later Frank'd walk out of the bedroom, calm as anything, gun held in both hands and aimed at the ground six inches wide of his right foot.

One day I was digging through his steamer trunk in the coat closet and came upon a picture of him from the war. Tiger-stripe fatigues, aiming a Stoner 63 into the middle distance. He had face paint on and wore a squint and his half smirk, his cheeks stubbled. It looked like something out of one of my comic books. I wondered hard and long about that picture. Was he posing? Not Frank.

I took the picture and hid it in the frame behind the one of my dad.

There were more photos in that trunk, images of Frank's past, but I didn't look through them. Maybe I liked how Frank was mysterious. Maybe I wanted to keep him that way.

They got married in a backyard ceremony with a few friends and some cold-cut platters from the deli. Callie wore one of those awful wedding dresses with the poofy shoulders, but Frank didn't seem to mind. His voice caught once when he was giving his vows, and until that moment it had never struck me that Frank might need anyone or anything.

When he worked late, which was whenever Caruthers was in town, Callie and I'd eat on the back deck. After, in the moth-spotted glow of the porch light, I'd watch her sketch, leaving charcoal smudges on the glass of iced tea that went everywhere with her. It always seemed like magic the way the lines and shading suddenly took shape as a bowl of fruit, an old man's face, a woman's bare body. She'd look over and smile at me a touch self-consciously, using the heel of a hand to shove her curly hair out of her eyes. 'Isn't this boring?'

I'd just shake my head.

When Kinney and Caruthers got reelected, Frank's responsibilities in the LA office increased. Any chance I got, I'd sit in the garage and watch Frank wand down his truck for bugs. I loved listening to him talk on the radio, loved the protocols and call signs. When the Vice President came in for a weekend, Frank'd say, 'Looks like Firebird's gonna pull a double-header at the west nest.' It was like something out of a spy movie – just as cool, just as reassuring.

I made the high school baseball team and became a pretty good utility infielder. I could go the other way and pull for power, and I had a backhanded pickup worthy of a Venezuelan. If I kept on it, I could maybe be a bench player at a Division I, and my grades wouldn't present a recruiting coach any hurdles. The UCLA baseball coach pushed for me and Callie prepped me endlessly for the SATs. When I opened the acceptance letter my senior year, she pressed a fist to her mouth and turned away so I wouldn't see her crying.

I worked hard, practiced late. Sometimes I'd come home to find Frank sitting in his armchair in the dark, watching Zapruder's film of the JFK assassination over and over, memorizing those twenty-six seconds. I'd always slide past him into my room. If it was anyone else, I'd think I'd gone unnoticed.

One night, as I sneaked by, he paused the tape. 'What do you see?' he asked.

I froze behind him. Lifted my eyes to the familiar rise of grass, the grainy limo, Jackie's pink hat.

'JFK's head getting blown apart?' I said.

He made a sad, thoughtful noise deep in his throat, and I felt like an asshole. He nursed his coffee – Frank loved his coffee. He used to drink bourbon, but he'd

23

stopped drinking after he hooked up with my mom because he knew the smell upset her.

Instead of continuing to my room, I walked around and sat on the couch. 'Why, what do you see?'

'Clint Hill.'

'Who?'

He pointed. 'Secret Service agent on the left front running board of the Queen Mary. The car behind the presidential limousine.'

He clicked the remote again and the limo coasted forward. The silent horror of the two shots, the red mist by JFK's face. But this time I didn't watch the President. I watched Clint Hill sprinting toward the still-moving presidential limousine. He leapt but missed his grip on the trunk, then stumbled a few steps behind, refusing to fall. The limo accelerated. Hill lunged again, grabbing on and tugging himself forward, one foot shoving the bumper. He seized the First Lady's arm, forcing her down out of view, then he pivoted to look back at the motorcade. The screen shook in Zapruder's panicked hands, losing the procession. When the lens swung back, Clint Hill had wedged himself against the spare tire compartment, trying to lie across the President and First Lady. His body was rigid, braced to absorb a bullet, and it stayed that way until the limousine vanished under the Triple Underpass.

I'd never noticed him before, yet there he was, and his actions knocked the snot-nosed cynicism out of me.

The screen went black and Frank turned off the TV. We sat in the darkness tinged with English Leather and Maxwell House.

'I was a kid when this happened,' he said.

'You were older than I am now.'

'I was a kid,' he repeated in that same, distant voice. 'They got Jack, then Bobby and Martin Luther King.'

'The same guys?' I asked.

His lips pursed, maybe amused, maybe distressed at my daftness. 'No, not the same guys. But JFK had a protection detail. That' – he angled a finger at the dark screen – 'can never happen again.'

'Is that what you think about when you guard Caruthers?'

His chin rustled against his collar. 'Every minute.'

'Is he worth dying for?'

Frank thought about that awhile. 'He is. If people can shoot our elected leaders, we don't have much of a democracy. I protect the Man to protect my vote. And everyone else's. Even the fifty percent of eligibles who don't bother showing up come poll time. But Caruthers, Caruthers is a little different. I respect him.'

'Why?'

He took another slow sip of coffee. 'Hard to say, really. It's not about platform or policies, though both matter. If there's one thing I've learned, it's that people don't damn themselves in an instant, but with a thousand small decisions. One compromised choice leads to six more and it goes from there. They decide they can cut a corner, or the ends justify the means, and then since they decided it once, they decide it again. All you can rely on is a man's character. Not what he says or promises, but what he *does*. What you *do* is the measure of a man. And Jasper Caruthers, I guess I like what he does. He could be a great man. He's got a shot at being President, too.'

25

'What makes a great man?'

'The man himself.' Frank smiled that half smile, but it faded when he took in my expression. 'What's wrong?'

'Nothing.'

He studied me. 'We say what needs to be said in this family.'

It was the first time he'd ever called us a family. My mouth twitched a few times as I tried to figure out what I wanted to say without embarrassing myself. 'Why do you think Caruthers's life is worth more than yours? That just seems stupid to me.'

He nodded gravely. 'No one's life is worth more than anyone else's, not even the Vice President's. Caruthers does what he does to serve the country, and this is what I do.'

He got up, set down his empty coffee cup, and I rose to head back to my room. As Frank passed, he hugged me. I was stunned – my arms didn't rise from my sides. His shirt was warm with body heat and I could smell the aftershave mixed with the sweat of a day's work and I felt my throat close though I didn't know why.

He said, 'Don't worry,' then he wiped his mouth and walked down the hall to his and my mom's bedroom.

That night I moved his picture in front of my dad's in the frame on my nightstand. He didn't say anything about it.

After that, things began to change. Over the next few months, Frank got more and more paranoid. He checked the phone lines for taps. He came up with different hiding places for various weapons so he'd never be caught defenseless. A K-bar beneath the trashcan

26

flap, a .22 in the icemaker. He said they'd taught him –
in the military and in training – where to hide things,
but who knows where some of it came from. For the
first time, he missed a day of work. Then another. Callie
and I confronted him once, worried, but all he said
was, 'There have been some unusual concerns at work.'
That was all we could get out of him, but one night I
got up for a midnight glass of water and overheard him
sitting in his truck in the garage, talking on his car
phone about a threat to Vice President Caruthers.

A week later, I caught Frank standing at the front
window, two fingers through the curtain. His other hand
rested on his hip-holstered Glock, and when I asked what
was out there, the gun almost cleared leather. As he shook
his head and headed past me, mumbling, I thought I
heard an engine turn over and then a car drive away.

I wondered why a federal agent was creeping around
his own house peering out windows, but I didn't say anything. Maybe I didn't want to think about the
implications. Maybe I was afraid of what the answers
would be.

What could be dangerous enough to scare Frank?

For a time, I stood in the cold hall, looking at the
master bedroom door, debating walking over there and
knocking. But I kept my mouth shut and my concerns to
myself. I'd wait. Whatever it was, Frank could handle it.

He was dead within the month.

The helicopter banked hard around a stretch of coastal hills, knocking me back to the present, and the giant nuclear power plant drew into view. There were maybe fifty police cars, lights blinking. Army cargo trucks and Hummers, even twin tanks guarding the western perimeter, cannons swiveled to face the dark sky over dark water. Cops and agents had surrounded the containment domes and set up a perimeter outside the rectangular building housing the spent-fuel pond. Powerful spotlights illuminated the scene in broad swaths of yellow.

The trail of destruction left by the terrorist's SUV told a tale of its own. A smashed gate arm at the checkpoint, a path blazed through the brush, and an overrun section of chain-link fence, flat on the ground, aligned with a second, identical breach in a second fence. Curls of tire lay on the ground past the fallen concertina wire, just inside the compound. A clipped generator box continued to throw up sparks. Thirty yards of concrete scored by the Jeep's metal rims. And at the end of the trail, angled up the three broad concrete steps and embedded in the doorway as if of a piece with the building, was the red Cherokee I'd been watching on TV mere hours ago from the anonymity of my bed.

We descended into a typhoon of dirt and sand. Soldiers cleared the makeshift landing zone, squinting against the gritty wind. My left knee was bouncing. There had to be more time for this situation to prove itself not real.

We set down with a thump and the overhead whirring finally began to die away.

No more time.

'We need you to do this now,' Wydell said. He held out the cell phone to me.

I reached out an unsteady hand and took it.

Sever leaned over and tore open the helicopter door. Several agents jogged toward us, assault rifles bouncing on their slings.

Wydell grabbed my shoulder. 'Get him away from that spent-fuel pond. Don't give him the phone unless he's away from the water. A few steps is enough. He claims to be loaded with explosives. Given this guy's volatility . . .'

I nodded, my stomach churning. 'You sure you guys know what you're doing?'

'Who do we call in case of emergency?'

Not the answer I was looking for.

An agent reached in and clutched my arm, tugging me. 'This is him?'

The seat belt jerked me at the waist; I fought the buckle free and stepped out. Kicked-up dust coated my lungs. I coughed and then a wet sea breeze blew the air clear, chilling me through my thin clothes.

The agent hustled me forward, Wydell and Sever behind us. Dozens of men stopped talking into phones and radios and to one another; scores of heads swiveled to watch me. I drew even with the line of Hummers and soldiers and agents at the perimeter, maybe thirty yards back from the spent-fuel building. The crashed Jeep was lit up as if on stage.

I heard Sever's gruff voice behind me. 'Go on.'

I turned and looked at him. Wydell, at his side, nodded urgently. 'Good luck, Nick.'

All around us, sharpshooters crouched behind Hummers and cop cars. A young Latin soldier had the end of his crucifix pendant between his lips, sucking it. I stared back at the empty, unprotected ground between the perimeter and the building. A stretch of concrete that even the soldiers and agents didn't dare set foot on.

I stepped out from cover, my Pumas padding across the concrete, the broken plastic of my left sneaker giving off its maddening click. A spotlight tracked my movement. Twenty yards. The wet wind came off the Pacific, biting at my arms, my neck, my bare ankles. I was shivering. In my thin T-shirt and pajama bottoms, I felt naked, oddly self-conscious and dissolved into my surroundings at the same time. I sensed every part of my body and everything around me – the cool air filling my chest, the grind of stray sand particles underfoot, the tuning-fork vibration of my arms. Ten yards. I braced for flame to burst out of the building and engulf me. The scrapes in the concrete from the tire rims grew deeper as I approached. And then I was there.

The violence of the Jeep's collision with the door frame

was striking. The double doors had been flung back into the building, one tilting from a hardy hinge, and the wall around had crumbled to accommodate the broad snout of the vehicle, which perfectly plugged the hole it had created.

I stopped and looked behind me. The perimeter seemed miles away. All those trained men and women, safely tucked behind cop cars and cargo trucks. I felt suddenly isolated out in no man's land.

I climbed the three wide steps, reaching the bullet-riddled back of the Jeep – a few of the plant guards with machine guns must have figured out, late, where it was heading and opened fire. The rims had been worn down, one bent on the axle.

My voice sounded thin. 'It's Nick Horrigan!' I shouted. 'Don't shoot me. I'm just here because you asked for me.'

To get in, I had to slide through the Jeep's shattered back window and claw my way through the crumpled interior, not-so-shatter-free glass pinching my hands. The front half of the vehicle was buried in the embrace of the caved-in wall. The deflated air bag had been shoved aside, and the windshield had been kicked out so the guy could slide protected from vehicle to building. There was blood on the steering wheel, the dashboard.

I rolled down the gnarled hood, still hot to the touch, and tumbled to the floor amid a scattering of windshield pebbles. Checking that the cell phone remained in my pocket, I stood. The spa-blue water, lit from within, set the walls and high ceiling aglow. Monitors embedded in consoles flashed readings. The reek of chemicals and something more sinister burned my nose, the back of my throat. Tanks and generators lurked at the dark edges, adorned with neat mazes of pipes and endless coils. Set with respectful clearance to the center of the enormous building was the pool.

At its end, like a swimmer contemplating a dive, stood a man in ripped clothing, dimly lit from the rising glow. The man from the photo, though older and in far worse shape. His shoulders were slumped unevenly, as if from injury, his head lowered on his neck. His face was badly lacerated, a section of cheek lifted to crowd his left eye. Unruly blond hair, dull with age, swirled up and out. His eyes jerked back and forth, almost uncontrollably, but his posture remained perfectly still.

Slung over one shoulder was an army-green rucksack, his hand buried in it up to the wrist.

My throat was so dry the words seemed to stick. 'I'm Nick Horrigan.'

With two fingers, he beckoned me forward. His elbow was torn open, probably from the crash, and blood pattered at the lip of the pool. A crimson drop hit the crystal blue water and blossomed.

I couldn't move at first, so he beckoned again.

I headed forward on legs that decided they didn't belong to me. The air, dense with humidity, felt almost liquid. I drew even with the pool and stared into the perfectly still aqua water. Down at the bottom, packed maybe ten inches apart, were the spent-fuel rods, benign-looking bundles. Not a speck of debris in the pool – it was maintained with a care suitable to the awesome lethality it contained. My Pacman shirt, damp with sweat, clung to me.

The blue light played over the man's bloodied features. That wide, wild mouth. He hardly moved as I approached, but his dark pupils swiveled, tracking my movement.

'Do you know me?' I asked.

He raised a hand, pressed a ssh finger to his lips. I stopped. I was maybe ten yards away. His toes were over the edge of the pool. He swayed a little, then took a step back. I let out a breath I hadn't known I'd been holding.

His weary features barely moved. 'Did they give you something?'

His voice was a low rasp; it took me a moment to realize I'd understood him. 'What? Oh. A phone.'

I pulled it from my pocket.

His hand slid out of his rucksack, matching the movement of my own. He held a black, cigarette-sized box with three bars of red light and a recessed button.

I stopped breathing.

He eyed the phone in my hand, grimaced as if disappointed that I'd broken my end of some bargain, and lowered his thumb to the ominous little box.

My entire body went rigid. 'Wait a second!'

He pressed the button.

When I lowered my hands, which still existed, I saw the man staring at me with a puzzled expression.

He looked from my face to the small black box in his hand, seeming to put the two halves of the equation together. 'Pink-noise generator.'

I took a gulp of humid, bitter air. Sweat burned my eyes. I used the collar of my T-shirt to wipe my forehead. 'Pink noise?'

'Subaudible. Pretty much plugs up any frequency they're listening in on.'

'I'm not wired.'

'Yeah, but you can bet your ass that cell phone they gave you is.' He crouched and set the little generator on the floor at his feet, right at the edge of the pool. He flicked his bloody head. 'Come here.'

I remembered Wydell's warning to get him away from the water. I wanted his rucksack moved away too. 'I'm not going near that pool,' I said.

'The radiation won't hurt you. Not unless the water boils off.'

'Is that what the bomb's for?'

'There is no bomb,' he said impatiently.

'I . . . *what*? What are you doing then?'

'I needed the bomb threat to get you here.' He took a crooked step toward me, away from the pool. I responded with a half step back, drawing him farther. He raised a hand to the laceration on his cheek, the loose section of flesh shifting under his gentle touch. His grimace held more resignation than pain. 'They'll kill me the minute they get me in a scope. I'm not getting out of here alive, and if I do, they'll make sure I disappear.' He drew nearer, walking on a tilt, until we were at arm's length.

I was breathing hard, trying not to bounce on my shoes, but my body wouldn't obey. When he swayed closer, I snatched the rucksack from his shoulder and shoved him away. He stumbled back a few steps and made no move to retaliate. I was shocked at myself, the panicked burst of courage, how easy it had been. With shaking hands, I rooted furiously through the rucksack, but it contained only a handgun, two stacks of hundred-dollar bills with purple bands, a notepad and pen, and a change of clothes.

I dropped the rucksack. 'There's no bomb?'

He shook his head and started to say something, but a coughing fit doubled him over, blood spraying from his mouth. The coin-sized drops looked like oil in the dim blue light. Finally he straightened up.

'Who *are* you?' I asked.

'I'm Charlie. I knew your stepfather.'

'*How*? How do you . . . ?'

He swayed on his feet, his eyes glassy with pain or from the crushing pressure of the situation. 'I made an awful mistake. But maybe you can set it right. I trusted Frank. I trusted him with my life. He's the only guy I ever trusted a hundred percent.'

'If you were friends, how come you didn't come to the funeral?'

I was bluffing; I hadn't gone either. I'd gotten dressed for the service, but hadn't been able to stop vomiting to make it into the car with Callie.

'I was scared shitless,' Charlie said. 'You would've been too. That's what this is about. That's why I needed you here. Frank always talked about you. Years ago. Years. If there's anyone I can trust to do the right thing, it'd be Frank's kid.'

'I'm nothing like Frank Durant. I'm not even his kid.'

But Charlie didn't seem to hear me. 'I prayed to hell you still lived here. I didn't know who else . . . what else can be done. But if anyone can figure it out, it's you. At least from what Frank said. I don't have anyone else.'

35

'How do I know this isn't a set-up? How do I know you and Frank were really friends?'

He moved toward me again, ignoring my questions, digging in his pocket. 'Here. Here. Take this. Hide it.'

Something glinted in his blood-streaked hand. A key.

He grabbed my arm, shoved the key into my palm. It was brass, maybe two inches long, more sturdy than a house key. 'Hide it now. On your person.'

His sleeve had shoved back almost to the elbow. On his forearm, in a faded tattoo blue, was the familiar *kanji* script.

Trust No One.

I stared at the tattoo, stunned. Then I crouched and wedged the key through the cracked plastic window in the heel of my sneaker. With a push, it fit into the air pocket. More drops of blood tapped the floor, the tops of his shoes.

His voice sounded loose, pain-drunk. 'Your life is now on the line. I'll explain to you. I'll explain to you everything you need to kn—'

The phone rang in my pocket, shrill off the concrete walls. We both started, and I jerked upright. We faced each other, a few feet apart, bathed in the antiseptic glow of the pool. I pulled out the phone again.

He gestured for it. 'I'll buy us another few minutes.'

I handed it to him. He took it and staggered back a half step. Moving his injured arms gingerly, he unfolded the phone.

I flashed back on Sever pulling the phone from its black-foam nestle in the Pelican case.

Charlie winked at me with that flesh-crowded eye.

'Trust no one.' He spat blood, raised the cell phone to his face, and said, 'What?'

A white flash of an explosion replaced his head atop his shoulders, the concussion sending me in a slow-motion float back through the roaring air, and then into darkness.

5

A few weeks before my eighteenth birthday, Callie left for a class she had saved up for at the Art Institute of Chicago. It was May, but already sweaty summer weather, and I headed out to see *Backdraft* with a few teammates. We stopped off after at our weekend hang-out, the original Bob's Big Boy, one of Glendale's few cultural landmarks.

Isabel McBride. That's what the shiny new nametag, positioned left of her cleavage, announced. She was in her late thirties with lush auburn hair, prominent breasts – grown-woman breasts – and a fringe of bra lace showing where her shirt was unbuttoned. She had a firm, lipsticked mouth and a few creases by her eyes when she smiled, which she did at me every time she leaned over to serve or clear. We all laughed and whispered and shot knowing glances to show how un-nervous we were and when I went up to the register to pay, she caught my wrist and said, 'I get off shift at one. I have a daughter at home but I could slip out to meet you and maybe teach you a few things.'

'I'm seventeen,' I blurted. 'I live with my mom.'

She glanced down at my Glendale High letterman's

jacket and said, 'Baseball? Meet me at your pitcher's mound.'

I nodded, having lost the capacity for speech.

When I got home that night and opened the front door, Frank was standing in the hall as if he'd been waiting there for hours, though I knew he'd responded to the scratch of my keys in the locks. 'Good,' he said, turning back to his room.

I was thinking about Isabel McBride. The way that shiny hair curled around her nape to touch the top of her chest. The faint wrinkles in her neck that her tan had missed. She'd had a *child*. Though I was less experienced than I wanted to admit, this opportunity had stepped forth as if from the pages of a stroke mag and there was no way I was going to miss learning whatever she was interested in teaching me.

'Frank,' I said, 'lemme keep the window open tonight. It's like a hundred out.'

He stopped and scowled at me, as tired as I was of the old argument. He looked more weary than usual, yet wired at the same time. 'Comfort doesn't matter,' he said. 'Security matters.'

I lay on my bed and read, urging the clock on my nightstand to move quicker. At twenty to one, I slid from my sheets. I carried my shoes, wearing my socks to stay quiet down the hall. Frank had left his door open, and I could hear his even breathing issuing from the dark room. I stole into the kitchen, managed to get the waterproof magnetic box out of the garbage disposal without making too much noise. The key inside fit an alarm panel in the kitchen wall, by the door to the garage. I disarmed

39

the system and slipped through the back door, locking the knob, but forgoing the heavy-duty Medeco deadbolts that slid home with wall-vibrating clunks.

Ten minutes later I was navigating the dark campus, positive that she wouldn't be there, that it was all a joke, that I'd made it up. But there she was, a feminine figure on the pitcher's mound, her hands clutching a purse behind her back. She'd gone home and changed and she wore a sundress that blew against her splendid form, showing both curves of her thighs.

'Hi,' I said, as I approached. 'I'm not really sure—'

She put her hands on my face and kissed me, her tongue flicking inside my mouth. Her body leaned into mine and we were both responding, the first time I'd experienced a woman confident in her sexual appetite. She tugged me by the hand and we walked to the out-field grass, still damp from the evening's sprinklers. Her hands were at my belt and then I was in her mouth, arching my back, making noises, unsure of everything. She fought down my jeans and pulled her dress up to her waist and reached in her bag. 'Here,' she said. 'Put this on.'

I struggled with the condom, trying to unroll it upside-down at first and with all the tugging and the slow burn of my mortification, I came. I felt myself flush, and I turned away and threw the thing and collapsed onto my back. She stroked my chest and leaned over me. Her perfume was too sweet and her hair brushed my skin, raising goosebumps.

'You have a really nice body,' she said.

'Didn't help me out much tonight, did it?'

'It got you this far.' She laughed. 'That's one of the benefits to being seventeen.'

'What is?'

'Wait five minutes and I'll show you.'

I did and she did and I lasted at least twice as long. I lay back in shock and amazement and she petted my face. She'd popped in some gum and her breath smelled of watermelon. 'You're a sweet boy,' she said. And then she stood, stuffing her panties in her purse, tugging at her sundress. 'I have to get home to my daughter. But come by the restaurant some time.'

'I will,' I said. And then, in case she hadn't heard me, 'I will.'

I jogged home in a daze. At the side gate, I slipped off my shoes. Moving stealthily alongside the house, I checked my watch – *2:18*. My breath caught when I turned the corner.

The back door was open.

A rustling issued from inside. I was running, full of dread. I stumbled over the step but kept my feet and saw a dark form in the middle of the living room. I hit the light switch and there Frank was, at the end of a short, bloody trail he'd scraped along the floorboards, propped against his armchair. Both hands pressed to the dark, glittering hole in his gut. He was trying to talk but there was blood at his mouth and his features were jerking around and I could see steam rising from between his fingers. The Glock was a few feet to his right, an ejected casing beside it.

The kitchen door leading to the garage was open, fresh air sucking through the rectangle of darkness past

41

my face and out the open door at my back. Fear sent me into a scramble for the gun before I remembered I'd never shot before. I was crying and pleading and apologizing, trying to place the gun in Frank's hand so he could protect us, but he could no longer grip. Then I heard the garage's side door bang open, clapping against the outside wall I'd crept along moments before.

Frank raised his hand, pointing limply to the circular key I'd left protruding from the alarm pad in the kitchen and his lips wavered some more and he choked out the word. 'W . . . ? W-why?'

His other hand went loose over the wound and the blood streamed out, dark, so dark. The next thing I knew I was cradling him, my hands over the entry wound. I was sobbing so hard his face was a smear, but I could see he was looking up at me with shock and bewilderment and one of his feet was ticking back and forth and then he wasn't looking at anything anymore.

42

6

M y head swam with nightmare images dredged from a thick slumber. I grasped for my time-worn mantra: *You're not seventeen anymore. You're safe now.*

My memory clicked and my eyes flew open.

The nurse's face resolved from the bleached white of the room. Blonde, pinched waist, clipboard – the whole nine. I was naked, it seemed, under a papery hospital gown.

'The agents told me what you did,' the nurse said, 'and I just want to thank you.'

I squinted into the sudden bright. 'How did I get—?'

'Do you know your name?'

'Nick Horrigan.'

'What month is it?'

'September.'

'Who's the President of the United States?'

'Andrew Bilton.' *Unfortunately.*

'Do you remember what happened to you?'

A rush of images. The bullet-riddled Jeep. The aqua glow of the pool. The bundles of spent-fuel rods under the glassy surface.

43

'Guy named Charlie. There was an explosion.'

'You sustained no serious injuries, except some bruising and the small wound in your right cheek. Don't be surprised if you have some tenderness for a few days, maybe a whiplash that rears its head in a week or two.'

The digital clock said *9:18 am*. My brain was still playing catch-up, but I had a vague recollection of an interview I was supposed to be at in twelve minutes. I had graver concerns now. My fingers rose to my cheek, found a bandage and some tape.

She said, 'I wouldn't take that—'

But I'd already peeled it back. I sat up, my stomach muscles burning. The skin on my face and chest felt raw, as if sunburned. The floor was cool beneath my bare feet.

The nurse said, 'I think you should take your time getting—'

I trudged across the room to the mirror, my ass hanging out the hospital gown flap. A hole in my cheek, the size of a pea, with surprisingly little blood. The skin dimpled in around it. 'Shrapnel?'

'You could call it that,' the nurse said. 'It's actually a bone fragment.'

My eyes ticked right, picking up her reflection in the mirror. 'Not mine?'

'No.'

I swallowed hard.

'It's embedded in your cheek bone and it won't do any damage, so rather than have you undergo an invasive procedure, the doctor figured she'd let it be.'

A little piece of Charlie Terrorist permanently lodged in my skull. My head throbbed a few times, hangover

44

style, and I shuffled back and slid into bed. I took a few deep breaths. 'Where's my stuff?'

'You mean your clothes?' The nurse pulled a plastic tub from under the bed and set it beside me on the sheets. My Pacman shirt had been sliced off my body by the paramedics. It was torn beyond that too, the ripped fringes charred from the explosion. The heap of pajama pants was in similar condition. The Pumas sat neatly under the rags.

'The doctor'll be in soon on rounds to take a look at you and probably discharge you.' She offered her hand, which I shook. 'A pleasure meeting you, Nick.'

She left me alone in the private room. I was high up, maybe the fifth floor, my window overlooking Beverly Boulevard. Cedars-Sinai Hospital. Circling the room, I tried to slow my panicked thoughts.

I picked up the nightstand phone and called my place to see if anyone had left a message. After two rings, someone picked up.

'Hello?' I said.

Dead silence. Not even breathing, but I could hear enough background noise coming over the line to know it wasn't just a dropped call.

'Who is this?' I asked.

The line went dead. I called back, got my voice-mail recording, and punched in my code. No messages. Had I misdialed the first time?

Your life is now on the line.

I shook off a shiver. Everyone lives with a shadow, whether it's a lump under the skin or an abusive ex-husband or an addiction that comes knocking when it's

45

hungry. For seventeen years, I'd done everything to forget what was hanging over my head. I'd tried my best to rebuild my life. Bad weekend volleyball at Santa Monica Beach. Happy hour at El Torito with 'the gang' from work. The occasional date. It had been quiet for so long that I told myself I might be out of the woods. The past few years, I'd even relaxed into believing, *Yes, I can have this.* But no matter how hard I pretended, deep down I knew it couldn't be true. And now, finally, the spooks had come out of their holes.

I grabbed my left sneaker from the tub and shook it – the rattle was still there. Charlie's key. I pinched my eyes, rubbing hard. Kanji script appeared in the darkness behind my lids – Charlie's *Trust No One* tattoo. Okinawa. War buddies. I recalled his rasping words: *I trusted Frank. I trusted him with my life.*

I found a remote on the nightstand, clicked on the overhead TV. The morning news showed helicopter clips of the car chase down the 405, but only stock footage of San Onofre; the airspace over the nuclear power plant must've been cleared last night. Standing on the Culver City street where the shootout had taken place, the reporter didn't mention my name or Charlie's, merely claiming that a high-speed pursuit ended in a stand-off at San Onofre, and that the terrorist had been killed. A whirl through other channels revealed similar footage and vagueness.

MSNBC, however, was running highlights from the presidential debate. Not surprisingly, they were largely of Senator Caruthers. Caruthers had made changes since the days Frank helped protect him. The move to Capitol

Hill was the most obvious, but there were subtle refinements, too. He wore his razor-sharp suit more casually, the soft-power-green tie picking up his striking eyes. A slight lean on the podium now offset his perfect posture. Despite being heir to a textile fortune, he managed to project a man-of-the-people image. He was who we'd want to be if we were rich.

'Since I've promised a transparent campaign,' Caruthers said, 'let's state the obvious. Why are we in Harlem? We're both courting the black vote. The difference between me and my opponent is, I've actually come here to meet with community leaders numerous times in the past decade under circumstances far less contrived. How many times has my opponent?'

A cutaway to Andrew Bilton in his gray suit, lips pursed as if in amusement at youth's folly, though he and Caruthers were both in their sixties. An old, bitter rivalry, reaching back a decade and a half to when Bilton, as rising-star California governor, acted as party hatchet man against the fiery then-Vice President, cutting down Caruthers's first bid for the Oval Office.

I remembered my disappointment back then, watching Bilton paint Caruthers as too progressive for the time. Sneering from talk show couches, riling up packed union halls, Bilton was paying his dues by acting as the public face of his party's negative campaigning, while allowing the nominee to remain above the fray. And Caruthers had failed to preempt and respond in the fashion he'd now perfected. There'd be no catching him short this go around.

From the TV, Caruthers continued, 'Well, Mr

President, this is your first visit to Harlem, is it not?' A welcoming smile. 'I'd recommend the deep-fried catfish at Sylvia's on Lenox.'

Before the erupting crowd, Bilton wore the same post-surgical expression that had frozen Quayle's face after Lloyd Bentsen told him he was no Jack Kennedy. I'd seen it live, but the replay was just as enjoyable.

Bilton produced his same even smile and I almost felt sorry for him. A dutiful frontman for his party, he was a pleasant-looking guy who filled out a suit nicely, spoke in clean, on-message paragraphs, and gave off an old-fashioned, subdued authority. But against Caruthers's aquiline nose, brilliant green eyes, and explosive charm, he seemed reduced to a divorce lawyer playing himself on a commercial.

I checked the clock again. Did I *have* to wait for the doctor to get out of here?

To soothe myself, I clicked over to Cartoon Network. A favorite – Bugs as a snake charmer teased an electric razor out of a clay bowl to pursue a hapless Elmer Fudd across an opera stage.

I love Looney Tunes. I love how Acme makes everything from flypaper to disintegrating pistols. I love how when a character goes through a wall, he leaves behind a perfect silhouette. I love how steaks are always shaped the same and make everyone drool.

I love how no one really dies.

A tap at the door, and Reid Sever entered. I stiffened, unsure and a bit rattled. The door sucked closed behind him and he took note of my reaction and smiled – not an expression that came naturally. 'Congratulations, hero.'

Telling my muscles to relax, I pulled my ruined clothes into my lap.

'We'll pick you out something nice from the gift shop. Or we can send an agent to your place, get whatever you need. Hell, after what you did for us?' Sever gave a little shrug. The civilian clothes accented his solid build. 'Your bill's covered, too. We understand your COBRA insurance isn't the greatest.' He waited for a reaction, but I didn't give him one. 'Listen, I have a couple questions I have to run through with you. I'm sorry to do it so shortly after you've come to, but . . .'

'Go ahead.'

'Did the terrorist give you a fake last name also?'

I dug through the pajama bottoms, found my money clip in the pocket. 'I'm not following.'

'The nurse said you referred to him as Charlie. Did he give you a last name?'

It took me a moment to get my head around the nurse's reporting back to Sever. Or was the room bugged?

'No,' I said slowly. 'Just Charlie.'

'His real name was Mike Milligan.'

'The guy I met in there may have been a nutcase, but he wasn't a terrorist.'

'You've dealt with a lot of terrorists?' A follow-up smile sprang up fast on Sever's face, an attempt to extenuate his tone.

I fanned my thumb across the money clip. At the center of the bills, I always kept my driver's license and credit card back-to-back to protect the magnetic strip. But the credit card was flipped the wrong way. A lazy effort by whoever had searched my pockets, but then I was just an average dipshit who wouldn't notice. My heart rate ticked up another notch.

'Did you guys talk at all before we called?' Sever pressed. 'You and Milligan?'

I pictured the loose flesh beneath Charlie's eye, how it hadn't moved with the rest of his face when he'd winked at me. *Trust no one*.

I said, 'There wasn't much time.'

'So does that mean *no*, or *a little*?' A tight smile. 'He asked specifically for you. He must have said *something* when you first got there?'

'Nope. You pretty much blew him up first.'

'Well, we can all exhale now.'

'It's over?'

'Yup. Our intel shows Milligan was just a loose cannon looking to cause a disruption before the elections. We're convinced he was acting alone.'

Before I could respond, the door opened and Wydell entered breathlessly, as if he'd rushed over. He nodded at Sever, who stepped back deferentially, ceding the stage to his boss. Wydell crossed and sat bedside. 'How you feeling?'

I just looked at him.

'You did a great thing.'

'Listen, Mr Wydell—'

'Joe.' His lean features had arranged themselves into an accommodating expression.

'Okay, *Joe*. You almost killed me in there. And you lied to me—'

'We never lied to you, Nick. We misled you, and I apologize for that, but we needed you calm. You're not an

50

agent, and unlike everyone else in LA, you're not an actor. We couldn't send you into that building knowing you were delivering a cell phone packed with C4. It wouldn't have worked, and if you think about it, you know that. We weren't only concerned with the bigger picture. Your own safety was at stake.' Wydell studied me, waiting for a reaction he didn't get. 'A major terrorist act was prevented, thanks to you.'

'A major terrorist act,' I repeated.

I sensed he wanted to ask if I knew that there'd been no bomb, but there was no way he could without showing his hand. Instead, he said, 'This can be an enormous opportunity for you. Son of a former Secret Service agent, the whole thing. We have a press conference in an hour. We'd like you to be included.'

'I'm not gonna talk about my relationship with Frank.'

'You don't have to. There's plenty else to talk about after what you accomplished last night.'

'I'm not going to any press conference. I don't want my name released.'

'Anything you *do* want? This is a pretty big moment for you. A lot of powerful people will be looking to express their gratitude.'

I thought about what Frank had said that night I'd come upon him watching the Zapruder film, how people damn themselves with a thousand small decisions. *One compromised choice leads to six more and it goes from there.*

'I don't want anything,' I said. 'You guys tricked me. I wasn't a hero. I was just the dupe who carried the bomb.'

'I think that's the least flattering interpretation possible.'

The bedside phone sounded and Sever picked it up

on a half ring. He'd been waiting right beside it. 'Yes, he's here.' He pressed the handset to his considerable chest. 'President Bilton wants to express his gratitude to you.'

I swallowed dryly. 'As in, the Commander in Chief?'

'That's right. He'll have a window in about half an hour.'

I glanced from my scorched clothes to the clean white walls, my chest feeling tight. 'Sorry, but I need to get out of here. I, uh . . .' Claustrophobia gripped me and I couldn't finish the thought.

Sever looked at me, his mouth slightly agape. Then he muttered something into the phone and hung up.

Wydell fixed his dark brown eyes on mine. 'If you want to stay off the radar, that's fine by us. But it's important – no, *essential* – to national security that we don't confuse the press or the public. Do you understand what I'm telling you?'

'Not really.'

'The threat is over. It's important that the public be made to feel at ease again.'

'Listen,' I said, 'I don't want to have to go home and puzzle out what you're trying to say. So just be clear what you mean. Please.'

His brow furrowed. 'Okay. If you choose not to be officially recognized, we'd like you not to talk about the events of early this morning. Least of all to the press or media. It's a closed chapter that's best left that way. If there's anything that you have to say about it – anything at all, ever – our understanding is that you're to come to us first. And as I said earlier, if there's any way we can thank you for what you did, please let us know.'

'There is one thing I'd like,' I said.

'Anything.'

I looked across at Sever. 'Evelyn Plotkin, my neighbor. The one you shoved back into her apartment. She's a nice lady. Collects figurines. Member of Amnesty International. T-shirt with a picture of her grandkids on the front. That sort of stuff. I'd like you to apologize to her.'

Sever's tan face flexed, accenting the muscle beneath his cheeks.

Wydell said, 'That's it? That's all you want?'

'That's all.'

He nodded at Sever. 'I think we can arrange that.'

I pulled on my sneakers. 'Oh – sorry. One other thing.'

Sever looked less obliging now. 'What's that?'

I stood, cinching the hospital gown around my waist as best I could. 'Can you help me get home?'

I followed them out, Charlie's key rattling soundlessly inside the heel of my shoe.

7

A few ribbons of yellow crime-scene tape had been stretched haphazardly across the open doorway, a spider web that had lost its momentum. My door rested flat in the middle of my torn-up living room. I stood for a few moments in the hall, contemplating the mess. I was wearing an *I Heart LA* T-shirt and baggie muscle pants from the hospital gift shop. My head was throbbing – I could feel the pulse intensified in the cut in my cheek – and the hallway lights seemed unusually bright. My mouth tasted bitter, like the rind of some fruit. I had been looking forward to getting home so much it hadn't occurred to me what would be waiting.

I stepped through the tape, picked up the door, and rested it carefully back in place. I walked around and checked all the locks. Stupid, I know, given that the door was leaning against the frame, but old habits are hard to kill. I closed all the blinds, then surveyed the condo. When I got home, I usually checked that none of my things were out of place, another part of the ritual, but what was the point? Every drawer had been dumped. My books, bills, and papers had been rifled through and dropped unceremoniously.

The TV had been moved to the carpet and Frank's old steamer trunk flipped, jaws to the carpet, its contents strewn around my bedroom. I hadn't gone through them in years. My first baseball trophy, broken at the base. The Punisher's debut in *Spiderman*. My dad, still smoking, still smiling in Kodachrome. All these artifacts, imprinted in my memory so strongly that seeing them felt like déjà vu. But they were also somehow altered, diminished. The shine of the trophy had worn off. The baseball cards looked faded. My father's smile wasn't as relaxed as I'd remembered, and it held an element of self-righteousness.

Callie's sketches had landed over by the Ikea bureau. The back porch of Frank's house. A pear on our battle-scarred kitchen table. They transported me back in time as swiftly and vividly as the smell of fresh-mowed outfield grass. I unrolled the portrait of Frank and sat cross-legged on the floor with it. I'd forgotten how capable Callie was. She'd accented Frank's lips and given him the benefit of the doubt on his nose, making him not more handsome, but perhaps more refined. Yet she'd captured precisely the creases in his face, the depth and vigilance of those dark pupils.

An image knifed into consciousness – me cradling that face while the body beneath it shuddered and failed. Half my life I'd spent running from that spotlit moment and the fallout from it.

The ache in my knees drew me back into my present confusion. Tufts of couch stuffing, key in my shoe, the charcoal portrait of Frank in my lap. The acid flicking at the walls of my stomach reminded me why I'd consigned the sketch to the trunk, why the trunk had stayed closed. I rolled up the drawing and put it away with everything else, then set the TV back on the trunk to prevent it from leaping open like a horror-movie effect.

My discomfort came to life as an itch under my skin. I clicked the remote, hoping the background noise would make me feel less alone. A Reelect-Bilton spot oozed from the TV with an inspiring symphonic track. The Commander in Chief decked out in a sweater and khakis before the Oval Office desk, his high-school sweetheart still sedated at his side, surrounded by three generations of Biltons – grown children, it-generation grandkids, and a few burbling great-grandsons. 'Senator Caruthers says he doesn't "understand family values". Do you really want someone in the White House who's proud to make that claim?'

Three channels over, I found Wile E. Coyote on a precipice, about to misjudge his pendulum swing.

I took a deep breath, contemplated my next move. I'd missed a morning interview, not good considering I was beholden to my ex-girlfriend for setting it up. Induma, a software engineer when we'd dated, had sold a storage-management application to IBM or Oracle for an obscene amount of money and for stock options that turned out to be worth more than that. She now acted as a part-time guru, helping troubleshoot for the hundreds of companies and institutions using her system. They included Pepperdine, which offered a joint MBA/Master of Public Policy I'd had my eye on for a while.

In the last eight years, I'd worked my way from soup-kitchen ladler to co-executive director of an umbrella charity that channeled money to various programs for LA's homeless. At thirty-five, I had just convinced myself I was ready for something bigger. Last week, I'd left to explore options and start studying for the standardized tests required for Pepperdine's joint degree program. And Induma had hooked me up with an informational interview with a dean of admissions; I didn't want to screw up my chances, but even more, I didn't want to make her look bad.

I picked up my cordless phone to give her a call. A chill tensed the skin on my arms and I threw the phone down on the bed. I found a screwdriver among the dumped-out tools at the bottom of the coat closet, and pried the phone's casing open. I lifted out the perforated disk of the receiver. No C4. And no bugs, but I knew from *Law & Order* that these days they tapped calls from outdoor junction boxes. Deciding to play it safe, I left the phone dismantled on the kitchen counter.

I headed into the bathroom, sat on the edge of the tub, and at long last, wiggled the key from the sole of my shoe. Brass, like I remembered. Thicker than a house key. Stamped on the front, three uneven numbers: *229.* On the back: *US Gov't, Unlawful to Duplicate.*

An office in the Secret Service Building? A government vault? A safe-deposit box?

A knock at the front door startled me. As I sprang up, a thud vibrated the floor. Jamming the key back into the air pocket of my sneaker, I scrambled out into my bedroom.

A ginger-haired young man in his early twenties stood at an uncomfortable forward tilt, peering apologetically into my apartment, his fist still raised from knocking. He wore a white shirt, almost the shade of his skin, and a red paisley bowtie. The front door lay flat on its side just inside the threshold. We regarded each other, startled. I looked like an idiot or a schizophrenic – muscle pants, gift-shop T-shirt, eyes glassy with fatigue.

'Uh, sorry. Mr Horrigan?'

'Nick.'

'I'm Alan Lambrose. One of Senator Caruthers's aides. The Senator got into town late last night after the debate, and he'd like to thank you in person.'

'Is that really a bowtie?'

'It is. It's sort of how I'm known. Senator's aide with a bowtie.' He smiled brightly and fanned a hand down the hall. 'I have a car waiting for you, if that's okay.'

I walked into the living room, the Aztec pattern of the muscle pants flashing with my movement, and gestured around. 'Not the best time.'

'Is there some way we can help?'

'Sure. I'd like my door fixed.'

'We'll get that taken care of. And we'll see that you're reimbursed for the damage.'

'Look,' I said, 'I get it. There's fifteen minutes of fame to be had. Everyone's eager for me to have them, and to get a picture shaking my hand.'

'Everyone?'

'Every presidential candidate.'

Alan's pale lips firmed to suppress a smile, the first break in his wonkishness. 'I won't lie to you,' he said, 'and pretend we're not pleased you didn't wait around for Bilton's call.'

'How do you know about that? Did Wydell tell you?'

'I don't know Wydell, but I can tell you that it became Service scuttlebutt before you left the hospital.'

That struck me as odd, and made me wonder at the reach of Caruthers's influence. 'I'd always thought the Service was about discretion,' I said carefully.

'Times are different, I suppose,' Alan said. 'Everything's gone to shit and politics.'

'Right,' I said. 'Well, please thank Senator Caruthers for the offer, but tell him I'll take a pass. I need to, you know, figure out what to do here about my place.' I hoped I didn't sound as helpless as I felt.

'I didn't mean to upset you.' Alan withdrew.

I tried shoving some of the stuffing back into the couch, growing increasingly frustrated. I wanted to restore something to its former shape, even a damn couch. But the more I fussed with it, the more the fabric tore and stretched, and after a while I gave up and sat, splay-legged and discouraged.

When I looked up, Alan was in the doorway again, sliding his cell phone back into his pocket. 'The Senator told me I was an asshole for playing the political angle. He said he has no interest in publicizing his meeting with you. He just wants to meet you because he was such an admirer of your stepfather.'

I considered this skeptically. But I remembered how Frank had always spoken about Caruthers. 'Can I take a shower?'

'I'm sorry, the Senator's on a bit of a schedule today.'

He turned away obligingly while I changed. I kept the *I Heart LA* shirt, but switched out the muscle pants for jeans.

'Watch your step there.' He held the crime-scene tape up for me as I ducked through the doorway, a boxer entering a ring.

I followed him down the hall, on my way to meet the next President of the United States.

Waiting for the elevator, Alan raised a hand, touched my shoulder. 'You mind my asking why you're so reluctant to be noticed?'

'Yes,' I said, my thoughts yanked back seventeen years. I minded quite a bit.

8

The open back door. The bloody streak across the floorboards. Frank, dead in my arms. Propped against his armchair, cradling his body, I went in and out. My arms cramped. My shirt was saturated, his blood growing cold against my skin.

Then the phone was at my face, an operator squawking in my ear. Two buttons bore the mark of my bloody fingerprint, though I couldn't remember dialing.

There were sirens, and then cops and agents were there, though I didn't recall them arriving. At some point much later, Callie appeared, sitting on Frank's armchair, trembling. The detectives were telling her that Frank had been shot by his own gun. His watch was missing and Callie's fake-diamond bracelet and our shitty VCR. A botched robbery, probably a junkie. The perp had come in the back and left through the side door of the garage, which they'd found unbolted and swaying. With everything he was, Frank Durant had been killed by a third-rate lowlife. Yes, he had. He'd been killed by me.

When I told the authorities why I'd snuck out, Callie gave a muffled sob and walked out of the room. It cut me to the bone, that little sob and the universe of disappointment it contained.

Night after night I sat in my room, listened to my mom crying through the thin walls. I can't describe what those sounds did to me. Some of my earliest memories of Callie were after my dad died – the only few months I'd known her to smoke – standing outside with a long-burning cigarette after she thought I'd gone to sleep, her shoulders shaking. And I thought, *This is her life again. This is her life now. And it's because of me.*

I stayed home from school. I didn't show up for play-offs. Caruthers himself called Callie to express condolences. She and I didn't speak much – I could barely be in her presence, let alone meet her eye. I was completely lost, and there was no Frank to come in and figure out what not to tell me.

She finally started taking sleeping pills and going down a little after ten o'clock at night, but I was still in such bad shape I could barely close my eyes to blink. I wandered the dark house, searching out traces of Frank. His coffee mug still in the sink, the dark ring inside. English Leather clinging to the dated sport coat over the back of the kitchen chair. His footprints in the matchbox garden. I felt his absence as broken glass in my stomach, my betrayal as the pounding of my heartbeat in my head.

Once the food in the fridge spoiled, I threw it out and went to the convenience store to pick up some iced tea and frozen burritos for whenever Callie started eating again. Walking home at twilight, the 7-Eleven bags swinging around my knees, I became aware of a car creeping behind me. The side-view mirror of a parked truck afforded me a glimpse. Dark sedan, tinted windows, no front plate. It moved with me, matching my pace, for about a half block. My fear mounting, I kept on, fighting to hold my gaze ahead. Finally I could no longer resist, and when I whirled, the sedan screeched into a U-turn and sped off. I stared after it until I felt the plastic grocery bags cutting off the circulation in my fingers. The back plate had been missing, too.

That night I found Callie sitting in Frank's armchair, staring at the bleached spot on the floorboards, a white puddle to match the one Frank had left behind.

'Mom?' Just calling her that made my voice falter.

She looked up blankly.

I said, 'Frank was scared of something. Some*one*. I think whoever did it was waiting for the opening I gave them that night.'

Her anger caught me by surprise. 'You don't have to do this, Nicky. It's a morbid fantasy. You heard the detectives. It was some druggie burglar.'

'We live in *Glendale*, Mom. How many junkies have you seen around here?'

'I don't want you to be responsible for Frank's death, either. But this, your scenario, it isn't real. Frank was *always* worried about security. It's just part of who he is. Was. It just got worse. And worse. Don't take on his paranoia.'

'Whoever killed him was in the house when I was coming up the side run.' I pointed past her head at the facing wall, but she just pressed her eyes closed. 'They think I saw something. Or that Frank told me something. They're waiting and watching, like they did with Frank. I don't know that it's safe to be near me.'

She was crying again. 'Please don't make me do this with you. Not right now. Please, Nicky. It's *nuts*. The detectives said – and even the agents – they said it wasn't . . .'

'There was this car today. At a stop sign. A sedan, and the windows were—'

She was on her feet. 'There's *nothing*. It was *nothing*. Or – or the PD and the Service said they'd send a car by. To keep an eye. That's what they do after a murder. Or it was just some car and you want it to—'

'There was no license plate. They peeled out as soon as I—'

'Stop it! Just – *stop*. I can find a way to live with . . . your mistake, and with Frank's dying, but I will not live in this house one more day with this toxic paranoia.' Sobbing, she darted to the front door, threw back the deadbolts. She shoved the kitchen windows open, smashed at the alarm pad with her fist, then sagged against the counter, holding her hand. 'Not one more day,' she said hoarsely. 'Do you understand?'

'Frank was *scared* of something, Callie. And we both know he didn't scare easily.' I couldn't shake the flurry of images – Frank fingering aside the curtain, wanding down his truck, that grainy flash by JFK's head. 'He couldn't get backup either. So the Service is either involved, or this is something too big for them.'

She was yelling, now, to match my tone. 'Too big for the Secret Service? Do you hear yourself?'

'You don't see them digging into this. One of their agents was *murdered*. And they don't want to touch it. You *really* think some crackhead could've wrestled

Frank's gun away from him? The Service is rolling over for some bullshit story. And so are you.'

She came at me, leering, her face twisted with loathing. '*You* fucked up, Nicky. *You* did. You got Frank killed so you could screw some slut on a pitcher's mound. So don't go making this about conspiracy theories and cover-ups.'

I swallowed dryly. My flesh tingled, wanting to be numb. It felt anything but.

She sobbed for a while and then looked around as if she'd just realized where she was. 'I'm sorry. I'm sorry. Right now, I just . . . I just . . .' She took a deep breath, held it, and after she let it out she sounded more weary than I'd ever heard her. 'Kathy's coming to pick me up. Italian. You oughta come eat with us.'

I couldn't answer because I was afraid if I talked, I'd start crying. So I shook my head and walked away. In my room, I plugged Tetris into Nintendo and watched those puzzle pieces fall. I made no move to play, to align them; I just let them pile up until they reached the top of the screen and blinked defeat. All those broken shapes, all those parts of an elusive whole. I watched them tumble and tumble until I no longer felt overwhelmed, until I felt just a glazed sort of surrender. A half-hour later I heard a honk and she called through the door that she was leaving. The first time she'd gone out since Frank's death.

I came back out after she left and walked around, closing the windows, relocking the deadbolts. I paused by that front window I'd watched Frank stand at so many times. Mimicking his position, I slid two fingers through the gap in the curtains. I knew what would be waiting out there as I knew the next twist of a recurring nightmare. My hand shaking, I drew back the curtain.

A dark sedan was parked up the street at the curb.

My skin tightened as if against the cold. The phone rang, startling the hell out of me. Walking backward to keep an eye on the front door, I reached the phone and picked up.

A gruff voice said, 'Your mother was just seated at a corner table at Giammarco's.' He breathed for a moment on the car phone, letting the implications sink in. Then he said, calmly, 'Come outside.'

I held the phone in a sweaty hand until it bleated in my ear. Then I set it down. I waited for my mind to kick into gear, but it wouldn't. There was just terror, superimposed across the blankness that was everything else. But I already knew what I had to do. I'd placed Frank at risk. I couldn't do the same with my mom. On trembling legs, I walked outside.

I wouldn't see that house or my mom again for nearly nine years.

9

It was my first time riding in a limousine and I was still adjusting to how uncomfortable it was. I was seated on a curved section of leather bench, my knees wedged against an acrylic bar. Somehow Alan managed to work two cell phones without breaking the cadence of either conversation. He finally finished the calls and rubbed his eyes with boyish indulgence. 'Sorry. As you can probably guess, it's a critical time.'

'He hammered Bilton in the debate last night,' I said. 'November's gonna be a landslide.'

'Debates don't always matter. We have a seven-point lead, but Bilton's just starting to dig into that war chest and we're waiting for the October surprises.'

I kept an eye on our route to make sure we were heading where he'd said we were. 'Yeah, but you have to admit. It feels like this is Caruthers's time.'

'I agree. I just think it'll be tighter than everyone's predicting. Jasper Caruthers is threatening to a lot of people. Institutions. Corporations. The Pentagon. There are a lot of voter blocks with a vested interest in seeing him lose.'

Alan tapped the divider and pointed left and the limo slowed and signaled. Cops shoved sawhorses back against a dense press corps and we pulled into the turnaround under the famous cursive sign: *Beverly Hills Hotel*. We stepped out into a dry heat, palm trees nodding over-head, and a woman scurried forward and handed me an impressive-looking laminated pass with my DMV photo and a security seal. Before I could acknowledge her, Alan was prodding me through the second security perimeter, magnetometer wands and agents scrutinizing us as an air-conditioned current blew past.

We moved through a number of well-appointed halls, Alan nodding at post-standers as I robotically raised my pass on its lanyard, and then we were through a back door and out at the edge of the dais with a huddle of campaign workers, Caruthers no less than ten yards away, addressing a ballroom filled with rapt listeners. Five agents composed the inner security perimeter, positioned back from the podium and down in front of the dais. Though they were at only a five-foot stand-off, you'd barely register them if you weren't looking.

After years of trying to blend in, I felt completely exposed up there before all those eyes and lenses. I took a half step back behind the curtain.

Caruthers turned, noticing me, and winked without breaking cadence. 'I made a promise a year ago when I announced my intention to seek the Presidency that I would run a transparent campaign. That I would do my best to bring voters *inside* the process' – he spread his arms to quell the applause – 'because I assume that you're as fed up with smoke-blowing as I am. We've come through a period of unprecedented irresponsibility in the White House. We can't torture to stop violence. We can't disregard our Constitution to promote democracy. We cannot cede long-term environmental strategy for short-sighted gain. It's been said a thousand times, but that makes it no less true: the ends do not – *cannot* – justify the means. We've seen it time and time again – and nowhere as clearly as in our woeful foreign policy of the past decade – a single decision made for the wrong reasons coming back to bite us in the ass. A single bad decision can open a world of lamentable consequences.'

People rose in bunches to clap. I wondered if any of them, like me, were thinking of choices they'd made and aftermath they'd lived with.

'We need to question these decisions. We need to question our leaders. The next debate, up the road here at UCLA, will give students and citizens an opportunity to address their concerns directly to the candidates. Please take advantage of it. Ask tough questions. Call us to answer.'

He bent his head reflectively. 'My favorite reminder of my years as Vice President is my passport. A lot of people don't know this, but the President and Vice President of the United States, just like everyone else, have to turn over their passports to immigration control before entering a country. As you can imagine, mine is filled with stamps. They remind me of the privilege of the post. But more important, they remind me that no man is above the law. Every American, no matter his post, no matter his privilege, can be faced down, called to answer. We must call this President to answer for the blunders he has made. And you can do that most powerfully with your vote.'

The dais literally shook with the standing ovation and Caruthers waved and grinned, then moved toward me, agents rotating around him like electrons. The focus of the entire ballroom seemed to follow him as he strode over and then he clasped my hand in both of his, his amused eyes snagging on my shirt which he seemed to sense wasn't my fault, and said, 'Nick, thank you for coming. I promised June I'd hurry back to the condo – will you please join me?'

At first I wasn't certain I'd heard him correctly over the noise, but I nodded anyway. He waved again, camera flashes dotting the sea of faces, and then he was gone through the back door.

I was frisked and wanded twice between the lobby and the door to Caruthers's apartment. The limo had dropped Alan and me off before the tallest building along the Wilshire Corridor, LA's stretch of pseudo-high-rise condos where retirees intermingled with pining Manhattanites and Angelenos too rich to live on ground level. I wasn't surprised when the elevator stopped at the ninth floor – Frank had always said that was the highest story accessible by hook-and-ladder in case of emergency. They'd spent months trying to convince Caruthers to move seven stories down from his penthouse when he'd been elected Vice President. When they'd finally appealed to June, she'd closed the deal in twenty-four hours.

Two more agents in the hall checked out my pass and Alan's face, then opened the double-doors leading to the condo. The first thing that struck me was the space. I'd never been in a residence that large, particularly not one in the middle of a building. Several pods of chairs and tables and sofas, a bar, a dining area, wall-to-wall floor-to-ceiling glass – tinted and ballistic – three or four plasma TVs, a treadmill, and at least five doors leading back to hallways or other rooms. The place was alive with voices and movement. As Alan whisked me through different clusters and discussions, I strained to make out snatches of conversation, but as we passed, the volume dropped as if electronically regulated. Instinctively, I kept track of the exits, the turns, the routes back out to freedom.

We landed in a conference room with an intimidatingly long marble table, a statue-still Secret Service post-stander, several ominously titled 'state operatives', and a heavyset woman with horn-rims and an air of unflinching competence, introduced as the architect of the campaign. Adorning the walls were pictures of Caruthers – lost in thought in the Oval Yellow Room, on the distinctive trails around Camp David, at dinner sharing a joke with Gorbachev. At the end of the table was the man himself, cocked back in an Aeron chair, facing the window, shirt sleeves cuffed, phone pressed to his ear. Seated beside him and also facing away, June spoke simultaneously into another line. Her willowy form was accented by her sleek outfit, its flaring sleeves and pant cuffs echoing the lines of her sweeping red hair. A former prep-school dean, she was as tall as her husband and widely thought to be even smarter. They'd each been married before and their divorces made much of by the opposition. Even their well-advertised silver anniversary hadn't inoculated Caruthers from pious question-raising about his suitability as a role model.

Alan gestured toward the couple. When I raised my hands in bewilderment, he gestured again. Nervously, I walked toward them, passing a number of empty chairs. I sat one chair away from them, past the table's curve, but the Senator and his wife were too immersed in their conversations to notice me. Midday light came in through the window, framing their forms. I looked out with them across Westwood, Bel Air, the ribbons of smog caught on the Santa Monicas. Was I really here, pulled up to a table with Jasper and June Caruthers? Or was I still unconscious from the blast and dreaming this?

'I'm sure you could if you wanted to, Governor. I've certainly been made a fool of by lesser men than you.' Caruthers hung up, chuckled to draw his wife's attention, and swiveled to face me as if he'd known I was there all along.

'Nick, glad you could make it. I'm sorry to ask you to run around like this.'

He was the most important person I'd ever been in close proximity to, except maybe when I'd sat next to Barry Bonds on a Southwest flight. Caruthers had a shaving nick at the point of his jaw and a fleck of a cherry mole on his forearm. Both inexplicably surprised me. 'No problem, Senator.'

He removed a box of gum from his pocket and popped a piece through the foil backing into his mouth. 'Voters hate smokers,' he said. 'So I've been addicted to nicotine gum for twenty-five years.' He tapped his wife on the shoulder and she signed off and slotted the phone. 'What's all that about?' he asked her.

'The temperature in the auditorium for next week's

debate,' she said, offering me a disarming smile that said she'd get to me in a minute. Her modest chin added to a deceptively demure appearance, but she was one glance to sharp or sexy. 'We want seventy-three, they want seventy.'

'Why?'

'Bilton is a sweater.'

'Oh, for Christ's sake. Have it at sixty. I'll make him sweat anyway.'

June's attention moved to the cluster of workers at the far end of the table. 'We'll need antiperspirant for his forehead.' She ran her freshly manicured fingers through Caruthers's hair, pushing it up from his forehead. 'Something that won't chalk.' As she rose, Caruthers feigned indignation, which she met with an amused grin. 'Remember,' she said, 'this is why you married me.'

'Your ruthlessness?'

'No. To save you the humiliation of sweating like a pig on prime time.'

'You forget: I have the resilience of a used-car salesman.'

'I don't think *Vanity Fair* intended that as a compliment, darling,' she said, even as she shifted her focus to me.

I half-rose from my chair and received her feminine handshake.

'Nick, it is such a pleasure. Thank you for what you did this morning even if the boys in black didn't deal with you entirely on the up-and-up.' I followed her stare to the door, but the agent's face remained impassive. She leaned over her husband, kissed him, and headed out before I could stammer a response.

I felt disoriented, yanked out of my quiet existence into a plot I couldn't keep pace with. Everyone was being too damn polite, which told me that whatever I'd fallen into was as lethal as those innocuous-looking bundles of spent-fuel rods resting at the bottom of that pool. One thing was for sure; I was well out of my depth. I wiggled my sneaker ever so slightly – Charlie's key was still in there, insistent as ever.

Caruthers regarded the crew waiting on the far side of the room. 'Anything else?'

The woman in the horn-rimmed glasses said, with barely-contained anger, 'Please do not ever again say *ass* on broadcast television.'

'Come on. Voters like a little moderate swearing.'

'Not in Colorado Springs they don't.' She studied his frown, decided to press the point. 'Don't make me remind you and everyone else you stepped in it on the family-values business.'

Alan redirected to cut the tension. 'We're still waiting on finals, but it looks like the San Onofre thing bumped Bilton's numbers.'

Caruthers waved him off, leaning to confide in me, 'When people are scared, they cozy to the incumbent. If nothing else, Bilton is soothing for his consistency. When he dies, his tombstone will read, *Here lies Andrew Bilton. He was appropriate.*' Caruthers swept a hand in your-name-in-lights fashion, and I couldn't help but smile.

Alan said, 'Well, he's up three in the polls this morning. Masterfully handled operation, can't switch horses midstream, blah blah blah. They're spinning it as Bilton's idea to direct Secret Service resources to the threat.'

74

Caruthers scowled. 'Bilton wouldn't think of that if it was typed out on his teleprompter.'

'Well, it's his Service, sir. We're just borrowing it right now.' Alan shot an after-the-fact glance at the post-stander, whose face still betrayed nothing.

Caruthers and I were elbow-to-elbow at the end of the table, like two senior board members. 'All right – thank you everyone. Please give me a moment with Nick.' He waved them out. 'You too, James.'

The Secret Service agent at the door didn't budge. His even stare took my measure. 'I'd prefer not to leave you alone in a room with anyone, Senator.'

'I agree wholeheartedly. But this isn't anyone. It's Frank Durant's boy.'

'Okay.' The agent withdrew, but as he went through the door, I heard him say, 'Though we don't want you ending up like Frank Durant.'

Caruthers scowled after him before settling back in his chair. And then it was just me and a presidential candidate and the Westside laid out beyond the broad window.

He eyed me gamely. 'Are you a Democrat or a Republican?'

'Neither,' I said. 'I didn't vote in the last election.'

'Yes, you did,' he said. 'And your candidate won.'

It took a few seconds for me to pick up his meaning. Caruthers seemed to be pithy like Frank, even away from the cameras. He had the same talent for cutting to the heart of a matter, for leaving you reflective rather than defensive.

'Okay, fair enough—' I caught myself. 'With all due respect . . .'

He was leaning forward, genuinely interested in me now, or else doing an excellent job faking it. 'Please, by all means, continue.'

'All the dogma and feigned moral indignation, it just wears at me. In my old job, I saw a lot of policy changes, and God knows Bilton has gutted social services, but I've found that whatever politicians promise, it usually doesn't trickle down to the people who need it.'

He licked his lips, seeming to enjoy the frank exchange. 'Not a fan of government?'

'Government can be a nasty thing when you're on the wrong end of it.'

He rested a hand on my forearm, a gesture that from anyone else might have seemed condescending, but his eyes were so alive, his face so receptive and oddly vulnerable, that it didn't bother me. 'People are fed up with the bullshit. And rightly. I hear some of the agents on the team think something more went down in that nuclear power plant.'

Just like that. No transition.

We stared at each other. My mouth was dry and my blood was moving at a good clip. I thought about his sending the Secret Service agent outside and wondered who he trusted and with what.

'So that's why you wanted to talk to me?'

The phone chirped and Caruthers tapped a button to silence it. 'You're the only person who was actually inside that nuclear plant. You say you're tired of bullshit, and we both know the official line on San Onofre hardly smells like roses. If you want to talk, I'm someone who will listen to you. The administration is very eager to label this terrorism because it drives their stock up. But I have to wonder if a guy like Mike Milligan with a bomb is looking for something more than just turning Southern California into a radioactive wasteland.'

I said, tentatively, 'You believe there was a bomb?'

A silence. Then he laughed. 'Oh, that's clever. Really clever. Quite a spin job they foisted on the public. To the tune of three percentage points.' It was hard to gauge his surprise, but it seemed genuine. He rubbed his eyes and slumped back in his chair. For the first time I could recall, he looked his age. Four of the buttons on the phone were now blinking. 'So what do you think is *really* behind this?'

I shrugged. 'Why do you think I would know?'

'Milligan asked for you.'

'Not really. He asked for Frank Durant's stepson.'

'Still. Why?'

'I don't know. If you think the agents know something more, can't you just demand the information?'

'I'm a member of the Senate, but only a candidate for the Presidency. The Service and I have a strictly protector-protectee relationship. As Alan pointed out, the agents are only guarding me since I'm in the race. They're under no obligation to present to me investigative details about every nutjob who wants to disrupt the election.' He smirked. 'Beyond that, it's the rules of the game. Bilton's the Man now. Eight years around the White House taught me the need to protect sensitive information from political rivals.'

I said, 'So you think there's sensitive information.'

'That's another of the rules – *any* information is sensitive. Case in point: Mike Milligan with a bomb is a terrorist. Without, he's just a criminal . . .'

'And a dead terrorist is more useful to the incumbent in an election news cycle.'

Caruthers offered me a slow nod, just down. 'If you need anything, or if this thing takes a spin on you . . . well, Alan gave you the number at headquarters? I'll make sure you can reach me at any time.' He saw my discomfort and his face softened. 'I understand you don't want to get sucked into all this. I get it. Believe me, I get it. But the offer will be there.' He cocked his head, the light coming through his fair hair, the pronounced nose punctuating his thoughtful frown. I couldn't help but think of his Service call sign, Firebird. 'I've been told that you don't want any recognition for your role in last night's events,' he said. 'Is that right?'

'The nail that sticks out gets hammered,' I said.

He fixed those trademark green eyes on me. 'You sound like your stepfather.'

'That's because it's his line.'

'Maybe I've been in politics too long. People who don't want something make me nervous.'

'Sorry. I don't mean to make you nervous.'

'Please. Christ, maybe I'll learn something from you.' Caruthers's smile softened. 'Frank Durant. What a tragedy that was.' His eyes gleamed with a memory. 'One year back then we were at President Kinney's ranch for New Year's. After dinner, the President brought a glass of port over for Frank – I mean, he didn't send it, he carried it himself. Frank was working, so he politely refused. The President pressed him a bit, but Frank held firm. It couldn't have been an easy situation. Finally President Kinney said, "Special Agent Durant, I know you're working, but

78

it's just a half glass." And Frank said, "As the twig is bent, the tree inclines.""

I smiled and felt the familiar tug in my chest.

Caruthers said, 'He didn't talk much, but he deployed his words well.'

I looked away so he wouldn't see the emotion in my face. 'Frank spoke very highly of you,' I said.

Caruthers nodded kindly, but he was a man used to taking compliments, and didn't understand the weight Frank's assessment carried. He rose and offered his hand. 'I hope I see you again, Nick.'

'Nice meeting you, Senator.'

When I walked out, I glanced over my shoulder. Caruthers was standing again at the window, silhouetted against the light, lost in his thoughts or troubles.

10

Though I was a high-school senior, I was trembling like an eight-year-old. First the sedan beyond the curtain. Then the gruff voice over the phone, the implicit threat against Callie – *Your mother was just seated at a corner table at Giammarco's.* I had little choice but to go outside and face whoever had come for me.

I edged through our front door into the cool night. The sight of that dark sedan nearly made me take off in the opposite direction, but I thought of Callie and willed myself not to bolt, not to freeze, not to slow. I became horribly aware of every part of my body – my arms swinging unnaturally, my feet rotating to slap concrete, my shoulders ratcheting up toward my neck. The sedan's windshield was tinted; I might as well have been staring at a wall of obsidian.

When I got within five feet, the back door popped open. Just a few inches. The handle felt cool under my fingers. I got in. Two men up front, mid-40s, high-and-tight hair. The smell of the leather interior.

The guy in the passenger seat turned around, placed a thick hand next to the headrest. My heart was pounding so hard I could barely hear my voice. 'I'm here,' I said. 'I came. Please leave my mom alone.'

The driver was more slender. He laughed. 'I'm afraid you misunderstood. We weren't threatening your mother. We don't want to involve her in this. I'm sure you don't either.' His voice – the one I'd just heard on the phone.

He pulled out from the curb. I was too terrified to ask where we were going. They listened to the radio. Small talk about college hoops. Slim had a girl on the side who was turning into a hassle.

We headed toward downtown. I was certain I was going to be shot and dumped under a freeway. I finally worked up the nerve to speak. 'I don't know anything. I didn't see anything. I swear to God.'

The big guy said, 'Radio sucks out here, huh?' and twisted the dial.

We pulled up in front of an imposing, almost futuristic gray building with endless floors, bulges, and tiny windows. Slim said, 'Out.'

But there were no interior door handles. Slim came around, tugged me onto the sidewalk. A big sign read *Metropolitan Detention Center*. I knew from Frank that it was a federal facility. My legs sagged under me and the big guy grabbed my arm and helped me inside. At the guard console, Slim removed some folded papers from his jacket pocket and handed them across. 'We have signed clearance.'

The guard nodded. The way he nodded – deferentially – put a fresh charge into my anxiety.

He waved the two guys through and then we were in an elevator, then moving down a dark corridor past men shuffling in leg cuffs. They booked me, printed me, and put me in an interrogation room. I sat in the chair, trying not to cry. They circled around me.

Slim's footsteps tapped the concrete. Paused. 'We know.'

I swallowed dryly. 'You know *what*?'

'What happened to Frank Durant.' He came back into view, using a thumbnail to pick at his teeth. 'You killed him.'

I couldn't get out any words.

'*Unless* . . .' The big guy turned the other chair around and sat on it backwards. 'Unless you stop trying to upset your mother. You see, Frank was killed by a burglar. That's the story. And if he *wasn't*, then he was killed by you.' He slung a pistol, encased in a crime-scene baggie, over the chairback. Frank's Glock, still covered in blood. I hadn't seen him carrying the gun; it had appeared magically. 'Your prints.'

Slim was leaning against the far wall. 'Can you imagine? After all Frank did for you. Took you in. Treated you like his own.'

Tears ran down my face. Hot. My voice came out hoarse. 'I would never have.'

'Then I guess that burglar whacked him.'

Slim jerked his head. They both got up and walked out. Leaving me there.

I waited what seemed like a long time.

They came back in and led me out. Down a concrete corridor with sweating walls. We came up on a giant rolling door built of bars. Beyond, a general holding tank. Sinewy men with pale skin and tattoos doing pull-ups.

Mexicans bickering over smokes. Bandannas tied over perspiring ebony skulls. I had never felt smaller. I had never felt younger.

The big guy put his hand on one of the door's bars. 'Want a night to think it over?'

I shook my head, wiped my nose.

They steered me through the concrete maze and down to the street. In the back of the sedan, I cried a bit, but tried not to make noise. We weren't driving back to Glendale. We were driving to LAX. Slim pulled over at Terminal One. The big guy handed me a torn piece of paper, then dialed the car phone and stretched it back to me.

'Read,' he said.

My throat was closing up, but I fought it open. Callie's answering-machine greeting finished, and after the beep, I read from the slip of paper, 'I know I'm responsible for Frank's death. I can't figure out how to face you every day. I'm sorry. I hope you'll forgive me.'

The worst part was they'd got it right.

The big guy flipped an envelope in my lap. Filled with thousands of dollars of traveler's checks. I felt my last ray of hope extinguish. I thought about the financial-aid package waiting for me at UCLA. I thought about the baseball team. The attention I might get. The opportunities.

He said, 'You don't talk about this to anyone. *Ever*. Or we'll know. And we'll know who you talked to also. We won't be nearly as accommodating next go 'round. To you *or* her. Bear that in mind.'

I said, 'I will.'

'You stay gone. A good long time. Understand?'

I nodded.

'If they require guardian clearance for you to buy a ticket.' He pointed at a phone number that had been written on the envelope flap. 'You're two days shy of your eighteenth birthday. Forty-eight hours.'

I had forgotten.

He knuckled his broad nose and it made a faint popping sound. 'By the time they declare you a missing person, you'll be an adult. Able to uphold your commitments.'

So that's what I was now. A missing person.

My stomach roiling, I got out, clutching the envelope. Cars honked; cops ticketed; people hugged each other goodbye. In a stunned haze, I stepped into the terminal and the glass doors whistled shut behind me.

11

A fter my meeting with Caruthers, I went home to change out of the hospital-gift-shop T-shirt. Then I headed over to the First Union Bank of Los Angeles, on Montana Avenue between a handmade soap store and a juice place with little doormats of wheatgrass in the window.

I waited until I was in line to pull the brass key from my sneaker, and I hid it in my fist until I reached the teller's window. The security cameras were making me sweat. The emergency exit was just past the loan desk – if I hopped the rope, I could be into the alley in a few seconds. My paranoia had returned, so forcefully it seemed impossible there'd ever been the quiet life I'd been torn out of last night.

'My stepdad just died and my mom found this key among his possessions. How can we figure out which bank it belongs to?'

The bank teller looked at me over her glasses, then took Charlie's key and examined it in the flat of her palm.

'Doesn't look like a safe-deposit key to me.' She took my disappointment for greed. 'Oh, honey, even if it *was*, I doubt the box would be filled with something your mom would want. You'd be amazed the things people keep locked up. Most of them sentimental.'

'Why don't you think it's a bank key?'

She tilted it. 'Well, at least ours don't have as many grooves. They're flatter, with square teeth and a clover-leaf head. Plus this one says it belongs to the US Government, but we're privately owned. Banks generally are.' She handed it back. 'I'm sorry I couldn't be of more help, and I'm sorry to hear about your father. I just lost my mom, so I know how hard it can be sorting through the possessions, trying to figure out how to do right by a loved one.'

Her gentle smile made me feel like a heel. I thanked her and left.

The locksmith a few blocks down didn't even give me the chance to lie to him. He was a burly man with a bot-tlebrush mustache and an indistinct accent. 'I not can copy for you. Our blanks not are thick enough, bro.' He rolled the 'r' in *bro*, infusing it with an 'l' sound.

'I don't actually need it copied.'

'Unlawful-to-duplicate key require seven-pin key blank. Illegal to have seven-pin key blank, bro.' A massive eyebrow contorted suspiciously, pinching his right eye. His nametag, which read ASK ME, MY NAME IS: RAZ!, didn't match his apparent gravity. 'You are cop?'

'No, I'm not a cop.'

'You not can lie about, you know.'

'I know.'

'How do you know?'

'Because I'm a cop.'

Raz eyed me, then smirked. 'Listen, bro. Perhaps I get

seven-pin key blank from Canada? Perhaps I copy, but it will cost extra, eh? The risk for illegal.'

'I actually don't need it copied. I was hoping you could just tell me what kind of key it is.'

He sighed, indignant, then knocked the key against the countertop. 'It is good key, pure brass, not cheap alloy.'

'I just found it. It was my stepfather's. What do you think it goes to?'

He screwed up his mouth, his mustache arching like a displeased caterpillar. 'I have to guess, I say post-office-box key.'

'Thank you.'

'You want to copy, you come back here.'

I shook his warm, oversize hand and came away with his business card. I said, 'I promise, bro.'

Crime-scene tape had been strung across the smashed-through garage door of the run-down little house in Culver City, and bulletholes pockmarked the soft wood of the façade. I'd parked a few blocks away and come over on foot, feeling safely anonymous in the thickening dusk.

I kept to the far side of the street and walked past the house, keeping my head down and my pace swift. In the footage I'd watched on the hospital-room TV, the reporter had positioned herself by the front walk where the yellow tape had come unmoored and was fluttering provocatively.

I went around the block and came back, pausing behind an empty van. The parked vehicles appeared to be empty, and I spotted no one lingering or watching the house. I wasn't surprised that the media had decamped after shooting their initial reports last night. But no ongoing surveillance from the cops? That pretty much confirmed that the terrorist story sold to the press was the flimsy cover I'd suspected it to be.

I remembered a lesson I'd learned in another life on the bleached-white tundra. Liffman's Rules: When you don't know what to do, wait longer.

It was a fairly busy street, so I walked to the corner gas station, drank a cup of dense coffee, and returned to see if anything had changed. As I turned the corner, a police car appeared, slowed a bit in front of the house, and continued on its way. So they were making a cursory show of keeping an eye on the place, at least, but it still hardly felt like a terrorist watch. I wondered who made those decisions and at what level.

I stuck my hand in my pocket, clenched it around Charlie's key. I'd checked it at the five closest post offices, starting with the one with the house's ZIP code. The key was appropriately sized for the PO box locks, giving me a stab of excitement each time it slid home, but it had refused to turn. Even if my locksmith bro had guessed right, there were countless other PO Box 229s in Los Angeles, let alone the country.

To figure out whatever Charlie wanted me to know, I wasn't sure what else I could do. Besides break into a crime scene.

Back in my hiding spot behind the van, I realized that I was balking because I was scared. This just wasn't the kind of thing a reasonable person did. But nothing about this situation felt reasonable.

I walked briskly up the sidewalk toward the house, timing my arrival with a break in traffic. I slipped through the crime-scene tape blocking the gaping hole the Jeep had made when it had blasted through the garage door, and crouched in the silence, listening for shouts or approaching footsteps. I heard nothing but the drip of a faucet in the rust-stained sink, rats moving in the walls, the sound of my quickened breathing. By ducking under that tape, I'd crossed a line. In the dark quiet, the danger seemed suddenly more tangible.

After ten minutes, or twenty, I rose and poked around the garage, careful to keep back in the shadows. Several jars on a warped shelf held dried industrial glue. A jackhammer tilted in the corner, its red handle gleaming. A few oil-slick wrenches beneath a dusty work bench, a stack of *National Geographic*s near the step, a faded plastic sandbox on end. I knew it was a rental even before I pushed through the creaking door into the empty interior.

I stood in silence, listening to the sounds of the house. There was literally no furniture. A plastic McDonald's cup in the sink. Grease-stained wrappers in the tipped-over trash bucket. Empty drawers on top of the stove, refrigerator shoved out from the wall – the search had been thorough.

I stepped into the living room. Beams of yellow from the streetlights shot through countless bulletholes, skewering my body as I passed through.

In the tiny bathroom, the medicine cabinet had been torn from the wall and thrown into the tub, bits of mirror twinkling in the faint light like gems. The folding closet doors in the bedroom had been ripped back on their hinges, one of them snapped, and a few items of clothing dumped on the floor. An army-green sleeping bag lay bunched in the corner, as if to make as little an intrusion on the square of dusty carpet as possible. As if Charlie had wanted to curl up there and disappear.

I paused in the doorway, the loneliness of the life lived here settling into my bones. Even if the Service had cleared the place out, it was obvious that Charlie had lived like a squatter. Like someone biding time. Until what?

I walked over and straightened out Charlie's sleeping bag, then lay where he'd slept. A neighbor's porch light glowed through the vertical blinds. The low vantage and the room's bareness added to a feeling of purposeful desolation. As if he was punishing himself for something. As if he didn't believe he deserved more than this.

The tiny den across the hall was empty, the closet bare, save for an attic hatch. I pulled myself up and peered around the crawl space. I could see where numerous boots – law enforcement? – had stamped through the blanket of dust.

Dust.

I dropped down and hurried back into the garage, flattening against the wall to the side of the blow-out garage door. With a finger, I drew a line in the dust on the lids of the glue jars. And again on the top cover of that stack of *National Geographic*s. I forced myself to wait to see if there would be another police drive-by. It seemed an eternity, but finally the car materialized, slowed, drifted off.

Then I scurried past the gaping hole to the jackhammer in the corner.

I touched that gleaming handle.

No dust.

I searched the slab for any signs of chiseling or new concrete. None. Back inside, moving quickly. A cockroach skittered across the worn-out linoleum, but there was no sign that the flooring had been peeled back.

I closed my eyes, running through possibilities. I thought about how Frank had installed that alarm monitor beside his bed so he could sleep knowing it was right there.

Racing back into the bedroom, I tugged the sleeping bag from the corner and ran my hands over the carpet, feeling for bumps in the concrete beneath. Perfectly smooth – it would have had to be or it would've been discovered in the search. In the stripes of light from the blinds, I noted how the carpet edges lifted ever so slightly from the walls in the corner. From this angle I could see it had been pulled up for about three feet in either direction before being smoothed back in place.

It took a few pinches to get a grip on the carpet, then I peeled it back. It came easily, revealing a floor safe embedded in the concrete slab.

I was breathless. The house had been searched, but no one had bothered to lie where Charlie had lain in his sad little corner, had bothered to inhabit his world of asceticism and paranoia.

The lock took a tubular key. I'd hauled Charlie's key around on my person all day and it didn't match the safe he'd slept on top of every night. It made me wonder how many more secrets a guy like Charlie had.

I sat back on my heels like a little kid. A muscle car

blew by outside, the engine spatter loud through the thin walls. A draft rippled the vertical blinds, making the strips of light roll across my face, the walls, making the room come alive. I felt a surprising calm, the still excitement I used to get when I read a ball coming out of the pitcher's hand and knew I'd hit it before it was halfway to the plate.

I rose and headed into the kitchen. I pulled the McDonald's cup from the sink, reached down through the rotting rubber guard into the garbage disposal. My fingers brushed a magnetic box. I pulled it out, slid back the grimy lid, and held the tubular key to the faint light.

My head buzzing with childish excitement, I retraced my steps, sank to my knees on the tugged-back carpet, and lowered the key into place. It fit snugly, the gears shifting in the floor safe. I blew a breath through clenched teeth. The weighty door lifted silently. Hooked to the inside handle, a rope trailed down into shadow. When I tugged, whatever it was connected to gave surprising resistance. I pulled up the rope hand over hand, not sure I wanted to see what would rise into view.

A rucksack, just like the one Charlie had brought with him into San Onofre. It was full, stuffed so the fabric was taut. I undid the buckles and flipped it over before I could lose my nerve.

Out tumbled stack after stack of hundred-dollar bills, bundled neatly in purple bands.

12

With $180,000 slung over one shoulder, I walked as casually as I could back toward my condo. The nearest parking space I'd found was five blocks away, not bad considering it was past nine o'clock and folks had slotted their cars for the night. I paused to glance in store windows and pretended to tie my shoelaces to check if anyone was following me. All these years later and here I was again, as edgy as a fugitive.

As I approached the corner mart, a woman with pursed lips confronted a massive man, his rotund form draped with layers of ripped, dirt-blackened clothing. Even the real-estate prices hadn't driven the smart home- less people out of temperate Santa Monica.

The woman pulled a dollar bill from her purse and handed it to him. 'Do *not* spend this on alcohol.'

'Absolutely not, ma'am.'

His benefactor's Lexus chirped twice and she climbed in and drove off. He heard my footfall and turned at my approach, scratching his bloated belly. Despite a leonine mess of curly hair and a nose swollen to absurdity from weather and alcohol, he had astute, intelligent features.

His face lit up. 'Nick, I'm two bucks shy of a pint.'

I dug in my pocket, came up with a few crumpled bills. 'Do *not* spend this on alcohol.'

Homer smiled, showing off his true-yellows. The bills disappeared into his paw-like hand.

I'd met him not at the various soup kitchens and shelters I'd worked at, but on the street. Homer was one of the stubborn ones, who preferred rooting in garbage cans and sleeping under the open sky. Foolishly, I admired him for that. Working with the homeless could drive you nuts because you wound up liking the right people for the wrong reasons. But I think I took to Homer – and my work – because I'd also lived in the awful crush of imposed anonymity. A few times, I'd been one bounced check from the street. Homer's wryness about his fate had touched a nerve with me from the start. He was as amused as he was resigned, in on the existential joke. Where I'd fought tooth and nail not to slide over the edge, he'd long ago embraced despair, and that made him a seer of sorts, a guide through an underworld I'd only glimpsed.

But Homer also stood out because, in a community of fragmented minds and souls, he'd managed to keep some part of himself intact. On an outreach shift a few years ago, I'd turned my back on a bulky schizophrenic living out of a park utility shed, and the guy had taken a swing at my head. Homer, who'd followed me along in hopes of free lunch, had tried to flop on his shoulders, but misjudged his jump and landed on a water fountain. The guy rang my bell pretty hard before I recovered and subdued him with the help of a coworker. Homer seemed utterly unshaken by the episode; his only injury was when he'd hit his funny bone on the water-fountain spout. He'd shrugged off my gratitude, but I'd never looked at him the same. Whoever said it was the thought that counts was sure as hell right when it came to going up against a two-hundred-eighty-pound schizo off his Risperidone.

I hurried into the store, Homer at my heels, and snatched an *LA Times* from the stack. 'Have you eaten?' I asked.

'No.'

'If I give you a couple more bucks, will you buy a sandwich?'

He shook his head.

'Come on, then.' I detoured to the refrigerated aisle and Homer perused the selections with maddening thoroughness. Hacmed watched us closely from behind the counter. 'How's Italian sub sound?' I asked, shifting the cash on my back and trying to move things along.

'A lotta fat in mortadella,' Homer said.

'Do you have one without mortadella in the back?' I called over.

'For Jesus' sake, Homer, is there not expression about beggar and chooser?' Hacmed looked at me and I looked back and he sighed and went through a curtain that looked like something from a drive-through carwash.

While Homer waited at the counter, staring at the alcohol cabinet, I searched out the prepaid cell phones and grabbed a few from the hook. Hacmed returned and we paid and walked out, Homer sliding the pint of whiskey into a ragged pocket and munching away, bits of bread clinging to his beard.

'Can I get a shower?' he asked.

'Thursdays only,' I said. 'That's the deal. You can wait until tomorrow.'

'I don't see what the difference is.'

'The difference is if you shower whenever you want at my place, then you can start paying rent or putting out.'

'Okay. Tomorrow.' He slid down the wall, kicking his legs out at a flung-doll angle, and readied himself for the next passer-by. 'Do I look sufficiently abject?'

I gave him the thumbs up and rushed home, reading the paper. Front and center, the article about the San Onofre face-off was vague, all quotations coming from 'high-placed government officials'. It mentioned neither Charlie/Mike Milligan nor me. A terrorist whose name couldn't be released due to security considerations had been thwarted in a plot to blow up the nuclear power plant. Bland as the story was, it had pushed the debate round-up, more flattering to Caruthers, below the fold.

Evelyn Plotkin was in the lobby sorting through her mail and dumping the flyers into the trash bin. She had on a neck brace.

'Evey. Are you okay?'

She was holding her eyeglasses up before an envelope, but she let them fall back around her neck. 'Not really. I'm feeling very weak. I haven't eaten all day.'

'Why not?'

'I didn't want my mouth to be full of food if you should call to let me know you were all right.'

I'd already hurried into the elevator, but I dug deep for patience, shouldered out, and walked over. She appraised the small wound on my face with heightened gravity, then gave me a warm, clutchy hug, the kind only mothers give.

'I'm sorry,' I said.

'Who did that to you?'

'The Secret Service. There was a mixup. They confused me for someone else.' I got on the elevator again, but stuck my foot out just before the doors closed. 'By the way, did one of the agents call you to apologize?'

She looked at me like I was out of my mind, and laughed.

The elevator closed, shutting me in with my anger at the Service for ignoring my only request. I rode up, the rucksack sitting heavily on my shoulder. The hoarded cash likely took Charlie out of whistleblower contention, which meant his involvement was less than honorable. Given the two $10,000 stacks with matching purple bands Charlie had brought with him to San Onofre, I figured he'd started with two hundred grand. A heist? Extortion money? Terrorist funds? Or a payment? For what service? Aside from $180,000 and a key, Charlie had barely left behind an imprint. He was a phantom. A cipher.

None of that troubled me much. His association with Frank did.

The crime-scene tape across my dark doorway reminded me of the mess awaiting me. I yanked it down and stepped in, dumping the rucksack.

A rustle startled me around, the shadow on my wrecked couch resolving slowly as a feminine form, and then Induma's voice came out of the darkness. 'Love what you've done with the place.'

'Jesus, you scared the hell out of me.' I righted a tipped-over floor lamp and clicked it on. 'Why didn't you turn on a light?'

She shrugged. 'Didn't want to be presumptuous.' She was leaning on the torn arm of the couch with her legs tucked beneath her, her dark skin beautiful even in the clinical halogen glow. She was yoga-fit, but carried enough extra weight to curve where she was supposed to. Her high cheeks tended toward plump, and an emerald glittered in the side of her nose. She was Indian before it came into style, growing up right here in Brentwood, and she spoke with a casual LA intonation that caught most people by surprise.

In the year that we dated, just before her money really started flowing in, we never really discussed my life from before I moved back to LA. Induma had something of her parents' Buddhist restraint. She never pushed for more answers than I offered and was glad to give me space as long as I adored her – which wasn't hard – and as long as I was honest. And I was honest, but at the same time, I let myself off the hook for lies of omission.

Standing the front door on end, I pushed it to the frame. She gestured at it. 'How will I get out?'

'Oh yeah, right.' I placed it a few inches offset from the jamb.

'Wendy called, said you no-showed for your interview. I figured something was up.'

'I'm sorry – I meant to call.'

She glanced at the phone, still in pieces on the kitchen counter. Her mouth tightened but she didn't comment. 'The nice hysterical woman downstairs gave me a version of what happened. It sounds like you're in the middle of whatever you've spent your life afraid you'd be in the middle of.'

I said, 'Yes.'

'Come here.' She rested a hand on my cheek, tilted my head to get a better look at the wound. Her concern turned to anger. 'Is there someone – a lawyer, cop, whoever – you know who can help you navigate this?'

I thought about it. 'No.'

'Is there anyone you'd *want* to call?'

'Bugs Bunny.'

Her burgundy lipstick set off her smile, the perfect whiteness of her teeth. 'What's *he* do when he gets in a jam?'

'Cross-dresses.'

'Hmm. Maybe it's time to look for some new allies. Or new candor with old ones.' She leveled that cool stare at me, in case I hadn't figured out it was a challenge.

I cleared my throat, then cleared it again. 'If I gave you an address, could you look online and find out about whoever's renting the place?'

'Probably.' She cocked her head, grinned pertly. 'What address?'

'It belonged to the guy who was killed last night at San Onofre.'

'Okay,' she said, processing. 'Okay. Guy have a name?'

I jotted down the address on a junk-mail flyer and handed it to her. 'I was told it's Mike Milligan.'

She took the paper with a flick of her hand. 'I'll help you on two conditions. First, you're coming over for dinner tomorrow night. I'm making *puliyogare*.'

'Will Alejandro be there?' Her boyfriend was dense and exceptionally good-looking, so of course, I was mortally jealous of him. She nodded, and I said, 'Fine. The second condition?'

'You tell me who you really are.'

Her directness put me back on my heels. 'This is something that happened to me. That's *happening* to me. But it's not who I am.'

If the vehemence of my voice startled her, she didn't show it. 'Okay,' she said. 'But there was always a part of your life that you avoided. You can't deny that. It's why we never got past where we did.' She kept her eyes on mine, unafraid to press the point. 'And now? This?' She gestured to the turmoil of my condo. 'It's a whole different thing. I need to know what I'm prying into for you, what's really going on. I never got to know all of you when we were together. And that was fine. But if I'm gonna help you, I need to know now.'

My apartment felt suddenly stuffy and I realized I'd broken a sweat. 'I . . . I can't do that.'

'New alliances, pal. They come at a price.' She extended the paper, holding it pinched between her thumb and forefinger, ready to drop.

I'm not sure how long I stared at her, but she didn't drop her gaze. I'd always told myself that if I had my past to relive, I'd make different choices. I looked around at the mounds of hurled clothes, the clumps of couch stuffing, the strewn papers, the offset front door. Maybe this was, bizarrely, my shot at a fresh start.

I crossed and sat on the gutted couch. Induma shadowed me, sitting also and leaning against the arm to face me. My throat was dry and my thoughts jumbled, but patience was one of Induma's virtues.

I made a few mental runs at the beginning before I forced it out. 'My stepfather was murdered when I was

100

seventeen.' Saying it out loud gave it a profound power that I couldn't have imagined. But I was talking. The words poured out. I told her everything. The Zapruder tape and Isabel McBride on the pitcher's mound and the way the calluses on Frank's heels scraped the floorboards as he died. I told her about the dark sedan trolling the street, the phone call telling me to come outside, my trip to the Metropolitan Detention Center, the envelope stuffed with traveler's checks.

And then I told her the rest.

13

The cold interrogation room, the car ride with Slim and the big guy, the coerced drop-off at LAX – they left me unable to catch my breath. At the Alaska Airlines counter, my hands shook so badly I could hardly count out seven of the traveler's checks from the envelope. I didn't know that one-way cost more than round-trip, and it took the agent to say, 'Then just buy a round-trip and don't come back.'

She looked mystified by my expression. I could only imagine what I looked like.

A moment later, she frowned down at my driver's license. 'I can't issue you this ticket. You're not eighteen for two more days.'

I showed her the number written on the envelope and waited, melting in sweat, as she called and explained the situation.

'Oh, okay, sir. Right away, sir.' The reverence in her voice and her lack of eye contact seemed to seal my fate as a nonentity. She hung up, printed my ticket, and handed it to me without further comment.

I spent half the flight in the cramped bathroom, sitting on the toilet and rocking myself while impatient passengers banged on the flimsy door. My running made me look guilty, but it also kept Callie clear, and that was a trade I was willing to live with. But how would I know when it would be safe to see her again?

We set down in Anchorage, the wind on the tarmac cutting me at the neck, the shins. I didn't even have a jacket. I followed a heavy-set woman who'd been on my flight to the terminal and boarded the same bus. I suppose I was clinging to anything familiar. She got off an hour in and I watched her vanish into the white morning haze, my breath steaming the window. I rode on, watching the permafrost roll by, as blank and lifeless as I felt. I woke up half dead at the end of the line in Ketchikan.

It was light til 10:30 at night. I got a job in a cannery, cutting the heads off salmon. No one asked questions. All those felons in Alaska, everyone on the run from something. Deadbeat dads and bail skippers. My own private Siberia.

I worked the line next to a massive bearded guy named Liffman who wore an eyepatch and a maniacal grin. He brandished his knife with skill and zest that left me wondering.

After a few weeks, at bedtime, I called Callie just to hear her voice. I had to assume the house was bugged, since they'd known about my conversations with her, but I needed to know that she was safe. After she said, 'Hello' a third time, I hung up. I couldn't sleep, so I pulled the phone onto my little rented bed and curled around it, as if it held some imprint of my mom's voice.

I watched the news obsessively for Caruthers's assassination, but as the months dragged out, I tuned in less and less. Winter got so cold it froze the ears and tails off cats. I jerked awake at 2:18 every night, my arms clutching at Frank as he bled out. After six months, Callie's home line was disconnected, so I risked a call to her at work.

Leaning against the payphone at the back of the pool hall, sticky with sweat and trapped air, I pressed the familiar buttons. I'd gulped down a few beers to shore up my courage, and my buzz turned the whole thing into a dream – the sound of her, my shaky words, so much resentment and pain that neither of us could stop talking to breathe. She demanded to see me. When I told her it wasn't safe, she yelled at me until I eased the phone back onto its cradle.

I spent a sleepless week worried that they'd monitored the call and were coming to throw me in jail, but there wasn't anything I could do about it.

A few nights later, I came across Liffman outside the bar, shooting a pistol at a moose crossing sign. His night-vision goggles were crooked, and he staggered under the weight of the booze, but he cracked that sign again and again. The cops had wisely parked at a good distance, and sat smoking on the curb, waiting for him to pass out. But Liffman, I'd learned, never passed out.

As he fumbled with a reload, I approached. Callie had never let Frank take me shooting, but I'd been around his guns enough to be calm in their presence. 'Liffman.'

'Yuh, Nicky?'

'What do you say we get you some sleep so tonight doesn't cut into your drinking tomorrow?'

It took a few moments for him to decipher the words

through the booze, then a smile cracked his wind-chapped face and he slid the gun into his pocket and trudged home. The cops waved as we passed.

The next day at work, while whacking the head off a Sockeye, he gave me that missing-tooth grin. 'You ready for when they come for you?'

I kept working.

He lopped off a few more heads, flicked them to the bin, the pink spray specking his corded forearms. '*I* am. I'm ready for those motherfuckers. DEA, IRS. Shit, when the black suits come sniffin', I'll be a trace in the wind. Or a round in their chest.'

When the whistle blew, I followed him out to his truck. He never turned around, but he unlocked the passenger side first, left the door standing open. I got in.

I said, 'I don't want to be at the mercy of anyone ever again.'

We drove out to the nowhere tundra and sat on his hood, draining a six-pack and squinting into the white. He pulled a pistol from his parka pocket and aimed it at my face. His head was crooked, his black curls hanging down like a curtain fringe. He was smiling, and it wasn't a pretty smile.

I said, 'Liffman.'

'Wanna learn how to shoot?'

'Yeah.'

He walked off twenty paces and crunched the bottles into the snow. We shot. He drank the next six pack himself. We shot some more. When I came back around, I heard a flicking sound and he had a knife out, low and mean at his side. He faked a swing at my head, the blade whistling by so close I could feel the air move.

'Knife fight?'
I said, 'That too.'

Every six months I sent Callie a card at work telling her I was alive and okay, delivered through a remailing service in Utah so it would bear a different postmark. Another lesson from the school of Liffman. The service would alert me if the letter bounced back as undeliverable, so I'd know if she quit or moved. I was terrified she'd get sick and wouldn't be able to contact me, or that she'd die scared and alone. Those sporadic cards served as my lifeline to her.

I moved to Washington and snagged a job driving a delivery truck for a bakery. And then, two years later, to Oregon, where I worked mornings on a road crew and earned a night-school BA.

I felt like a hermit crab trying out new shells, looking for a fit. I didn't realize it consciously at first, but I was inching my way toward Los Angeles.

Nine years after that first flight, I finally came home. When the plane touched down at LAX, I was so ashen the kindly schoolteacher next to me offered his air sickness bag. The first weeks were awful. Some nights I lay awake, curled around a pillow, eyes on the door, until sunlight fell through the dusty motel drapes. Other times I prayed they would come just to get it over with. But slowly, perspective returned. They had to know that if I hadn't talked all this time, that I had nothing to say. Surely, *they* had moved on.

I waited a month to track down Callie. She was living in a big white house in Pasadena. Frank's hefty life insurance policy had bought her a nice piece of property. Coming up the walk, I almost threw up in the tulips. When Callie opened the door, she stood perfectly erect, her face motionless except for the tears streaming down her cheeks. We hugged and sat and talked, and I told her some of where I'd been. I lied too – those lies of omission that had become part of who I was, blank spaces at the center of me. I said I'd fled because of guilt alone, and given what I'd done, that was plausible enough.

She gave me Frank's steamer trunk, which she'd filled with some of my personal things and held onto all these years. But after six months, we hardly saw each other. I still didn't want to risk telling her the whole truth, so there were buried landmines everywhere. And Callie had a whole other life that I didn't fit into, no matter how hard she tried to let me. I drove by her house a few times, sat in my car, and watched the impassive face of the large white house. And I heard an echo of the big guy's voice, just after he flipped me the envelope filled with traveler's checks. *You don't talk about this to anyone.* Ever. *Or we'll know. And we'll know who you talked to also. We won't be nearly as accommodating next go 'round. To you* or *her.* I could no longer bring myself to stroll up that nice suburban walk and ring the doorbell. On my third or fourth trip, as night fell and the lights began clicking on upstairs, a neighbor slowed in passing to cast a suspicious glance at my crappy little Honda. The drawn reflection I saw in my rear-view was alarming even to me. I had become that troubling watcher in the night. That dark, idling car at the curb, beyond the curtains. The thought of someone outside my mother's house, scaring her, finally drove me off for good.

I tried to resume my old life. But I quickly learned, it wasn't there waiting for me. My friends, too, had moved or moved on. Seeing them brought home just how much I'd lost. How bad the damage was, burned into my character like a convict's brand. One day I'd been a seventeen-year-old with a Nintendo and a decent life forecast. The next I was a grown-up on the run. Secretive, itinerate, alone with my guilt and those dwindling traveler's checks. And then just my guilt.

I drove to Bob's Big Boy one night. I didn't get past the parking lot. The big picture windows were lit up like Norman Rockwell. All those kids eating and drinking, talking about movies and lying about getting laid. I was brought up short like a bum contemplating a lavish window display. I didn't think about everything I didn't have, but everything those kids did. Envy flared, of course, but when it burned away, I said a silent prayer for them, that their lives would stay blissfully uncomplicated, that for many more years they would be able to take everything for granted.

I had to start over. And I gave it my best shot. Make new friends. Build a different life. Cut my bitterness with gratitude for what I still had. I tried to live up to Callie's hopes for me by not spending my life looking over my shoulder. Now and then, when I'd see a dark sedan or hear a voice of a certain tenor, I'd feel a flicker of the old fear, a snake's tongue moving along my spine. At any moment, they could pounce on me and throw me in a cell, charge me with a murder I didn't commit.

But they didn't. I got a job helping people who were homeless. I managed to become a part of society so if I did get hauled off, I could feel like my life had been worth something.

I had finally found calm, or at least my version of it.

And then I awoke one night to see the end of a black rope coiled on my balcony.

14

The silence told me I had finished talking. I emerged from the stupor of my thoughts as if rousing from a deep sleep, pressed into the present tense by the couch arm in my lower back, the floor beneath my feet, the sensation of nearly unbearable vulnerability, as if I'd been skinned and dangled above salt water.

Induma glanced away, her dark eyes darker than usual. Then she slid down the torn-up couch and embraced me, pressing my cheek to her chest. I couldn't move. We stayed like that a few minutes and then I raised my hand and put it on her forearm.

She set her other hand on top of mine and said, 'I will help you.'

She stood and straightened out her clothes. With effort, she produced a smile for me. The door thumped to the carpet, and she was gone.

I jolted awake at 2:18. Experience had taught me to lie flat and draw deep breaths, to picture the soothing roll of the ocean. Soon, the panic lifted and I came back to my body, safe in the darkness.

Clever, the tricks our minds play on us. The mean-spirited reminders they think we require. Given the past twenty-four hours, it was no surprise that the habit had reasserted itself, but still, the thought of it stung. I'd convinced myself it was behind me, that I'd rebuilt my life, that I'd grown beyond this. The return to the old pattern seemed proof that I'd failed. My deficiencies had been waiting there all along, hibernating just beneath the surface like a bad memory.

It was ungodly hot, my pillow drenched. My air conditioner was awful. It made a lot of noise and didn't put out much, like a sitcom wife. It didn't help that I kept the windows and sliding glass door closed and locked even in muggy summer nights. I lay on my slashed mattress, restless and miserable.

But comfort doesn't matter. Security matters.

I spoke Frank's name to the darkness as I sometimes did. I knew it was weird, embarrassing even, but I did it because it was the only thing I had left of him, really. I did it to keep him alive. Now I was doing it out of habit. For years, it was the one thing I was sure of. Tonight, it didn't feel quite that way.

How were Frank and an old war buddy linked to a rucksack of cash? The bills were new, dated last year, but even so, it didn't mean they weren't merely the latest move in a ploy stretching back to Frank's last months. Frank was a man with secrets, but I'd known him well, better than I'd known anyone except Callie. Whatever his involvement with Charlie, or with whatever had surfaced in the weeks before his murder, he would have acted above-board. I tried to convince myself and got mostly there. Mostly.

I was exhausted, yet wide awake. I turned on the TV, my analgesic of choice. Daffy Duck was being stared down by a little mob guy with a big hat. I mouthed the line with him: *okay, duck, no more stallin', see?*

It was no use. I got up, dressed, and double-checked the locks and windows. About ten years ago, I realized I wasn't checking for my safety. So why? Compulsion, certainly. Partly out of respect for the dead. I knew my way around this apartment in the dark; I'd walked it with my eyes closed.

After Induma had left, I'd cleaned up, bagging my broken possessions and dumping more down the chute than was necessary. I'd hammered the front door into the jamb with two nails, which I now tested with my thumb. They'd prove at least as effective as the deadbolt had been last night. Cracking the dishwasher, I checked the bundles of hundred-dollar bills that I'd laid beneath the bottom tray. I closed the door, setting a paperclip on the right top corner so it would fall if someone looked in there.

I opened the sliding door, passed through the torn-out screen, and straddled the balcony parapet. The three-story drop was menacing, but the telephone pole was within easy reach, one of the reasons I'd selected the apartment. Liffman's Rules: Always leave a get-away. Timing my lunge, I grabbed the footholds without having to go airborne, then pulled myself across onto the pole. I climbed down and walked to my Ford pickup.

I told myself I wasn't sure where I was going, but of course I knew.

Aside from a different shade of paint, a goose mailbox,

and the realtor sign hammered in the front lawn, Frank's house looked the same. I parked up the street, walked back, and stood staring at the house from across the way. I thought of a rucksack stuffed with a hundred eighty grand and Frank's tattoo and how he'd hugged me that one time and called us a family. I thought, *please don't be a lie.*

I slipped through the side gate and circled the house, peering inside. Some furniture was there, and a few boxes, but whoever had been living there was mostly moved out. The old porch swing remained. I placed a hand on the peeling wood but couldn't bring myself to sit. Then I confronted the back door I'd stumbled through that night to find Frank. I wondered if this was the feeling killers got when they returned to the scene of the crime to roll in the dirt of their misdeeds.

The door was locked, but the pivot latch on the kitchen's sash window was tired, and pulled open readily with an upward jostling of the pane. I stepped inside, easing the window shut behind me.

I walked into the living room and sat in a slip-covered armchair, setting my feet before the spot where I'd held Frank while he died. I stared at the rag rug for a while. I'd driven by the house when I'd first moved back, and one or two other times when I really missed him, when I wanted to breathe the air he'd breathed, walk the streets he'd walked. These walls held my favorite memories. And, of course, some others, too.

I slid off the chair onto my knees and turned back the rug, revealing the bleached stain on the floorboards. It had yellowed over the years. It smelled of dust and rot. I wondered if the last owners had been oblivious to the blood spilled here.

I smoothed the rug back into place and walked silently into the kitchen. The old alarm keypad, still cracked from Callie's fist, no longer hooked up to anything. Padding up the hall, I saw that my old bedroom had been converted into a sewing room. For a time, I stood beneath that high rectangle of window and stared up at the smog-smeared night sky.

Comfort. Security.

Caruthers's words came back to me from yesterday afternoon: *a single bad decision can open a world of lamentable consequences.*

I asked myself the same questions I'd been mulling over half my life. What if I'd just let the phone ring that night? What if I hadn't climbed into the back of that sedan?

My footsteps seemed amplified in the small house. Same Medeco locks on the back door. I looked in the master bedroom, which was nothing like I remembered it. No sweaters cramming the top shelf of the closet. No scattering of half-read books on the nightstand. No stack of sketch pads on the bureau, cloudy with charcoal. I went back out and faced the front door. The same. The window dressings had changed, and I wondered if the security catches Frank had installed were still there. I pulled back the curtain and fright hit me so fast and hard I crouched in still shock.

A short way up the shadowy street, a car was pulled to the curb in front of my truck. A figure stood at my driver's-side window. He either sensed movement from the house or was looking for it, and the dark oval of his head wobbled slightly as it rotated. He was looking at me.

I jerked my hand back, letting the curtain fall closed, my breath sucking in with a screech. An engine turned over.

And then something unexpected happened. My reaction shifted, away from fear, to a fuck-it urge for confrontation, no matter the stakes. Seventeen years ago I'd exited this house on trembling legs, but now I found myself charging the front door, spoiling for a fight. By the time I was off the porch, the car was already around the corner, the whine of its acceleration rising in pitch but fading with distance. When I reached my truck, there was nothing but crickets and the machine-gun strafing of a high-power sprinkler. A spasm of energy spun me in a full circle but I spotted no one anywhere.

My mouth dry from the scare, I hurried back, closed and locked the door, and left the way I'd come in. Back at my truck, I pulled a flashlight from the glove box, slid under, and examined the undercarriage, as Liffman had taught me. The gas tank also showed no signs of tampering.

When I climbed in the truck and set my hands on the steering wheel, they were still shaking. I squeezed, doing my best to still them. When I looked up, I noticed a slip of paper tucked under the windshield wiper. Like a valet stub. But I hadn't valeted, not in months.

I climbed out and tugged it from under the rubber blade. A film-processing slip from a photo place on Ventura Boulevard. A single roll. Ready for pickup tomorrow at noon. The order number and pickup time were preprinted, the name and phone number spaces left blank. The only human mark was the black circle around *Thursday*. The film had probably been dropped in an overnight box rather than brought to a counter and filled out.

I got back into the truck and stared through the windshield at nothing. My fear bled into curiosity and back again. A panicky urge overtook me. To drive away from all this. Keep moving until I wound up at a new city, a different apartment, a cannery in Alaska. But no matter how hard I tried to give in to the urge, some part of me wouldn't allow it this time. I had reached some turning point that I hadn't even known I was approaching.

I headed home. After monkeying my way up the telephone pole, I checked the locks, the paperclip, and the two nails through the front door, then sat on my mattress, staring at the damn photomat slip. My bones ached from last night's explosion, and my shirt chaffed the raw skin of my chest.

When I closed my eyes, I saw in the darkness those familiar ideograms, blue ink faded into flesh. *Trust No One.*

To find the answers that I needed, I'd have to source Charlie's connection with Frank beyond Okinawa. How had Induma put it? *Maybe it's time to look for some new allies. Or new candor with old ones.*

I got up and moved the television off Frank's trunk and onto the floor. The lid creaked as I pried it up. I dug around until I came up with what I was looking for. A creased photo of Callie from so many years ago. At the beach, squinting into the sun, one hand pinning back her thick, unruly hair. That face, almost as familiar as my own, though I hadn't seen it for years.

It was time.

15

On the front walk, I felt exposed in the bright light of morning, though I'd circled the block three times to make sure I wasn't being followed. A moment's pause didn't help me regain my composure, but I made my legs carry me up onto the porch of the neat white two-story. My thumb rested against the doorbell, barely touching it, refusing to press.

Finally, I rang. A three-chime doorbell. I ran my hand through my hair, shifted from foot to foot. The wound in my cheek from Charlie's bone frag made me self-conscious.

Approaching footsteps. My mom's voice calling back into the house, 'I got it, sweetheart.'

The big door swung in and her smile caught on her face. My mom looked good, probably, for her age, but all I could notice at first were the differences, the incontrovertible evidence of the passed years. Her hair was a little coarser, the auburn sheen a shade too rich to be natural. She looked youthful in her ponytail and man's shirt, which was flecked with dried paint and unbuttoned to reveal a tank top. She wore foundation to cover the wrinkles, I assumed, but it muted her freckles too. I didn't like that. Callie's freckles were my favorite part of her.

Sorrow rippled through her features and left them blank. 'Five years,' she said. 'Your visits are getting almost frequent.'

'I think four. Remember that lunch?'

'Right. Lunch.' She lowered her head, pressing her crown to the edge of the door. 'You get my Christmas card?'

'Yeah. You get mine?'

'I did.'

She stepped back. I followed her in, Charlie's key clicking around inside my sneaker. We passed through a tiled foyer with mirrors and dried flowers in vases, and into a spacious kitchen. Porcelain rooster by the Viking stove, blue-checkered tablecloth, butter churn in the corner. I couldn't put the new country-contemporary décor together with Callie.

A short, wiry man sat on a wicker stool at the center island, reading the paper and eating poached eggs. His curly hair was receding, with strands of gray at the temples. It was poofy, needing a cut. He stopped mid chew, regarded me over the top of the sports section. Halfway down the staircase to the right stood a girl, maybe thirteen years old. She was stooping so she could look down into the kitchen and see who'd arrived. Despite the heat, she wore a hooded zip-up sweatshirt over a baggy thermal shirt – charcoal on black. Maroon and blond streaked her dark brown hair, which fell lifelessly to crowd her face. Her sleeves were pulled down over her hands, and she pinched the banister, ready to retreat.

Callie stopped by the double doors of the refrigerator and gestured at me, at the man, back at me.

'This is my son,' she said.

The girl's jaw dropped. Two scampering footsteps and she was gone.

The man set down his newspaper, dotted his mouth at the corner with a paper napkin. He came around and shook my hand. 'Steve Yates.' He looked at Callie, nodded supportively, and excused himself to the next room, leaving his breakfast behind.

She said, 'My husband.'

'Right. Congratulations. I got that card too.'

'And you didn't want to come?'

'I didn't know it was an invitation.'

'We didn't do a big thing.' She flared an arm. 'Third marriages, you know.'

'Six months ago?'

'Yes. Steve and Em moved in over Christmas break. Changing schools in the middle of the year was . . .' She used the heel of a hand to shove a wisp off her forehead and then she said, 'Why are you here, Nicky? I mean, I've been trying to see you forever now. You're hardly one to just drop by.' Her eyes moved to the cut on my cheek.

'Some stuff's come up.' I was looking at Steve's breakfast more than at her.

'Like what?'

'I'm not sure.'

'You're not sure what's come up, or you're not sure you want to tell me?'

'Both.' I looked at her directly. 'Whatever Frank was afraid of? It came back.'

But she barely responded. Her eyelids fluttered an extra beat when she blinked. That was all. I couldn't read the emotion, hidden as well as her freckles.

'Okay,' she said. 'Are you gonna talk to me?'

'Until I know what's going on, I don't want to put you—'

'In danger? Nice of you to make that decision for me.' She crossed her arms, tight, like she was cold. 'So what do you want?'

I said, tentatively, 'Frank's pictures. That were in his chest. What'd you do with them?'

She stared at me, her lips trembling. The question had offended her, or my arrival had. I wondered how much I'd changed, if I disappointed her.

Finally, she said, 'They're in a moving box. In the attic. I put them there when I got the trunk ready for you.'

I forced the next question out. 'Can I see them?'

'Why not, Nick?' she said irritably. 'Why not?'

We had a frozen moment, then I asked, 'Where's the attic?'

'On top of the house.' She watched me, deciding whether to be helpful, then added, 'Upstairs, end of the hall. The boxes are labeled. Help yourself.' She grabbed her husband's plate, still half full, and walked out to bring it to him.

I made my way hesitantly up the stairs. Music blared through the closed door to the left, Alanis Morissette wailing about an ex-boyfriend, with no small measure of bitterness. Scrabble letters glued to the door spelled out *Emily's Room*. Feeling like an intruder, I continued down the hall toward the attic hatch. A bathroom, a guest room, and then open double doors to the master. I stood under the hatch, peering into the bedroom where my mother slept. A large, four-poster bed with a floral duvet faced a window overlooking a gazebo and swimming pool. A shoulder holster was slung across a dressing chair by the bathroom door. An easel by the bay window held a half-finished portrait of Emily. The lips were tight and angry, and her posture suggested that she was an unwilling subject. The drawing itself was a bit generic – not Callie's best work. It reeked of obligation all the way around.

A string dangled from the hatch overhead. When I tugged, the hidden ladder unfolded like the leg of some insect. I climbed up, heat hitting me along with the scratchy smell of insulation. A ventilation fan embedded in the roof chopped the morning glare to hypnotic effect.

Four boxes sat by the air-conditioner unit, all magic-markered *Frank* in my mom's hand. Two held old suits and a few dress shirts that I guessed Callie couldn't part with. Books filled the third. I lifted a few to admire the familiar spines. Presidential memoirs and military histories, a couple Leon Uris novels. The fourth box was the lightest, its contents shifting around when I lifted it. A few layers of pictures, loose in the bottom. I sorted through them. Black-and-white wedding photos – Frank's parents? Pictures of him as a kid. In one, he wore trousers and a little flat cap and pointed a wooden gun at the camera. Until that moment, it had never occurred to me that Frank had once been a kid. I scooped up more pictures and flipped through several handfuls.

Down at the bottom, I found the pictures from the war. There was one of Frank and other soldiers at a camp in the jungle. He was stretched out on his back, smirking, his legs crossed, boots unlaced. I studied the other men's faces but none were familiar. A few photos later, I found him. It was a mess-hall picture, guys in white undershirts hunched over trays of cubed meat and noodles. Frank leaning over his food, fork raised to punctuate a point he was making to the men around him. The others bent toward Frank. At the table behind him, his head turned to listen, sat Charlie. The wild blond hair was shaved in a flattop, but I recognized the piercing eyes, that wide, unruly mouth. He seemed an outsider, pivoting to get in on Frank's conversation, and something in his body language suggested an underdog's reverence. I couldn't help but wonder if Frank trusted Charlie half as much as Charlie trusted him.

The fan huffing overhead, I sat looking at the photograph until sweat trickled down my ribs. Then I shoved it into a back pocket, stacked the boxes neatly, and climbed down. As I passed through the hall, Emily stepped out of the bathroom, nearly colliding with me.

'Hi,' I said. 'Sorry.'

She looked up at me. Her brown eyes were doleful and sort of pretty. 'It sucks here,' she said.

'I bet.' I extended my hand. 'Emily, right? I'm Nick.'

She brushed past me into her room. 'It's just Em.' She scowled at the Scrabble letters on the door. 'Your mom glued those there when we moved in. She got my name wrong.'

I thought about that portrait in Callie's room, how neither of them probably had the desire or stamina to finish it. 'She's probably just trying to help you adjust.'

'She's always hovering over me, trying to feed me and stuff.'

'She means well,' I said.

'Then why haven't you talked to her for, like, nine hundred years?'

'Because of a bunch of shit I got into when I was younger.'

She stared at me curiously for a moment, then flopped down on her stomach in front of a Scrabble board and a two-volume dictionary. A few tournament certificates and ribbons were tacked over her desk.

I stayed in the doorway. 'You're a Scrabble champ? That's pretty cool.'

'Cool. Yeah. I have to beat the boys away with my thesaurus.' She glanced back at me over a shoulder. 'Look, why don't you just get out of here?'

When I got back downstairs, Callie was doing the dishes. I cleared my throat, but she didn't turn around.

'Do you know what company Frank was in?' I asked. 'In Vietnam?'

She kept scrubbing. 'Frank didn't talk much about the war. You know that.'

'Do you have anything that would say where he served?'

'Yeah, Nicky, I keep his obit framed in the powder room.' The pan hit the counter with a clank, then her shoulders lowered and she relented. 'I believe it's on his headstone.'

'Where . . . where is that?' I was ashamed not to know.

She caught the hitch in my voice and turned. 'The Veteran Cemetery. Wilshire and Sepulveda.'

Above the breakfast nook hung a wedding picture of Callie and Steve, Emily scowling from the side in a dark blue velvet dress. So much of Callie's life I had missed. What had I been doing the day my mom had gotten remarried?

Like his daughter, Steve had seemed a bit tentative in the house, a touch formal. Six months he'd lived here. It wasn't easy transitioning into a new place, feeling like a guest in your own home. I thought about that shoulder holster on the chair upstairs. It struck me how tall Frank was, or how tall he always seemed. 'What's Steve do?'

'He's a cop.' She added, defensively, 'He's a wonderful man.'

'I expect so. You wouldn't marry a man who wasn't.'

We looked at each other a moment, awkwardly. She'd rebuilt a life, just as I had. Though I was happy for her, seeing her brought back the ache I'd tried for years not to feel. We were no longer who we'd been when we'd known each other. The old cues, the connections, our stupid inside jokes – they weren't there when I reached for them. I could see in her face that she felt it, too. That hollowness.

She said, 'We were so close, Nicky.'

'Yeah,' I said. 'We really were.'

As I passed, she took my arm, stopped me. She said, 'I'm ready to listen now. I want you to know that.'

'Listen to what?'

'Why you really ran away.'

I thought about the photomat slip in my pocket and the key in my shoe.

She said, 'What?'

I shook my head.

'How about the short version?' She let go of my arm. 'Do you owe me anything?' She asked it not passive-aggressively, but with genuine curiosity.

My chest cramped; my throat was dry. It was like my body was rebelling so I wouldn't be able to get the words out. 'The night I left, they came and arrested me,' I said. 'For Frank's murder.'

'They did *what* to you?' She was instantly, protectively furious.

'They booked me into MDC. Have your husband check the records.'

'You should have talked to me, Nicky.' She looked crushed. 'We could've gotten you a lawyer. There would've been no case. *No case.*'

'They'd manufactured one, including my prints on the gun.'

'Everyone *knew* you picked up the gun. They couldn't make anything of that.'

'After what happened to Frank, I was willing to believe they could do a lot of things. And I wasn't gonna trust the assholes with badges to handle it on the up-and-up.'

We both turned at a movement in the doorway. Steve standing, holding his dirty plate. His stare was the first coplike thing I'd noticed about him.

I nodded at her, then at Steve. 'Thanks for letting me look at those pictures.'

I walked out, but Steve barely moved so I had to brush past him. My footsteps knocked the tiles of the foyer, then I swung the door closed behind me and hurried down the walk and to my truck, hidden around the corner.

I walked among the thousands of headstones, the perfect rows fanning by like ploughed furrows seen from a moving car. The photomat slip remained safely in my pocket. A few more hours before I could pick up the roll of mystery film. I told myself that's where my uneasiness was coming from.

The grounds administrator had pointed me to the general area but it was difficult to keep my bearings among the identical Department of Defense grave markers. Traffic on Wilshire and the 405 was distant enough to recall the ocean, a white-noise accompaniment to the grassy swells and shade offered by venerable trees. It would have been peaceful were it not for all the dead.

I nearly walked past Frank's gravestone. I hadn't expected it to be any different from all the others, but I also somehow had. No wreath, no flowers. Just his name, indented in a plug of marble. My chest tightened and I realized I was breathing hard. Fumbling out a notepad, I jotted down the information I needed. *Company C, 1st Battalion, 8th Infantry, United States Army. Vietnam.*

Slapping the notepad closed, I turned swiftly to go, almost striking an old man making his fragile way up the row of graves. His cheeks were hollow, his jaw pronounced and skeletal, and he wore an ancient cloth hat weighed down with military pins. He looked into my face, then glanced past me at the headstone and shook his head, his lips bunching. 'Them boys caught a lot a' shit they didn't deserve,' he said.

He winked jauntily and continued up the row. I was staring at the grass and then it got blurry and I forced my eyes back up to the date of birth, the date of death, the name stamped in block letters on the cold white marble.

16

I sat in my car in the sweltering Valley heat, the photo package in my lap. The cheery yellow envelope featured sample photos of a hot air balloon and a golden retriever shuddering off sprinkler water. But I wasn't looking at the samples. I was looking at the one slot on the front form that had been filled out, the handwritten block letters that spelled out NICK HORRIGAN.

Breaking the gummy seal, I extracted the inner envelope. I ran my thumb under the flap, hesitant to lift it. What if it contained pictures of a mangled corpse? Someone being shot? A child being molested? I hadn't considered a frame-up. Charlie probably hadn't either. My heart thudding, I glanced around the parking lot, but didn't notice anything out of the ordinary.

Bracing myself, I tugged the set of pictures from the envelope. Whatever I was expecting, it was nothing compared to the jolt I got from looking at my own face.

A zoom-lens close-up of me walking down the street, hands shoved in my pockets.

I jerked my head around, craning to take in the full parking lot. The mother loading groceries, the kids angling in on tacos outside the comic-book store, the

129

businessman at the meter – all of a sudden, no one was outside suspicion. It wasn't until I looked back at the photo that I saw that it captured me passing in front of Charlie's house. The picture had been taken from a good distance. Blurred at the edge of the frame, I could make out a sliver of the Dumpster that the photographer had hidden behind. A second shot showed me ducking the crime-scene tape into the garage. Then there I was, coming back out with a rucksack hanging heavily off my shoulder.

With shaking hands, I flipped to the next picture.

A nighttime shot of the Sherman Oaks Post Office, no more than ten blocks from here. The flash illuminated the Magnolia Boulevard address painted on the beige wall.

The burn in my chest alerted me that I'd been holding my breath. I shook my left Puma, felt the rattle of the key there inside the air pocket.

The rest of the pictures were black. Unexposed.

Eager as I was to get moving, I headed back inside the photomat, passing the overnight drop box outside the front door where the film had been left last night. The guy behind the counter was overweight, a wispy blond beard framing his round face.

I handed him the film and asked, 'Is there any way you can tell what kind of camera was used to take these pictures?'

The guy studied them. 'Not really. He's got a pretty good zoom lens going, maybe a Canon, but you can't really tell.'

'You mean a zoom lens separate from the camera?'

'Yeah, there's no way he got this clarity from a built-in.'

He handed the pictures over and I caught the faint lettering on the back of the top print. *Kodak Endura.* I pointed to it. 'What can you tell me about this type of film?'

'That's just the kind of paper it's printed on. But let me see the negatives.' His tongue poked out as he squinted at them. 'Kodak Ektachrome 100. A daytime-balanced color-transparency. Fine grain, high sharpness, makes your colors pop.'

'So someone who uses this knows what they're doing? This isn't a film you'd pick up to snap casual pictures?'

He shook his head, used his cupped hands to slide his dangling hair back over his ears. 'Nuh-uh. Mostly commercial photographers use it.'

'Would you choose this film if you were a paparazzi? Or a cop on stakeout or something?'

He gave me a weird look. '*Paparazzo*'s the singular. And not really. More like if you're shooting clothes or curtains or something where you need really accurate color.'

I thanked him and walked back to my pickup. Five minutes later I was parked outside the post office, staring at the same view as the photograph in my hand. Casting glances over my shoulder, I entered. The sudden chill of the air conditioning underscored the dead heat outside. There was a line of annoyed customers, people bickering over forms. I veered left, into the banks of PO boxes. The second alcove held box 229, a double-wide bottom unit. The half walls afforded privacy and muted the sounds from the rest of the building. I crouched and worked the key from my shoe.

I slid it home, paused for good luck, turned it.

The little door swung open.

The box was empty.

I sat, putting my back against the wall, allowing myself a few moments of despair. Then I sighed and started to swing the door closed so I could retrieve the key.

A yellow edge protruded ever so slightly from the roof of Box 229. Getting down on all fours, I peered in. Taped to the top of the unit, a manila envelope. I reached in, tugged it free, and opened it. A half sheet of paper covered with columns of numbers slid out. I scanned down the rows. *1.65, 4.05, 3.49, 1.80, 2.71* – they were all numbers less than five, not a single integer. Only one stood out, both in size and in its own column: *99.999*. The top part of the page had been torn off, and the paper was brittle with age. An electronic date stamp on the bottom read, *December 15, 1990*.

About five months before Frank was murdered.

Holding the stiff sheet in my hand, I slumped back against the wall. 'Well,' I said, 'this clears up everything.'

17

I drove home with the torn page of numerals staring at me from the passenger seat, in case it decided to explain itself. Rolling down the window, I let the stale Valley air blow across my face.

Your life is now on the line. That's what Charlie had said when he'd shoved the key into my hand. Over a sheet of numbers? This grid of digits had put a charge into the Service, scrambled a Black Hawk, led to a stand-off at a nuclear power plant? Were they nuclear launch codes? Kickback tallies? Or a cipher for government documents? And who the hell was leading me to this stuff? Charlie's confederates? Or his killers? It was like that Tetris game I used to play on Nintendo, puzzle pieces falling one after another, defying order.

Miraculously, I found a parking spot on my street. When I got off the elevator upstairs, Homer was slumped against what appeared to be my new front door, his coat loose around him like a sack.

'You're late,' he said. 'But I exercised restraint.'

As I regarded the new door with surprise, Evelyn emerged from her apartment, a pendulous knock-off Gucci at her elbow. She disapproved of Homer's

Thursday appointments with my shower, and did her best to ignore us.

Homer stared at her with great humility. The smell coming off him was sour, whiskey pushed through dried sweat. 'Ma'am, can you spare a dollar? I haven't eaten in two days.'

Evelyn set her deadbolt with a decisive click, casting a dubious gaze over her shoulder. 'Force yourself.' She disappeared into the stairwell.

I set my hand on the door. Shiny brass doorknob, Medeco lock. 'How am I supposed to get in?'

'Try the knob?'

It turned easily under my grasp, and swung open on well-greased hinges.

Sever sat on the remains of my couch, his agent-perfect suit riding high at the shoulders. My first reaction was that he'd come, at long last, to arrest me for Frank's murder. I tensed, fought an impulse to bolt. But he wore an accommodating grin.

I did my best not to look over at the dishwasher that hid Charlie's cash.

He struggled to his feet and pulled two sets of keys from his pocket, that tan outdoorsman's face crinkled around the eyes. He looked far less comfortable confined to a suit than he'd seemed in his SWAT-gear with an assault rifle dangling from a shoulder. He was the perfect counterpart to Wydell, intelligent muscle to Wydell's muscular intelligence. 'I wanted to make sure I put these directly in your hand,' he said. 'And that I kept this guy out of here until you got home.'

Homer shrugged, his shoulders even more massive

beneath the layers of cloth. 'So I didn't exercise *that* much restraint.'

'You *do* know him?' Sever asked me.

'I do.'

The sun was shining through the sliding glass door, making Sever's scalp tingle through his flattop. I'd forgotten how tall he was. The linebacker's weight behind his boots when he'd swung off my roof and knocked me in the chest. His mouth gathered solemnly, and he started to say something, then thought better of it. He tilted his head at Homer.

I said, 'Give us a sec here?'

Homer curtseyed, even pinching out a phantom dress on either side, and withdrew, closing the door behind him. For our benefit, he hummed as he strolled up the hall.

Sever reached for his hip holster and I froze before his hand continued to his pocket, pulling out a fat cell phone not unlike the one I'd delivered to Charlie. Holding up a finger at me, he pushed a button, listened, then said, 'Yes. Yes, it's a secure line. Put him through.'

He offered me the phone.

I hesitated. After all, Charlie hadn't fared so well after taking their proffered call. But, knee-jerk reaction aside, I grabbed the phone.

'Nick Horrigan?'

I recognized the voice, but still couldn't believe it. I said, hoarsely, 'Yes, Mr President?'

'So good of you to take my call this time.'

I wasn't sure what to do with that, so I bit my lip and waited.

Bilton continued, 'I understand you want to stay out of the limelight.'

'Yes, si—' I caught myself. 'Mr President.'

'That's good. I respect that. Lord knows there are enough types willing to air their dirty laundry for a chance to swap Kleenex with Barbara Walters. Do you have any dirty laundry, Nick?'

I swallowed just to get some moisture to my throat. 'I think we all do, Mr President.'

'Yes,' he mused. 'Some more than others. As I was saying, I'm pleased that you're not a glory hound. I'm proud of the contribution you made at San Onofre. You'll find, Nick, that some people will want to meet with you, to exploit your role for the sake of their cause or campaign, to pry around in what is clearly a matter of national security. You wouldn't want to meet with someone like that, Nick. Certainly not twice.'

Information moved quickly between the camps, it seemed, through the common link of the Secret Service. But who was reporting back to whom?

Bilton continued, 'If you mess around on certain stages, the spotlight finds you eventually. And that spotlight is hotter than a desert sun and illuminates twice as much. So again, I'm pleased that you've decided to take the high road on this.'

My heart was racing. On the one hand, it seemed like standard political bullying from Bilton: *don't help my rival in his campaign to defeat me, don't contradict the fabricated version of events at San Onofre which is helping us in the polls, or I will make you pay*. But there seemed a more menacing lining as well. Would I be made to pay like Charlie?

While I was trying to figure out how to reply, he said, 'Goodbye, Nick,' and hung up.

As I handed back the phone, Sever seemed amused by my expression. 'The Man likes to do that. The off-guard thing. Apologies, but you know, following orders and all that.' His hand disappeared beneath his jacket and came out with a fat envelope, which he offered to me. 'This is so you can get some new furniture and the like.'

I tilted the envelope, took note of the hundreds crammed inside. The sight brought me back to the oiled leather smell of that sedan, where I'd clutched a similar envelope filled with traveler's checks. The one thing I'd carried into my new life.

I tried to read Sever's eyes. What was really being offered? Hush money? Payment for me to stay away from Caruthers, to abstain from giving him any information that might help his campaign? Was the cash for me to disappear again? Given the context, it would seem Sever was playing bag man for Bilton. But I had put in my sarcastic request for a new front door to Alan, a member of Caruthers's camp. And here a door was, with a cash offer behind it. Yet that seemed too straightforward. Was Sever really testing the waters, or was this a smart misdirection?

I handed the envelope back. He raised his eyebrows inquisitively.

'As the twig is bent,' I said, 'so the tree inclines.'

He shrugged and returned the envelope to his pocket. 'We'll hold onto this for you. In case you change your mind, want a new couch.' Passing me, he grinned a strained grin, handing me the keys. I wondered if Wydell knew about this little field trip. 'You need anything else, give a call.' He tapped his fist on the jamb and nodded farewell.

I took a minute to regain my composure, then called in Homer, locking the door behind us as he trudged to the bathroom. The minute I heard the shower running, I checked the dishwasher. The paperclip was still there, resting on the top right edge of the door. The bundled hundreds remained inside, untouched beneath the rack of dirty dishes.

On my disposable cell phone, I called Raz and asked him to come change out my locks. 'I be there in two hour, bro. I give you good price.'

I had no sandwich meat, but I found a mac and cheese in the pantry, so I started boiling water. After I'd stirred in the fluorescent orange powder, Homer emerged from the bathroom, shrugging into his massive coat. His cheeks and forehead were flesh-colored again, but already his hands bore streaks of dirt from his clothes. Beads of water stood out in his matted beard.

He trudged over and stared at the pot and the glass of water, disappointed. 'You don't even have a soda?' he asked.

'Why don't you dip into your 401k and go buy a Pepsi?'

He sighed resignedly. 'Fair enough. But macaroni and cheese?'

'Hey,' I said, 'it's been a long couple days.'

'Something to do with why that guy's been hanging around?' He registered my surprise. 'Oh yeah. Up the street. Sitting in his car, talking to himself – earpiece, you know.'

'The guy who was just here? How often?'

'I seen him once or twice the past two days. And now up here. Why's he so interested in you?'

'Mistaken identity.'

'Don't think so,' Homer said firmly. His beard shifted as he chewed, then he noticed I was looking at him and said, defensively, 'You notice things in my profession.'

'Profession?'

'Homeless drunk.'

'What kinds of things do you notice?'

'People on the run. People with something to hide.' He lifted the spoon from the pot and ticked it at me, and I noticed how much he resembled Liffman while looking nothing like him at the same time. 'What are you hiding?'

'A hundred eighty grand in the dishwasher.'

His smile held little amusement. 'You like to avoid questions.'

'What are you, the homeless shrink? Eat your fucking food.'

'You call this food?' But he lowered his face and ate in silence.

After a while, I said, 'Sorry.'

'You should be. That's no way to talk to a guest.'

'Don't push it.'

He finished scraping cheese goo off the bottom of the pot and handed it back. I set it steeping in hot water. Later, it would need a good scouring, as would the bathroom, which generally looked like two street dogs had fought in there by the time he got through with it.

His assessment of me continued to chafe. 'How can you tell that about someone?' I asked.

139

He gestured around the condo. 'Look at this. Look at you. A perfectly all-right-looking guy. Reasonably smart. Everything's there for you. But it's like you left something behind somewhere along the way.'

My face grew hot. 'Left something behind?'

'Some people dig in and fight. Some of us run. You're a runner. Like me.'

I knew better than to ask what *he* was running from. We'd covered that ground, and he skirted his past almost as well as I did. 'Maybe once,' I answered, a little too sharply.

'People don't change.' He lifted a snowy eyebrow at me, observing the impact of his words. 'Truth hurts?' he asked, not unkindly.

'C'mon,' I said tersely. 'I'll walk you out.'

'Of course.'

We headed down and out onto the street, and Homer started trudging off. I stared after him. *Was* I a runner like him? In light of Bilton's not-so-indirect threats, did I dare to keep digging? Could I stop?

I called after him and he turned back. I asked, 'You're buddies with the homeless guys who live around the VA, right?' The VA was a bigger operation with federal funding, so I didn't have any contacts over there.

'*Buddies* might be a stretch but we have common interests.'

'Such as?'

He frowned thoughtfully. 'Abandoned shopping carts, empty soda cans, Night Train.'

'A lot of Vietnam vets around there?'

'Ya think?'

'Can you ask the administration if they have a system for keeping tabs on soldiers from specific infantries? I'm trying to find anyone who served in Company C of the 1st Battalion, 8th Infantry. I need to get a name of one of the guys they served with.'

'Half those guys are prob'ly dead or on the street, and I doubt the government gives a shit where the other half lives, but it can't hurt asking. *Sir.*' He snapped off a salute and a smirk, and kept walking.

When I turned back to my building, a glint overhead pricked my peripheral vision, something on the balcony of the unrented unit next to Evelyn's. I glanced up in time to see a long-lens camera withdraw from view, disappearing behind the orange-tile balustrade.

18

I teetered on the ledge between balconies, doing my best to ignore the pavement three stories down. Hugging stucco, I inched farther along. I'd climbed from my balcony to Evelyn's, and on toward the unrented unit from there. It was a reckless play, but I was god-damned tired of being spied on, and angry enough to risk a deadly plummet in order to force a confrontation.

Two abandoned lawn chairs sat by the sliding glass door, which had been left open. The screen cut the sunlight, but I could see there was no one in the living room. I eased down onto the balcony and through the screen door, which gave off the faintest chirp in the tracks. The sound echoing in my head, I froze for a solid minute, so tense my shoulders cramped.

The living room was empty and smelled of fresh paint. Outlets still taped off, sheets of drywall on the counter. The condo, a mirror image of mine, was undergoing a remodel to be put on the market. The workers had taken off for Labor Day last week and not come back. Sensing movement in the bedroom, I crept over, flattened myself against the wall beside the jamb, and peered in.

She sat crossed-legged in the middle of the faded

carpet, facing away. Her brown hair was pulled into thick girlish braids and her head was bent as she fussed over something in her lap. The camera? A gun? Her arms, poking from a black tank top, were pale and thin, though not without muscle. A sun tattoo stood out on the back of her slender neck. Her posture and manner seemed that of a child, though she was probably in her mid-twenties.

I stepped into the doorway. 'Why are you following me?'

She yelped, a camera popping from her lap onto the carpet. 'Damnit.' She clutched at her chest. 'You scared the *shit* out of me.' Her bangs were cut high and ruler-straight across her forehead. Her eyes, big and unreasonably pretty, were moist from the scare. She crawled over and checked the camera, twisting the zoom lens free and examining it with concern. 'I'm not following you.'

I walked over and crouched in front of her. The realization that she was scared made me uncomfortable, but I felt no urge to reassure her. Her nose was nicely sloped and she had pouty lips, but her face was lean, shadows touching her cheeks. She reached for one of the many pockets in her cammy pants and I grabbed her wrist, my fingers nearly encircling it.

'Careful,' I said. 'Slowly.'

I let go and she withdrew a roll of film. I took it and slid it from the little black tube. *Kodak MAX Versatility Plus, 35mm 800-speed.* The kind used to snap me before was Ektachrome 100. 'Let me see the rest of your film, please.'

She pulled a handful of plastic canisters from her pockets. 'Look, I'm sorry, okay? I'll just get out of here. You don't have to call the cops.'

A pillow, blanket, and overnight bag had been shoved in the corner, along with some Styrofoam take-out boxes. Her nervousness seemed genuine, and it didn't quite add up.

I checked the other rolls of film and the one in the camera. They were all the same high-speed type, not the kind left for me at the photomat. Not that that meant anything. So I went through her bag, but it held only a change of clothes, some toiletries, and more camera gear. A lens case bore a printed label – *Property of Kim Kendall*.

'Who hired you to follow me?'

'I told you. This has got nothing to do with you.'

'Don't bullshit me. I saw you taking pictures of me.'

'I'm not taking pictures of you. I was taking pictures of *him*.'

'Okay. Let's just call the cops and have them straighten this out for us.'

Her mouth tensed. 'No, seriously,' she said. 'I'll prove it.' She stood and tugged at my arm. 'Come here.'

I followed her into the bathroom. A chemical reek hit my nostrils when she shoved aside the shower curtain. Photographs hung dripping from the retractable clothes-line, which had been pulled out and notched at the far end of the tub. Homer slumbering outside the liquor store. Homer napping on the grassy stretch along Ocean Avenue. Homer passed out at a bus stop on Wilshire. Evidently, Homer slept a lot.

I plucked a photo off the line and studied it. 'Who is he?'

144

'Wendell Alton. He was a dentist. Couldn't control the drinking. Lost everything – his family, house, his practice. He hasn't paid child support in years. We just tracked him down.'

'Homer was a *dentist*?'

'Homer? Right. Yeah, he was.'

'And you are?'

'Usually? An art photographer. But that pays about as well as you can imagine. So I do jobs now and then for a couple private investigators.'

'And this job?'

'Just to figure out what Alton's up to. To capture his life, report back. I'd learned that you let him come over once a week to shower and whatever. So I set up here to show him coming and going. And for a home base, you know? It's harder than you'd think to shadow a homeless guy. All they do is lie around in the open.'

'So what's going to happen to him?'

'Not up to me. I just turn in the pictures. His wife wants to come after him, that's her business.'

'Isn't there a statute of limitations?' I was more upset than I should have been. 'The guy's suffered enough, hasn't he?'

'A statute of limitations on abandoning your family?' She looked at me like I was subhuman. 'Try that on the mom who's been working three jobs for the past decade. Or the kid.'

'So he'll pay now? From jail?'

She shrugged. 'Probably not. But he can't just run away from his past and expect it'll never catch up with him.'

I leaned against the sink, feeling a bit nauseous.

145

'Why were you looking at all my film out there?' she asked. 'What were you expecting to find?'

'Nothing. I . . . nothing.'

'Are you gonna call the cops?'

'No. Just – listen, go easy on Homer. Tell his wife and the PI or whoever. He's an okay guy. Just beaten down. Going after him isn't going to solve anything. Just . . . leave him be.'

Her big light eyes were flared with what I imagined was uncharacteristic empathy. I felt more paranoid than usual as I walked out.

19

Slotted in the driveway next to Induma's recreational Range Rover was her Jag, a nice old-school one from before all the luxury cars started looking like Camrys. Her house, a done-to-a-turn Craftsman backing on the murky Venice canals, lit up in greeting as I strolled through the waist-high bamboo lining the walk. Less than a block from the beach, the air had a pleasing sea-dirty tint. I was a few minutes late, having driven freeway loops and parked three blocks away to make sure I wasn't being followed.

The lights, with their high-tech sensor pads, continued to illuminate my walk in segments until I was on the porch. Induma loved her technology. At the door, I realized how nervous I was. I hadn't been over since we'd split, and I was looking forward to seeing her more than I wanted to admit.

Before I could knock, she shouted, 'Come in.'

Stepping into a waft of humid air and layered scents, I set down the bottle I'd brought of her favorite dessert wine. Induma, like the kitchen, was a mess. Shiny hair piled atop her head, flecks of lassi on her face, dishtowel

147

crammed quarterback-style down the front of her sweat pants. Lids rattled atop steaming pots. Papadum disks dripped vegetable oil onto paper towels. A timer buzzed. On a sheet of tin foil on the kitchen table sat a giant lump of clay, shaped vaguely, bizarrely, like Chewbacca's head.

Induma kneed the oven door closed. 'Out of my way. Sit here. Eat this.'

She slid a dish of *puliyogare* across the counter, pointed at it with a dripping wooden spoon. Rice with roasted peanuts and curry leaves, flavored with tamarind. I took a bite. She was a vegetarian but her food was excellent anyway.

'Lord,' I said.

She winked at me. 'I know. Handro'll be right down. He's cleaning up.'

'Cleaning up?'

'He's into sculpting.'

That explained Chewbacca on the kitchen table.

'He any good?' I asked.

'God-awful.'

I wanted to ask her about Charlie's house, but there was a comfort to being near Induma, and I wanted to enjoy it before Alejandro descended. I took a turn around the kitchen and the contiguous living room, noting the wonderful, domestic accoutrements. A ring-stained cork coaster on the coffee table. Sheet of TV channels taped to the inside of an open cabinet door. A dog-eared fashion magazine. What I was admiring, I realized with a touch of envy, was how *lived-in* the house felt. I was older than my dad was when he had me, but I'd never been able to settle into a place, let alone a family. I was frozen, a bug in

148

amber. There's a kind of fear, a kind of loss, that goes into your cells. Becomes a part of you. Walls you off, keeps you from getting to the things you want the most. Nothing brought that home like the feeling I got when I glanced over at Induma.

Alejandro pattered down the stairs, pulling a T-shirt over his head leisurely enough to show off his ridged stomach. He was clearly more handsome than me. And more Latin. At the sight of me, his striking face lit up with a sincerity that made me feel guilty.

'Nick!' The suave accent turned my name into *Neek*. He sauntered over and offered me an embrace that reeked of Polo Sport. He flipped his shaggy dark hair from his eyes with a practiced toss of his head, then gestured proudly at the lump of clay on the table behind us. 'My latest piece. You like?'

'Wookie?'

He frowned. 'Self-portrait. I still work on the nuance.'

'The nuance,' I said. 'Right.'

Putting his arm around my shoulders, he turned me away from Induma in a two-man huddle. 'I need your advice. We have our year anniversary Sunday and I want to do something special.'

'Look, I don't think I'm the guy to—'

'I know you two used to, you know, but it don't bother me. Really. You friends now. You know her so well. Give me the advice for a good date.'

I glanced back. Induma, busy at the stove, caught my eye, suppressing a grin.

'You wouldn't think it, but she loves action movies,' I said. 'Rent something with Steven Seagal.'

'*Really?*'

'I know. Weird, right? And you know what else she digs? Chicken wings.'

He eyed me hesitantly. 'But she a vegetarian.'

'Except for chicken wings. The ones at Hooters, especially.'

Finally, he got it. He pointed at my face. 'A*ha*! You fucking with me.'

'No, I'm serious.' I wasn't, of course, but I figured someone who didn't know Induma at least that well didn't deserve to date her.

He slipped around the counter and gave her a soft-lipped kiss. I looked away uncomfortably, but still managed to watch. She kissed him back, then hip-checked him to the side and glanced in the oven. A sandalwood Buddha laughed at me from a wall alcove.

'Baby, I take the Jag in tomorrow for the service.' Alejandro jogged over and plopped down on the gargantuan sofa in the living room, clicking the remote until Telemundo soccer highlights appeared on the wall-mounted plasma.

Induma set two square Pottery Barn plates on the counter between us and we started to eat. She had a beautiful dining room, but we always ate over the counter, me parked on a stool, her leaning so as to keep the oven in reach.

Behind us, Alejandro leapt up on the coach in excitement, then groaned, his shoulders slumping. In his distress, he'd yanked off his T-shirt. 'How hard is the penalty kick? Twelve yard! How hard can this be?'

Induma said to me, 'Rhetorical.'

A curved bank of windows past the TV overlooked a strip of lawn and the imitation canal beyond, but right now the glass just reflected back the house's interior, so we saw two Alejandros leaping up and down, shouting Spanish curses at the screen and holding his head in woeful disbelief.

'That address you asked me to look into?' Induma said quietly. 'It's a rental property, owned by an old Jewish broad in Encino. The last lease ended two months ago, Korean family. If someone new was renting it, they did it with cash.'

So Charlie had spent less than two months there. He'd moved in to do whatever it was that had gotten him the money. Or to lie low with the bundles of hundreds.

'Given how low the vacancy is in Culver City and the fact that the owner was busted for not reporting income in. '05, I'd say it's likely she took cash under the table,' Induma added. At my expression, she blushed – a rarity – and shrugged. 'It's not hard to check certain things if you know where to look. Or who to ask.'

'Still. You're pretty good.'

'No. Just Indian. We cultivate relationships all over the place and can scare a computer into behaving itself most of the time.' She eyed shirtless Alejandro, now pleading with the TV. 'Two of my three most useful skills.' She smeared some mango pickle on a wedge of papadum, popped it in her mouth, rolled her eyes with ecstasy. 'Now, the late Mike Milligan was part of a few separatist groups, real bad news. Ruby Ridge survivalist stuff, mountain men who hoard guns and thump *The Turner Diaries*. They got him on DNA for a murder in the eighties – left a hair on

151

the body – but he sold out some other guys in his organization and got early parole. The unofficial word is that he was the terrorist killed at San Onofre, but the government is neither confirming nor denying publicly.'

Certainly didn't sound like Charlie, but I had to ask. 'Was he in the army? Vietnam?'

'He was.'

'Which infantry?'

'I couldn't find that. Some Vietnam-era service records are still classified, and the rest are a mess. I'm way stronger on law-enforcement databases than military stuff.'

I set down my fork on the Easter-blue plate. 'You're sure this Mike Milligan was the guy, not just another bullshit part of the cover story?'

'Anything's possible, but this is pretty good intel. And there are enough documents and trails for him that I doubt it's someone they just invented. I guess a lot of these separatist types are former military. At least according to the assistant police chief.'

'You went to the assistant police chief? LAPD?'

She shrugged. 'When we installed my encrypted backup software at the crime lab, I was there every day for two months. I don't get speeding tickets either.'

'You didn't mention me, right?'

'Oh – that's what you meant. Only by name and Social. Come on, laugh. All right, don't laugh. No, of course not. And don't worry. He has strong incentive to keep my confidence. Unless he can find someone better to call the next time his fingerprinting database decides to hang from hitting a thread-unsafe code section.' Her not-so-poker face showed what she predicted the likelihood of that to be.

The doorbell rang and I came up off the stool. 'Are you expecting anyone?'

Her forehead textured with concern. 'No, but relax.'

Alejandro flew by, slipping in his socks. 'It's for me. It's for me.' Some murmuring at the door, then he returned with a Domino's pizza box.

I said, 'You're not eating with us?'

'He doesn't like Indian food,' Induma said.

Alejandro seemed upset at the prospect of having hurt her feelings, though I knew from her expression that he hadn't. 'No, baby, I just in the mood for Italian, thassall.'

'He thinks Domino's is Italian food,' Induma said.

I hopped up and got the bottle of dessert wine from the accent table in the foyer. She snatched the bottle from my hand, glancing at the label, her face lighting up. 'Olallieberry. Brilliant.' Rising to her tiptoes, she kissed me on the cheek.

Smiling, she poured two glasses. Took a sip. Closed her smooth, beautiful eyelids as she savored the taste. We drank and looked at each other a bit. She opened her mouth to say something. Closed it. Then she said, 'Why did you think you couldn't tell me about all this when we were together?'

I swirled the wine around, peering down into the glass as if it held great interest. Induma didn't say anything, but I could feel her gaze on me. I cleared my throat and said, softly, 'Can you get him out of here?'

'Alejandro?' she called, not moving her stare from me. 'Yeah?'

'Give us a minute?'

'Okay, baby. I go to the gym.' He came into the edge of my vision, kissed Induma, and then his footsteps padded away. The front door closed, cutting off his whistling.

She said, 'Were you worried I'd think you were a murderer?'

I shook my head.

'Couldn't you trust me?'

The bareness of the question, the vulnerability in it, knifed right through whatever protective shell I thought I'd built up. 'God, yes, I trusted you.' A touch of hoarseness edged my voice: 'But I was scared what might happen to you.'

She returned my stare evenly. 'So it was all for me, huh?' she said pointedly.

'Not all.' I studied the counter. 'I guess I wasn't used to what it was like to be, you know, close to someone. I never really learned that as an adult.'

Induma's lips pursed. She said, 'Will you tell me the rest?'

It wasn't quite a test, but there was a lot riding on my answer. A pot boiled over on the stove and hissed, then it stopped hissing. I said, 'Yes.'

Induma's mouth tensed; she was pleased. I filled her in. When I was done, she drew back from the counter – her first movement through it all. Her back cracked. She moved the scorched pot from the burner and turned off the stove.

She asked for the torn sheet of numbers and perused it, as mystified as I was. Finally, she handed it back with a shrug.

'I wish we had more information on the guys who arrested you when you were seventeen,' she said. 'Last names, anything.'

I pictured Slim and the big guy. How the big guy twisted the dial with those wide fingers. *Radio sucks out here, huh?*

I said, 'I always figured they were flown in from another office just to shake me up and get me out of the picture. Only told what they needed to do and not much more.'

'Yeah. I guess there's always someone willing to follow orders without asking questions.'

'You think I could still be nailed for Frank's murder?'

'I doubt it. It would be hard to convince a grand jury or a judge that the same evidence they'd had for seventeen years suddenly makes a different case.'

'But it's always there. The threat of busting me. No statute of limitations for murder.'

'Yeah, but if the authorities were going that route, they wouldn't have tried to make you the hero of San Onofre. I'd guess that charging you for Frank's murder would open up a lot, call attention to the wrong things for the wrong people.'

'If I become a problem, it would probably be easier just to kill me like they did Charlie.'

Her jaw firmed. She didn't like considering that, but she also didn't argue with me. 'Well, for the moment, no one's trying to kill you. And whoever directed you to that PO box doesn't have official clout or they would've just charged into the post office and searched number two-two-nine.'

'Unless they needed *me* to find what's in it.'

'Either way, it seems like whoever's watching wants to give you some leash and see if you'll lead them to whatever they're looking for.'

'Which is exactly what I don't want to do.'

'If you let this whole thing drop, you're probably safe. You've spent years avoiding all this. Why pursue it now?'

'The way this reared its head? It's not just going to vanish.'

'Yeah, but *you* could.'

I thought about those 2:18 wake-ups, how they'd returned with the vengeance of a shunned relative. 'I've been running for seventeen years. I know now I'm not gonna get away.'

'But are you ready to face it?' Her expression registered her skepticism.

I had no ready answer. The question gnawed at me. I redirected: 'Can you look into the backgrounds of the Secret Service agents for me? Sever and Wydell?'

'What do you mean *backgrounds*?'

'They're both in the LA office now, in Protective Intelligence. Is there some way to find out if they ever worked a protective detail out of DC? Then we'd have a pretty good idea if they had strong loyalty to a particular political figure. Like Bilton.'

'Or Caruthers,' she added.

'Sure. Him too. Though it seems less likely.'

'But worth looking into, no?' She noted my discomfort. 'Why does *that* bother you? Would it really upset you if Caruthers was behind this?'

'I could care less if Caruthers is behind this,' I said. 'I care if *Frank* is.'

There it was.

The anger in my voice underlined how deeply the notion cut me. I looked away, fearing how much showed in my face. I said, 'We don't know if either candidate is or isn't involved. All we know right now is that the Secret Service is hooked into this thing differently than they're letting on.'

'Meaning?'

'Wydell claimed that the Service wasn't called in until Charlie asked for me at San Onofre. The more I turn this over in my head, the more it seems like the time frame's too tight between then and when they stormed my apartment. I think Wydell's lying. My guess is the Service was there with LAPD for the shootout in Culver City.'

She said, 'You're still calling him Charlie.'

'Whatever his name, I don't believe the profile.'

Induma said, 'Let's pull it up then, see if there's anything more specific you can use.'

I followed her to the living room. She set her laptop across my knees, but leaned over me to navigate through the folders. I turned to look at her as she typed. Our faces were close.

The document chimed into existence, pulling my focus back to the screen. A rap sheet, complete with booking photo. Mike Milligan had pockmarked cheeks and sullen eyes.

He looked like a terrorist all right, but he looked nothing like Charlie.

20

Back at my apartment, I stood well away from the sliding glass door and scanned the neighborhood with night-vision binoculars. I'd picked them up from the overpriced spy store on Sunset that catered to weekend warriors and paranoid music executives. The store's gear wasn't as top-shelf as what Frank used to bring home, but it was better than the mail-order junk Liffman used to play around with.

No one was watching me. No one who I could pick out, at least.

Now that I had a functional front door double-locked behind me, I moved the sheet of numerals and the cash from the dishwasher into Charlie's rucksack. Then I stored the whole thing beneath the counter in the giant pasta pot Evelyn had given me for Christmas last year.

Collapsing onto my ripped mattress, I felt wrecked from the day and from the menace I'd churned to the surface. Charlie's head – and certainly his dentistry – had been blown to pieces, but there'd been plenty of his DNA to scrape off the power-plant walls. They'd managed to switch or lose a lot of evidence and slot

Milligan, a loner with the right rap sheet, into fall-guy position. Had they murdered Milligan too? Or had he been the best candidate who'd died at the right time? Either way, I had to get back into Callie's attic and go through the rest of Frank's things to see if any other photos or documents could tell me anything about Charlie; I needed the real name of the man who'd pulled me into all this.

I turned on the TV to shut off my head, and channel-surfed. My thumb stopped when I saw Jasper Caruthers on *The Daily Show*, palling around with Jon Stewart. After a NAMBLA joke that Caruthers wisely skirted, Stewart settled down into a straight-man role.

'Why do you believe you're less susceptible to special-interest groups?'

Caruthers shifted forward in his chair, his mouth firmed in a bit of a grin. 'You may not have heard, but I'm obscenely wealthy.'

Even Stewart cracked up. When the applause finally died down, Stewart said, 'In your ex-wife's exposé—'

'Which one?'

'Which ex-wife, or which exposé?'

'I've only got one ex-wife, unless June's been busy this afternoon.'

'This one.' Stewart held up a book whose title screamed from the jacket. 'She makes a number of new claims, including that you drove under the influence of prescription drugs once when you were first dating. Is that true?'

'Absolutely. I've also watched pornography, smoked pot twice in college – *and* inhaled – cheated at checkers, gave up on a marriage, and shoplifted a candy bar from a newsstand. If anyone thinks that makes me unfit to contend with a nuclear-armed North Korea, please don't vote for me.'

I smiled in the darkness, and couldn't help wondering what the staffer with the horn-rimmed glasses would have to say about the pornography crack.

Wearing his bankable smirk, Stewart signaled to quiet the audience. He feigned incredulity. 'How old were you when you shoplifted the candy bar?'

Caruthers settled back, laced his hands over a knee. 'Fifty-five.' He waited through the laughter, then said, 'I was seven, I think. Or eight. My father was driving me to school on his way to work, stopped off for a morning paper. We were two blocks from my school when he caught me with the candy bar and he turned around, drove back, and made me return it.'

'That was before three-strikes legislation.'

Caruthers chuckled. 'Well, it still scared the hell out of me. My father had an appointment with . . . I think it was with the president of Sears Roebuck that morning. And he made himself late over a ten-cent candy bar. Personal accountability. It was ground into me from an early age.' Caruthers shook his head. 'To this day, I see a Mr Goodbar, I break into a cold sweat.'

I found myself liking Caruthers more than I wanted to. Frank had certainly thought a lot of him. Could he have admired him so much that he'd gotten pulled into something shady on his behalf? Whatever Frank and Charlie had gotten into, it didn't appear to have been 'proper', to hang a prissy word on it, and it didn't seem like Frank. At least the Frank I knew.

The swirl of unease left me feeling achy and heavy-lidded, a stress hangover. I couldn't keep my eyes open and I finally gave in, hoping to grab a few hours' sleep.

I jerked awake with more unease than usual. Not the familiar heart-thrumming anxiety of that small-hours ritual, but a sense of imminent danger. The air sat cool and heavy across my sweat-clammy face.

Rolling to my side, I glanced at the clock. *1:37 am.*

I stopped my hand, which was instinctively reaching for the lamp. A slight chill blew across my face. Moving air.

As quietly as I could, I slid from the bed onto the floor. Once again in my pajama bottoms, shirtless, I moved through my dark apartment silently. Six steps and a shuffle to the bedroom window. The lock was fine. Nine strides across, three and a half diagonally into the bathroom – window closed, security hook secure. I picked my way into the living room. Both new front door locks were as I'd left them, the chain notched safely in its catch. I sidestepped the couch, arriving at the sliding glass door, muscle memory guiding my fingers to the handle's security lever.

Unlocked.

My entire body tensed. I stared down at that raised metal lever as if I could make the fact of it go away. I sensed something – some vitality – in the darkness over my shoulder. With deep foreboding, I turned. A man's outline, barely discernable in the darkness, stood backed to the kitchen counter. The form tensed, registering my focus, then sprang at me.

His shove hurtled me into the wall. I collided hard,

bouncing off and swinging. He'd already thrown the sliding door open and was halfway out, but I clipped his chin. He reeled back, the door screeching along the tracks. Though the overhang shadowed the balcony, the lower half of his face passed through a band of yellow light from the opposing streetlight and what I saw froze me with shock. I was still for just an instant, but it was time enough for him to get off a kick to my chest.

My view tilted and then the carpet was there like a horizon. Through the swirl of dust raised by my cheek, I saw the dark form leap recklessly from the balcony and strike the telephone pole. A grunt at impact, limbs scrabbled for purchase, and then he lurched down out of view.

I got up, clutching my ribs, each inhale aching. Staggering to the balcony, still short of breath, I peered down in time to see him sprinting away, flashing into view at intervals beneath the streetlights. His footfall – rubber soles shushing across asphalt – rasped back from the unlit carports in half echoes.

I'd caught my breath but still felt winded. Not from the pain, not any more, but because the wide, wild mouth I'd seen illuminated in that band of light belonged to Charlie.

21

It was impossible. A twin brother was too farfetched. And yet there was no mistaking that mouth. Before the concussion wave had knocked me unconscious in the power plant, I'd *seen* the explosive flash at Charlie's head. There was no way that he'd emerged unscathed. But I never actually saw him dead. Maybe his head hadn't blown up at all. Maybe the memory had been implanted by government drones. Maybe the trauma had tipped me into a delusion sleep, and I'd awakened with bits and pieces of a story forged from my reinforced paranoia.

Had I dreamed it *all* up? My fingers found the little wound in my cheek. Score one for reality. I went in the stark white light of my bathroom and peroxided the cut, then checked the skin of my chest and arms. Still faintly red from the blast.

Something had happened to me. And to Charlie. But what?

I paced my claustrophobic condo, checking and rechecking locks, fighting with myself about whether it was safe to stay. My sense of isolation, I realized, was compounded by the fact that I'd dissected my home telephone. None of my friends had a way to reach me, and I was hardly in the mood to call around and give people the number of a disposable cell phone which I was soon going to throw away.

Shortly after 7 am, I resolved to go and check into a motel under a fake name until I could figure out my next move. I shouldered the rucksack with the money and threw open the front door, nearly barking my surprise at the cheery DHL delivery guy staring back at me. He handed me a padded envelope and an electronic clipboard. In elaborate, illegible cursive, I signed *Foghorn Leghorn* and sent him on his chipper way.

I returned the rucksack to its home, then fought open the adhesive flap of the padded envelope. A Nokia phone slid out into my palm. I stared at it, spinning my tires and looking for traction.

It rang.

I dropped it and vaulted the counter into the living room. Crouching, I waited. No explosion, just three more linoleum-rattling rings and then silence. They were probably waiting to hear my voice before pushing the red button. It started up again, shrill and unnerving. A seeming eternity until it silenced. Slowly, I crossed to the sliding glass door and nudged aside one of the vertical blinds with my knuckle. No dark sedans, no hovering helicopters, no glinting sniper scopes on the opposing roof.

I grabbed the screwdriver next to my disassembled home telephone, then tentatively rounded the counter and regarded the Nokia, working up my courage for the five-step approach. Finally, I picked up the phone. It shrilled in my hand, putting a charge into my heart rate, and I dropped it and stumbled back, tripping over a cereal box. Through the V of my bare feet, I watched the angry, clattering Nokia until it silenced. Then I pounced on it, using the Phillips head to crack the cheap plastic casing. I sorted through the electrical entrails and the battery compartment, but found nothing resembling C4. The wires had come loose from the circuit board and I stared at the broken unit, dismayed. I'd likely just dismembered my best chance to find out what the hell was going on.

My name and address were typed on the packing slip, but the sender information remained blank. No account number. The envelope boasted of same-day service. I called DHL from my cell phone and, after a costly wait, determined that the package had been dropped off at a Mailboxes 'n More on Lincoln first thing this morning. When I reached the store, the owner was indignant that I'd believe his business to be so sluggish that he'd remember an individual customer. The paperwork, of course, showed that the sender had paid cash.

The store was a few miles from my place. The sender had known to call the Nokia immediately after it was delivered, which meant he was watching.

I took the disemboweled phone downstairs and set it on the square of lawn in front of my apartment, near the curb so it was visible from my bedroom window. Then I set up camp with a cup of instant coffee and my binoculars by the vertical blinds in my bedroom. The lenses aimed through a sliver of light, I sat on my chair until my ass grew numb. Facing windows, parked cars, passers-by – nothing seemed out of the ordinary. A Labradoodle sniffed at the phone casing and found it not worth his interest. A skateboarder stopped to examine the tangle of wires before passing on. By one o'clock, my bladder had reached bursting point and caffeine had my stomach roiling. Finally, a big white truck pulled up to the front of my building and the driver ambled up the walk. In the core of the building, the elevator whirred to life.

A few moments later, my doorbell rang.

Gratefully, I rose, my lower back and knees aching. The same delivery guy smiled the same grin and handed me the same padded envelope. I signed *Pepé Le Pew* and thanked him.

A transparent Nokia slid out from the box, a tweenie model designed to show off the electronic entrails. I felt understood.

It rang within seconds, and I clicked the green button. 'Hello?'

A gruff voice I didn't recognize said, 'I have something you want. The Hyatt on Sunset, West Hollywood. Mezzanine level. Show up at seven. Alone. Do not come earlier. Do not tell anyone you're coming. I'm watching you. Do you need me to repeat any of this information?'

'No. Are you the one who took pictures of me—?'

'Seven o'clock.'

The line went dead.

22

E mily answered the door and scowled at me. 'We gave at the office.'

'Is Callie here?' I asked.

She pointed to the bronze placard screwed into the wall. 'No solicitors.'

'Where's Callie?'

'Sorry, we're full up on drama this week.' Under my steady gaze, she finally broke eye contact, popping her jaw. 'At work.'

I was surprised. 'Where's she work?'

'Gallery.'

'Why are you home?'

'Assembly day. Drug awareness. They're teaching us to "just say no". I've perfected saying *no*, so I figured I'd take a pass.'

'I just need to get something from the attic.'

She held out her arms as if preparing for an aria. Her moth-eaten maroon sweater had baggy sleeves that turned her arms into wings. She cleared her throat, readying her instrument. '*No.*' A fake smile. 'I told you.'

'Why not?'

'My dad said not to let you in if you came back.'

'Look, I just need to look through the boxes in the attic one more time. Then I'll leave you alone.'

'Tempting offer.' She thought for a moment, then waved me in.

I followed her up the stairs. 'What was it like running away forever?' she asked over her shoulder.

'It was a weird situation.'

'Still. Sounds heavenly.'

'*Heavenly*. Eight letters across, twelve points.'

She smirked. '*Seventeen* points. Or sixty-seven with the bingo bonus.'

'It's really that bad? Living here?'

'I liked my old school. My old friends. Our old house. Just me and my dad. Your mom's all uptight about wiping the counters and stuff. And they're so . . . *gross* together. All kissy and stuff. Who wants to be around that?'

Not me.

We reached the second-floor hall and she pointed at the hatch and disappeared into her room. I took a moment to collect myself; I was still a bit jumpy from the cell phone exchange. The Mystery Caller had sent the second Nokia from a different location and paid cash again. No one at that store had remembered him either. Both of the Nokia accounts had been prepaid, and were equally unsourceable. Whoever I was up against knew the steps of this particular dance.

I climbed up into the attic, squinting in the faint light, at first unsure of my eyes. The boxes containing Frank's possessions were gone. I searched around to see if they'd been moved behind a beam or to the far side of the air-conditioner unit. Bewildered, I kept looking around as if the boxes were going to warp back into existence. Who the hell was shuffling through the darkness like a stagehand between acts, leaving telltale photographs, speaking cryptically over delivered phones, stealing boxes out of attics? Finally conceding reality, I climbed back down and knocked on Emily's door.

'What?'

'Can I come in?'

'I guess.'

I opened the door. She was lying on her belly, facing away, playing Space Invaders, using one of those new joysticks that holds a thousand retro games right inside it.

'Do you know what happened to the moving boxes in the attic?'

'Yeah, I keep Lojack on all your mom's junk. Let me pull up the GPS screen right now and we'll track 'em in real time.'

'This is important,' I said. She ignored me so I crossed and unplugged the joystick.

'You're an asshole.'

She looked genuinely hurt. Her eyes were tearing – I'd violated her trust after she'd done me a favor by letting me in. I'd been there myself. How had Frank always known how to handle me?

'Listen, I'm sorry. I shouldn't have done that. I know it must be hard being uprooted like this—'

'You don't *know* anything. Spare me your condescension.'

'Em, I need to know if someone came and took those boxes. This isn't a game. This could be dangerous. For you, your dad, and Callie.'

She studied my face a long time, deciding if she could believe me. Then she said, 'I don't know anything about any boxes. I swear. If they're gone, someone could've come this morning and taken them when I was at school and my dad and Callie were at work.'

'I want you to lock all the doors and windows after I leave, okay? I'm gonna look into some stuff, and then come back tonight and talk to your dad and Callie.'

She sat up, cross-legged, pushing the fringe of her sweater down nervously with both fists. 'Okay.'

'Promise me you'll lock up everything. I'm gonna give you my cell phone number—'

'I have my dad's cell phone. He's a cop. Unlike you.'

She followed me down and closed the door behind me. I waited on the front step, listening for the metallic thunk. I waited some more. I was just stepping toward the doorbell when Emily called out, '*Kid*ding,' and threw the deadbolt.

My pseudo martial-arts class, taught on sticky blue mats in the basement of my gym, finally moved on to Aikido throws, my favorite part of the session. I like Aikido because it doesn't focus on punching and kicking, the crass offensive. Instead it teaches you to use your opponent's energy and momentum against them. The quick sidestep, the locked joint, the tug-and-throw that sends your off-balance attacker hurtling by. I had the skills and the reflexes for it. Fat lot of good they'd done me last night.

170

After, I ran on the treadmill, hoping the pounding would clarify my thoughts, separate the specks of gold from the silt. But my troubles pursued me even here, staring out from the mounted TVs. Occasionally misspelled closed captions gave to-the-minute poll coverage. President Bilton was still trailing, but he was closing the gap. His running mate, Ted Appleton, a labor-and-farm guy from Pennsylvania, was hardworking and almost as bland as Bilton himself. But he had the same old-boy skills – the deflection, the dismissive chuckle, the snide implication – that wore overloaded voters down into submission, like besieged prom dates who'd run out of excuses not to put out. Watching Bilton and Appleton waving to filled Mountain-State bleachers, I was struck by the dangerous complacency of their calculated campaign and know-better personas. Even from my own apathetic viewpoint, Caruthers's energy seemed a possible antidote.

I showered, and dressed in front of my locker, ignoring the usual guys who liked to walk around naked and pretend that no one noticed because we were all so grown-up.

In the rooftop parking lot, I chirped my auto-unlock and climbed into my pickup. Before I could get the key into the ignition, the passenger door opened and Wydell slid into the seat. He held a notepad on his knee on which he'd written, *Don't talk. Your vehicle is wired.*

He said, 'I suppose you're wondering why a Special Agent in Charge would bother to pay you a personal visit.'

171

I stared at him and he gestured impatiently.

I said, 'I'm wondering why you're harassing me.' On his pad, I wrote, *Who?*

He nodded good job, and spoke while he scribbled. 'You did us a favor three nights ago and I'd like to repay it before you learn what hardball is.' He tilted the pad to me. *We put it in this morning.*

'I've played hardball. I was scholarship material.' *So why warn me?*

He paused from scribbling, scratching his nose above the jag where it bent left, a gold cufflink peeking into view. 'You could've been a contender. But that was a long time ago.' *Problem. Mole in the department.*

'You just pop by to Doctor Phil me or do you have something useful to say?' I circled *Who?* twice, emphatically.

'It's come to our attention that you've been looking into matters as pertain to the San Onofre incident. Is that true?' *Don't know. Major sting in works. Answers soon.*

'Not in the least. You'd think guys in the intel business would get their facts straight.' *Mole for who?*

'For a disinterested guy, you're opening a lot of old doors.' *Not sure.*

'I guess almost dying in a fiery nuclear blast can serve as a wake-up call. I'm reassessing some things.' *Whole Service compromised?*

'You're not digging around where you shouldn't be?' *Extent unclear.*

'Not that it's any of your goddamned business, but no.' *Is Sever dirty?*

'Keep it that way.' *I can't protect you. Stay away.*

He tucked the pad under his arm and got out, slamming the door. I watched him walk away until he disappeared into the shadows of the overhang.

23

After bucking Sunset traffic for forty nerve-grinding minutes, I pulled up to the Hyatt a hair before seven. I valeted and took in the trendy stretch of the Strip. Next door, people were already lined up for The Comedy Store, and across the street, thin women in strappy dresses and chunky heels teetered into Skybar, laughing into cell phones too small to see.

After the gym, I'd returned to the spy shop and bought a magnetometer wand, feeling unsettled at my growing kit of implements of paranoia. In an alley by my building, I'd wanded down the truck as I'd seen Frank do so many times and found, embedded in my visor mirror, the digital transmitter that Wydell had warned me about. I'd taped the bug to the wheelwell of a neighbor who always complained to me when our mail got mixed up.

The Hyatt had been tarted up in keeping with its hipster surroundings. I moved swiftly through the slick lobby and mounted the broad steps to the mezzanine. I could feel the pitch of tension rising inside me, prickling my skin. Ducking into the bathroom, I splashed water on my face. A sign by the paper-towel rack urged workers to wash their hands. It was written in Spanish only. I found that presumptuous.

At the right edge of the mezzanine, a glossy sign on an easel announced *Opaque, A Unique Dining Experience.* A number of well-dressed couples chattered nervously on modern couches, but no one seemed to be waiting for me. Arty black-and-white photos of LA cityscapes punctuated the hall beyond.

I walked over to the podium. A calligraphed sign next to a stainless tray said, *Please check cell phones and pagers here*, and a number of customers had. A handsome man with a blond goatee glanced up from the reservation book.

'Hi. I'm Nick Horrigan. I'm not sure—'

'Yes, we're expecting you.' A firm accent, Swiss or German. 'Jocelyn will lead you to your table.'

'Lead?'

A heavyset black woman shuffled over, skimming a hand along the wall, smiling a bit too broadly. As she neared, I saw the vacant stare and realized she was blind. The host took my hand and hers and joined them with odd, New-Age ceremony. Sliding my hand up her arm to rest on her shoulder, Jocelyn turned away, leading me, and asked, 'How are you doing tonight, sir?'

'Baffled.' We came around the corner and whisked through a heavy velvet curtain into an unlit, narrow corridor comprised of more curtains stretching up to the high ceiling. The velvet behind us whispered back into place, leaving us in total darkness.

No visible exits, no easy escape route. My worst nightmare.

I broke a sweat, debated a retreat. Jocelyn, of course, took no notice. My concern rising with every step, I followed her through another curtain into what felt like a larger space. My heightened senses picked up faint giggles, rings knocking against wine glasses, the smell of charred meat.

I'd blundered into a conceptual dining experience, an evergreen Los Angeles trend. The crap they dreamed up to justify twenty-dollar cocktails – aquarium-tank floors, fruit-infused shoshu bars, scorpion toast served within eyeshot of Santa Monica Airport's private runways. And now, darkness. You could slit someone's throat over a glass of Syrah in here and never disrupt the atmospherics.

I balked.

'It'll be worth it,' she said, misreading my hesitation and gently tugging me along. 'They brought the concept over from Switzerland. They say you won't believe what it does to your tastebuds.' We shuffled forward past invisible dining tables. 'Now if you need anything, just call for me. Jocelyn, right? Likewise to go to the bathroom. Give me your hand. There you go. This is the edge of your table. This is your chair. You'll find a glass to your right – got it? Bread and salad in front of you. Butter in the dish.'

And she was gone.

A small table. For two. Feeling around my place setting, I stared into darkness. I wouldn't have been able to see a gun barrel inches from my nose. A waft of air conditioning. The tinkle of breaking glass. Behind me, a man guffawed and said, 'I just spread butter on my thumb.' I tried to read the air. Someone was sitting opposite me.

I heard the whirr of night-vision goggles auto-focusing

and felt my heart seize. Being scrutinized when I was blind pitched me up to a whole new level of discomfort. I felt a bizarre urge to cover my face, but instead, I braced myself – for his stare, a bullet, a blow to the nose.

'Don't worry,' he said. 'I won't hurt you.'

I tried to gauge the voice. Strong, but nervous. Gravelly from first-hand smoke. Older than me, but not by much. Before I had time to ponder why he was nervous, he said, 'Please, take a bite. It *is* pretty amazing.'

The scents around me were especially distinct; of course, I hadn't eaten all day. I tore off a piece of roll. Flaky, warm, hint of anise. Absolutely incredible. 'Okay,' I said. 'Obviously I shouldn't bother asking who you are. But what should I call you?'

'Shallow Throat.' He chuckled. 'Call me the Voice in the Dark.'

'So, Voice, you're a pretty controlling dinner date.'

I heard a click, then he set something on the table.

'Pink-noise generator,' I guessed. 'You think I'm wired.'

'You, the table, the walls.'

'The walls?'

I shoveled my fork through the salad. By the time the tines got to my mouth, they were empty. I used my fingers, which somehow made everything taste better. Baby greens with pear slices and some kind of blue cheese. I chased a toasted walnut around the plate.

"Talking concrete," he said. 'When we speak, we bounce amplitude waves off the walls. The Russians figured out how to embed crystals into concrete, crystals that oscillate with the amplitude waves, throw a signal a hundred fifty yards. It's no-shit stuff – they got it into the

177

US embassies in Moscow and Brussels when they poured the walls. Anyone could be listening to anyone else. At any time.' Someone shuffled by. I heard the whir again, and then the Voice said, 'He'll be eating quickly.'

Jocelyn said, 'I'll bring 'em as fast as they come out.' She leaned over me. 'Done with your salad already? All right, then. I'm gonna reach past your right shoulder. There we go. Now hang on.' She withdrew and returned moments later. 'And hot plate coming. Okay now.'

Somehow, miraculously, she filled our water glasses.

The hot scent of steak rose to my face. I pawed around my plate. My fingertips told me the filet was wrapped in something. Pancetta, maybe. I sawed with a knife, then tore with my fingers, slid a lump past my lips. My workout had left me ravenous. As I chewed, I realized that if I was still scared, I wouldn't be eating. Despite the ominous stage setting, the Voice didn't seem menacing. Just firm and concise.

'I need my money,' the Voice said.

'I thought you said you had something *I* want.'

'You only got one part of it.'

'One part of what?' I asked.

'Of what he wanted to give you.'

'Charlie?'

'So you know his name.'

'Just his first name,' I said. 'What's his last?' My fingertips had moved instinctively to the dimple in my cheek from the explosion. Realizing the Voice could see me, I lowered my hand.

'That's not important,' he said.

'What is?'

'You found the PO box?'

I stopped midchew. 'Yep. I got the photomat slip. When did you pick up my trail?'

'I knew where Charlie's safe house was. I waited for you there. It was the logical first place someone would look. After watching you for a bit, I figured out you needed my help.'

'But you didn't know where Charlie had hidden the money. You saw me leaving his place with the rucksack. That's why you broke into my place last night. To get the money.'

'*My* money,' he said.

'You were the one who paid him?'

'He got it for me.'

'So that *was* you in my place last night.'

He said, 'I didn't mean to hurt you.'

'You didn't hurt me. You just pissed me off.'

'I intended to help you. Did the PO box have whatever you were searching for?'

'You didn't look?'

'I didn't have the key,' he said.

'Why didn't you ask me for it?'

'I don't want the key. I want the cash.'

'Yeah,' I said. 'I opened the PO box. All it had in it was—'

'*Don't tell me.*' The conversation around us silenced, then slowly started back up. After a time, the Voice said, quietly, 'Whatever comes with that key, I don't want it.'

I pushed the plate away, leaned back in my chair.

Jocelyn was back in the vicinity. 'How you doing here?'

'Good, thanks.'

She cleared and set down another plate. I sat cross-armed for a few moments before curiosity got the better of me. I stuck my fingers into the plate, licked them. Chocolate profiteroles. Something to the side of the plate was moist and firm. I fished it out of the sauce. Explosion of strawberry. I'd have to bring Induma here someday. If I got the chance. So many dates I'd planned in my head since we'd broken up. All those elaborate fantasies of reconciliation that I never acted on. Rarely did I go to a new restaurant, a garden, an arthouse movie that I didn't think about having her with me.

I could hear the Voice breathing, the sound of it bringing my attention back to the situation at hand. 'I'll play along,' I said. 'What's the other part of what Charlie wanted to give me?'

'You got one key. There's another.'

'Another key. Okay.' I set down my fork angrily. 'Forget any keys, or cash, until I know what angle you're coming into this from.'

'I knew Charlie.'

'Knew him how? Tried to kill him? You're his twin brother? What?'

'I owe something to his memory. Do you know what it means to owe someone? After they're dead?' The voice trembled, ever so slightly, with emotion.

The white noise around us seemed to swell until I could hear each distinct element. 'You're his son,' I said.

'You're not nearly as clever as you think you are.'

'Well, that's bad news,' I said, 'because I don't strike myself as particularly clever.'

'Charlie had a lot of respect for Caruthers,' the Voice

said. 'He was going to try to help him. He told me he had something Caruthers needed for his election bid.'

That *Caruthers* needed. My stomach sank at the name.

The Voice continued, 'Charlie's only fault was . . .'

'What?'

I could hear the flicks of his fingernails against his scalp, nervously scratching. 'He thought he could get money for it,' he said.

'Two hundred thousand dollars, maybe,' I said.

'Or maybe four. Half up front. Half later. But there was no later.'

'Extortion money,' I said.

'I suppose some people might consider it that.'

'So Caruthers paid him some of the money, then brought down the hammer.'

'I don't know who paid,' the Voice said. 'I don't know what it was. But money was delivered. And then he was killed.'

It sounded like he was fed a version of the truth from Charlie, but was that version correct? The Voice had said he didn't want whatever came with that key; he'd been kept insulated from the hard facts, which made it hard to untangle reality from conjecture. But everything he'd told me pointed to Caruthers. Which, in turn, pointed to Frank.

I nudged the plate away. My mouth was dry. 'How was Frank Durant mixed up in all this?' I asked.

'Frank Durant? Hell if I know. I know he and Charlie went back to the old days. Thick as thieves, those two.'

His choice of wording did not seem accidental. In light of the night-vision goggles, I tried to keep my face impassive, but it was a struggle.

Fortunately, the Voice didn't seem to notice. He continued, 'Charlie did this for me, but it turned into more. He wanted to do what was right. He wanted whatever he had to be made public.'

'But his conscience only kicked in once he got double-crossed by Caruthers's buyers,' I said sardonically. No response from the darkness. I added, 'And you won't see it through.'

'I can't. I can't be seen. It's not safe for me right now. This is all . . . it's all my fault.'

'How are they into you?' I asked. Again, no answer. I said, 'So you have the other piece.'

'No. Just the other key. There's another PO box, another item. He kept them separate. Insurance. But you can't carry insurance against these people.'

'How do I get the key?'

'We swap,' he said. 'The money for the key.'

'When?'

'Soon. I had to see if I could trust you first.'

'Can you?'

'Yes.'

'How are you reachable?' I asked.

'I'm not.'

Jocelyn came back. 'Bet you're done with that dessert?'

I waited patiently while she cleared, humming to herself. Then she said, 'I'll be back in a minute with some coffee.'

I waited for her footsteps to fade, and then I said, 'So how do we do this? Voice? *Voice*?'

But I was alone, talking to the darkness.

24

Slumped against the wall of the elevator, I ran through the ambiguities and half-answers I'd gotten out of the Voice. For every question I'd knocked off the list, four more had popped up. After being led out of the darkness by Jocelyn, I'd asked the staff about my mysterious dinner partner. Of course no one had seen anything – the blind waitstaff at least had an excuse – but the host's goatee had twitched with a faint smirk that said he was exercising Swiss discretion.

The doors dinged open and I stepped out into the hall. Kim Kendall was leaning against my door frame, shoulders pressed to the wood, her body an arc beneath them. Her thick hippie braids squirmed on her shoulders as she rolled her head to take me in. Her full lips, pronounced on her slender face, twitched, and she said, 'His wife's gonna let it drop. The homeless guy. Wendell Alton. What do you call him again?'

I walked toward her. 'Homer.'

'Right, Homer. I thought you'd want to know. I mean, you seemed so worried about the guy, Nick.'

'How do you know my name?'

'I work for a PI, remember? You didn't think I'd spy on

your and Homer's little charity get-togethers without putting a name to the face.'

I put the key in the lock next to her. 'It's not charity.'

She put her hand on my arm. 'How about you shut up and be flattered I came back here?' She shoved herself off the wall and kissed me on the cheek, catching me off guard. Those lips felt as good as I'd imagined they would. The effect was enhanced by relief – relief to be doing something normal again, after chasing down spooks, getting calls from the President, being summoned to pitch-black rendezvous.

She said, 'What's a girl gotta do to get invited in?'

I fumbled my keys into the locks and we entered. She looked around and said, 'The hell happened here?'

'Tasmanian devil.'

She walked straight into the bedroom and fell on the mattress, propping her head on her fist and looking at me. Her waistband had slipped below one pale hip, and I could see the side thread of her G-string. She said, 'I brought you something.'

She reached into her pocket and pulled out a black-cord necklace. The perceive-no-evil monkeys, carved from boxwood, formed a small, circular pendant. 'I saw it on Melrose and figured it was appropriate. For you not ratting me out.'

I draped it over my hand. 'This is cool. Thanks.'

'Let's see it on.' She lowered it over my head. Her translucent green eyes, up close, showed sparks of orange.

'Lemme check it out in the mirror.' I got up, went into the bathroom, and closed the door. The pendant had a seam along the edge where the sculpted face was attached to the backing. I took a can of shaving cream from the shower and set the pendant on the counter. Reaching for the raised toilet seat, I flipped it closed just as I hammered the shaving cream can down on the three monkeys. I poked through the wood pieces and saw the little silver bug, half the size of a Tylenol capsule, glued in the hollow.

'It looks really good on!' I called out.

I swept the wood shards into my pocket and walked out quickly, breezing past her toward my front door. 'Hey, Kim – right? I just realized I parked my truck on the wrong side of the road. Street cleaning tomorrow at seven am. Lemme move it real quick.'

I figured she'd be thrilled at the chance to poke around. The cash and sheet of numbers were hidden in the kitchen, and I doubted she'd make it out of my bedroom if I hurried.

I moved swiftly down the hall, dropped the bug down the trash chute, then tapped at Evelyn's door. She answered, *New York Times* in hand, folded back to the dimpled crossword. 'Ten letter word for unkempt?'

'Thanks a lot,' I said. 'Listen, I locked myself out of my apartment again. Can I climb over your balcony?'

A mournful sigh. 'You know that scares the hell out of me, Nick.'

'I know, but Eldy's not in until Monday with the master keys.'

'Fine, but I'm not watching.' She aimed the newspaper at me. 'You be careful.'

I thanked her and slipped onto her balcony, then climbed one apartment over in the other direction. I moved through the vacant living room into the bedroom. Kim's pillow and blanket were still there, and the overnight bag. The bathroom smelled of darkroom chemicals. I clicked on the light. My face stared back from all around. Photographs, clipped to the shower rod, taped to the tile, hung from the clothesline above the tub, some of them still wet. She'd captured me putting the disassembled Nokia phone on the lawn. Wanding down my truck in the alley. Removing the bug from behind the visor.

I collected the photos and walked back down the hall to my place. Quietly, I opened the door. As I'd hoped, she was still in my bedroom. I heard her flop back to the mattress. 'That didn't take long,' she called out.

I walked in and threw the pictures on the bed, then the broken pieces of the pendant. She sat up quickly. 'Shit,' she said.

A quick knock, then Evelyn took a step into my living room, clutching the newspaper section. For once, I'd left the door unlocked. She tilted her eyeglasses, peering into my bedroom. "*Disheveled*," she said triumphantly. She frowned, lowering the crossword. 'You made it in one piece?'

'I did. Thank you.'

'Is someone there with you?'

'This is a bad time,' I said. 'A really bad time.'

She nodded and withdrew, holding her gaze on me.

I looked back at Kim. She was staring at the photos spread across the mattress and I could have sworn it looked like she felt bad.

'Do I know you?' I asked. 'Is this personal?'

'No. I was paid. To watch you.'

'By who?'

'I don't know.' She noted my face and said, 'Look, I swear. I feel really bad about this.'

'You're sweet.'

'You have every right to be pissed off. But you can't let anyone know you caught me. This guy seems dangerous, all right? I wasn't lying – I *am* an art photographer. I do take PI jobs on the side. But never like this. This guy scares me.'

'Tell me what you know.'

She took a deep breath, studied the ceiling, exhaled hard. 'I was tight on cash, so I pulled a posting off a website two days ago. Someone wanted a photographer like me, around my age. Had to be female. The guy had me meet him on a fire road by Runyon Canyon that night. He told me to park, turn off the car and lights, unlock the doors, angle away the rear-view mirrors, and wait. So I did. He was twenty minutes late. Probably watching me, making sure I was alone. Just when I was about to drive off, he slid into my backseat. He told me your name and address and said he wanted me to spy on you, take pictures if I could. Get close. He knew the condo here was getting renovated, but he'd had someone pay the owner to rent it for a few weeks. He told me to let myself get spotted by you, then have the pictures of the homeless guy waiting. Build trust, all that. He left cash and the necklace on the back seat. A lot of cash. He said to give you the necklace later. Then he told me to wait five minutes before leaving and he walked off.'

'Was the cash in hundreds, banded?' I asked.

'No. Twenties. Normal money, not fresh from a bank or anything.'

'How old is he?'

'I didn't see him, obviously. He sounded older than me, though. Older than you.'

'Did he have a smoker's voice?'

'No. Smooth, quiet. And calm. Too calm.' Her eyes moistened and then she blinked and they were as they'd been before. 'Look, I just want to go back to my stupid life.'

And I wanted to get the hell out of my condo, but if I did, the Voice wouldn't know where to find me, and I'd be giving up my shot at that second PO box key. If there *was* a second key. I'd gone all-in on a single hand and couldn't leave the table taking anything with me. I blew out a breath and refocused. 'How are you in touch with him?'

She sighed, stared up at the ceiling again. 'I have a pager number, okay? If I input the number where I'm at, with a 1 after, he calls back. That's all I've done so far. But if I type a *2* after, it means I'm leaving something at our drop point.'

'Which is where?'

'Echo Park. There's a garbage can next to the pretzel stand on the north side of the lake. I'm supposed to tape photos beneath the lid. But only if I get pictures of you meeting with other people. Everything else he's just had me describe over the phone.'

I fished a piece of paper from a drawer and found a pen on my nightstand. 'Write down the number.'

She looked at me. 'If you find him, you can't tell him.'

'Write it down.'

She jotted it down on a piece of paper for me. I dialed, got the two beeps of the pager right away, and hung up.

'Listen,' I said, taking a page from Wydell's book, 'let's pretend I believe you. You're scared. You should be. You don't even know who this guy works for. People have died already.'

Her eyelids flared convincingly, and she blanched.

I said, 'Is there anything else you can tell me?' Her eyes darted away, so I said, 'What?'

'I don't know if it's anything,' she said. 'I don't even know what it means. But one time I dialed the pager from a pay phone and after I input the number, I hit 4 instead of 1 by mistake. Right when I hung up, the phone rang.' She'd gone cadaver-pale, and her voice had thinned out with fear. 'Before I could say hello, he said, "Godfather's with Firebird, so all's clear. Get it to them."'

Firebird. My mind went blank when I heard the word: Caruthers's old Secret Service call sign, from back when Frank worked with his protection detail.

The Voice in the Dark's information, though scattered, had pointed to Caruthers, but the phrase Kim had overheard seemed a solid indication that the senator was directly involved. As I sat there absorbing it, I began to wonder – was the snippet too pat, too convenient? Who the hell was Godfather? The handle seemed a bit on-the-nose for a mobster. The 'accidental' message relay could have been disinformation. Call signs weren't classified; they were easy enough to find out and inevitably obvious, usually a jokey take on some feature of the principal.

Everyone knew Reagan's was 'Rawhide'. When the Service had the Pope back in '87, the newspapers even reported his call sign as 'Halo'.

'That's exactly what he said?' I asked.

'No. But it was something like that. And I remember the code names for sure.'

'What did you say?'

'Nothing. I was scared. I mean, *Godfather*? So I hung up. I knew I wasn't supposed to hear whatever. He called back. The phone rang and rang. It scared me, so I took off. I almost hit someone backing out.'

I watched her closely. My gut said I should believe her. Still, they could've played her to mislead me.

I said, 'Wait until morning. Then page him to call you back. Tell him you gave me the necklace, but I told you I left it in my truck when I moved parking spaces. I had you follow me to the beach, but I lost you on the way. You spent a while looking for me, then went back to your place for the night. When you came back to the vacant apartment, you saw I'd broken in and gone through your stuff. I might've gotten his pager number, which you kept written down on the back of a business card in your overnight bag.'

'What if he hurts me anyways?'

'You don't know anything. You're as useless alive as you are dead.'

'Thanks.'

'If you cross me on this,' I said, 'I'll make sure he knows you told me everything.'

The fear in her eyes confirmed she'd been telling the truth, at least about some of it.

I stuck out my hand and we shook.

Trust no one.

The dark palm trunks rose, breaking up the distant lights of downtown like the bars of a cell. Lotuses floated, black latticework along the lake edges. Toward the middle, the fountain spouted, misting and slapping water. Bedded down in a scratchy stand of bushes, I swept my night-vision binoculars again past the garbage can next to the pretzel stand. A drug deal seemed to be going down by the Oriental bridge, but that's Echo Park for you. A homeless woman lay on her substantial stomach at the lake's brink, letting her tangled hair dangle in the water. A black teenager wheeled by on a dirt bike so small his knees rose to his chest when he pedaled. Aside from an elderly man dumping a lemonade, no one had gone near the garbage can, despite the fact that I'd paged Kim Kendall's employer to the drop two hours ago.

My excitement was palpable as I hid there in the pseudo-brush, waiting to see who would stroll up and check behind that trash-can lid. Sever? The agent I'd met at Caruthers's? Charlie, back from the dead again? Or, more likely, a perfect stranger, like Slim, who was no more to me than a windshield was to a bug.

I thought about how Kim Kendall's employer had kept her waiting twenty minutes in her car on Runyon Canyon while he got the lay of the surrounding darkness, and my mind flipped to Liffman's shaggy beard and eyepatch and another of his countless rules: Even when you're spying on them, they could be spying on you.

I widened my search to see if I could spot another

watcher. The park, rendered video-game green through my binocs, seemed to flicker with hidden life. Druggies. Stray cats. I traced the rim of the lake, rechecking the nighttime loungers, then explored the tree trunks and the shadows around the stairs. When I swung the lenses south up the concrete embankment, at first I was unsure what I was seeing by the bushes at the base of the fence. The image resolved swiftly, tightening my hands around the binoculars.

A sniper sitting, partially obscured by branches, peering through a scope directly at me. He tensed, surprised to find me looking back, and pulled his head away from the eyeguard. I stared with panicked horror at the face of my mother's latest husband.

25

I drew my hand across the back of my neck and it came away with blood. Branches had whipped my skin as I'd flung myself back into the bushes at Echo Park. I'd sprinted away in a stooped combat run, doing my best to get tree trunks and outcroppings between me and the sniper rifle. Now, crouched in the darkness along Callie's big white house, I waited and watched for headlights. They came, boring into the night, and then an Explorer turned into the driveway.

I'd raced to Pasadena, figuring that Steve would spend at least a little time trying to track me down at the park. He wouldn't expect me to hurry back to the snake's nest. Through my jittery drive, the ramifications had begun to settle in. A conspiracy so serious they'd had someone marry Callie just to keep an eye on her.

Steve parked the big SUV in the driveway and hopped out, brazenly carrying his rifle case with him. He had his handgun in a hip holster, as I hoped he would. As he headed for the door, I sneaked up behind and, unsnapping the thumb break, tugged the Glock from his holster. I pressed the barrel to the back of his head. Satisfying.

He dropped the rifle and raised his hands.

I could barely hear my voice over the blood rushing my ears. 'Not an inch.'

'Nick? You gonna shoot me?'

'Should I?'

'What are you into?'

'You tell me. Is Emily home?'

'She's at her mother's. Why the hell do you—?' He jerked around so I hit him on the side of the head with a stock-enforced fist. He reeled but didn't go down, and then he put his hands on his knees and coughed. A spot of drool hit the pavement.

'Because she doesn't deserve to see you like this,' I said.

I marched him up the walk and rang the doorbell. He was as wiry as I remembered, but more dense. A powerful little guy. After a time, I heard footsteps and then the porch light went on. I hid the gun in the small of Steve's back in case Callie looked through the peephole, but instead she called out in a worried voice, 'Who's there?'

'It's Nick,' I said. 'And Steve.'

She opened the door and I shoved Steve in past her and followed. 'Nick. Are you okay? What are you *doing*?'

Steve staggered a bit and leaned against the wall. Then he bent over and dry-heaved. He wiped his mouth. 'I need to sit down.'

Callie swooped to his side, glaring at me. 'What did you do to him?'

We moved into the family room, a bizarre little procession, and Steve slumped on the couch and held his head. I felt a stab of concern, so I aimed the gun at him to shore up my ill-will. 'Your husband was pointing a rifle at my face a half hour ago.'

Callie held up her hand, firmly, as if stopping traffic. 'Wait. *What?*'

'Jesus,' Steve said, 'I'm dizzy.'

I was breathing hard, revving up instead of calming down. 'He hired a girl to spy on me. I tricked him into coming to a drop site. I got there early, with night-vision binoculars, and caught him set up with a sniper rifle, about to shoot me.'

Callie said, 'No, he wasn't.'

I moved the gun away from Steve, aiming at the carpet between him and Callie. 'Are you in on this too?' It felt awful giving in to myself that way, but there was also an odd feeling of release, of yielding to something sweet and tempting.

Callie looked at me, stunned. 'You're losing touch, Nick. You're more paranoid than Frank ever was.' She started to say something else, but she stopped, her mouth slightly ajar. Then her whole body began to shake. She hugged herself around the stomach and bent over a little and took a few deep breaths. Then she straightened up and said, 'Nick. Look at me. You have to choose. Sanity or paranoia. Life or death. Look at me. Think what you just asked me.'

'This is real, Callie.'

'*What's* real?'

I jabbed the gun at Steve and he flinched away. I was yelling through my teeth. 'He came after me tonight. He had a sniper rifle aimed *at my head.*'

'I asked him to follow you, Nicky!'

'What? *Why?*'

'Em told us what happened. Your stopping by. It

sounded like you got yourself into something awful. I asked Steve to keep tabs on you. I was worried. You're my *son*.'

Steve was pressing both hands to his head.

'So he took that to mean he should come shoot me?' I said.

'I'm LAPD SWAT, Nick. How do you surveil someone at night if you're SWAT?' Steve raised his face. A blood vessel had burst in the corner of his eye. 'Through a night-vision scope.'

Doubt wormed its way in. 'You just *happened* upon me? In the bushes at Echo Park?'

'No. I tailed you from your apartment. I didn't really care to, but your mother and Emily talked me into it. I was watching from the moment you set up in the bushes. You took a leak on your way in. If I was gonna take you out, I could've shot you whenever.'

Was there *anywhere* I'd been in the past three days that I wasn't being watched by one party or another?

My conviction wavered. Could it be true? That Steve had followed me and we'd chased each other out of Echo Park before the puppet master showed himself? 'Okay,' I said, imploring Callie, 'he also cleared Frank's stuff out of the attic, a picture tying Frank to someone the government doesn't want to admit exists. It's all missing.'

'*That's* part of this – this fantasy you've concocted about Steve?' Callie said. '*I* moved Frank's boxes to the garage after you left. For the trash and Salvation Army. They'd been up there, untouched, for so many years. And then you came by, all the old ghosts . . . I figured it was time.'

196

For a few crushing moments, I regarded the Glock in my hand. Then I walked over and set it on the couch cushion beside Steve.

He was still holding his face and he didn't look up. 'Any other questions?' he asked.

'Yeah. How's your head?'

'Not very fucking good.'

'I'll get you some ice, honey.' Callie glared at me as she swept past. 'I think you can leave now.'

'Can I wait to make sure he's okay?'

'I'm dandy,' Steve said. 'Now get the hell out of here.'

'Can I at least get you some Advil, something?' I asked.

Steve was murmuring under his breath. Callie came back with ice wrapped in a dishtowel. She pressed it to Steve's cheek and temple. 'Our medicine cabinet, upstairs.'

I ran up the stairs, fumbled through the cabinet. I got the blue-and-yellow bottle and turned to go when a framed sketch above the towel rack stopped me cold. Callie's portrait of me was incredibly lifelike. Soulful eyes. Smooth, youthful skin. A heavy mouth – more pensive than sad, but still, not the mouth of a seventeen-year-old. Had I really looked like that? Finger smudges on the glass showed where someone – Callie – touched my face from time to time. How could she keep the sketch up? And right here, where she'd see it every day? Stepping out of the shower. Brushing her teeth. A part of her life. What did that do to her?

I heard her shout for me and I ran downstairs with the Advil. Steve was on his feet, shaking off Callie. 'I'm fine, honey. I promise, I'm fine.' He grabbed the pills out of my hand and walked by, smacking my shoulder with his. I stared at Callie as the sink ran in the kitchen and we heard him slurp down the pills. She stood erect, chin slightly raised, like an English actress. She did that sometimes with her posture, used it to hold herself together. Stray hairs caught the light from behind her. That tough, pretty face, made tougher and prettier by the years. I thought about what it would be like to have an estranged son pistol-whip your husband and shove him through your front door. The accusations I'd made. I couldn't get that sketch out of my head, how she'd hung it where she had to see it every goddamned day.

'What?' she asked sharply.

I just shook my head, not trusting my voice.

Steve trudged out of the kitchen and through the front door, returning a moment later with the rifle he'd dropped in the yard. Without slowing, he said, 'I'm gonna shower off this fucking day.' His footsteps thudded up the stairs. Callie and I looked at each other some more, and then at the walls, and then at each other again. A car drove by outside, the engine fading.

She said, 'You want to be like Frank?'

I looked away. I couldn't meet her eyes. But I felt that stare coming on, still coming on. 'I could never be like Frank.'

'All these years, the stars are still in your eyes, blinding you to what's right in front of your face. Frank wasn't Clint Hill. He never jumped on the trunk of a limo. Never held the President's head together. Never got a Purple Heart in Vietnam. You know what Frank was great at? The day-to-day. Showing up. Knowing when to give space. The quiet heroics. And you. You didn't show up for his funeral. You didn't show up for your own graduation. You didn't show up for college. You haven't shown up for a damn thing in seventeen years.'

The edges of her words seemed to ring off the walls for a while, and then the silence of the house reasserted itself. The pipes feeding the shower upstairs hummed gently in the walls.

'Well,' I said, 'I'm showing up now.'

She studied me a long time but her face didn't soften. Not a bit. 'Frank's box with the pictures is in the garage.' Her voice quavered, but only once.

It took me a moment to get the feeling back in my body, to take that first step. She followed me, angrily, through the kitchen, to the door to the garage. By the trashcan, I found the cardboard boxes. After a quick search of the others, which held nothing of relevance, I carried the photo box back out, through the entryway, Callie behind me. I stepped down onto the walk. My face was burning. My hands, poked through the handholds on the box, felt numb.

Her voice, behind me. 'Wait . . . I – just *wait*.' She'd been drawn a few steps out onto the porch. 'You should've come to me, Nicky. When they arrested you. I would have done *anything* for you. You were everything I had left. Why didn't you just talk to me?'

I readjusted my grip on the box. 'They made clear they'd hurt you if I did.'

Callie took a half step back. Then she leaned one hand against the pillar and sort of collapsed, her hair down over her face so I could see only her downturned mouth.

Her sobs, rising up from some cracked-open place inside her. I stood dumbstruck, holding the box, watching her, unsure what to do.

She kept crying, her hair tangled in her eyes, her tears, and then I was running, the box kicked aside on the concrete walk but I wasn't running away, I was running to her. I stepped up on the porch and bent to her and she pulled at me, hard. My shoe slipped but I held her weight and she rose and then she was gripping me, sobbing, the crown of her head pressed into my chest and she was shaking and sobbing and I was holding her.

26

His fluffy hair reined in from the shower, a red amoeba swelling on his cheek, Steve shifted on the couch beside Callie. 'Now that we're all pals again,' he said, 'why don't you tell us what the fuck is going on?'

So I did, from the flight to Alaska to the Voice in the Dark. It didn't come smoothly or easily, but it came. Callie interrupted frequently with exclamations and questions, but I didn't mind.

When I finished, Steve leaned back and crossed his arms. 'I made some calls today, checked up on your story. About the two mystery agents who came to arrest you for Frank Durant's murder.' He ignored Callie's look of surprised indignation. 'There *are* no records of your arrest. Or your being booked. Or interrogated. There isn't even a record of out-of-district officers or agents going to MDC that night.'

Callie's cheeks had gone red. 'You heard Nick's story. That wasn't an official arrest. It was thugs threatening a teenage kid.'

'Listen,' I said, 'whether you believe me or not, please don't tell any of this to anyone.'

Steve said, 'Like to the *Enquirer*?'

'Like to your SWAT buddies when you explain how you got the bruise.'

Tilted back against the couch cushions, Callie blinked a few times, catching up to her thoughts. 'So you came back to look for more pictures of Charlie?'

'Or anything else that might have had his name or given any clue as to who he was.' I set down the box, discouraged. Most of the pictures were bent, a few wrinkled with moisture from the front walk. I'd checked them as I'd gathered them up, but there weren't any others of Charlie. 'If he's from the army, it's not like you'd know him, and I'm having trouble getting to anyone else who could give me anything on him.'

Callie grimaced. 'Yeah, I didn't know any of Frank's friends from the war. You know how he was about that. Closed off like a fist.'

I pulled the one picture of Charlie from my pocket and offered it to her anyway. She frowned down at it, holding it at arm's length, a new mannerism. Or at least new to me. 'Wait,' she said. 'Oh yeah, sure. He's a guy Frank knew from the service.'

I leaned forward, excited. 'So you *did* meet him?'

She looked at me funny. 'Of course I met him.'

'Why "of course"? You just said you didn't know many of his friends from the war.'

'Oh,' Callie said. 'Not that service. The *Service.*'

Steve's head snapped around. It took a moment for me to find my voice. 'Charlie was in the Secret Service?'

'Yes. Right. Charlie. We saw him at the occasional event. He may have come over once or twice. We even went to a barbecue at his house.'

202

'What's his last name?'

'Jackson? Johnson? I can't remember.'

'So he was a buddy of Frank's?'

'A colleague. I don't remember them being particularly close, but you know how agents are. The bond.'

I recalled Charlie's desperate eyes, picking up the aqua glow of the spent-fuel pond. *I trusted Frank. I trusted him with my life.* Given the tattoo, I'd assumed the army, but there was also plenty of risk to go around in the Service. And evidently, plenty of trouble to get into as well.

I asked, 'And Frank never mentioned they were in the war together?'

'No, I don't think so. Or I didn't remember. But you know Frank. That doesn't mean anything. It doesn't mean it was a secret.'

'Isn't that a bit of a coincidence? Two guys from the same platoon wind up working together in the Service?'

Callie gave me the look she used to give Frank.

Steve said, 'The Service recruited heavy after the war. And the CIA, the Marshals, the FBI. A lot of soldiers were steered the same directions by the same people, sent each other resumés. We tried to help each other out.' He looked at his folded hands – he hadn't meant to let that 'we' slip, not with me in the room.

'When did they work together?' I asked.

'Up until the end,' Callie said.

We sat with that one, all three of us, and then I asked, 'What did you know about Charlie?'

'Nothing, really.'

'People always remember more than they think.' Steve

looked interested despite himself. 'Think about when you went to his house.'

'Oh – he had a son,' Callie said. 'Troubled kid. I want to say drugs. A few years older than you, Nicky.'

'Did they look alike? Same mouth?'

'I don't really remember. Just that he was so *scowly*. Charlie wasn't exactly all polka dots and moonbeams himself.'

'Was he married?' Steve and I asked at the same time.

'Going through a divorce. A rough one, maybe. He had a few tense late-night talks with Frank just before Frank was killed.'

'He came to the house?' I asked.

'Phone.'

Steve's jaw firmed and our eyes met. Tense late-night calls and then a bullet to Frank's gut. I took awhile to work up the nerve. 'Do you think there's any chance Frank got pulled into something dirty?'

Callie said, 'Never.'

Steve looked at her, and I could see the skepticism in the set of his mouth, the sympathy in his eyes.

Callie implored me, 'You don't believe that either.'

'No,' I said quietly, 'I don't. But I don't like the way this is looking. There's some compelling stuff pointing to Caruthers. You know how Frank was about him. And now Charlie working under Caruthers, too. Plus, everything surfacing now, right before an election—'

'How do you know it's not Bilton behind it?' Callie asked. 'That would be more in character. Bilton's the one who got a bounce in the polls from the San Onofre threat.'

I said, 'Bilton has no link to Frank. Or Charlie. Or any-thing Frank was dealing with seventeen years ago.'

Callie said, 'I'd believe the whole Secret Service was dirty before I'd believe Frank was.'

I felt diminished, as if in asking the question I'd given up something precious. I considered what she'd just told me about stars in my eyes and wondered what the costs of that might be for her, for me. If our image of Frank came apart, what else would have to come apart with it? More than just the past seventeen years.

I slid the photograph into my pocket and rose. 'Thank you. I'm sorry, again, for everything.'

Callie stood nervously. 'Maybe we could see each other sometime . . . calmer. Em seems to have taken to you.'

'Could've fooled me,' I said.

Steve said, 'I don't want him near my daughter.'

Callie shot him a glare. 'Then I'll see my son when she's not home. Shouldn't be hard – she sleeps over her mother's every chance she gets.' She looked back at me, a bit desperately, and I felt the pull of old fears. Contact meant trails and trace evidence and sedans with killed headlights in the night. And then a phone call. Sweat stung the faint lacerations on the back of my neck. Callie was studying me still, trying to figure out what to say. 'Maybe we could cook or something.'

'I don't cook,' I said, as gently as I could.

Callie made a noise in the back of her throat, and they walked me to the door. I was glad I'd parked blocks away so I could breathe the sharp night air for a bit.

I stood nervously at the threshold, then moved awk-wardly to hug my mom. She embraced me and then we pulled apart and stood there for a moment, unsure what to do next.

I offered my hand to Steve but he just glared at me. 'If half of what you're saying is right, you've got a long, nasty haul between you and the truth. And from what I've heard, you've never finished anything in your life.'

Moths swirled around the porch light, pinging the glass. 'Maybe this,' I said.

'What?'

'Maybe I'll finish this.'

I heard them arguing in hushed tones as I headed down the walk, the picture of Frank and Charlie snugged in my back pocket.

27

My windows were locked, the front door dead-bolted, the blinds closed. Spread on my sliced mattress was the shrapnel from whatever had sailed in and exploded my life. A black-and-white photograph of Frank pointing with his mess-hall fork, Charlie turning to listen from one table over. A hundred eighty grand, neatly bound with purple bands. A torn sheet of numerals in nine columns. A pager number, scrawled in a con girl's signature on a scrap of paper.

What the hell did all this have to do with my stepfather?

Sitting cross-legged, I propped my face on my fists and studied my neat display. Blissful stillness. No helicopters, no zoom lenses, no sniper scopes, no loud locksmiths and transparent Nokias and limousine rides. The lights were off, the items illuminated only by the muted TV and the streetlight spill around the blinds.

The Voice had to be Charlie's son. Nothing else explained as well the shared mouth, the hitch in his words when he explained his debt to the dead. *Charlie did this for me.* Why *for* him? Callie's description was a start. *Troubled kid. I want to say drugs. A few years older than you, Nicky.*

It was a story of a father and son. Sonny got into trouble, owed the wrong kind of people the wrong kind of money. More money than Pop could spot him on a Secret Service pension. So Pop came to the rescue, hauling out a seventeen-year-old secret and putting it up for sale when it was at peak, election-year value. To a point, he'd known how to handle himself. He had army training. Secret Service training. He knew who the right people were in Caruthers's inner circle, and how to contact them. He started going wrong when he didn't figure out his two-hundred-grand downpayment was bait to set the hook. And the Powers That Be had lived up to their title. When he found himself cornered, Charlie's last desperate shot was the stepson of an agent he'd worked with, an agent he'd admired.

Charlie's last resort, sadly, was me.

Seventeen years ago, Frank had been pushed to his snapping point. By what? Had he and Charlie stumbled across something while digging up dirt for Caruthers? Or covering something up for him?

Frank had skipped a few days of work there at the end, for the first time in his career. He was into something bad and was figuring out how to get clear of it without putting me and Callie at risk. He was cautious, guarded, strategic. What he didn't count on was me following my dick out the door that night, giving the wet-work man his window of opportunity.

But if Charlie also knew the secret, why had he been spared the visit in the night? Maybe *they* didn't know he knew. Or maybe he'd cut a deal. Regardless, all these years later, would he have been willing to reopen Pandora's box because his kid had gotten himself into a fresh round of trouble?

Would Callie?

I closed my eyes, breathing the sensation swirl of paranoia – the phantom smells of English Leather and too-strong coffee, Frank sunk in his chair, that grainy Zapruder footage playing across his impassive face. Had Frank damned *himself* with a thousand small decisions?

An overheard message pointing to Firebird. An agent showing up at my condo to urge me onto the phone with the President. Frank and Charlie calling each other late at night just before Frank's murder. The Voice in the Dark, spinning tales of extortion. The facts were colorful, and they fell into different patterns depending on which way I twisted the kaleidoscope. There were more variables than I could pin down. So, of course, I called Induma.

She picked up after a few rings, her voice rough from sleep. 'Yuh?'

'Hi. Sorry. I . . .'

'What? *Nick?*'

'I need your help.'

'Okay. I'm here alone.'

'Alejandro's not spending the night?' I regretted asking the minute it left my mouth. Between Kim Kendall's deception, braining Callie's husband, and my latest round of dirty hypotheses, I was irritable, out of sorts. I made a fist, pressed my knuckles to the wall.

But she answered evenly. 'No. He's out clubbing. With club people. You know how I like club people. Now what's going on?'

I shorthanded everything that had happened since I'd

seen her last, and the theory I'd managed to work out about Charlie's extorting Caruthers to get money for his son. Then I asked if she'd dug anything up on Wydell and Sever.

'Just that they've both been in the LA office for years,' she said. 'Wydell for six, Sever for five.'

'You couldn't find out which protective details they were on before that?'

'I'm an open-source-software geek with a few police connections through the crime lab, but I can't do everything. I've called in a handful of favors, but what you're asking for is too sensitive, Nick, for obvious reasons. It's not like they list this stuff online.'

'Did you find out whether the Service was at the Culver City house with LAPD for the shootout?'

'I couldn't. That operation would've been run through LAPD's counterterrorism unit, which is as close to airtight as it gets.' She sensed my frustration and said, 'Look, I don't have to tell you this is all mirrors and shadows. Given that you're risking your ass, it's probably worth asking: are you willing to pursue this even if it proves that Frank was dirty?'

'Frank could've been killed for *not* going along,' I said, a bit too quickly. She let the silence work on me. It made a more effective argument than I had. I thought of the Voice, coming at me out of the darkness, asking if I knew what it meant to owe someone after he was dead.

'That's not an answer,' she said.

I pressed my teeth into my lower lip until I felt the sting. 'I have to know what happened. Whichever way it goes. I have to know what got Frank killed.'

'He's dead. It's not like he has a name to clear.' Induma waited out the pause. 'Maybe it's time to start taking care of people who are alive.'

She didn't often get judgmental. I stood quietly, thinking of Callie and what this could do to her if it proved to be as ugly as I feared.

Induma asked, 'If he *was* dirty, would that change who he was to you when you were a kid?'

'It's who he is to me *now*. That didn't die on the living-room floor. So maybe you're right. Maybe this isn't just about Frank. Maybe he made his own goddamned bed. But he wasn't the only one affected by his choices. And if all that went down for no good reason, or worse . . .'

We were silent for a while, together. 'Okay,' she said softly. 'I spent a good amount of time plowing through databases after you called with those names earlier. I can't get clearance for a lot of them, obviously, but I'm strong on financials.' An uncharacteristic hesitation. 'I checked federal pension records, and I can't find a Charlie Jackson or Johnson in the Secret Service back then. In fact, there were only three Charlies and Charleses and Chucks even *in* the Service in a two-year span around Frank's death. Two were black guys and the third was fifty-two years old *then*.'

'What does that mean?'

'Look, this kind of search? Where I have access to a federal pension database? If I can't find him in there, the guy doesn't exist.'

'I *saw* him.'

'I'm sure he told you he was Charlie—'

'My mother *met* him. He had a tattoo. The mouth. Not a face you forget. He *exists*. I have a picture of him.'

211

'*Now* you tell me you've got a picture?'

'That helps?'

'Of course. I can take a run with some facial-recognition software, see if it picks anything up on the other California and federal law-enforcement pension databases. It's not a lock, but it'll help the search criteria. I'll come pick it up.'

'It's not safe for you to come here.'

'They won't mess with me if they don't know who I am. And once they do their homework and figure it out, they *really* won't want to bother with me. I'm high-profile, and not a little politically connected. Dragging me – or my corpse – into this will only complicate whatever they're trying to get done.'

'Still, why take the chance.'

'Fine.' A silence, and then, convincing herself, 'Fine. Put the picture in an envelope, tape it beneath the lid of the Dumpster at that corner mart by your place. I'll get it in a few hours. Let's meet at Starbucks at noon tomorrow. Free Internet.'

'The one on Montana?'

'The *other* one on Montana.'

After she hung up, I shut the phone and held it at my side. I closed my eyes but didn't like what I saw there either. Leaving aside the photograph and the slip with the pager number, I gathered together the items on my mattress, stuffing them back into Charlie's rucksack. It fit snugly into Evelyn's giant pasta pot in the kitchen cupboard.

I grabbed my keys, left, and walked the few blocks, stopping occasionally at windows and newspaper vending boxes to check behind me.

Homer was sleeping off a drunk, slumped against the convenience-store wall, one leg flung over the parking-space bumper block. A car pulled in right in front of him, headlights glaring into his face. He raised an arm against the light, wagging sluggishly. The driver hopped out, chatting on his cell phone, and scampered inside.

Homer was cursing and rearranging himself. He looked like a brown puddle. He got nasty when he boozed hard, not like the affable bums you see in movies. His eyes were bloodshot and sinister, his crows' feet white lines in his dirt-caked face. I thought about what Kim Kendall had told me about his wife and kid, how he'd let his past run him into the ground. I seemed to be on pretty good course for the same destination.

'Hey, Homer,' I said. 'Did you talk to anyone at the VA for me about tracking down those soldiers?'

'. . . ffffuckin' think you are . . .' he said, in a dry-throated mutter. 'Leeme the hell alone.'

I stepped past him into the shop. When I laid two more throwaway cell phones on the counter, Hacmed leered at me. 'You start a telecommunications company, Nicolas?'

I set down some cash and went outside. Homer was out cold on his back, his mouth a ragged oval. His head was shoved up against the parking-space bumper block. I did my best to move him but his girth and odor out-matched me. I finally managed to roll him onto his side, his forehead clunking to the asphalt. I wedged a folded piece of cardboard beneath his sweaty cheek and left him snoring prodigiously.

The corner mart's rear wall, papered with flyers for

213

independent films and sex-caller lines, abutted a rank alley with a Dumpster. I taped the picture of Charlie and Frank beneath the lid, then studied the slip of paper with the pager number.

Ten digits on ragged paper. My sole channel to the Powers That Be.

I flipped open one of the cell phones I'd just purchased, dialed the pager number, then punched in the digits printed on the back of the cheap plastic earpiece. I hung up and waited. A half-peeled ad proclaimed, *Have Sex With Locals Now!!!!* I wondered how they decided to stop at four exclamation points. The breeze wafted a faint sewer smell from the grate, but faint was enough.

The shrill ring startled me. I answered in a low voice, 'Hello?'

Silence. A whisper of static coming through the live line. A faint rustle, a puff of breath catching the receiver. And then nothing.

'Hello?' I said again, wanting back just a single word to match against my memory of Sever, the Voice, Charlie. But there was just a click, and eventually, a dial tone.

I smashed the phone on the ground, threw it in the Dumpster, and headed for home.

I came awake in terror, gasping for breath, shoving at my sheets. For a few wretched moments, I tumbled through scenarios, disassociated. Was I holding Frank on the blood-glistening floorboards? Hurtling back from the blast that consumed Charlie's head? Battling an intruder by the sliding glass door? The fabric between past and present had torn, and I was in free fall between them.

Finally, I realized that I was in the grip of night terrors. I didn't have to check the clock to know what time it was. My witching hour.

I spoke the facts out loud to try to calm myself: '*It's 2:18 and you're safe in your bed. It's 2:18 and you're safe in your bed.*'

But still I couldn't slow my breathing, my thoughts, my furious heartbeat.

The ghouls had fled their cages and there was no herding them back.

28

Starting early the next morning, I sat with my back to the wall, knees drawn to my chest, watching the front door. I was waiting for a knock, the delivery of another transparent cell phone. But it kept not coming. I walked around my place, peering yet again through the blinds down at the morning-bright street. Finally I made a handful of calls, pushing back my upcoming appointments – a job interview, a teeth cleaning, a get-together at Maloney's to watch the Dodgers–Giants game. I reached the dean at the Pepperdine MBA/Public Policy program and apologized for missing our meeting. Reacquainting myself, even briefly, with my normal life only underscored how far off the tracks the last few days had sent me.

By 11:30 am, I had a pretty good case of cabin fever and was glad to head out to meet Induma at Starbucks. I got there a bit early, and made my way through the rush to the pay phone in the back. Customers were cycling past the counter rapidly, on their morning schedules, ordering in abbreviations and using the proper, ridiculous terminology. Shouldered to the wall near the bathroom, pressing the receiver to my face, I felt more out of place than usual. Maybe I was having another hiccup of envy for the incessantly well-adjusted, with their BlackBerries and leather folios and buckets of caffeine. I tugged the well-traveled paper slip out of my pocket and dialed the pager number Kim Kendall had given me.

The first ring cut short. '*This number is no longer in service. If you believe you have reached this recording in error—*'

Hanging up, I noticed Induma pushing through the crowd, holding her laptop down against her thigh. She wore a cashmere sweater, hooded and blood-orange, that brought out the hidden hues of her caramel skin. Using a napkin, she wiped down the table, bussed the empty cups, then sat. As I approached, she kept her eyes on the screen. Her slender fingers flying across the keyboard, she kicked out a chair that rocketed into my hands. 'Sit down. Is this him?'

On the laptop screen was a picture of Charlie, a match of the one Wydell had flashed in my face after they'd raided my place. Loose scowl, blue blazer, slicked-back hair. A training-school headshot, archived on a state employee pension site that Induma had somehow accessed. *Special Agent Charlie Jackman. California State Police.*

Confronted, at last, with proof, with a name.

'That's him,' I finally managed. 'That's him. He was real. He was there.'

She studied me with her large brown eyes. 'I never doubted it.'

'What the hell is the California State Police?'

'What the hell *was* the CSP. They were merged into

217

CHP in '95. And guess what fell under their jurisdiction?' Induma's gaze was steady across the top of the computer. 'Protecting high-ranking state officials.' She took in my stunned reaction, nodding. 'That's right. They were a security police agency. Seventeen years ago, Charlie Jackman was a dignitary protection officer who worked close-in detail for—'

'Governor Andrew Bilton,' I said. 'Holy *shit*. Charlie didn't have dirt on Caruthers—'

'—he had it on *Bilton*.'

The Voice in the Dark's words, considered from this angle, made as much sense. *Charlie had a lot of respect for Caruthers. He was going to try to help him. He told me he had something Caruthers needed for his election bid.*

For the first time in days, I felt hopeful. The farther this stayed from Caruthers, the farther it stayed from Frank. I thought about how Bilton had tried to reel me in early, arranging to talk to me after I'd regained consciousness in that hospital room. How his self-assured voice had sounded later on the phone, the threats he'd buried beneath that superficial charm: *if you mess around on certain stages, the spotlight finds you eventually*. How his links to the Secret Service were now vastly stronger than Caruthers's. How the message divulged by Kim Kendall pointing to Caruthers – *Godfather's with Firebird* – had smelled like disinformation.

'Charlie brought the dirt on Bilton to Frank,' I said, 'thinking Frank would broker a deal for the Caruthers camp to buy it. As Caruthers's guy, Frank would've *had to* bring any intel to him. But for whatever reason, Caruthers didn't bite – maybe it was too hot, maybe he didn't want to stoop to dirty politics. When Bilton's guys caught wind and came looking, Charlie hung the blame on Frank.'

'That's certainly,' Induma said, 'one possibility.'

'And?'

'The other, just as obvious, is Charlie brought it to Frank because he needed an outside man to blackmail Bilton. Working for Bilton, he couldn't do it himself.'

A new dark cloud. Another array of considerations. I sagged back in my chair.

'There are two choices here,' Induma said, quietly, 'Frank either brought it to Caruthers for the right reasons, or to Bilton for the wrong ones.' She watched me consider this for a moment, then directed her frown back at the computer screen. 'Why did your mom say Charlie worked for the Service?'

'Because it seemed like he did. He was another dark-suit earplug guy when she met him.'

'Well, Charlie pulled a pretty good disappearing act. He took early retirement a week after your stepfather was killed. Then he pretty much vanished. No tax returns, no mortgages, no phone numbers. And I know where to look.' Turning back to the screen, she slid a finger across the touchpad, tapped with her thumb. 'Charlie had one son. Mack. Thirty-eight.'

'Mack Jackman?'

'I went to elementary school with Ronnie Ronald. "Mack Jackman" is rock-star cool by comparison.'

The screen loaded. A home page. *Mack Jackman Commercial Photography*. It featured numerous catalogue pictures of furniture. A beechwood leather couch.

A pale-sea-green faux-suede chaise. A dining-room table, chocolate wood and frosted glass.

Induma said, 'The film used to take your picture outside Charlie's? Kodak Ektachrome 100. What'd the guy at the photo place tell you? "Fine grain, high sharpness, makes your colors pop."'

'If you're shooting something where you need really accurate color,' I said. 'Clothes or curtains.'

'Or furniture,' Induma said.

I clicked the *art shots* button on the website, and a few black-and-white cityscapes appeared that I recognized from the hall outside Opaque. The Voice in the Dark, tight with restaurant management as I'd thought; the smug Swiss host had made clear his unwillingness to give up anything, and the waitstaff could hardly play eyewitness. I wondered if there was some connection between Charlie and Kim Kendall, the other art photographer in the mix.

'I checked the web page's source,' Induma was saying. 'The page elements are stored in date-sorted directories. He used to add docs from the server every few days, but he hasn't added a new one since June.'

'Which, in English, means . . . ?'

'This site hasn't been updated in three months. Not much of a way to run a business. He went off the grid. No new leases, no new jobs, no forwarding information.'

'Money trouble,' I said. 'Hiding from whoever he owed. Then his dad swooped in to save the day.'

Induma tapped the laptop with a thumb. 'I couldn't source that pager number you got off that girl. I obviously don't have clearances for all the law-enforcement databases, but still. Whoever set up that pager knows what he's doing. How to not be seen, not leave trails.' She folded her laptop and stood. 'When's Mack contacting you? To give you the other key?'

'I don't know. But not soon enough.' I jotted my cellphone number on a piece of paper, and she tucked it into a pocket. I took her arm. 'Thank you.' The cashmere was soft against my fingers. I rolled my thumb across the fabric. 'You were wearing this when I met you.'

'You remember?'

'With dark blue jeans and open-toed sandals. Your toenails were painted a deeper shade of orange, and your hair was pulled back in a tortoiseshell clasp.'

She stopped, laptop against her thigh. I watched her chest swell and settle beneath the sweater.

I said, 'I'm sorry I didn't tell you everything then.'

Behind her, around us, people jostled and scraped by and sipped on the go. Her lips twitched – a bittersweet smile – and then she turned and disappeared through the door.

29

D ripping with sweat, I sat on the bench before my locker. I'd hit the weights, jumped rope for twenty minutes, then run myself to exhaustion on the treadmill. The workout should've cleared my head, but instead I felt jumpy, antsy to get home to see if DHL had dropped off a transparent cell phone at my government-issued front door.

I tugged open the locker. Through the curtains of my hanging clothes, my money clip sat on the thin metal shelf. Still fat with cash – I'd stopped at an ATM – but something was different. A piece of paper was tucked beneath the clip, parallel with the top bill. I withdrew the fold of cash, pulled the silver clip free, and stared down at a familiar film-processing slip.

One roll, ready for pickup.

The photograph looked like shit, but it did its job. Pronounced against a blur of yellow stucco were five large painted numbers. The picture had been taken at a slant, encompassing the corner street sign. All the info, in one neat little snapshot.

I lowered the photograph and stared at the real thing.

Precise angle, precise distance. I was standing where the photographer had been when he'd snapped the shot – across the street on an apartment-complex driveway leading sharply down into an underground garage. As I leaned against the retaining wall, my head was just above street level. An inconspicuous spot. Which was good, given the dark sedan pulled to the curb in front of the neighboring building.

The picture was one of only two that were exposed in the roll, waiting for me at the photomat I'd visited last time. Logic dictated that Mack was the guy who'd taken them. After all, he'd left me the first film-processing slip. But two things bothered me. The quality of the picture, poor by the standards of a professional photographer. And the film was a standard 35mm, not the high-end Ektachrome he'd used before.

I slid the second photo out from behind the first. A head-on of an apartment door. Above the peephole, in tarnished brass – *2G*. Anyone or anything could be behind that door, and anyone or anything could have been leading me there. But I had to go.

I glanced back up the road at the dark sedan. Tinted windows. Engine off. But I knew the car wasn't unoccupied. The mole Wydell had warned me about?

Bracing myself, I stepped out from cover and walked briskly up the sidewalk, heading away from the sedan, hugging the buildings. The glut of apartments here, south of Pico near Lincoln, had been untouched by the Westside richification. Peeling paint, crumbling stucco. Tree roots had buckled the concrete in several places. I was sweating, desperate to look over my shoulder. I tried to hurry, then tried to slow down. No car door opened behind me; no engine roared.

Turning the corner, I passed my parked truck and looped back behind the complex. I hopped over a locked gate onto the pool patio. The door from the courtyard into the building was unlocked. I took the stairs, easing out onto the second floor. A damp hall, carpet still holding on from the '70s. Down the length, past a laundry room, through a firedoor, and there it was. 2G.

The door was slightly ajar, the latch resting against the plate.

I stood and listened. Nothing.

I didn't like that unsecured door one bit. Before I went through it, I wanted to check out the rest of the floor, scout some exits, make Liffman proud.

I reversed down the hall to an emergency stairwell that dumped out into a side alley. On my way back to 2G, I ducked into the laundry room. Dry heat. Shoving the window open, I glanced down. Six feet below was a pool shed.

Cautiously, I made my way back up the hall. Through that open sliver in the doorway of 2G came a sharp odor. I knocked and the door wobbled open a few inches. No answer.

I stepped inside. The reek of gasoline. The sun was low and fat in the street-facing window, making me squint. A figure in a chair, head bowed. Newspaper spread on the floor under and around him.

The place was torn apart. Drawers emptied. Couch cushions slashed. Chairs flipped over. A familiar tableau.

The big window was open, a faint breeze lending body to a limp, shoved-back curtain.

'Mack?' I eased forward. The front of the man's shirt was stained. A crimson bib.

My shoes padded on the moist newspaper. The print wadded and blurred, soaked in gasoline. The man was bound to the chair, cloth strips tying his wrists and ankles. Wild blond hair, just like Charlie's.

My breath came back to me as an echo, as if off the walls of a cavern. I reached out an unsteady hand, gripped the hair, and raised the head. The resemblance was shocking. Not just the Mick Jagger mouth, but also the wide brow and intense, neurotic eyes. The Voice in the Dark, a dead ringer for his father as a younger man. The major difference being the second smile etched across his throat.

Stunned, I let go of Mack's head, and it flopped forward again, chin to chest. Mindful of the window, I dropped to the floor. His bare foot was inches from my head. I fought my stomach back into place. I hadn't seen a dead body since Frank's, and the smell alone about undid me.

The abraded flesh, the restraints, the gasoline dousing – no question he'd been persuaded to talk. Which meant he'd talked about me. And likely revealed his photo-slip gimmick, which they'd imitated with a lousy picture shot on cheap film.

I'd either sneaked in past whoever was watching, or walked into their set-up. Despite the open window, the gasoline fumes were starting to get to me. I crawled over to the window and peered down at the street. The sedan was still parked in its spot, the impervious black windshield throwing off a glare.

I turned, my back to the wall beneath the window, regarding the tossed apartment. Mack's killer or killers looking for whatever Charlie had been trying to sell. Or for the banded hundreds, still crammed in the pasta pot beneath my kitchen counter where even Mack didn't know they were. Mack had told me he had a second key from Charlie. Maybe his father had taught him where to hide things, as Frank had taught me.

I crawled to the sink and, staying low, reached up over the counter into the sink and worked my hand into the garbage disposal.

A magnetic box under the lip.

I yanked it free, fought it open. Another key. Brass, just like the other one, but this was numbered *228*. Probably right next to the PO box that had held the torn page of numerals. I'd been within a foot of whatever this key guarded. Oblivious. I flipped it over, read the familiar print: *U.S. Gov't, Unlawful to Duplicate*. I shoved the key into the case, the case into my front pocket.

What else could I find that they hadn't? And how much time did I have?

With mounting panic, I scurried toward the bedroom, skidding over fallen books, the titles staring up at me in bold – *Living Sober, Twelve Steps and Twelve Traditions, The Big Book*. A stripe of wet carpet ran under and ahead of me, a guiding trail. My face was down near the floor, close enough that the vapor stung my eyes. Mack stared at me from the chair, a dark smudge at the edge of my vision.

In the bedroom, a file cabinet by the double-futon had been knocked over, photographs and papers scattered. I dug through the mess on the floor. Loose film cases, holding Ektachrome 100. Another contained a dime bag of weed. So much for living sober. Among glossy 8x10s of armchairs and bookcases, I found a picture of me climbing down the telephone pole the night I'd gone to Frank's old house.

The nightstand light had tilted over, throwing an ellipse of gold across a book. *Twelve Steps*. No dust jacket.

I'd slid over another book wrapped in that dust jacket on my way to the bedroom. Clambering on all fours back to the main room, doing my best to ignore the slumped, bound form across the way, I flung the books aside until I found the dust-jacket lettering – *Twelve Steps*. I tore off the cover to reveal what it was hiding – a leather-bound journal.

My fingers moved furiously through the pages. A ledger. Some pluses. A lot of minuses. Next to each sum was what I assumed to be a basketball score. *LA 98, Miami 102, -$8,000. NC 88, Duke 90, -$8000.* Interspersed were steep interest charges. The debt, as of last month, was *$383,918.00*.

The Voice in the Dark had been clear. *I need my money.* Not, I *want* my money. As soon as the other addictions had fallen away, a new one had grabbed him.

I forced my eyes back to Mack. From behind, were it not for the cramped angles of his bound limbs, he looked as if he'd nodded off. Bound and doused with gasoline – the style seemed more crime syndicate than Secret Service. Had Mack been killed not by Bilton's crew, but by his bookie's people? But why would they want to lure me to the scene with a photomat slip? The answer came with a shudder: Mack would've told them I had the money.

Bookie murder or Service hit. Neither option a comforting one.

I scrambled back into the bedroom to continue my search. As I crossed the threshold, something fell from the back of the ledger. An old-fashioned envelope, yellowed and brittle. It was unopened, a date scrawled across the seam in faded blue ink: *5/91*. The month of Frank's death. Crouching, I tore at the flap, the paper slitting my finger. A Polaroid fell out into my waiting palm. Bilton at a campaign field office, wearing a smile and a too-narrow brown tie, his arm around a beaming woman in her late twenties. She wore turquoise dangly earrings, and her hair was center-parted behind a poof of bangs. A sign behind them proclaimed BILTON FOR GOVERNOR! Nothing on the back.

Our future President popping up in the back of a gambling ledger with a woman other than his wife. Who was *she* in all this?

No time to ponder – someone could kick in the front door any second. Pushing the photo into my back pocket, I looked desperately around the bedroom. In my excitement, I'd risen from my half squat. Standing in full view of the window. The angle still hid me from the street and the sedan below, but I stared with dread at the windows of the apartments across.

A wink of light from the opposing rooftop caught my eye.

Before I could react, I heard something strike the kitchenette, simultaneous with a pneumatic thump from outside, like a tennis ball leaving a court cannon. I looked through the doorway. Something pinged around the small corner kitchen, sending up chips of tile. It had shot in through the open window one room over. I watched it spin on the cheap linoleum, then stop.

A miniature rocket, no bigger than two inches, narrow stem connecting the warhead to a fin assembly. It looked like a fat, olive-drab dart.

I don't remember leaping. I only remember flying in the air toward the back wall when the overpressure lifted me from behind, flipping me over. Shrapnel studded the walls instantly. Air sucked past me, drawn toward the front door, then the room seemed to pulse, and flames billowed up everywhere at once, clouds of brilliant orange. I scrambled to my feet as the flames advanced, curling the pictures at my feet, scaling the walls.

I shot a frantic look out the window. The roof across, now empty. Down below, the dark sedan remained in its place, but the door was thrown open, the driver's seat empty. My hand shot to my pocket, instinctively checking for the magnetic case, but it was gone, the pocket torn. I spun around desperately, the fire flicking at me. The box lay shattered by the flaming futon. Falling to my knees, I jabbed at it. Melting plastic pieces and the top half of the key. It had snapped, a perfect break right in the middle of the brass teeth, but where was the bottom? The fire closing in, I ran a hand through the carpet, until a hot pain bored into my palm. There it was, in a nest of burnt fibers. Before I could talk myself out of it, I seized it. Hot metal singed my fingertips, but I clutched it and ran toward the front door.

The fire grabbed at my pants, my hands. Mack's corpse was alight, the smell sickening. Flames ate through the cloth restraints, his corpse sagging as each gave way. I flew past and staggered through the front door into the hall.

A few neighbors were out, older folks staring shocked, a kid on an old-fashioned scooter. A sturdy man was pinning the fire door open with his heel, shouting for everyone to clear out. Past him, way down the hall, a tall, powerful figure wheeled into view around the turn.

Reid Sever.

We stared at each other, me in a half crouch, him frozen in his dark suit. And then I was on my feet, sprinting for him. His hand went to his hip but I crashed left into the laundry room and flew out the window, landing with a bang on the pool shed six feet below. My shoes slid out from under me and I ass-bumped hard and skidded off the edge, landing in a full sprawl on the concrete. The severed top of the key bounced free from my hand, knocking the ground with the ring of a flipped coin. I rolled once and caught it just before it would have disappeared into the murky pool.

Glancing back, I saw Sever leaning out of the laundry room, readying for the drop, smoke billowing from the neighboring window. I bolted. Over the fence, up the street, fighting my car keys out. Two blocks away and accelerating, I still couldn't catch my breath.

I had to get home before they beat me there and seized the rucksack holding that torn page of mysterious numbers.

30

Across the street from my apartment building, an agent sat behind the wheel of a fleet Chevy, his lips moving. I couldn't make out the earpiece, not from this distance, but he wasn't talking to an imaginary friend. Was he in the corrupt cadre with Sever, or was I now official Secret Service business? Either way, more agents were en route. I wouldn't have time for finesse.

I'd left my pickup one block over in a corner spot, facing the intersection, ready to haul ass in the likely event that I was pursued. Stepping forth from behind the mail truck I'd followed up the street, I walked briskly to my building.

As I entered the lobby, I heard the Chevy door close behind me. I turned calmly into the stairwell, out of view, then I bolted, taking the steps three at a time. I reached the third floor before the door banged open below, and then the agent shouted up at me, the words indistinct with stairwell echoes. Spilling out into the hall, I nearly collided with Evelyn, tugging her cat along, a leash on its rhinestone collar. Stuttering an apology, I sprinted into my condo, slamming and locking the door behind me.

Moving furiously, I swept pans and lids out of the

cabinet, clawing my way to the giant pasta pot in the back. I snatched out Charlie's rucksack and threw it on, sprinting to the sliding glass door. Behind me, I heard a yell, then splintering wood. The agent tumbled into the room as I whipped the sliding door shut behind me and leapt off the balcony, striking the phone pole harder than I'd intended. I grabbed one of the metal bars, but my other hand swiped and missed. Swinging out monkey style, the pavement a gray swirl below, I caught a glimpse through the glass of the agent rushing to the balcony. Clamping my legs around the pole, I half slid, half fell to the ground. I risked a glance over my shoulder as I ran past the Chevy with its dinging open-door alarm. The agent was straddling the three-story drop between the lip of the balcony and the top foothold of the telephone pole.

The two dark SUVs screeching onto my street interrupted my momentary relief. Rucksack flapping on my back, I sprinted through the opposing alley, banged through someone's back gate, and tumbled out onto the street where I'd left my truck. There it was, parked a half block up by the intersection. A sedan was parked parallel to it and Sever was on his feet, peering through the passenger window. The tan, square face lifted, started to turn my way.

I pivoted abruptly and started walking away, but then I heard Sever shouting into his radio, so I dashed off again. Into the street, a bicyclist swerving and cursing at me, then across someone's terrace, and through the lobby of a condo building. I spilled out the back into an alley, looking around wildly. The rev of unseen engines, eager and predatory. Two agents ran by the mouth of the alley, headed for my building. I was standing in full view but they didn't happen to look over. I jogged the other way, rounded the corner toward Hacmed's store. Stepping out onto the street, I stared at the back of Sever's head. He was standing in the V of his open car door, gazing out at the street. I was so close I could see the white flesh beneath his freshly cropped hairline. I froze. Behind me, around the corner, I heard the crackle of approaching radios.

A dark form lunged at me from beside the Dumpster, hurling a ragged jacket over my head. I heard a muttered word – '*Quiet*' – and the jacket settled over my shoulders. The weight and stench were staggering. Homer threw an arm over my shoulders and tugged me, stumbling, right past Sever and out into the crosswalk. As Homer bellowed at me in a false slur, I looked at the asphalt, reducing the view of my head from behind. Just a couple of tottering vagrants. I waited for a shout, a firm hand on my shoulder, pounding footsteps.

Behind me, I heard the agents convening around Sever's car. Sever said, 'Concentric circles. Let's go.'

Homer and I crossed the street, the jacket's hem drooping to my calves. I had a moment of weak-kneed gratitude for my worn-out Pumas, a footwear accent to the slum attire. We stepped into the humid kitchen of a Chinese take-out joint, Homer nodding at the cooks, who looked up as one from their woks and greeted him with kind familiarity. Sidling past sizzling kung pao and vats of rice, we moved through a side door to the rear lot, with its three demarcated parking spots. We threaded between cars and trash barrels, moving west, staying off the main streets and finally winding up in a peaceful yard behind a church. A giant cardboard box, warped from water, sat by the rear door, filled with clothes.

I shrugged off Homer's aromatic coat and handed it back to him. Then I sat on the church's back step and put my hands on my knees. My arms were still shaking. I couldn't get the stench of Mack's burning flesh out of my nostrils.

'You probably just saved my life.' My voice was thin and cracked.

Homer said, 'They'll be looking for a guy in a white shirt,' and pointed to the box.

I dug through. Christian-themed T-shirts. I passed over *Soak Up The Son* and *Tougher Than Nails*, settling on the more ecumenical *Forgive Us Our Trespasses*, with its gray scrolled letters on black. As I pulled it on, a police siren rose to ear-splitting pitch. On the far side of the fence, the vehicle whipped past, and then the sound faded. I had to consciously lower my shoulders.

Homer said, 'I checked at the VA for you about finding guys who served with whatever infantry, but admin was unhelpful and stupid.' A world-weary nod. 'The federal government in action.'

'Thanks,' I said. 'I got the name I needed anyway.'

'We'll head to the beach, wait there 'til night. The tunnels beneath PCH fall between patrol routes, so the cops never check 'em. Plus they're a pain to get to, have to leave their patrol car. Or unmarked government sedan.'

We traced an equally circuitous route, winding up north of San Vicente, where the streets dipped toward sea level. Homer rushed me down a run of stained concrete steps and then we were safe in the tunnel, a few nervous beachgoers on their way back to their cars scurrying past the homeless. It was dank and otherworldly, our footfall bouncing back as innumerable echoes. The stale air magnified the stench of urine. Homer coughed, the warped sound commanded through the tube until the wind across the far entrance sucked it away. He hooked my arm and we stopped at the midway point, sliding to sit, our backs to the curved wall. A ragged man wearing spectacle frames with no glass in them stumbled past, followed by an obese woman air-playing a stringless tennis racket like a fiddle. Several more colorless forms, rank with sweat and waste, negotiated and joked and played with their odd, broken props – a homeless circus. The breeze shifted, breathing fresh ocean air through the concrete throat. Pacific Coast Highway thrummed overhead, timpani on endless vibration. The circle of sky at the end glowed with the kinds of colors they name crayons after. It was a weirdly beautiful scene.

I turned to Homer and said, 'Thanks for bringing me here.'

He said, 'Remember to tip the help.'

Across from us, a skinny, ancient man slumbered under a blanket of newspaper. A headline shouted, *Incumbent Surge – Bilton Coming on Strong*. The consequences of what I carried in the rucksack sent my thoughts rippling outward until the implications grew too vast to comprehend. As the sun descended to the glittering plain of the Pacific, our shadows stretched grotesquely up the curved tunnel walls.

I tilted my head back until it tapped the sweaty concrete. Buried in a piss-drenched tunnel beneath a freeway, on the lam with a homeless alcoholic with an alias. I'd been seen leaving the burning apartment by numerous eyewitnesses. They could hang Mack's murder on me. They'd been ready to hang Frank's on me for less.

The shooter on the opposing roof could have killed me. But instead of launching the rocket into the bedroom at me, he'd shot it through the open window into the front room. Sever had been waiting in position to grab me. They were planning to sit me in an interrogation room like the one they'd put me in seventeen years ago, and use their new-found leverage to squeeze me for answers. Or maybe they had a different plan to make me talk – a chair, restraints, and a gallon of gasoline.

I tugged the two pieces of Mack's key from my pocket. They lined up perfectly at a skinny part between teeth – no missing slivers. A stutter-beat of stress at my temples. I said, 'We gotta go.'

Homer's breath whistled through his nostrils. 'Wait for dark,' he said. 'For dark.' He patted my knee, an uncharacteristically avuncular gesture.

His head nodded forward, and I couldn't help thinking of Charlie's son. The dead weight in my hand as I'd pulled his face up to reveal the gash across his windpipe. Mack hadn't told them what they needed to know, and now they needed me to produce it.

At the tunnel's end, in the constricted, desperate glimpse of sky, the sun dropped from view. Silhouettes disappeared into blackness. All around, the rustle of humanity heightened, somehow connected, bodies rasping

237

and murmuring in concert, an elaborate wind-up toy. Among the faceless shadows, all fleeing, all fallen, I felt my eyes well and then tears spill. I kept my throat locked, a hand clamped over my mouth to staunch the dread. Not a sound, just trickles of moisture across my knuckles and an invisible fist in my throat. It wasn't fear, not exactly, but something denser and more awful. It was a cold kind of horror and the weight of a pressure I couldn't withstand.

I'd been kidding myself that I could ever enjoy a normal life. I needed to walk away while I was still on this side of dead, shoulder the rucksack of cash and hop a bus to another city, another state. Leave it all behind again. No matter how awful the prospect, I could start over. I'd done it before.

But then I'd never know. Then maybe no one would ever know.

It was dark now, the tunnel filled with grumbling and snoring. I glanced over and prodded Homer awake. 'Can you get me to Montana Avenue without being seen?'

'Of course.'

'How?'

'I'm the only person who's not a cleaning lady who actually rides public transportation in this town.' He grumbled his way to his feet, then swayed a bit, rocked by malnutrition or boozy fall-out. 'And nobody *sees* anyone riding a bus in Los Angeles.' He belched, pressing both hands to his enormous gut. 'What's our business there?'

The jagged pieces of the post-office key poked at the inside of my fist. 'I need to see a man about a lock.'

31

I caught Raz closing up. Stepping from the shadows, I clutched his arm and said, 'Can you make a whole out of these halves?' I opened my fist and let the brass pieces glitter. 'I'll pay you well.'

His burly arms paused from securing the shop's front door. 'You into some crazy shit, bro.'

He pinched his dense mustache with a thumb and forefinger and led me back inside. I'd left Homer up the street outside the Duck Blind liquor store with a forty of King Cobra. He'd drunk it before I'd finished paying, and he'd elected to stay out back, digging through the trash-cans in case anyone had left a swig in the bottom of a discarded bottle.

The shop was dark and cramped, and Raz kept the overheads off, out of respect for the illicit nature of the undertaking. Clicking on a boom-mounted light, he held up the pieces of the key and made a big show of squinting at them. 'This will be tough to remake for working key. I do not have seven-pin blank, bro. I told you I must order from Canada.'

'I didn't know I'd need it.'

'Yes,' he sighed sadly. 'Yes, they never know until they

need. I will use other type. I will try. I will try for you.' His wide fingers fussed over a tackle box filled with key blanks. 'This is illegal, to copy this key.'

'Yes,' I said, 'it is. But I need to get into that PO box.'

'Like other PO box?'

'Yes.'

'What is inside these very important PO boxes?'

'I don't know what's inside this one.'

He pouched his lips and leaned forward, appraising me. 'I help you, bro. But why? I don't know what you do with this key. Maybe I should better call cops on you.'

He paused for dramatic effect. Then he clamped the key bit into the milling machine, adjusting screws, gripping handles. 'But I don't. That's how it work. Like for my grandfather. First, they have him turn in his hunting rifle. For war effort, bro.'

He bent forward and the cutter head revved up and bit metal. Setting the second piece of the broken key, he did his best to align the angle. He spoke between blazes of sparks, short sentences offset by the shrieking cuts. 'Then they tell him he and my grandmother will be relocated. For own good. Always for own good. They were escorted. Escorted, like one of your prom date. Across Anatolia. On the way, they rape the women. Starve many to death. No water. They die in ditches. The skin, like paper over the ribs.'

He ran the key along the deburring brush. More sparks flew, creating an orb of light in the dark shop that illuminated his face, his wide, firm cheeks. He did not wear eyegear. For a moment, he looked like a boy. He whisked his fingers over the teeth of the new key.

Then he shook his head, dissatisfied, threw the key into the trash, and started over with a fresh blank. 'You know this story. It is same story. Crusades, World Wars, Croatia, the Sudan, Iraq. This is mankind.'

Again with the deburring brush, again the sparks flew, his face a ruddy portrait in focus. 'On the march, a peasant woman hide my grandparents in chicken coop. Why? I do not know. If she was discovered, she would be killed. People help people sometime. They don't know why. But this is *also* mankind.'

He sat back on his creaking stool, stuffing showing through the split vinyl at the sides. He looked at the latest key, his mouth twitching. 'I am sorry, bro. Here I go on like windbag about help but I cannot. I cannot make working key from pieces. Not with substitute key blank. I can order proper key blank from Canada.'

'I don't have time to wait.'

Raz mused on this weightily, chin set on the boulder of his fist so his cheek rose in wrinkles beneath the eye. 'I have idea. Way to get PO box open. One time only. You will have one chance. It is confidence game. You must commit. You can commit?'

I said, 'I can commit.'

I cased the block by the post office and found no one waiting, but given their technology, if they were hiding I wouldn't see them. The bus stop was two blocks away, waiting to whisk me back into oblivion. I looped back to Homer, sitting on the curb in a strip-mall parking lot up the street.

'I'm gonna go. Meet me at the bus stop in five?'

He waved me off dismissively.

Tentatively, I approached the Sherman Oaks Post Office, moving behind trees and parked mail trucks. Every passing car put a charge into me. Finally, a break in traffic. I slipped through the front doors and put my back to the wall. The lobby with the counters and registers was locked up, but the wing to the left with the banks of boxes was open as advertised, if dimly lit to discourage night-time visitors.

A movement from outside caught my eye. Homer strolling boldly down the sidewalk. He shoved through the front doors, regarded me, and said, 'What? I got bored.'

I let out my breath in a hiss.

He dipped into the trash can by the door, found wrapped taco remains to his liking. 'You really think if they're watching, you tiptoeing in like Sylvester J. Pussycat's gonna keep you under the radar?' He moved on to the supply table, stuffing priority mail envelopes inside his jacket for insulation or just because he could.

I headed back into the banks of PO boxes. Crouched in the weak glow of the energy-saving fluorescents, I held the two pieces of the key in my hand and stared at the stamped numbers: *228*.

I'd assumed the PO box was at the same location as the last one. The sequential numbers seemed to suggest that, but if the last four days had taught me anything, it was not to expect the obvious. I'd have only one play at this, and it would be hard enough without worrying about failing because I'd taken my shot at the wrong post office.

I sat on the floor, pinching the broken tip of the key

between my thumb and forefinger. A skinny run of brass, all teeth, ending on a slant at the fracture. I nosed the end into the slot and guided it in a few ticks, but didn't let go, just as Raz had counseled. I held my breath. Readying the second piece in my other hand, I brought the broken edges together until they aligned. Then I firmed my grip on the fat head of the key, counted to three, and shoved. The key purred into the lock. I held it there a moment, gripping hard, praying it had aligned properly in the channel. Then slowly, I twisted. Miraculously, the lock turned. Keeping the pressure steady, I tugged gently. The rectangular door opened an inch. I slid a finger through the gap and pulled it open, the top piece of the key falling from the lock, clattering on the tile.

The box appeared to be empty. I reached inside, found the manila envelope taped to the roof. Mack had given up a lot before he was killed, but not this. The envelope tore free. I ripped open one end and a stiff sheet slid out into my hand.

An ultrasound.

I stared down at the flashlight-cone illumination, the messy grays and blacks, the alien blob of a fetus head. White letters stood out from the black top margin: *J. Everett 10:07:28 am December 12, 1990.*

To the side, beneath some technical jargon and medical measurements, a note read, *18 wks, female.* No hospital, no medical group, no Social Security number.

I dug in the rucksack and removed the torn page of numerals I'd pulled from the neighboring PO box two nights ago. Still I could make no sense of the digits. I peered inside the manila envelope I'd just retrieved, and sure enough, it held a strip of paper. I tugged it out, and it aligned perfectly with the torn top edge of the larger sheet.

A lab report. At the top, the mother's name was listed as *Jane Everett*, the father, *Unidentified Male*. And to the right, *Baby Everett*. Below the names were column headings for the grid of numerals – paternity indexes and specimen numbers and probe/locus figures. Bold print announced *Mother's Alleles, Child's Alleles, Alleged Father's Alleles*, and finally, *Percent Probability of Paternity*. My eyes tracked down beneath that final heading to the one anomalous number: *99.999*.

An arm around a campaign worker. A pregnancy. And an illegitimate child, fathered by Andrew Bilton, Mr Family Values himself. Was that really enough to lead to all that had been done? In an election year, with the presidency of the world's most powerful nation at stake? Certainly.

I fought the Polaroid of Bilton with the young woman out of my pocket. Hello, Jane Everett.

Her baby would have been born just before Frank's murder. She'd be a high school senior. Seventeen years old, the same age I was then. And the same number of years I'd lived with the aftermath. We'd been in this together, somehow, from the beginning. Like me, she carried with her a burden. Even if she didn't know the fine points of her inheritance, she contained the concealed history in her DNA, held the weight of it in her bones.

I felt how Frank must have felt, as if a live grenade had been dumped in my lap. But burning beneath the surface of my thoughts was a new consideration. Baby Everett. I'd been old enough in 1991 to make my own choices, to walk out of that house and into the jaws of the consequences. She'd been a newborn. More than anything, I wanted her to have a shot at a life different than the one I'd been dealt.

Bilton would be safer with her in the ground. And he'd have no shortage of friends willing to put her there.

Was she in hiding? Had Charlie been telling me, in his own cryptic way, that I had to save her? Was that the grave responsibility he'd entrusted me with?

I sat on the floor, gazing down at the ultrasound, waiting for the buzz in my head to subside. I thought of the buses pulling into that stop a half block away and all the places they could take me. I put the documents and the picture into the rucksack, stood, and walked past Homer. He paused, holding a wadded priority envelope in either hand, and watched me pass.

I walked out into the biting night breeze. To the right, I could make out the bus-stop shelter, glass walls and soothing blue bench. I gazed at it for a moment, then turned left and found the pay phone. My hands were surprisingly steady as I dialed.

When Induma picked up, I told her what I'd found. She was silent for a long time, then she asked, 'What are you gonna do?'

'If they're coming after me this hard, you can bet they're trying to erase all evidence. I have to find that girl. Baby Everett. Before they do.'

'Baby Everett,' she repeated, as if trying out the name.

'She may not even know she's in danger.'

'How do you find someone if you don't know her name?'

'Start with her mom,' I said. 'Are you still willing to help me?'

'Of course,' she said, 'but we have minimal search criteria. I'm sure there are a lot of Jane Everetts out there in the right age range, and we don't even have it narrowed down to a city. With Charlie, at least I knew we were looking at law enforcement in California.'

'So what do I need?'

'Someone with powerful correlation and analytics software, a shit-ton of bandwidth, a datamining engine, and warrant power over classified hospital records.'

'Hospital records for the birth.'

'Right. The birth and the maternity stay. You need someone with official clearances and serious hardware for that kind of run-down.'

'You can't call in another favor at LAPD?'

'They froze me out. I guess the inquiries the assistant chief made on my behalf touched a nerve. He sealed me off – no threat there – but there's not going to be any more prying in the department. At least not on my behalf. And given *your* relationships with law enforcement, that doesn't leave you a lot of options. At least not a lot of options you'd want to risk.'

The wind whipped my face. I said, 'This isn't just about Frank anymore.'

'No,' she said, 'I guess not.'

When I went back inside, Homer was lying across the counter, trying to sleep. I didn't mind the quiet. I sat and breathed the silence until headlights swept through the window. The Range Rover. It kept going.

Homer woke up and watched me with sleek, dark eyes.

246

He followed me obediently outside, and we walked up several blocks, through a park, climbed over a fence. Induma was pulled over, waiting. The Range Rover's window whirred down and Induma glanced over at me.

'This is Homer,' I said.

'Hi, Homer.'

Homer twirled one hand, Queen Mother-style, and gave a half bow.

I said, 'We're gonna need him.'

32

Induma dropped me two blocks away and waited with Homer back in the Range Rover. Wearing the rucksack, I scaled the back fence of Callie's house and crossed the patio.

I rapped on the back door, and a moment later, Steve tugged it open. The sight of him made my stomach clutch. The left side of his face was ballooned from where I'd hit him, a shiny saddle of red riding the yellow-black swell beneath.

My mouth opened, but no sound came out.

'Oh, great. Get your ass inside.'

From the other room, Callie called out, 'Is it him?'

Steve yanked me inside. He said, 'Not a *word* in front of Em.' He waited to walk behind me so he could keep me in sight. Callie and Emily were sitting at the table in front of their plates. My mom's had been polished with bread – an old Callie habit – but Emily's looked barely picked at. A tray of torn-up lasagna sat on a pig-shaped trivet I'd made my mom in high-school shop class.

Callie stood up, excited or agitated or probably both. 'Nicky.'

Emily said, 'Great. *Now* can I be excused?'

Steve said, 'Fine.'

She slumped over to the refrigerator, cracked open a Pepsi, then glared at me. '*What*? You want one?'

'Sure, thanks.'

She carried a can over and thumped it against my shoulder.

Steve said, 'I've lived with you for how many years, you've never once got me a soda.'

Emily said, 'You're not as helpless,' and walked upstairs.

Callie said, 'I told you she likes you. Sit down. Have you eaten?'

'Sure,' Steve said. 'Make yourself at home. We have a guest room upstairs too, you want to move in for a few months.'

Callie looked at him sharply, but I said, 'No, he's right. I've brought you guys nothing but trouble.'

'We're finally in agreement,' Steve said.

Emily's door closed upstairs, hard. Callie's voice dropped. 'You need to see something. It might be bad.'

Steve: '*Might* be?'

They led me into the living room. The curtains were drawn. Steve fussed over four remote controls until Callie came over and clicked two buttons. The TV blinked to life and then, thanks to Tivo, she was fast-forwarding commercials. She glanced toward the kitchen and frowned. '*Em!*'

A clunky black boot with an embossed skull protruded slightly from the doorjamb. And then, five or so feet above it, a scowling face. 'Be grateful I'm too stupid to pick up on the fact that anything weird's going on.'

'Upstairs, *now*,' Steve said. 'Go listen to Fall Down Boy or whatever.'

'God, you are *epically* clueless.'

The Goth boots put out some worthy stomping on the stairwell. Callie said, 'Three . . . two . . . one . . .' and cringed. A moment later, a door slammed so hard the floor vibrated. Then Callie thumbed the remote.

A local newscaster pointed his craggy face at us. 'In West LA today, federal agents staged a raid on an apartment, identified as operating headquarters for the group responsible for the failed attack on the San Onofre Nuclear Power Plant. One suspect was killed. A second escaped.'

I took a halting step back and sat, hard, on the couch.

The TV now showed firefighters getting the apartment blaze under control. 'The escaped suspect detonated stockpiled explosives before fleeing the raid. In a bizarre twist, preliminary forensics suggest that the terrorist whose body was recovered had been killed prior to the blast, and police are looking into the possibility that he was tortured and executed by his confederate.' Back to the solemn newscaster. 'Much of the evidence authorities were seeking was destroyed.'

Callie turned off the TV. 'No photo has been released. Of the escaped suspect.'

Steve said, 'Yet.'

My hands had made fists in the fabric of my shirt. 'There's more.' I almost didn't recognize my voice.

'I'm sure,' Steve said. He walked back toward the kitchen and we followed. Callie eased down into her chair as if it were just another family dinner, but Steve and I stayed on our feet.

'Please. Hear me out. I need your help.'

Steve let out a guffaw. '*My* help?'

'Just listen to me. And if you don't believe what I have to say, I'll leave and you'll never have to see me again.' At this, Callie stiffened. 'But if you *do* believe me, I sure as hell could use your help. Someone else could be at risk.'

Steve stared at me until I got uncomfortable. I counted twenty ticks of the kitchen clock behind me, which is a long time to be stared at. Finally, he glanced at Callie. She'd been watching us silently, not saying anything, which was so out of character that was probably what got him. He pulled the chair partway out, sat with his arm resting on the table, and angled his head at the opposing chair. I sat.

I told them the story top to bottom, filling in details I'd skipped last time, giving them my version of the confrontation at Mack's apartment. I showed them the ultrasound and the lab report and the Polaroid of Bilton and the woman. When I finished, I said, 'I need to locate the mother who had the DNA analysis done. Or at least find out anything I can about her. And her daughter. And I don't have anyone else who can do that for me.'

Steve said, 'You have to turn yourself in, Nick. It's the only way—'

'No,' Callie said.

We both looked at her, surprised.

'If he goes in and this thing is real, this'll be the last time *anyone* sees him,' Callie said. 'Help him, Steve. Please.'

'And what if he *did* kill that guy? Plus the money – who knows where he got that? I know he's your son, but let's be honest: you haven't known him for years.'

251

Callie said, firmly, 'I believe him.'

Steve's high forehead was glistening. He drew a hand through his curly hair, settled back in his chair, and grimaced.

I looked down at the dirty plate in front of me. 'Thanks, Mom.'

Steve took a deep breath, held it, crossed his arms. Then he said to me, 'I'm a police officer. I've never helped you. I've never been in contact with you. If I saw you, I would probably be obligated to arrest you. Do you understand?'

I nodded.

He tugged a detective's notepad from his back pocket, jotted something down, and showed it to me, the way people do in movies when they make some big financial offer. It was a phone number. 'Memorize this,' he said. 'It's my cell. Do not call it unless you are about to be killed.'

I studied the number and nodded.

He slipped the notepad back into his pocket. 'Leave me a phone number. Preferably a mobile. I can't just go in and start asking questions without raising suspicions, but I'm working a pm tomorrow and can grab some desk time when it's quiet. I'll check to see if there's a BOLO out on you – that's a "Be On The Lookout" – or if the pursuit is contained to the Secret Service. And I'll run Jane Everett through the databases, but you're asking a lot here, kid. Medical confidentiality is a mess and I can't produce a warrant even if we knew which hospital she had the baby at, which we don't. I have to go the other route – old-fashioned slogging – see if I can find a Jane Everett in her late forties or fifties who has a seventeen-year-old daughter. If she looks like the broad in the Polaroid, even better. Though she's young enough there she'd have aged a good deal. If I get something – and that's an *if* – I'll call you. In the meantime, you are to stay underground. And you were never here. Not without putting your mother and me – and Emily – at risk.'

I said, 'I was never here.'

'How about that?' Steve said. 'We agree on two things.'

Induma sat, legs curled beneath her, on the enormous sofa. I could tell she was upset because she'd pulled one of the oversize pillows into her lap. Jane Everett's paternity report rested beside her on the cushion, where she'd set it after a cursory glance. From the upstairs bathroom carried the sounds of the running shower and Homer singing, a gravelly outtake from *The Pirates of Penzance*. Alejandro was at his apartment for the night, a relief on many levels. Pomegranate candles were burning on the coffee table, adding a pleasant tinge to the air.

'We shouldn't have come here,' I said. 'They're gonna start digging into my relationships. We don't know when they'll come knocking.'

'*If* they get around to ex-girlfriends from three years ago – and that's an *if* – so what? They have no grounds for a search warrant, and if they are digging that hard, they'll know who's on my speed dial. At risk of sounding smug, this isn't an address you kick the door in on. You ring the bell, inquire politely, and then go off and shore up one helluva case.'

'These guys don't bother with warrants.'

'I am willing to take that risk,' Induma said. 'Now let's focus on making that risk worthwhile.'

Wisps of smoke curled from the red candles. 'My only way out of this is to get more evidence in my pocket. To hand it off to someone as an insurance policy. And to disappear before they disappear me.'

Induma looked away sharply. 'Run away again?'

'Not before I warn Baby Everett. The more this thing heats up, the more they're gonna want to tie up loose ends. And she's the biggest one.'

She didn't move her gaze back to me. 'You slipped them,' she said. 'But there's no saying you can do that again.'

'I'd better get well out ahead of them, then,' I said. 'Are your channels still open at the crime lab? Could you get a DNA analysis through there?'

She hugged the cushion harder, glanced down at the lab report. 'In case you get close enough to pluck a hair out of the President's head? Probably. I configured the damn storage network. If I say there's a glitch, the director gives me the run. But even if I can get into the DNA databases, I doubt Bilton's info is in there with the general population's.'

'It's gotta be on record somewhere in case his body has to be identified after an explosion or fire or if someone shot down Air Force One or something.'

Induma said, 'Even if we do confirm Bilton's DNA profile with the paternity report, he could still argue that the report's been doctored. You'd need to track down the original at the lab center or wherever.'

'How about the Polaroid?'

She gestured for it and I pulled it from the rucksack. Biting her lip, she tilted it to the light. 'It looks old, way pre-PhotoShop. Pretty goddamned convincing. Let's assume it's real. And let's assume this woman *is* Jane Everett. It's still not hard evidence of anything.'

'I'm not going to court. I just want leverage. And Bilton's response to the stuff I've found proves I've got it.'

'Still, it would be nice to have something *concrete* about any part of this whole cover-up.'

'I do.'

Her brow furrowed. 'What?'

'Homer was a dentist,' I said.

'Yeah?' She blinked. Then blinked again. 'Oh no. *Oh no.*'

Homer strolled down the stairs, wearing a pink puffy bathrobe. His shaggy hair, when wet, touched his shoulders. The sash was stretched to its limit, barely holding the flaps in place across his distended belly.

Induma said, 'Fetching.'

Homer said, 'We do our best.'

'I need you to do something for me,' I said.

Induma said, 'Buddha wept.'

'This thing in my cheek is a bone fragment. I need it. And I can't go to a hospital. I know this isn't exactly your field, but I want you to cut it out of my face.'

Homer stared at me, then shrugged. 'Okay.'

I went to the kitchen and returned with a variety of kitchen knives. Fortunately, Induma had quite a selection. She said, 'I think there's an actual scalpel upstairs. Alejandro bought it for one of his sculptures.'

'Great. You have a digital camera, right? We should film the thing coming out of my face so we have proof of where it came from.'

Homer appraised the knives, then watched Induma lay down a sheet on the sofa.

I said, 'Listen, you can do this. I know it feels like you can't. But you can.'

He looked calm enough. I must have been reassuring him for my own benefit.

He said, 'Do you have any anesthetic?'

'For you or for me?' I said.

He didn't smile.

I looked at Induma. 'I don't think we have any.'

She said, 'One of Alejandro's club buddies left a gram or so of coke in the glove box of my Jag. I haven't flushed it yet.'

I said, 'You want to blow cocaine in my face?'

'No,' Induma said, '*you* want me to blow cocaine in your face.'

She got the folded square of magazine page holding the coke, soaked the scalpel in alcohol, and we settled down, Homer standing over me in the *Some Like It Hot* bathrobe, eyes closed, no doubt trying to recall the principles of facial surgery. I lay on the sheet like a corpse, gripping Induma's hand in mine, waiting for the blade. The scalpel neared. His hand was trembling. He wiped his brow and stepped back.

'Do you have any Scotch?' he asked. 'I need a highball to settle the shakes.'

As Induma started for the bar, I gazed up at his pale features.

'Better make it a double,' I said.

I slid out from under Induma and she grumbled but immediately appropriated my space. The imprint of her body had reddened my left side. Some of the feeling prickled back into my skin. At least the numbness hadn't been from some surgical mishap.

I fought my way to my feet, lightheaded, the makeshift implements spinning like cartoon recall. The silver and crimson blur brought back last night's endless probing, a memory as sharp as vomit in the back of the throat. It had been horrible, and cocaine hadn't lived up to its reputation. Despite Homer's best efforts, the procedure had gone on and on, a bottomless splinter dig, steel tips scratching bone. It wasn't until first light competed with the lamp that the piece of Charlie had popped free and Induma had wept with exhausted relief.

The digital camera was still peering from its tripod, though the red light no longer glowed. At the end of a single, grueling take worthy of Hitchcock, Induma had held up the bloody chip of bone with tweezers before the lens to document that the fragment was the one that had been lodged in my cheek. She'd encoded and uploaded the mpeg, along with scanned copies of the ultrasound and paternity test, to a secure off-site server.

Eager for an update on Baby Everett, I checked my cell phone, but there was no message from Steve. I moved unsteadily past the tripod into the bathroom. The first glance was horrifying, but after a few swipes with a towel soaked in warm water, most of the black crust lifted. The wound was fearsome in its depth, but it remained relatively small, a little bigger than a bullet head. After popping two extra-strength Tylenol and four Advil, I found a first-aid kit in the cupboard. A circular Band-Aid covered the wound, rendering my face, aside from its expression of squinting agony, normal.

The noise of the sink must have awakened Induma and Homer, because by the time I got back out, they were sitting up, blinking at each other like hungover acquaintances unsure if they'd slept together the previous night. Beyond the tinted windows, surfers pedaled by with boards under their arms. Carefree LA in full Sunday swing.

'What time is it?' Induma croaked.

'Almost five.'

Homer shoved himself to his feet, stumbled to the bar, and refreshed his glass with Johnnie Walker Blue Label. He gulped it down, then rubbed his eyes and shook his head. The bathrobe was hanging open now, but no one seemed to notice.

'Gotta get dressed,' he said, then staggered into the other room to find his rags.

Induma and I just looked at each other. She wore a pert little smile that seemed to say, *can you believe what we did last night?* We both held the stare, pleased at our shared secret – a blood oath and an inside joke all in one. It was more precious unspoken, just us in the imperfect stillness, like me and Callie on Frank's back deck with the moths and the gold smudge of the porch light, Callie with her iced tea and sticks of charcoal, me watching her work, blissfully unaware that I'd never feel so contented again.

Homer finally returned, the appropriated pink bathrobe peeking out among the layers of dirty clothes. I

259

doubted Induma would want it back anyway. I threw on a shirt to walk him out and grabbed Charlie's rucksack – I didn't want it out of my sight.

Homer downed another glass of Scotch before bending to kiss Induma's hand. We walked out and he tilted his face to the sun.

I said, 'I'd give you a ride, you know, but I should probably stay off the street. Take some money for the bus.' I reached in the rucksack, tugged five hundreds from beneath one of the purple bands, and held them out.

He exhaled, relieved, his shoulders dropping. 'I thought you were actually just gonna give me bus money.' He took the bills, rubbing them together like gold coins.

I felt a flood of affection for him, for what we'd been through, and I said, 'Listen, I feel like I ought to tell you I know. About your wife and kids, all that. And I'm sorry.'

He did a double-take, his jowls bouncing beneath that scraggly beard. 'I was never married.'

'It's okay. I found out by accident. About how you were a dentist and then you started drinking, left everything behind.'

'A *dentist*? What are you talking about, Nick? I sold weatherproofing.'

Shaking his head, he folded the bills into his pocket and walked off, leaving me poleaxed on Induma's front walk.

Induma was still laughing. 'You had a drunk former weatherproofing salesman perform faciomaxillary surgery on you.'

'Faulty intel. It happens to the best of us. Besides, I was high on cocaine at the time. Impaired judgment.'

260

'Especially this week. Homer's vocational history came from the same woman who sold you that "Godfather's with Firebird" line?'

'You try getting wrapped up in a government conspiracy. It can wear a person down.'

'I just hope she shows you the secret handshake next time.'

'There's an obvious joke I'm not gonna make.'

'Hey. Chivalry isn't dead.'

We were at the counter, me on a stool, Induma leaning. Our old positions. We'd showered and squared away the living room. Then, when we realized we were starving, she'd whipped together some *vadai* – which, to her chagrin, I characterized as Indian falafel. Now we sat and drank green tea.

She followed my eyes to the chip of Charlie's bone, in a Ziploc on the counter next to the chutney. I said, 'I wonder what bone it's from.'

'Sacroiliac, I'm thinking. I'll run it in right now. That all you care about or you wanna do a DNA, too?'

I couldn't help but grin. We sipped our tea some more, enjoying the sun-warmed room, prolonging the inevitable. 'Might as well while they're at it.'

'Okay. Two days to process. And no, there is no quicker way.'

'Baby, I take the Jag.' I thought it wasn't a bad Alejandro. 'I bring it in for the service.'

She snorted. 'You sound like Ricky Ricardo. Where to?'

'I want to see if I can flush out who's on my tail.'

'Just don't leave cocaine in the glove box. It's becoming

a pet peeve.' She pushed back from the counter. 'I have to get ready. Handro's taking me out.'

'Right. The anniversary.' I cupped my hands around the warm mug, stared into the tea like it held something fascinating. 'He's a lucky man.'

'Yes,' she said, 'he is.'

I watched her walk up the stairs.

34

With its throngs of UCLA students, Westwood has even more coffee shops per block than the rest of Los Angeles. At a sidewalk café table, I found a dark-skinned guy tugging on a hookah and slurping a boba drink with tapioca balls.

I said, 'Want to make a hundred bucks easy?'

He said, 'Okay, but I'm the top and it's another fifty for a reach-around.'

'Let me rephrase.'

'Please.'

'Here's my credit card. The hundred bucks is just to walk across the street to that Starbucks, charge a cup of coffee, and bring it back here.'

'Where you get the card?'

'It's mine.' I showed him the name and my driver's license. Then I peeled five twenties off my roll.

'What if they ask for ID?'

'They don't ID for three-fifty.'

He took another toke. 'You think I look like somebody name "Horrigan" you smoke more than I do.'

'I'm paying you a hundred bucks to try.'

He shrugged and rose, snatching the bills from my

hand. He took two steps away, then came back. 'What kind of coffee?'

'A Mocha Valencia.'

'What?'

'A Toffee Nut Latte.'

'Huh?'

'A cup of coffee.'

'Coulda just said so.'

I waited for him to scurry through the slow traffic and get into line, then I crossed the intersection, entered a little jewelry store with tinted windows and a good view. The cut in my cheek radiated pain when I shifted my jaw, but I didn't want to leave to get more Advil.

The kid came back across the street with the coffee, found the table empty. After looking around, he sat back down and resumed smoking and checking out girls. Another few minutes passed, then he started drinking my coffee.

I'd been perusing the same cabinet for too long. The clerk came over with an aggressive smile. 'Maybe I can help you decide on something?'

'Sure, I'm looking for my girlfriend.'

'Earrings?'

I looked down. Earrings. 'Yes.'

'Do you know what she likes?'

Two sedans screeched up to the curb by Starbucks and Sever and three agents I didn't recognize hopped out and rushed inside. I'd figured Bilton's crew had put a flag on my credit card, and I'd wanted to note the faces of some of the other involved agents. As a branch of the Treasury Department up until the Homeland Security shuffle, the

Service knew money and how to track it. It had been nailing counterfeiters since the end of the Civil War. And now those considerable resources were pointed at me. This was bigger than just Sever and a few agent cronies. Bilton's crew was using the system against me. They wanted that paternity test and ultrasound. Maybe they even thought I could lead them to Baby Everett.

The clerk cleared her throat. 'Is she fair or dark?'

'Oh, sorry. Her skin color's caramel. A little darker, maybe. Beautiful black hair. Dark brown eyes.'

'Rubies are nice.'

'Yeah, but she has an emerald stud in her nose. I'm worried it'd look like Christmas.'

The agents emerged from the Starbucks and looked around. Sever locked eyes with the kid across the street. The kid was holding the mouthpiece at the end of the hose a few inches from his open mouth.

The clerk leaned across the counter. A little tenser. 'Pearls maybe?'

'Sapphire's her birthstone. The gold settings?'

'Yes. Those are chips, not full sapphires.'

Sever crossed the street. The kid gave him my credit card, gestured around. Sever listened for a while, and then laughed, the gleam of his white teeth pronounced against his tan face. Sever spoke into his radio, and the agents reconvened.

'Should I wrap them up? Sir?'

The agents climbed back into their cars and drove off. '*Sir?*'

I offered her a smile. 'Do you take cash?'

*

265

Induma was sitting on the couch in the dark when I came through the back door an hour later. The clock on the Blu-Ray player showed 9:30 pm, but it felt later than that. As I neared, I saw that she wore a black tank top and a pair of men's Calvin Klein briefs. One night when we were dating, she'd put on my underwear on her way from bed to bathroom and found them so comfortable she'd made a habit of wearing them to sleep. I couldn't help but stare at her dark, smooth legs.

'Glad you're back safe,' she said. But she looked upset.

'What's wrong?'

She blew out an exasperated breath. 'For how low-maintenance Alejandro is, he drives me fucking crazy sometimes.'

I dropped the keys on the counter, mostly to stall. I waited until I could at least feign casualness. 'Does the good outweigh the bad?'

'In the relationship? Yes. I mean, for starters he's gorgeous.'

'He's not *that* gorgeous.'

'He's better-looking than *you*.' She smiled at my feigned indignation. 'Don't pout – that's hardly news. And he's nice enough. Heart of a golden retriever.'

'And the mind of a goldfish.' I relented under her look. 'Okay. At times, he's pleasingly good-natured.'

'So he's gorgeous—'

'You'd mentioned that.'

'I'm working to a point here.' She was smiling. 'But not matter how good-looking they are, you stop noticing. After a while, you get this . . . *disdain* for their familiarity. Sweat stains on their shirts. Hair gel blobs on the countertop. Open mouth when they sleep. I never had that with you. No part of you was dirty to me. Was it me? Was it just me?'

My hands were balled and I was unaccountably cold. I could catch the faintest scent of her perfume – Jo Malone orange blossom. 'No,' I said. 'It wasn't just you.'

'But that wasn't enough for you.' Glow from a garden light fell through the back window, catching her face in a pale yellow band. There were so many things I wanted to tell her, but before I could find the shape of them, she continued, 'Despite the problems, Alejandro's always there when I need him. This relationship – it works for me.'

'Does it?' I asked. 'How?'

'With all my money, everyone wanting something, I guess I want to hold some part of myself safe. Where no one can touch it. With him, there's never that risk.' Her voice was soft, even vulnerable, but her stare was as level as ever. 'I learned that from you.'

I crossed to her. She bobbed a bit on the cushion when I sat next to her. I said, 'That's the last example I'd want to set.'

'Well, you set it. With me. Over and over.'

I said, 'I'm sorry.'

'I made my own choices. I'm not looking for an apology.'

'That doesn't mean I don't owe you one.'

She bit her lip, waved me off. Her eyes glimmered a bit, or maybe it was just the way the glow caught her face.

I felt a black hole where my stomach was supposed to be. I would've done anything to rewrite the past, but here we were, with her upset and me wanting to say something – *anything* – that would help. 'I'm sorry your date went badly.'

'I wouldn't call it a date.'

'Oh.' My face grew hot. 'Uh oh.'

'He took me to Hooters. I mean, *Hooters*. And you know what his big surprise was? Chicken wings. I'm a vegetarian, for Christ's sake. I don't care that it's not some elegant restaurant – I mean, pack a sandwich and take me to the beach. Something that shows you've been remotely paying attention to who I am.'

I found my cuticle suddenly fascinating. 'I, um—'

'I asked him what the hell he was thinking, but he wouldn't say anything.' She looked over at me, noting my discomfort. '*What.*'

'I may be partially at fault here.'

'Talk.'

I would have done anything to avoid copping to my smart-ass role in their failed date. There was no way to come clean without revealing my feelings for her. But I owed it to her, and to Alejandro.

I cleared my throat self-consciously. 'He asked me for advice on what to do for your anniversary, and I, uh, I told him where to take you. Half joking. I'd like to say it got lost in translation, but I was also half not-joking, I guess.'

She glowered for a moment, then cracked up. When she finished laughing, she wiped her eyes and said, 'Why would you *do* that?'

My face burned. If I could have curled up and disappeared, I would have been long gone. I leaned forward, elbows on my knees, and stared at the blank screen of the TV.

She said, 'Oh, Nick.' Her voice was empathetic and disappointed all at once.

Then she rose and headed up for bed.

35

I woke up on Induma's couch, Egyptian cotton sheets twisted around me. Hot. Last night, I'd closed and locked the windows overlooking the backyard and the canal beyond. The night terrors had woken me at 2:18 am, but they seemed as distant now as a forgotten dream.

The cell phone, propped right by my face, showed no messages. I was impatient for Steve to get back to me with information on Baby Everett. Bilton's crew had every reason to go full-bore until they found her. If they hadn't found her already.

I showered in the downstairs bathroom, dressed, and swapped out the Band-Aid on my cheek. Sitting on the toilet with the rucksack at my feet, I removed five hundreds from my money clip and slid them imperfectly beneath the purple band of one of the cash bundles, replacing the bills I'd given to Homer. It had been bugging me since yesterday, and I was glad I could make up that money. Whoever's it was, I didn't want to owe them.

I stared at my cell phone for a while. No missed calls. If Bilton's henchmen were after Baby Everett, every passing minute gave them another chance to close in.

I dialed.

When I came out of the bathroom, Induma had old-fashioned bacon and eggs sizzling in one pan, soy sausages in the other. On the counter, a bottle of orange juice and an intimidating stack of pancakes.

'Are these some of those exotic Bangalore eggs?' I asked.

'Air-lifted this morning.'

'And the bacon?'

'Family recipe from the Mahatma himself.'

'I thought he was a vegetarian.'

'Eat your damn breakfast, honky.'

'I think only black people are allowed to say "honky".'

'What are Indian people allowed to call you?'

'Non-engineer.'

'Clever, for a fugitive.' She slid my plate across the counter.

When we were done eating, I helped Induma clean up, then put on my rucksack. She eyed it, looking worried.

I said, 'I can't wait any longer. I've got to find Baby Everett, get word to her, something.'

'You don't think Steve'll be able to find her?'

'Maybe not in time.' I took a breath. 'That's why I called Caruthers.'

'You called *Caruthers*?'

'His aide. Alan Lambrose – the bow-tied conduit. Caruthers just flew down from Sacramento, and he can see me in an hour. He offered to help when I met him. If anyone'll know how to locate a person . . .'

'We still don't know for sure that Caruthers isn't implicated in some other way. Trying to outbid Bilton for the ultrasound, whatever.'

'This'll be his test, I guess. If he has his guys grab me, we'll know he's implicated.'

'Nick. You're *wanted*. Caruthers ought to have his agents arrest you regardless.'

'Alan checked. He said there's no arrest warrant out on me.'

At this, her mouth opened a little.

I said, 'Bilton's crew is busting ass to track me down, but they're keeping it off the books for obvious reasons.'

She blew a wisp of hair out of her face, keeping her stare on me. 'They want you on terrorism charges, Nick. Which means if they do get you, you have no rights. You're willing to bet your life on Caruthers?'

'To warn Everett? What else am I supposed to do?'

'What if Caruthers's crew leans on you to give *them* the evidence?'

'I'm counting on it. I don't mind Caruthers playing politics as long as I can get to the girl.'

Induma laced her hands across the top of her head. Stared at me.

I said, 'If you need me, don't use your home line.' I dug in the rucksack, handed her the extra throwaway phone.

Still she said nothing.

'I'll be careful.'

She tossed me the car keys. 'That's all well and good, but you're just one small part of the equation.'

36

Standing in the middle of the street, sweating like an idiot under the midday sun, I turned a full circle. Alan Lambrose had given me a cross-street and a time. No phone number, no address. So here I was, on a quiet residential slope, like a street hustler waiting on a Cadillac.

From down Santa Monica Canyon came the purr of well-maintained engines, the crackle of asphalt beneath tires, and I turned nervously to face downslope, my grip tightening on the manila envelope. Rising into view first were the convoy SUVs with their tinted windows, wavering in the blacktop heat like a mirage. Then two joggers, barrel-chested with slim waists and weighed-down waist packs. Two motorcycle cops, Poncherelloed out with tan forearms and aviator sunglasses. And then, struggling up the slope, an additional Robo-jogger at either side, came Caruthers. His T-shirt spotted with sweat, he looked notably human amid the seemingly mechanized procession.

The lead jogger approached swiftly, smelling of deodorant, his hand in his unzipped waist pack. I recognized him as James, the Secret Service agent who'd stood post in Caruthers's conference room. How easy it would be for him to slap cuffs on me and shove me into one of the waiting SUVs. But instead, he said, 'Sir, if you don't mind?'

He waited stoically while his counterpart frisked me, then they nodded at Caruthers and gave us a ten-yard stand-off, facing away, ready for incoming threats. As Caruthers approached, slightly wobbly on his venerable knees, the SUVs pulled in around us, sealing us off from the open roads. Caruthers leaned over, catching his breath. 'I'm sorry about this, Nick. You know how it goes.'

'Doing their job.'

His eyes took in the Band-Aid on my cheek. 'They always do.'

'Still no warrant out on me?'

'Nothing official, at least through our channels.' He pursed his lips. 'You know that's probably *bad* news, right?'

Pain throbbed through my head, a party favor from the impromptu surgical shindig. I glanced nervously at the jogger-agents, intently facing away from us. 'Can we talk a bit more privately?'

Caruthers said, 'James,' and the men nodded and slid to the far side of the SUV perimeter.

I remembered the President's velvet smooth voice through the phone, his veiled warning for me to steer clear of Caruthers: *you wouldn't want to meet with someone like that, Nick. Certainly not twice.* What might this rendezvous bring down on me?

I gestured at the agents. 'They've seen me. Us, together.'

'We were seen together four days ago, too. What's the difference?'

'What I know now. Who they tell.'

'This is *my* detail, Nick. I trust these men. Plus I deal with people all the time. As do all my people. No one can know what came from whom.'

'They can guess.'

'They sure can. I'm not going to pretend there's no risk involved. You're too smart to buy that pitch. Listen, son, you called me. If you're too uncomfortable to talk . . .' He waved an open hand at the road.

Grimacing, I looked at all that assembled manpower, all those concealed weapons that could be swung my way at a moment's notice. Caruthers's challenge brought back Frank, sipping his coffee in the dark, the TV screen finally at rest after showing run after catastrophic run of JFK's limousine. *All you can rely on is a man's character. Not what he says or promises, but what he* does. *What you* do *is the measure of a man.*

I sidled a half step closer. 'Would you believe Bilton was behind a massive cover-up?'

I waited for the shift behind the eyes, the stalling-for-time grin, the nervous glance to the agents. But either Caruthers had a heightened tolerance for conspiracy theorists, or he'd learned never to rule anything out. He worked his gum. The coarse hairs of his eyebrows twisted this way and that over those intense irises.

'It's part of the job description of the chief executive,' he said. 'It depends—'

'—on what's being covered up.'

He nodded. 'Bilton's a gray suit and a trademark, a company man. He's subject to the pressures we're all subject to, but he yields to them a little more readily than the rest of us, flows with the prevailing current. He knows he is where he is because powerful forces wanted him there. So why reflect, let alone resist? His principles are convenient and poll-tested, and that means he can be convinced of anything.'

'That's a political answer.'

'I'm a politician, Nick. Now can we get on with whatever this is?'

'It wasn't Mike Milligan in that nuclear power plant. It was a former California State Police officer named Charlie Jackman.'

Caruthers's brilliant green eyes held on me until I looked away. He dotted his forehead with the hem of his shirt and blew out a breath. 'The crime-scene reports and DNA analysis say different.'

'They were *made* to say different.'

'Okay, so what was a former California State Police officer doing in San Onofre?'

'Jackman worked Bilton's detail when Bilton was governor.'

'Go on.'

I slid the ultrasound from the envelope and handed it to him. 'I believe this shows the illegitimate daughter of President Bilton.'

'Looks like a fetus.'

'And she was born seventeen years ago. There's a paternity test, too.'

He held the ultrasound to the sun. The human curl, bulb head and bean body. 'Jesus.' He looked around, as if for somewhere to sit, but settled for putting his hands on his knees, the stiff sheet bowing to the side. He was still

276

breathing hard from the run. 'Jesus, Nick. And the paternity test is conclusive?'

'All the attention I've been getting sure as hell shows it's real. But as for court-of-law conclusive? I'm not a lawyer. I'm not an agent. I'm just a guy who got pulled into the wrong situation.'

He cocked his head. 'We both know you're not as uncomplicated as you like to pretend. So let's drop the pretense.' His mouth was drawn, etched with innumerable tiny lines. The sun came through his hair, turning it gold.

I said, 'Charlie was in the process of selling the evidence back to Bilton. He got the first payment, but they tried to raid his place to get the goods. He bolted, then upped the stakes at San Onofre. So they blew his head off his shoulders, making me an unwitting accomplice and almost killing me while they were at it.' I tapped the ultrasound. 'If this leaked, it'd knock family values on its ass.'

Caruthers looked thoughtful, Charlie finding the golden ticket in his Wonka bar. Agitated, he pulled the nicotine gum from his mouth and winged it to the side of the road. It hit a mailbox post and stuck. 'Did you see this morning's *Times*? They're off my divorce now, and onto June's. Planted letters to the editor. Non-partisan advocacy groups are up in arms. Concerned Citizens for Traditional Values are, well, concerned. Bilton's nipping at my heels.' He handed the ultrasound back to me.

'*But*?'

The nearest post-stander's head swiveled at my tone.

Caruthers asked, 'What is this, Nick?'

'It's an ultrasound.'

'Right. It's not an issue. And you want this campaign to be about issues as much as I do. This is something Bilton could use and lose no sleep. We can't. Because I don't care if Andrew played grab-ass with some woman nearly two decades ago. If I pretend to care or if a leak traces back to my supporters, the voters'll smell the hypocrisy before Chris Matthews can open his yap.' He shook his head, irritated at his options. 'No, this thing is precisely the kind of petty political distraction I've spent the last two years decrying.'

'Charlie might not think it's so petty.'

'By your description, Charlie was an extortionist who threatened to blow a hole in a nuclear power plant. Now I'm sure Bilton had his Service henchmen dick around with this somewhere, but we're in spin terrain and a spin game goes to the incumbent. Here's another bit of transparency – I can't use something that's not airtight.' His green eyes took on a calculated, if self-amused, glint. 'I can always reconsider come the last week of October.' His smirk vanished, his face texturing with concern. 'I appreciate the risk you took in getting this to me. I hope I don't seem unappreciative.'

I waved him off.

His penetrating green eyes held on me. '*Right*,' he said. 'You need something. You wanted to trade.'

'Yeah, but you're not interested in dirt. Some politician you turn out to be.'

His lips curled with amusement. 'Maybe I can still help?'

'It's just, this girl . . .' I shook the ultrasound in an attempt to resuscitate my position. 'She's still just a kid.

278

Seventeen is a scary age to have people after you. I think she's in danger, and I don't have any way of tracking her down.'

'Last name Evers?'

'Everett.'

'And the mother's name is Jane? I can't exactly go running this up the flagpole, but I have plenty of avenues, and I promise you, I will figure out how to get the proper authorities on this.'

I nodded my thanks.

'That's all you're asking for?' His voice held a note of incredulity.

'Yeah. That's it.'

'How about that,' he said. 'You found something you want.'

The agents firmed, one after another. A Honda reached the slant-parked SUVs and turned, the driver intimidated into offering an apologetic little wave.

'If I get clear of all this,' I said, 'maybe I'll register.'

'Bilton needs all the votes he can get.' He smiled and turned to go.

'*Wait*, I . . .' It came out louder than I'd wanted it to.

He paused. I felt his eyes on me, and then he leaned toward me, trying to pick up my gaze. 'What?'

'So no one . . .' I had to stop, clear my throat. 'No one ever brought anything like this to you when you were Vice President?'

'Oh,' he said. '*Oh*. You mean Frank. No, I'm afraid he never did.' I must have looked crestfallen, because he paused to piece it together. 'Because Frank had no good reason *not* to show me that ultrasound seventeen years ago' – his face softened with sympathy – 'unless he was using it to extort Bilton.'

The breeze blew against my face, numbing it further.

Caruthers said, quietly, 'Frank and I never discussed something like this.'

My lips were dry. 'And should I believe you?'

'You're too smart to believe any politician, Nick. And I'm too smart to trust a conspiracy theorist. And yet here we are.'

He took a step away, then paused for a moment with his back to me before turning. 'I don't know if it's inappropriate to say in light of all this, but I think Frank would've been proud.'

I looked away so he couldn't see my reaction.

Caruthers nodded solemnly, and then stepped back toward the agents. The joggers swung over to his sides, running in place until he got moving. The SUVs purred around, in front of and behind him and he started steadily uphill, a lone man pulling a convoy.

37

I accelerated along Ocean Avenue, the Pacific whipping by beyond the cliffs to my right. I was gripping the prepaid cell phone so tightly my hand cramped. 'Why should I stay and risk my life for some seventeen-year-old girl I've never met? I told Caruthers about Baby Everett. I told Steve. They can handle it now. I'm not a cop.'

On the other end, Induma said, 'True. You're not.'

Craving open air, I screeched over into a slant parking space and climbed out, slamming the door behind me. 'Bilton's agents are on my heels. If I keep looking, I could lead them right to her. I could wind up getting her killed.'

'A valid concern.'

'I don't give a shit about politics. Or Bilton. I don't owe anyone anything.'

'No one's maintaining you do.'

'I've done everything I can.' My voice was shaking.

Induma just said, 'Nick.'

I crossed the strip of lawn and leaned against the rickety rail fence. Below and beyond, past the Pacific Coast Highway, stretched a quarter mile of sand and endless water. The sun was low, filtering through the puffy clouds in magenta and violet. It reminded me of the circle of sunset I'd watched from the tunnel where Homer had hidden me. I looked down at my shirt, the one I'd pulled from the cardboard box behind the church. That stupid scrolled lettering – *Forgive Us Our Trespasses*.

'Frank knew about Baby Everett,' I said, 'but he kept it from Caruthers.'

The weight of the implications hung between us. I heard Induma shift on the couch, maybe stand up. She said, 'You're trying to clear Frank. I know that. But if you're gonna keep prying at this, you have to do it knowing that you could damn well confirm your worst fears.'

The phone was trembling at my cheek. I said, 'I have to get out of here.' I hung up. Drew in a few deep breaths. Then returned to the Jag. I could leave it somewhere for Induma later, in some other city. I stared at the rucksack in the passenger seat, then at the broad curb drain, at the ready for all those LA hurricanes. Three steps and I could shove the rucksack through into the sewer and be rid of all this. Five yards and a push. I could leave the bundled hundreds curbside for the homeless folks camped out along the grass.

Instead I backed out and rode down the Santa Monica incline, merging onto the Pacific Coast Highway. Blending into traffic, I headed north, away from the city, away from Bilton and ultrasounds and the charred remains of Mack Jackman. I was now one of those cars I'd heard thrumming overhead from the tunnel, one of those fortunate souls with somewhere better to go. Just as Homer had told me four days and a lifetime ago, I was a runner, not a fighter. And just as he'd said, people don't change.

I had better reason to run now than I ever did. I was trying to run away from Frank's being dirty. I couldn't stay and face the possibility that everything I'd gone through these past seventeen years was for someone who wasn't worth it. The thought alone knocked the fight out of me, left me resigned to the only life I'd always feared I deserved – motel rooms and transient work, dark memories and 2:18 wake-ups. As bleak as that seemed, I'd take it over losing Frank all over again.

I flew through Malibu, past the fish-taco joints with the washed-out surfers counting gritty change from neoprene pockets, past the Country Mart where movie stars park their Priuses between jaunts on Gulfstreams, past the impeccable and untrodden green lawn of Pepperdine. I kept going, past rocky state beaches, past VW buses out of '70s horror films, past falling rock signs and even a few falling rocks. Somewhere around Paradise Cove, my cell phone rang.

I pulled it out of my pocket. Checked Caller ID. Induma. I flipped it open.

'They got Homer.'

The words moved through me, an icy wave. After a time, I said, 'Where?'

'They took him from his parking space outside Hacmed's store. Hacmed tried to call you. His stock of throwaway cell phones, I guess they have sequential numbers. He called the last one in line before the one on his rack. The one you left here rang, so I picked up.'

'Okay. Give me a . . . I need a minute. Sorry.'

I hung up and pulled over onto the hazardous shoulder, my hands bloodless against the black steering wheel. Vehicles shot past off the turn, rocking the Jag on its stubborn English chassis, one or two offering me a piercing blare on the horn as an after-the-fact fuck you.

I don't know how long I sat there, but when I looked up, the sun was a shimmering remembrance on the water at the horizon. A few seconds later, the dark waters extinguished the last dot of yellow.

I waited for a break in the headlights, then I signaled and U-turned, heading back to whatever was awaiting me.

With mounting dread, I drove to the corner mart, pulling the Jag around back. I stared across at the white parking-space lines.

What if they'd killed him already, just to send me a signal? He'd be easy to wipe off the map. I'd read the newspaper stories from time to time with perverse interest – a body discovered weeks or years after the desperate end, skeletonized in a chimney, bloated in a well, rotting in the trapped air of a by-the-month motel room. Lost souls who didn't punch in to work or have family dinners on Sundays. No one to miss them. No one to notice their removal. No one to care until a disruptive odor, a heap of chalky shards, or some other gristly matter gummed up life in progress or a real-estate inspection.

Before I could climb out of my car, I heard a call from the building. '*Psst!*'

Hacmed was gesturing at me furiously from the barely cracked rear door. 'Nicolas. You come here.'

I slid from the car and entered the storage room. He

284

put his hand on my chest, steering me into the corner, away from the overhead security camera's field of vision. 'They take Homer.'

'I heard. What happened?'

'It is my fault.' Agitated, Hacmed twisted his sweaty hands together. 'I do not have time to take cash register receipts to bank Friday. So I go first thing today. Drop them off. One hour later, two men show up at my store. Secret Service. They ask about hundred-dollar bill I deposit at bank. They tell me bank lady checked serial number against list.'

I sagged against the wall. I never should have given Homer those hundreds from Charlie's stash. Monitoring banks was actually part of the Service's infrastructure, since the agency had been set up to catch counterfeiters. I should've known that Bilton's crew would've tagged the serial numbers before paying off Charlie.

'They threaten me with being terrorist, with plotting to kill the President. They ask where I get this one-hundred-dollar bill. Only one I have is from Homer last night. I tell them. Homer is outside. They collect him. Shove him into car.' Hacmed's eyes were wet now. 'I was scared, Nicolas. I did not know what to do. What was I supposed to do?'

'There was nothing you could've done that would have made this turn out differently.'

'I could have made up story. Said it was not his hundred.'

'They would've checked the security tapes and found out it was him anyway.'

'They ask about you, too. If I know you. I say I recognize

picture, you are sometimes customer. But I do not tell them anything more. You be careful, Nicolas.'

The front door rattled, the ding nearly sending Hacmed through the ceiling tiles. He left me there, stunned, and scurried out to ring up the customer. Then he returned. I hadn't moved. I'd barely breathed.

It took me a moment to realize that Hacmed was speaking again. 'My brother-in-law, they take him for three month. He is cabinet maker. Nothing more. But they take him, because he is from Pakistan. No lawyer, no nothing. Just gone. Three month. I support my sister and their children. *Three month*. And then one day he is back. No explanation. They kept him in secret jail, asking questions, feeding him like dog. My brother-in-law is strong man. Homer cannot survive this.'

'They'll have to realize Homer doesn't know anything.'

'You think my brother-in-law knew anything?' He was practically shouting.

'No, no. What else did they tell you?'

'They are going to charge Homer with murder. *Murder*. They say he kill man in apartment, then lit him on fire, then blew up apartment. They say the bill proves he is involved with dead man. Homer tell them someone else give him the bill. They do not believe him. He has no money to hire proper lawyer. He cannot make bail. They will leave him to rot.'

'Who told you all this?'

'Secret Service agent came back one hour ago. Told me everything.'

'Broad guy, buzz cut, tan face?'

'Yes. That is him.'

'Nice of him. To give you all that info.'

Hacmed looked at me unsurely. 'What do you mean?'

'Nothing, sorry. Anything else?'

'They are processing Homer now. They are to release him into general population tomorrow. First thing. With rapists and killers.' Hacmed shook his head, on the verge of tears again.

Sever had gone to great lengths to make sure I knew that Homer would suffer worse than he already was unless I turned myself in. Either Homer or I was going to be charged with the murder of Mack Jackman. The decision was up to me.

'You must leave.' Hacmed ushered me to the back door. 'You must go hide.'

I said, 'Hacmed, listen to me. This is not your fault.'

He pulled his head back through the gap and regarded me with mournful eyes. 'No? Then whose fault is it?'

The slab of the high-rise towered over me, black windows framed with white concrete, an imperious honeycomb. I'd left the Jaguar three blocks away in a grocery-store parking lot, keys in the wheel well for Induma. Concrete planters and reinforced trashcans were positioned around the base of the building, measures against unresourceful car bombers.

Feeling oddly naked without my rucksack, I pulled the cell phone from my pocket and placed a final call.

Steve's voice answered me gruffly. 'I thought I told you only to call me if you were about to get killed.'

'Yeah, well.'

'Shit,' he said. The wind blew across my cheeks, the receiver, and then Steve said, 'Hello?'

'I'm here. You make any headway?'

'I'm hitting the databases every time I can grab a minute, but I have to do this quiet, like I said. Jane Everett's not the most common name, but it's not the most unusual either. A good number of hits so far, none matching the profile or the picture.'

I cleared my throat. 'Don't try to reach me. Don't call this number. Wait and I'll contact you. If I can.'

'Listen, Nick, your mother—'

'If you don't hear from me, tell Callie . . .'

'What?'

'Tell her thanks for believing me.'

I snapped the phone shut before he could say anything else. I set it on the concrete and smashed it with the heel of my shoe. Then I pried out the circuit board and bent it in half and dropped it through a sewer grate. The plastic casing I dumped in a trashcan.

Odds were good that I'd soon become an enemy of the state, with all the attendant privileges. Or one of those anonymous corpses, hidden in a heating duct, discovered weeks later when the weather shifted. Disappeared, but this time for good. Sadly, I felt like now I had more to lose than ever. So much had changed over the past six days. I had shared my past with Induma and Callie, and that meant I would miss them with more of myself.

A bus wheezed by on Figueroa, then slowed with a gassy exhale. The nighttime breeze swirled up hot-dog wrappers and a few early leaves. Leaning back on my heels like a rube in Manhattan, I contemplated the commanding building. It all but blocked out the sky.

I was sweating through my Jesus shirt.

Before I could lose my nerve, I walked into the lobby. A moderate amount of traffic to and from the elevators, even at this hour. By dint of habit, I put my head down and veered past the reception counsel. I didn't like signing visitor books, not that any of that would matter anymore. The rent-a-cops, distracted with phones and a shrill woman who'd misplaced a coat, paid me no notice.

I slid through the closing elevator doors. Thumbing the button for the thirteenth floor, I realized I'd turned away from the rear mirror and the security camera it likely hid. So many habits, stretching back so many years. But this was the end, the time to lay aside Liffman's rulebook and head into the belly of the beast.

By the time I arrived, my heart was racing and I felt pins and needles in my fingertips. I forced myself out, assailed by the bright fluorescents. At the end of the hall, beside the reception desk, hung the vast crest with its eagle and flag.

The woman looked up. Behind her was the open squad room, desks arrayed around waist-high partitions. Despite the loosened ties and sloughed suit jackets, the room was the picture of industry. Agents flipped through files, pulled faxes from machines, jabbed fingers at booking photos.

I kept on toward the receptionist. My palms were slick. I shrank from a passing agent as if he were infectious. The overhead security cameras felt like interrogation lights in my face. Shying from their glare, I reached the desk. Nowhere else to go now. The receptionist, nicely made up like a 1950s frontwoman, smiled at me expectantly. A few of the agents glanced up from their desks. I was having a hard time getting air.

'I . . .'

'Yes?' she asked.

A swirl of nausea, like the sickness that accompanied my 2:18 wake-ups, except more vivid under the bright lights. Beyond the partition, I recognized the wide shoulders of Reid Sever. He was facing away, bent to scrutinize a document. The strip of white flesh beneath the line of his buzz cut was pronounced.

'I'm . . .' My throat froze up. I couldn't get my name out.

'*What*, sir?'

'I . . . I'm . . .' My eyes tracked up to Sever. He – and every other agent in the room – was now staring at me. I was completely, pathetically immobilized.

Sever said, 'Nick Horrigan.'

38

'Release Homer now or I won't talk.' My arms ached. It didn't help that Sever was steering me by the cuffs, shoving me through one hall after another. Agents and secretaries paused at their monitors and over their cups of coffee to take note.

'You're not setting the rules,' he said, with that soft edge of a Southern accent.

'That was the deal. You know it and I know it.'

'We don't *have* a deal.'

'We both know this has got nothing to do with Homer. You used him to get to me. It worked. He's not valuable to you anymore. If you want me to talk, cut the guy a break and let him out before they dump him into general pop.'

Sever didn't slow. We passed a few open office doors, and then the cuffs bit into my wrists, and my shoulders strained in their sockets as I jerked to a halt. I could hear him breathing hard behind me, feel his fist tight around the handcuff chain. Finally, he tugged me back, pivoting me around another corner. A few more painful steps and we were outside a double-reinforced door, peering at a guard through ballistic glass.

Sever leaned close to the embedded microphone and said, 'Let him go.'

The guard rolled back from the window on his chair and disappeared. The buzzing of secured doors. A metallic rumble. A moment later, Homer was escorted through the door, a guard on either side, white latex gloves gripping him at the biceps. He was trembling, a mountain of shivering rags. His mouth worked on itself, his beard shifting. He saw me, blanched beneath the dirt, and tried to tell me something, but couldn't. The guards moved him past us toward the elevator and shoved him in. The doors slid shut and the guards walked by again, snapping off their gloves and chuckling to themselves.

They nodded through the window and the door clicked open and they disappeared.

Sever hadn't moved. He said, 'What's that bum to you anyway?'

'A friend.'

'You got some fucked-up habits, Horrigan.'

We were moving again. 'Where are you taking me?'

'Interrogation.'

'I want to talk to Wydell.'

Sever made a noise of severe irritation and the cuffs sank deeper into my flesh. Another hall, a doorway, past a female agent whose eyes lingered on Sever for an extra beat. I was the piece-of-shit offender, the foil for admirable men with admirable tasks and intentions. My arms pinned behind me, I approached a metal door. Sever didn't slow down. I hit it with my chest and it banged open. He hurled me inside and I staggered two steps and fell onto a wooden chair in the middle of the concrete box. The chair tilted up on two legs and then settled back with a clatter. Sever closed the door. Locked it. No security camera. No one-way mirror. Bare bulb overhead for that gulag effect.

Was this where people wound up who threatened the President?

Sever stepped in front of the dangling bulb, his face lost in shadow. My breath caught, but I smoothed out the inhale so it would be less noticeable.

I said, 'You can't kill me. People will know.'

'*Kill* you? What the hell are you talking about?'

I said, 'Check my sock.'

He tugged out the folded piece of paper from my sock and regarded my bad handwriting. *My name is Nick Horrigan. I was brought to San Onofre during the 'terrorist' incident last week. I did not kill Mack Jackman. I am not a terrorist. I turned myself in to the Secret Service at 725 S Figueroa the night of 9/15. At the time I went in, I had no injuries and was in good health.*

'The fuck's this gonna do for you?' Sever said.

'I've rented a motel room. With a fax machine that I preprogrammed. If I'm not released from here by midnight, that fax will send.'

'To who?'

'The *LA Times*, the *New York Times*, CNN, MSNBC, and Fox News.'

'No one can know you were at San Onofre.'

'That's the least of your concerns.'

'Yeah? So why don't you tell me what my real concerns are.'

'What *else* I'm sending in that fax.'

'What else *are* you sending?'

'I want to talk to Wydell.'

'You'd rather talk to me.'

'Why would I rather talk to you?'

He paused, wet his lips. 'I'm a better listener.'

'I'll take my chances on Wydell.'

'He's not here.'

'Where is he?'

'Overseeing the preadvance for the UCLA debate. Believe it or not, as the Special Agent in Charge, he's got other things on his plate. He can't get here. Can't be arranged.'

'You have 'til midnight to arrange it. Then it won't matter.'

'I may have to recommend a psych eval for you.' He studied me. My resolve must have been clear, because he grimaced and said, 'I'll see what I can do.' At the door, he paused. 'What makes you think you can trust Wydell?'

'I never said I trusted him. But I'll talk to him.'

But he'd already walked out, setting the deadbolt behind him. I went over to the door but the interior side had no knob. Not even a metal backing for the deadbolt. The seamless walls left me in a state of near panic. For the first fifteen minutes, I paced the perimeter, skimming my shoulder along the concrete, a hot pain pulsing in the wound on my cheek. At around the half-hour mark, I finally figured out to step back over the cuffs, bringing my arms in front of me. That relieved the stress in my shoulders, but little else. The recycled air grew dense and moist.

I was back on the hard wooden chair when Wydell entered, Sever at his back.

'No,' I said. 'Just you.'

Wydell nodded at Sever who sighed and stepped out. Wydell closed the door, then turned to me. The razor-sharp line of his parting left not a hair out of place. The knot of his tie was so symmetrical it looked clip-on fake. Sweat spotted his shirt at the crease of his stomach. A long, hot day. He moved toward me, the lightbulb playing off the shadows of that slender nose, bent slightly at the bridge from an ancient break. He stood over me, hands at his sides, too polished to cross his arms, though his impatience was clear.

His eyes picked me apart. 'I saw the note you're threatening to fax. I thought we had an agreement about San Onofre.'

'Things have changed.'

'Yes, you have a lot to answer for.'

'Is Sever the leak?'

'No. The leak has been plugged.'

'Who was it?'

'Oh, right. I forgot you had a Level 5 clearance.'

'How do I know *you're* not the mole?'

'You don't.'

'So why should I talk to you?'

'You asked for me, Horrigan, remember? We can put a name and a face to the third terrorist whenever the mood strikes. You're not in a position to play hard to get.' Wydell crossed to the door, opened it, and beckoned. He said, across the threshold, 'He's determined that we're both dirty, or maybe not.'

Sever came in, looking no more pleased with me. 'Maybe Mack Jackman was dirty too. Maybe that's why you slit his throat.'

'Or maybe Mack Jackman was dead when I got there.'

'Was he?'

'You tell me.'

Sever looked across at his superior. 'What is it with this guy?'

'You think I did what?' I said. 'Slit Jackman's throat, then tried to blow myself up and set myself on fire?'

'Ignited the munitions dump inside the apartment with a rifle grenade. To destroy evidence.'

I said, 'Convenient, that.'

'Not for Mack,' Wydell said.

'What are you talking about?' Sever turned to Wydell. 'What is this jackass talking about?'

Wydell's eyes never left mine. 'So,' he said. '*We* killed Mack Jackman. Is that it?'

I broke off the stare-down.

'You fled the scene,' Wydell pressed on. 'Not the decision of an innocent man.'

'After the explosion I wasn't feeling so welcome.'

'*Me?*' Sever was suddenly irate. 'You think *I* set the fire?' His confusion – and anger – seemed legitimate, that Southern accent amping up with the emotion.

'You fled the scene,' Wydell repeated. 'You were doing business with the victim.'

'How do you know that?' I asked. 'More pictures from Kim Kendall?'

'Who's Kim Kendall?' Wydell looked genuinely puzzled. I didn't answer, so he asked, 'Why were you – and your homeless buddy – in possession of marked bills?'

'Why were they marked?' I asked.

'We don't know. It was in the system. From the top.'

'Right,' I said. 'From the top. The West Wing keeping an eye on those hundreds, maybe.'

Sever had his back up again: 'What are you saying about the President?' Anger hardened his face. 'You're just full of comebacks here in private, aren't you? Not like out in the hall in front of other people where you were too t-t-tongue-tied to say your own name.'

Wydell opened the door, and reached through. When his hand reappeared, it was holding a Glock in a crime-scene bag. Frank's blood on the handle had gone black with age. 'You have a hell of a history, Horrigan, I'll give you that.'

Suddenly sweating in an interrogation room. Again. It felt like the last seventeen years had been narrowing to this needle-sharp point, waiting to impale me.

Wydell's face was tight with anger. 'This got dropped in our lap from above and I'm starting to feel a bit like a pawn in a political game. Is that what you're playing? A political game?'

The gun that had killed Frank swayed in the smudged plastic. I was having a hard time taking my eyes off it. I said, 'There's a reason why my prints are on that gun – read the crime-scene report.'

'So that's a yes?' Wydell handed the crime-scene bag back to whoever was waiting outside. The door closed with a decisive thump that said the room was sound-proofed. 'I don't know what channels this piece of evidence moved through to land on my desk the way it did. But let's just say it looks like magic. There's a lot of magic in politics. Evidence appears. People disappear. Like you did once. You sure you want to play in this sandbox? Because I sure as hell don't.'

Sever's glare hadn't left me. 'Have you been in touch with Caruthers?'

'No.'

'We think you have.'

'Give him a call. Tell him I'm here.'

'Why would we do that?'

'Maybe he'll want to know.'

'Who the fuck cares?' Sever said. 'We don't answer to some Senator. We *protect* him. But our primary charge is protecting the President of the United States.'

'Along with his interests,' Wydell added coolly.

'So get the Man a message. Tell him I have the evidence he's had the Service chasing.'

'What evidence?' Sever asked.

'The evidence that doesn't exist.'

Wydell said, 'And what is this non-existent evidence?'

'It's what's going to be faxed to major media outlets in' – I tilted my head to read Wydell's watch – 'two hours and fifteen minutes.'

Sever chuckled at me. 'It's a shame the President of the United States doesn't have any contacts in the media. I'm sure his forces are helpless against a random fax from an unidentified crank.'

'If you didn't kill Mack Jackman and blow up that apartment,' Wydell asked, 'why are we playing an extortion game with a fax machine?'

'So if I get choppered to a nonexistent facility or wind up with my head blown off, at least someone will know.'

'Know *what*?'

Sever brushed Wydell aside, an act of insubordination that Wydell seemed to condone under the circumstances.

298

Sever grabbed the arms of my chair, brought his face so close to mine I could smell his sweat. 'The system belongs to us. So we'll play this game. I'll charge you for murder – Mack Jackman's *and* Frank Durant's – and get bail set so high you'll sit in your stains until trial.'

I said, 'Give Bilton the message.'

Sever grimaced and stood. Wydell stepped forward, blocking that harsh throw of light from the dangling bulb. His hands tensed at his sides. I thought, *here it comes*, but instead Wydell just studied me with what seemed like genuine curiosity.

And then he asked, 'What do you want, Horrigan?'

'Answers.'

'No,' Wydell said. 'I mean, what do you get out of this?'

I shifted on the chair, looking up at him. 'Nothing.'

'That's what makes you so goddamned dangerous.'

They drifted through the door and then I heard the slam of the deadbolt. I could still smell the detergent from Sever's shirt. I banged on the door until the heel of my hand hurt, then I pressed my ear to the cool metal. Nothing but the hum of wires in the surrounding walls.

Twenty minutes passed, or forty. I was back in my little chair when the door opened. Sever entered first and placed a small table in front of me, and Wydell set a black, old-fashioned phone down on top of that. Its cord trailed across the threshold and down the hall. It was like room service, if the waiters hated you.

The agents stood against the wall and stared at me. I stared back. Wydell's impeccable suit wrapped around his slender build, that lank, gray hair with its sharp widow's peak and baby-boomer parting. And Sever, running-back broad, with menacing assurance etched in each line of his rugged face. They were the kind of white men they don't make anymore, of a generation that missed rap music and fusion cuisine and Hong Kong action movies; a generation of white quarterbacks and whiter airline pilots; men who grew up friendly with Negroes and Oriental girls, the white of golf clubhouses and martinis, white-bucks white; white like Frank, the white of authority, the white of the Secret Service. Wydell had maybe a decade on Sever, probably had already ponied up the downpayment for his retirement condo in Sarasota. Their gaze, the impenetrable stare of authority, didn't falter.

Carefully, I lifted the handset. It was the heaviest I'd ever held. I unscrewed the cap over the receiver, then the one protecting the transmitter, and checked inside. The cuffs made it difficult, but I managed. Sever and Wydell looked ready to fit me for a straightjacket.

The phone shrilled off the concrete walls, and we all started. I lifted the disk of receiver to my ear, cupped the transmitter entrails by my mouth. 'Hello?'

'I'm with the President.' A deep voice, one I'd never heard before. Mr Pager?

'At the moment?'

'No. I'm a member of his team.'

'What's your name?'

'That's not your concern.'

'I see he's no longer quite as eager to talk to me personally,' I said.

He continued as if I hadn't spoken: 'I understand

you're making wild claims against the President of the United States.'

'They're not so wild if you're on the phone with me.'

'President Bilton asked that we extend you the courtesy because of your role in the terrorist threat at San Onofre.'

'It wasn't a terrorist threat.'

For a while, I heard only the faint crackle of the line, then the voice said, 'Give the phone to the agent in charge.'

I offered the dissected handset to Wydell, who stepped forward and bobbled it to his face with great irritation. 'Yes, sir? No, sir, I'm not sure that's advisable. Yes, sir.'

He laid down the pieces of the handset respectfully on the table before me, then jerked his head at Sever, who followed him out. I pressed the receiver to my ear again, and somehow the man knew I was there.

'Talk,' he said.

'I know President Bilton fathered an illegitimate child in 1991.'

'You're delusional.'

'As I'm sure Agent Wydell explained to you, I have evidence of this. And that evidence is due to be faxed in about an hour and a half. I'm being held for crimes we all know I didn't commit. If I'm not released, right away, that fax will send.'

'Are you actually threatening me?'

'I don't even know who you are. I'm giving you facts on which to base a decision.'

'You're an exceedingly troubled young man. You should strongly consider professional help.'

'Then why bother talking to me?'

'Because of the role you played in last week's sensitive affair, President Bilton wanted us to hear you out and ascertain if you had credible intel. You do not. Good night, Mr Horrigan.'

The line went dead. The man had spoken with such smoothness and confidence that I felt my own conviction shaken. *Had* I gotten it all wrong? Had I put together the fragments to form a reflection of my own paranoia? Either way, the chips were all on the table and the roulette wheel was spinning.

I didn't have to marinate long in slow-motion panic. The door opened and Wydell entered, his lips thin with anger. He tugged a key from his pocket and unlocked my handcuffs.

'I don't know what kind of bullshit you pulled.' He threw down the cuffs on the table with disgust and walked out.

The door was open. Tentatively, I poked my head into the hall. A few workers, going about their business. Someone at a copy machine in a nearby office. I walked down the hall. The elevator doors were open, waiting – I assumed – for me. Sever was standing in the back, leaning against the metal rail. I was not surprised.

'You got some friends in high places,' he said.

I stepped into the elevator and he hit the button for the lowest parking level.

He said, 'Whatever black magic you worked on that phone call got you free and clear.'

'Free and clear?' I hit the lobby button and we whistled down in silence.

'You have a car?' he asked.

'No. I don't.'

'I'll give you a ride.'

Accommodating.

The elevator slowed, reaching the lobby.

Sever came forward, rested a shoulder against the panel of buttons. 'Why don't you come to parking with me?'

'Do I have a choice?'

'There are always choices.'

The doors slid open. Sever stiffened, coming off the wall. I stared out at the reception console, the street beyond the heavy glass doors. At the same time, I counted. *One . . . two . . . three . . . four . . . five*. Then the doors slid shut on my glimpse of freedom.

'I've been charged with recovering certain items,' Sever said, as soon as we were descending again.

'What items?'

'Whichever items you were planning on faxing at midnight.'

'No one seems to know what those items are,' I said, 'but they're sure getting a lot done.'

'Apparently they're classified.'

'I doubt it,' I said.

'Whether they're fucking classified or not, you're gonna tell me how we get them back.'

'Can I drop a line from Ketchikan, Alaska?'

The elevator doors dinged open. I stepped out into the dark garage, and Sever grabbed my arm. 'It might not be that easy.'

Behind us, the elevator doors remained open. *One . . .*

303

two . . . 'I didn't figure,' I said. *Three* . . . *four* . . . 'Okay,' I said. 'Let's take a ride.'

He smirked and let go of my arm. He stepped forward and I stepped back. Neatly, like a square dance move. I punched the lobby button again and the doors slid shut with Sever turning, baffled, five feet away, a red blush of anger coming up through the tan.

It seemed to take forever for the elevator to climb three stories. I bounced on my feet, urging it to rush. As soon as the doors parted onto the lobby, I slipped through, the rubber bumpers dragging across my shirt, and hustled past the security guards. One of the radios chirped and he raised it from his belt, but I forced myself not to run, not until I was through the doors. Then I was sprinting. Across Figueroa, dodging headlights, and then along the sidewalk, flying around corners, passers-by skipping out of my way.

I reached the grocery store parking lot and took the keys from the wheel well my own damn self. I couldn't get in the car fast enough, couldn't stop checking the rear-view. Blocks away, I finally unclenched my claws from the steering wheel and allowed myself a full exhale. Flying along, I rolled down the window to let the wind blast me in the face. Cleansing night air, even a few stars through a murky LA sky I'd been unsure I'd ever see again.

There was no fax machine or motel room, but there remained plenty of loose ends to tie down.

39

Homer was right where I might have guessed – in front of Hacmed's, sucking on a pint of Beam. I looked around before climbing out of the Jag, my wrists still tender from the cuffs.

He was halfway gone, lying on his side, his eyes pink, his lips – barely visible through the tangle of beard – twitching. On the ground next to his cheek was a small puddle of puke. Tracking my approach, he tipped up the empty bottle, letting the last drops fall. Then he threw it toward the Dumpster. It fell short, shattered with a pop.

He scooted himself back until he hit the wall and used it to shimmy up to a more-or-less seated posture. I crouched in front of him.

'You came in,' he said. 'For me. You came back.' He shook his head in disbelief. 'Why'd you'd do something so stupid?'

I started to answer, but he cut me off.

'I was scared, Nick.' He continued to shake his head. 'They were talking so *hard*. I didn't . . . I can't do much any-more. It was a lot of questions and people. I gave you up.' A tear cut a track through the dirt of his cheek. 'I gave you up.'

'You didn't tell them anything they didn't already know, Homer. They were using you to get to me. It's my fault for dragging you into this.'

'You didn't drag me into this. I *got dragged.*' His crow's feet deepened – a hint of amusement. 'There's a difference.'

'I involved you in this. Without giving you all the facts.'

'We can't know. How and when. What we do. The fallout. We can't.' A film came over his eyes. He wiped his nose from the bottom, shoving it up piggy-style with a ragged sleeve. 'You can't live without hurting people.'

'I guess not.'

'That's why I don't recommend it.'

'Recommend what?'

'Living.'

I thought of Homer in the park, jumping on the back of that red-eyed schizo, or at least trying to. I'd always thought it revealed some hidden reserve of courage. But maybe he just didn't give a shit anymore whether he lived or died. Here we were, two refugees from God knew what, defined by what we'd lived through and tried desperately not to acknowledge. I regarded those half-mast eyes. Losing traction, he slid down the wall a few inches.

I looked away at the street, half expecting to find Sever screeching up in a sedan. 'We have to get you out of here. Can you stay underground for a few days?'

'Please. I *live* underground.'

'Come on, I'll give you a lift to the tunnel.'

I took his arm and tugged him up, staggering under his weight. The odor was fierce, overpowering. His layers of tattered sleeve, damp with something I didn't want to identify, clamped across my shoulders, the bare skin of my neck. The reek of booze pushing through his pores made my eyes water. It was messy business, but I finally got him on his feet, propped against the wall. The low-sitting globe of his belly swayed. I started for the car.

'Buy me a bottle?' he said.

'You sure you need another?'

'Yes, I'm fucking sure.'

I held up my hands, conceding defeat, and went inside. Behind the counter, Hacmed was all amped up. 'Get him out of here, Nicolas. I will have to call cops. He vomit everywhere, scare off two customer. I cannot run business with drunk man in doorway.'

I said, 'The honeymoon's over, huh?'

'I am very glad he is well. That he is safe. But let us be honest, Nicolas. No one wants man like that around.'

I pointed at a pint of Jim Beam behind the counter, then pulled the last prepaid cell phone from the rack and set it beside the bottle.

Hacmed waved me off – an unprecedented act of generosity. 'For whatever you did to get him free.' As I turned away, he wagged a finger at me and said, 'And for whatever you do to get him now gone.'

Pocketing the items, I walked out. It took some doing to get Homer across the parking lot and into the passenger seat. He sat in silence on the drive to the beach, looking out the window. I had to keep mine rolled down to cut the smell. At one point, his shoulders shook, and I wondered if he was crying.

I pulled over by the concrete steps leading down to the tunnel. It looked different now. More mundane and sadly municipal. The damp air tasted of the sea and car exhaust. Overhead, cars whined by on PCH. He directed his pink eyes at the dashboard. I handed him the pint bottle. He didn't take it. I pressed it to his arm and finally he reached over and closed a dirt-caked hand around the glass.

'You came back.' His voice was gruff, cracked with dehydration. He got out and slammed the door, angrily. A dirt imprint remained behind on the leather seat. He stumbled past the headlights, pausing by my window, his gaze on the freeway and the maw of the tunnel below. His eyes were moist.

I knew so little about him. His past was all over him, like a pack of dogs, but I'd learned nothing of it. He was all present tense. Jim Beam. Corner mart parking space. Shower every Thursday. He hadn't been married. He hadn't been a dentist. Those were lies invented by Kim Kendall. Or maybe they were truths that Homer no longer acknowledged. I didn't know what he'd fled or why. I didn't know if he'd lost friends. I didn't know if he'd left behind a wife or a son or an elderly parent. I knew only that it was no business of mine.

He started to trudge off, then halted, his shoulders hitching as if the momentum break had caught them by surprise. Still he didn't look back. But I heard his voice clearly, even over the traffic and the rush of distant waves. 'If it happens again,' he said, 'just leave me.'

I watched him descend the stairs and fade into the mouth of the tunnel.

I was driving to drive, unsure of where I should land. I took San Vicente away from the beach, the coral trees rising out of the lawned median, catching fog in their twisted branches. Then I hooked up to Sunset and rode the turns past the northern edge of UCLA, the campus I used to daydream about during high-school classes. North through a canyon run, passing Bel Air mansions with their gothic fences, Tudor gables, and Santa Barbara-sandstone driveways, the confused architecture mirroring my own fragmented thoughts. I reached perilous Mulholland, blinking into headlights around the tight turns, a craggy rise to the side and then suddenly gone like a dropped curtain, revealing the breathless stretch of the Valley at night, glowing under a pollution haze.

The radio recycled Caruthers's afternoon chatfest with Sean Hannity. Caruthers: 'Back to family values, are we?'

The talk-show host's quick reply – 'You're the one who trotted out the discussion on the campaign trail.'

'That worked out well, didn't it?' Caruthers matched Hannity's chuckle, then his tone took on a note of subdued outrage. 'When President Bilton talks about family values, what does that mean? Are we interested in phrases or reality? For instance, there are those of us who are pro-life and those of us who are pro-choice. But none of us are pro-abortion. And there have been more abortions during President Bilton's three-and-a-half years in the White House than under any administration since Reagan's. Look at what actually impacts those figures. The *economy*. This President has consistently chosen image and hypocrisy over substance and effectiveness. There's a clear choice at hand. We can beat our chests and lecture sanctimoniously about values, or we can talk about the root causes and find solutions that actually make a difference.'

'I like chest-beating.'

'I've heard that about you.'

'Where to today?'

'Ohio.'

'Why?'

'Because it's a swing state. Where have you been?'

Hannity laughed. 'Another straight answer from the man with the transparent campaign. I was worried you were gonna kowtow to Midwesterners, praise the Buckeyes and Cincinnati's Rock and Roll Hall of Fame, pull a Hillary with a chocolate-chip-cookie recipe.'

'The Rock and Roll Hall of Fame is in Cleveland. And June does the cooking in our house.'

'What's her favorite thing to make?'

'Reservations.'

It was an old joke, sure, but the delivery made me smile anyway. The Senator always hit the marks, giving great press without sounding couched. Probably because he wasn't. He famously didn't rehearse. You got the sense that he didn't watch polls, though of course he did, and that he didn't choose sound bites the night before with a bunch of world-weary spitballers slurping bad coffee and chewing Rolaids. What voters would be betting on – or against – was his personality, which he was unafraid to present in relatively unfiltered fashion.

I veered off onto an unpaved apron, watched the dirt billow up from the tires and drift away like a dusty ghost, like Homer. I looked at the view, marveling at how I was embroiled in something that could impact matters discussed on radio shows and TV broadcasts and front pages around the world. I thought about how I'd sat beside Caruthers in his conference room, so close I could have rested a hand on his shoulder. How he was turned away so the midday light from the window had caught his silhouette. I pictured his shaving nick, that tiny mole on his forearm. He was just a man, like Frank. But like Frank, he seemed like he was more.

In the distance, a twinkle dipped through the haze, heading for the Burbank Airport. I watched until it merged with the pinprick lights of the Valley.

The crappy cell showed a surprising three bars. I called Induma on the phone I'd left there. When she picked up, I said, 'I'm okay.'

She was silent for a long time and I wondered about the expression on her face. Her voice was slightly uneven when she spoke. 'Come over?'

The customary fears stirred in me. 'Bilton knows I know now. It's in the open. This is a whole new level of exposure. I shouldn't be near you.'

'That's not just your decision to make.'

'This is life and death, Induma.'

'Everything is life and death.'

'Not like this. Look at what happened to Homer.'

'*Exactly*,' she said. 'Look at what happened to Homer.'

And she hung up.

Holding the phone in my lap, I tried to spot the plane down below, but I'd lost the points of reference to pick it up. There were no cars in earshot, and I could hear crickets sawing away down the hill. I pulled out onto the lonely road, and then I dialed again.

Steve answered on the first ring, and recognized my hello.

'*Nick?*' I could hear his relief in how he said my name.

'I'm alive,' I said.

'Then you'd better get over here.'

'Why?'

'I tracked down Jane Everett. She was murdered eleven days after Frank was killed. They found her body in a lot.'

The static over the line matched the thrum of ragged road meeting tire, a dazed, inadvertent composition. For an instant, I felt suspended, separate from the car, hurtling around dark turns three feet off the ground.

From a great distance, I heard myself say, 'Baby Everett?'

Steve cleared his throat once, hard, like it was bothering him. 'Two weeks old. I'm afraid they found her, too.'

40

W̶e sat around the kitchen table, Steve, Callie, and I, with new photos of Jane Everett laid before us. A college graduation picture that had run big in the press, and a candid shot taken eight years later, her pulling a Snoopy maternity shirt tight across her pregnant belly and grinning at the camera. She had large, expressive eyes and full lips that made her look younger than she was. There were fat dimples on her thighs, visible beneath the hem of the shirt, and her back was arched in an exaggeration of the weight pulling her forward. She looked happy.

A sentence kept running through my head like one of those news tickers at the bottom of Fox News: *the President had this woman and her baby murdered.*

The kitchen light was half-dimmed, and we'd spoken only in whispers. Not just because Emily was asleep upstairs, but because, I think, we were awed by what we were up against. Right now, it was just us, bound by this muted circle of light. If we spoke too loud, maybe we'd rouse the sleeping giant.

I lifted the *LA Times* print-out from the table and read the article again.

Oxnard, CA – The bodies of a 32-year-old woman and her 13-day-old daughter were discovered yesterday at 11:00 pm in a dirt lot in Oxnard. Jane Everett had been shot in the head, and her baby, Gracie, suffocated.

Neighbor Tris Landreth saw two men throw the bodies from the back of a truck into the deserted construction area. She immediately alerted the police.

Jane Everett lived and worked in Sherman Oaks, but Landreth claimed the new mother had been in the neighborhood before. 'I saw her around the trailers out by the 101 a few times a month or so ago. I remember her because of that great big belly. This is a horrendous, horrendous tragedy.'

The suspects were described as Hispanic in appearance. No arrests have been made. The Oxnard Police Department has requested that any additional information or previous sightings of Jane Everett be reported to (805) 385-7600.

Everett is survived by an older sister, Lydia (43), and her mother, Bernice (66). She is remembered by friends as a loving person who was interested in local politics and symphony music.

Given the exhaustion and stress, Callie was showing her age – her eyelids textured, the corners of her lips drooping, her skin faintly loose along the line of her jaw. She'd held me in the entryway as Steve closed and locked the door, relieved that I was out of danger for the time being. While she was clutching me, we both grew awkward about the physical display. We were two adults now, who didn't know each other well as such.

'At first, I couldn't find any information on Everett,'

Steve said. 'Credit header, utility bills, phone company, DMV, the usual. So I checked the death registry.'

'We finally have a name for the baby,' I said.

I noticed Steve's and Callie's heads pivot slightly to exchange a look, bewildered, no doubt, by my reaction to Grace Everett. She'd come into the world the same month I'd been forced into my new life. We'd been born of the same circumstances, products of similar fallout. Since I'd seen that ultrasound, we'd been in it together, me and her, at least in my head, and yet she hadn't been there after all. I'd made her my responsibility, and, foolish as it was, I couldn't help feeling that somehow I'd failed her.

'It sounds stupid, but I guess I thought maybe if I could save her, I could, you know . . .' But I couldn't bring myself to finish the cliché. My face grew hot, so I focused again on the papers before us.

Because of the baby, the murders had made quite a splash, but since they'd occurred two weeks after Frank's death, neither Callie nor I had noticed them.

Who had helped neutralize Bilton's problem? Who'd shot Jane in the head, cupped his hand over Gracie's tiny mouth and nose? How many others over the years had safeguarded what they knew? A secret like that rots outward until someone gives a damn.

I wanted Frank's death to make sense the way it used to. I stared at the printout and the photos as if they could make it so.

Steve flipped the article up, eyed the line of text at the bottom. '"Interested in local politics",' he read.

'That fucking bastard,' Callie said. 'His own child.'

'What's with the quotation about seeing Jane Everett

out by the freeway?' I asked. 'Isn't that a bit specific for a short news blurb?'

'It's all an inference game,' Steve said. 'Oxnard's always had a meth problem at the outskirts. Trailers are a favorite for cooking labs.'

'So the witness is lying? Putting Everett at the trailers?'

'Not necessarily. Bilton's people are smart. Maybe they figured out a way to get Everett over on that side of town where she'd be seen. Or maybe she really did have some drug involvement and they used that as a cover story.'

'The two men of Hispanic appearance play nicely into that.'

'Right. Wisely chosen as the dumping crew by Bilton's men because they match the meth-pushing pop in the region. Playing to racist fear is always good and distracting.'

'If the police suspected this was a drug-related killing, why didn't they just come out and say that?' Callie asked.

'Because the detectives can't go on record claiming they think a nice white girl from Sherman Oaks was meth-whoring on the wrong side of Oxnard,' Steve said. 'They want leads, sure, but they have to be careful. So they made sure the article was phrased to get the information out on the street without saying anything disrespectful.'

'Maybe Bilton's people oversaw the article. Or the investigation.'

'They wouldn't want their fingerprints on it. Plus, they didn't *need* to. They did something better.' He tapped the print-out. 'Everyone thinks they know what happened here. Half the people followed the wrong trail, and the other half didn't want to ask uncomfortable questions. This is the perfect way to bury a body in unspoken implications.'

'Two bodies,' I said.

'You watch your ass, Nick. This isn't just a spin game with poll numbers at stake. This is about accusing the President of the United States of murder.'

But I didn't feel afraid. Nor did I feel the usual swirl of paranoia. I wasn't jittery. I wasn't stressed out. I felt only a cold, calm rage.

I asked, 'Any of the family local?'

Steve scratched his curly hair. 'Everett's mom passed away in '01. Lung cancer. But I got an address for the sister at the office. I'll call you with it first thing tomorrow.'

I stood and zipped up my jacket. Callie looked at me disbelievingly. 'We're talking about the Commander in Chief, Nicky.'

I pointed at the witness's name on the article. Tris Landreth. 'Will you get me her address, too?'

I thanked them both and showed myself out the back door.

Sitting in the dark Jag four blocks from Callie's house, I dialed Alan Lambrose. He answered perkily, saying his name like it was something to be proud of.

I said, 'It's me. Nick Horrigan. I need to talk to the Man. Only him.'

'You got a reach number?'

I read him the digits off the back of the disposable

phone, hung up, and waited, chewing my thumbnail. I didn't wait long.

The same voice I'd heard an hour before coming across the airwaves. 'Nick? Are you all right?'

Having access to a presidential candidate was the kind of thing I could probably never get used to. 'Yeah, I'm fine. Where are you?'

'Franklin County. I'm told that's in Ohio.'

The phone brushed against the Band-Aid, sending a jolt of pain through my face. 'I need to see you. Privately. This has just jumped into a whole new league.'

'What is it?' Wariness in his voice.

'Not over an open line. But the threat of it leaking was enough to get me out of Secret Service custody earlier tonight.'

'You were in *custody*? Why didn't you contact me? We could have helped. Bullied the bullies.'

'I didn't want to drag you into it. Besides, I wasn't being offered a free phone call.'

His hand rustled over the phone, then he said to someone else. 'I'm ready. A minute.' Back to me: 'Can you convey whatever it is to Alan?'

'No, Senator.'

'I trust Alan implicitly. And he's in Los Angeles right now.'

Trust no one. I didn't respond. I just stared through the windshield, unsure of how to refuse respectfully, until Caruthers rescued me.

'I understand,' he said. 'I'll be back in LA tomorrow afternoon. Can we meet at the condo at three?'

'I'd like to meet in secret. No agents.'

'I can't promise no agents and I can't come alone, but I'll see if I can sneak out with a few aides and maybe just James. But we'll talk alone. I'll have Alan call you first thing with a location. I'm sorry, but I really have to go. Oh – and Nick? Watch your neck.'

41

Induma opened her door, wearing a sheer nightgown, and the breeze lifted the hem, folding it back against her dark brown thigh.

I said, 'He killed her. Thirteen days old. Had her dumped in a dirt lot with the body of her mother.'

Induma didn't ask a single question. She just unfolded her arms and I went to her, bowing my head and breathing in the scent of Kai lotion on her neck. Warm air behind her, the cold curling around us, tightening the skin of her arms, raising goosebumps. I felt her heart beating against the pit of my stomach. The strength of it, but also, its fragility. I didn't want to let go of her but finally I did.

She closed the door behind us and I locked it and threw the deadbolt. We went to the living room and I sat cross-legged on the couch while she listened patiently. I finished and there was a hum of silence, and then she said, 'What do you need?'

I said, 'Cartoons.'

We found him in short order, white chest puffed out, carrot at the ready. 'Of course, you know, dis means *war*.' The animated shenanigans flickered across my numb face. Cunning rabbits, French skunks, elastic mice, with their speech impediments and well-drawn plans. They were a comfort, not an amusement. They never made you consider the fragility of their hearts beating against your stomach.

How clear it all was in the land of Merrie Melodies. Pull-string cannons. Red TNT cylinders with sparkler fuses. Throw on a hat and an accent and you're a whole new rabbit. Or just put your head down and burrow until you wind up in a bullring or the South Pole or Ketchikan, Alaska. Only problem is, when you do that, you lose track of where you're going and wind up lost. Or worse, right where you started.

The credits rushed by in a syndicated flurry and then Induma clicked a button on one of four remotes surfing the cushions and the channel blinked and we were back in the real world. In anticipation of Thursday's debate, C-SPAN was re-airing the one from Harlem that I'd watched the night the Service kicked down me and my door.

Induma looked across at me, gauging my temperature, but I didn't mind watching. I wanted to see Bilton in all his banality-of-evil glory. I wanted to see Caruthers dismember him verbally and sweep the dais with his parts.

Jim Lehrer hunched over the moderator's podium, his doll eyes impartial and unblinking. 'Senator, I have a two-part question for you. Early in your career, you were for the death penalty and now you're opposed to it. My first question is: if June Caruthers were raped and murdered, would you favor an irrevocable death penalty for the killer?'

'Ah,' Caruthers said, 'the old Dukakis chestnut.'

'Please let me finish, Senator. And the second part is, why the change in your position?'

Caruthers's green eyes gleamed. 'If my wife were raped and murdered, I'd want to hunt down her killer and gut him. But in civilized countries, we don't let the victim's relatives choose the punishment. Imagine if we did. To answer your second question, before we even *get to* a discussion about the morality of the death penalty, we're hamstrung by the unavoidable fact that it is ineffective, biased, and incredibly expensive. This has become increasingly apparent to me. I *have* had some shifts in opinion over the course of my long career. And thank God for that. How many of you want a politician who refuses to learn on the job?' A wicked pause – 'Well, I suppose forty-six percent of you.'

A rumble of laughter, punctuated by a few hisses. The cutaway showed Bilton, the picture of mature restraint, jotting a note on the lectern.

Caruthers offered a collegial tilt of the head. 'My opponent would like to exploit a reasonable evolution of thinking to paint me as wishy-washy. Or as a waffler. Or whatever deprecation has currency this go 'round. But I hope that I will never hold consistency above conscience. And I *will* never claim not to have made mistakes. In fact, I just may have made enough mistakes to avoid some in the future.'

Bilton leaned toward the black bud of his slender microphone. 'Senator, most of the time it seems like you've made too many to keep track of.'

His constituency, bolstered by relief, applauded over-enthusiastically.

Induma hit *mute*. 'If smugness could be fitted for a suit . . .'

Bilton's lips moved as he continued his silent retort.

What did it take to order the killing of the mother of your child? His own flesh and blood, suffocated and dumped on a dirt lot?

I said, 'I can't believe that bastard might win.'

'This is about politics?' Induma asked.

'No,' I said, 'this isn't about politics at all.'

I bolted awake, scrambled up in the sheets on the couch, *2:18* glowing from the darkness beneath the TV. I carried out of sleep the image of Frank's foot ticking back and forth, metering the drainage from the gut wound. As I tried to untangle my breathing, the bank of windows rocked into view, the stretch of lawn, the fence of the boxwood, and the murky canal. Induma's living room. I was in Induma's living room.

I rubbed my eyes, felt the pinch of sleep. The rucksack was at my feet. The top was loose, and I could see the red jewelry box inside. I reached in, pulled out those earrings with the sapphire chips. Held them up to the faint light and pictured them against Induma's skin.

I thought about Frank and his thousand small decisions.

The stairs creaked a little on my way up. I paused outside her door. Opened it gently.

She was sleeping on her stomach, slid down off her pillow, her hair a neat half-circle against her cheek. The image of peacefulness. And then her eyes were open and she wiped her mouth and rustled up. She tilted her head for me to come in and I crossed on unsteady legs and stood a few feet from the bed, the jewelry box hard in my sweating hand and low by my side, hidden. She was leaning back, resting her elbows on the clutch of pillows behind her, her eyes dark and serious, her shiny hair spilled forward on her shoulders, the strokes of her collarbone pronounced beneath that velvet skin.

I said, 'There's no part of you I don't find magical.'

I wanted to get it all out because I knew if I stopped, I wouldn't be able to pick up again. 'I know I blew it before. With us. But everything that's happened has cracked my life open. And I got to see it for what it was. And what it isn't. I'd do anything to be with you again, and I'm ready for it to be different.'

The rustle of her shifting and then she was sitting upright. She said, 'Nick,' and I heard it in her tone and felt my insides crumble. My mouth was dry and I thought I might need to sit down but I couldn't, so I stood there on the cold floorboards to take what was coming next.

She said, 'I'll always love you, Nick, but I'm not where I was. Life doesn't wait. You don't just get to pick up where you left off.'

Far away, in one of the neighboring houses, I could hear canned laughter from a too-loud TV. My voice was hoarse. 'No, but maybe sometimes you get a second chance.'

'Look, I know you're raw right now, and that you believe everything you're saying, but how do I know this is where you'll stay? How do *you* know? You've got so much to put back together, Nick.'

I half turned, pushed that jewelry box into my back

pocket. Breathed. 'How do I do that? Put it back together?'

'You show up,' she said. 'Day after day.'

My face felt heavy, tugging my gaze to the floor. 'I want you to know,' I said. 'You were worth it. You were worth everything. I just couldn't figure out how to do it right.'

Emotion flickered across her face – sadness, but something else there too, something she'd been waiting to feel.

I took a moment to soak in the bedroom I'd once felt at home in. The three-wick candle, taller than the nightstand. The facing bathroom's burnt-caramel walls, matching the towels thrown over the lip of the clawfoot tub we used to dip into before succumbing to an exhausted, entangled slumber.

And then I turned and walked out, my steps heavy down the stairs. In the bathroom off the entry, I shoveled cold water over my face, tried to catch my breath.

Through the wall, I heard the creak of the front door.

Quietly, I unbuckled my belt and slid it free, wrapping either end around my fists.

Muted footsteps. Approaching.

I put my back to the wall behind the bathroom door. The handle dipped and the door opened. I was about to lunge when I saw Alejandro's reflection in the mirror.

I stepped out, lowering my hands. 'What are you doing here?'

'Shouldn't I ask you that?' He paused to acknowledge my makeshift garrote, then started digging through the medicine cabinet. 'Nice advice you give me. On the date. It's a joke to you, but now we fighting.'

'Handro, listen. You can't – you shouldn't have seen

me. You can't tell anyone that I was here. It could be really dangerous.'

'You Ethan Hunt now, eh?' He started humming the theme from *Mission Impossible*.

I said, 'I'm not fucking around. This could wind up getting us killed.'

His smile vanished, replaced by something like a scowl, and I was surprised by the steel in his dark gaze. 'Nick, I grew up in Boyacá. When I was a kid, Colombia had the highest murder rate in the world. Cartel, DEA – it was a ugly time. People point the fingers. People disappear. You heard about the necktie, no?' He made a cutting gesture beneath his chin and mimed pulling his tongue through the slit. 'Usually they don't bother with this. They just machete off the head.'

'Okay,' I said. 'I get it.'

'On my way to school, I pass trucks and workers. I keep my eyes straight ahead. I careful not to see anything.' He was looking through the drawers under the sink, a bit anxiously, not finding whatever he was searching for. 'I got to school every day. Some of my friends didn't. Some nights, I have to help look for them. Sometime we find a body. Sometime we find a head.' He finished with the last drawer and stood with exasperation.

'What are you looking for?' I asked.

'My pills.'

I reached for the towel I'd just used to dry my face. There was an orange bottle beneath it. I made out the pharmacy lettering – IN EVENT OF PANIC ATTACK – just before Alejandro grabbed the bottle and jammed it into

326

a pocket. Again, I saw something in his face I'd never seen before, and I thought about his happy-go-lucky demeanor and wondered how hard he'd had to fight to get comfortable in the world.

Alejandro shoved his lank hair from his eyes, grabbed the edge of the door. 'I been through this *mierda* Third-World style. So don't you question how *I* stand by a friend just because you don't know how to act like one.'

His footsteps padded out, and then the front door opened and closed quietly.

I stared at myself in the mirror, didn't much like what I saw.

I made sure Alejandro had locked the front door behind him, then returned to the couch. Resting my feet on the coffee table, I watched the windows. They had lever locks, simple throw-and-clicks with a catch that made them immune to jimmying. Good locks.

Seized by an impulse, I sprang up and threw those levers, one after the other, elbowing each window open on a slight tilt. Back on the couch, I listened to my heart thudding its disapproval. But I didn't get up.

I stared at those locks, breathing the fresh breeze, for what must have been hours. It's amazing what you can hear through a screen at night. I could sense the canal. Dragonflies buzzing, cicadas singing, the mossy reek of standing water. I could see the fluttering shadows of the Tibetan prayer flags nailed to the eaves.

With great effort, I averted my gaze from the windows, slid down on the couch, closed my eyes. The locks called to me, jealous for my attention, but I ignored them. The pleas rose to demands, a great, angry clamoring in my head, but still I didn't answer.

Security matters. But maybe comfort matters, too.

A thousand small decisions.

Sometime around morning, I fell asleep.

42

When she opened the door, I was struck by the lack of resemblance. Maybe it was the years that had passed, or maybe it had always been that way, but Lydia Flores looked nothing like her sister. At least nothing like how Jane Everett had looked at thirty-two. I stuffed the Polaroid of Jane and Bilton back in my pocket and smiled in greeting.

Lydia studied me through the screen, mottled by the morning light. 'Can I help you?'

'I hope so. I'm Nick Horrigan. I'm sorry to intrude on your morning, but I was wondering if I could ask you a few questions about your sister.'

She unlatched the screen and pushed it open. She'd be sixty now, but she looked older, with that timeless grandmotherly bearing. She wore a housedress and her hair was neatly done up in a bun. Her face was soft and round, made rounder by oversize glasses. Makeup – nothing excessive, but she was of the generation that really used it. Stockings and sling-back shoes, sensible but certainly not comfortable for hanging around at home alone. Somehow I knew that she'd been widowed – a sixth sense had emerged from an unknown part of my brain to make the diagnosis.

She said, 'Are you with the press? Every few years someone comes knocking. A retrospective or whatever they call it. Last year I got contacted by someone doing a psychology study about grief.'

'No,' I said, 'I'm not a reporter.'

But that didn't seem to deter her. She didn't even bother to ask who I *was* with. She led me back in through a narrow hall to a living room. The house was clean, but every surface was cluttered. A side table crowded with antique Limoges boxes. Porcelain cats on a doily. Plants everywhere, sprouting from decorative watering cans and hanging from crocheted slings, lending the air a musky quality. Framed pictures rising like feathers from the lid and key cover of a small upright piano. Lydia at the altar, Jane in the maid-of-honor spot though she couldn't have been more than thirteen. It was impossible not to recognize Jane Everett's lips. Lydia's husband, a kind-looking Hispanic man, looked to be at least a decade older than his bride. He aged with dignity across the piano. The last shot, a close of up him in a yellow sweater holding a tennis racket, was years old, bleached like the others from the facing window. He reclined at a club table, sipping iced tea, and his hair was silver, his teeth pronounced against a nice retirement tan.

I sat on a plastic-slipcovered couch. The seat was slightly warm and beside me was a crossword-puzzle book, folded back to a pencil-indented page. I'd taken Lydia's spot, though she'd been too polite to say anything. Across, on a flatscreen that looked anachronistic contrasted with the other furnishings, two soap stars were mashing their faces against each other in a way that looked distinctly uncomfortable.

When I realized Lydia was watching me, some prudish impulse made me turn my gaze away. The unplayed piano was too depressing, so I looked out the window beside it. A short, square garden met its end five feet out at the neighbor's aggressively tall slat fence.

Lydia followed my stare and said, 'The young couple added that fence when they moved in. It's at the property line, so there was nothing we could do.'

'Bad zoning laws.'

She slid sideways into an armchair, a graceful, feminine movement. 'Their house isn't even close. It sits a half acre back, but they wanted that fence there. They took it right up to code. My husband was furious. I lost him three years ago May. Ernesto. Heart attack.'

She said his name with a slight accent. A WASP woman marrying an Hispanic man wasn't so common back when they wed. I thought of those Hispanic males who'd reportedly dumped Jane's body, how neatly Bilton's team had taken advantage of people's prejudices. I felt like an intruder here in Lydia's cluttered little house, my eye to the peephole of a private life.

'I'm sorry,' I said.

'I find myself thinking about Janie more. With him gone.'

I realized that Lydia didn't care if I was with the *LA Times* or the CIA or Brownie Troop 9882. She just wanted to talk.

'It's a hard thing to forget.'

She firmed her mouth, looked up at the corner of the room. 'It was a long time ago.'

'Yes,' I said. 'It was.'

Her eyes lingered on the ceiling for a while. Then she angled her head sideways and spoke from the side of her mouth though we were across the room from each other. Confiding in me. 'I loved Ernesto dearly, as you can imagine. Forty-eight years of marriage. And there are still mornings where I . . . where I . . .' Her hand trailed off. 'But the *violence* of Janie's death. It doesn't sit. It never sat.'

'No,' I said. 'There's nowhere to put it.'

'They talk about closure all the time. Putting it behind you. Coming to grips.'

'Who does?'

'The TV. *Closure*. Like it's a thing. An actual thing that you can achieve. That you can hold in the palm of your hand.'

Her fingers fussed in her lap, taking up a fold of fabric. Her candor caught me off guard. Her loneliness. How deeply the loss still touched her.

'You never get there,' I said. 'I guess you just keep trying.'

'But these things *damage* you – I'm sorry, what'd you say your name was?'

'Nick.'

'They *damage* you, Nick. My niece . . .' Her fingers trembled, then she fished a tissue out of a sleeve and held it in a fist. 'Ernesto and I never had children. I took care of Janie growing up. Eleven years older. That's a lot. So I suppose I wanted . . . I don't know. Ernesto and I enjoyed our time so much. Janie was like my daughter. My niece would have been like – like another daughter, you see? Janie liked "Grace", but I was the one who started calling

332

her "Gracie". That part was – that part was mine. And after they died . . .'

'I understand.'

'Do you?' Her tone wasn't accusatory, it was deeply, intensely curious. Needy, even.

'Yes. I think I do.'

'You give something up, maybe. Like a penance. A part of your life. To honor what was lost. To not replace it.'

'I understand that, too.'

We sat in silence, not looking at each other. Another picture on the piano caught Jane in close-up, working some campaign event, election ticker tape and confetti frozen in a red-and-white blur in the background.

'What was she like?' I asked.

'She was *sweet.*' She shook her head slowly with the last word. 'You know how some people just have that heart? And quiet. Had a laugh that'd catch you by surprise. She made some choices that, well . . .' The tissue rose halfway to her face, then her knuckles whitened and she lowered it. She would not cry. 'She didn't know how long the future can be. How long it *can be.*'

I said, carefully, 'The father—'

Her lips tensed. 'I never knew who the father was.' She shook her head, quickly this time, as if fighting off a bad taste. 'She never breathed a word. Not even to me.' But her face couldn't hide the truth. I knew she was lying and she knew I knew.

The soap actors had pulled apart, the woman resisting in that no-means-yes way, and then, like a horrible joke, there was Bilton. His sweater-and-khakis spot, the business-casual Commander in Chief surrounded by his

333

progeny on the spotless Oval Office rug. Mr Morals, a sharp contrast to his twice-married challenger.

Lydia dug in her armrest pouch for the remote. I watched Bilton's well-shaven face. 'Senator Caruthers says he doesn't "understand family values". Do you really want someone in the White House who's proud to make that claim?' Dignified cursive across the screen announced, *Paid for by Andrew Bilton for President.*

Lydia finally fought the remote free and shut off the TV. We sat in the awkward silence for a moment, and then she said, bitterly, 'Janie deserved more from this life. And Gracie. She would have been loved. She was a person, too, and she would have had a family.' Lydia stared at the dark TV with disgust. Her eyes finally lifted to me. 'You said you were with the press?'

My throat was husky with emotion. I said, 'Yeah, I'm with the press.'

She rose and smoothed her dress in the back with a practiced slide of her flat hand. 'Please write about her kindly. There was some innuendo around her when she died.'

I said, 'I'm going to do everything I can for her.'

43

One more name on the rumpled piece of paper. Tris Landreth, the witness to the dumping of the bodies. The most recent address Steve had found under her name, from a cell-phone account, belonged to a run-down house in Van Nuys. The bell was broken, so I knocked, and a moment later, a heavyset woman in a plush bathrobe tugged the screen open.

I said, 'Tris Landreth?'

She scowled, waved a hand at me dismissively. 'I look like some *Tris* to you, son?'

'I'm sorry. I'm just—'

'She cleared out the guest house six months back in the middla the night. Give us *no notice*. And it ain't like she paid no security deposit we could cash in on neither.'

'Six months ago.'

'Yeah. And now everything "Tris Tris Tris" again all a'sudden. She a quiet lady. Why all these folks be up in here after her?'

My pulse quickened. 'Other people were asking for her?'

'The Five-Oh is who, son. Shit, worse. The secret-handshake guys. You know the ones.'

'When?'

'Last week. Dunno. Wednesday, Thursday. Shit, I ain't no calendar.'

I struggled to keep my head clear. 'Did she pack up her stuff? When she left?'

'What little she had, yeah. She was here almost a year, but she never really moved in, know what I'm sayin'? Had a suitcase for a dresser. Like she was just waitin' to pick up and go again.' A gruff voice called out from the back of the house, and she yelled back, 'I be there in a minute, baby,' and trudged off.

I stood at the door a few minutes before realizing she wasn't coming back.

I crossed the dead lawn and sat on the curb for a while, watching the kids play soccer in the street and the low-riders cruise by, vibrating with bass. Whatever Tris Landreth knew, I needed to know, too. *Just waitin' to pick up and go.* She'd been living a life I was all too familiar with. I thought about how isolated I'd felt up in Ketchikan, that soul-numbing loneliness that came from being cut off from those I loved, the semiannual cards I used to send through the remailing service to Callie, the freezing sleepless nights I spent waiting to hear if those cards had bounced back, if my mom had moved or gotten sick or died. I wondered, given that Tris Landreth had been too nervous to unpack her bags for a year, what had been keeping her in the area.

The liquor store at the corner had a pay phone in the back. I called the cell phone I'd given Induma, and it rang and rang before she picked up. I'd left early this morning to avoid awkwardness, and with her voice came a pang of embarrassment. And something heavier. Longing.

I said, 'Sorry about last night.'

'You've got nothing to apologize for.'

'Then I can impose on you for another favor?'

'That's what friends are for.'

'Rub it in.'

She laughed.

I said, 'Tris Landreth. The witness? She split.'

'And you want me to use the databases to locate her.'

'Steve already checked the databases. I need you to find out if she has any sick kids or elderly parents in the area.'

When we got off, I bought a Coke, went outside, and sat on the curb for a while. A young Hispanic couple was leaning against a truck in the parking lot and making out. Dark bands of eyeshadow stood out on her closed lids, and his hands were at her face. Effortless. I thought about how cold those floorboards had felt beneath my bare feet last night when Induma had told me that life doesn't wait.

The pay phone inside rang.

The shopkeeper gave me an odd look as I jogged back.

Induma said, 'No sick kids and no elderly parents, but looks like Landreth was raised by an aunt who's not doing too hot. The aunt lives in Northridge.'

I had a pen at the ready. 'You got an address?'

I entered the well-kept complex, and knocked on the appropriate door. After a lengthy wait and prolonged shuffling, an ancient woman answered. The apartment smelled of talcum powder and cats.

'Hi,' I said. 'I'm looking for Harriet Landreth. It's about her niece, Tris.'

'*Tris*,' she repeated, with impressive derision. She was severely hunched and had to crane her head to look up at me.

'Are you Harriet?'

'No, I'm Glenda, her older sister. I'm taking care of her.'

'Has Tris visited lately?'

'*Tris*? Visited *lately*?'

I might as well have asked if Peter O'Toole had swung by for a gimlet.

She regarded me warily. 'What *is* this?'

'I'm trying to find her. It's really important.'

'Well, Tris hasn't bothered coming around here. Harriet raised that girl like a daughter. When no one else wanted to, I might add. And now my sister's sick and do you think Tris bothers to come around? Not in *months*. And barely once a year before that.'

'Maybe there's an explanation for why she can't come.'

'If there is, Tris'll have it ready. It's always something. Always someone after her. Bill collector. Some ex.'

'You never know people's reasons for doing stuff, I guess,' I said. 'Maybe she's scared of something.' I didn't know why I felt so vehemently about defending her, and then of course I did.

'It doesn't matter,' Glenda was saying. 'Everyone's got reasons for everything. She left us. She left us holding the bag. I'm not interested in how she'll justify it this time around.'

I pictured Callie's face, hard with resentment: *you*

338

haven't shown up for a damn thing in seventeen years.
'You're right,' I said. 'It must feel pretty crappy from your end.'

Glenda's face seemed to draw into itself, the wrinkles moving but not really moving at all.

'Maybe I could talk to Harriet?' I asked. 'Just for a moment?'

'I'll see how she's feeling.'

The door closed in my face.

A moment later, the door opened again. Glenda was already shuffling back in. *America's Funniest Home Videos* played softly on the TV. A cat was leaping around a ball of yarn, accompanied by wacky circus music. The apartment smelled worse inside, something lingering under all that talcum powder. She headed down a shag-carpeted hall, calling over her shoulder, 'I just gave her artificial tears, so she should be okay to look at you.'

I asked, quietly, 'Artificial tears?'

She pressed through a door into the master bedroom. An emaciated female form indented the poofy sheets of the enormous canopied bed. Her skin was yellowed, like parchment, and the muscles under her face had atrophied. Medical equipment all around – poles and IVs and monitors. Her left arm dangled off the edge of the mattress. A nightstand held endless pill bottles. Harriet Landreth's eyes pulled over to us, but she couldn't turn her head. Her mouth tensed in a faint smile.

It was stronger in here, that scent, the one that draws vultures across desert miles.

Glenda crossed and picked up Harriet's right hand – dead weight – and set it on a tray holding a computer mouse with a tiny protruding bud. She guided her younger sister's finger to the bud until Harriet blinked twice.

'Hungry, love?' Glenda asked.

Harriet's eyes rolled to a computer screen, and her finger made some minuscule movements. A speaker emitted a loud, synthesized voice, startling me. I CAN'T EAT ANY MORE OF THAT SOUP YOU USE TOO MUCH SALT.

Glenda waved off her sister. 'Then I'll bring you plain chicken broth and you can quit nagging at me with that horrible voice.' She shook her head at me, morbidly amused.

The slow, electronic words issued again from her sister's synthesizer. WILL YOU PUT MY LEFT ARM BACK ON THE MATTRESS IT IS BOTHERING ME.

'You can't feel anything, love.'

PHANTOM PAIN PIN AND NEEDLES I CAN NOT STAND IT.

Glenda circled the bed, picked up the dangling arm, and set it on the sheets next to Harriet's side. As Glenda moved around, picking up dirty cups and plates, I stood in the bustle, overwhelmed and trying not to act it. A cord snaked from the computer monitor, leading to a digital telephone on the nightstand.

'You should have seen this cat on the TV. It jumped and jumped over a ball of yarn and then the Jewish comedian said it was raining cats and cats.' Glenda chuckled. 'Cats and cats.'

THAT SHOW WILL BE THE DEATH OF ME HA HA BAD ENOUGH TO WATCH BUT TO HEAR IT

340

DESCRIBED HAVE MERCY IT IS NOT AS THOUGH I CAN RUN OUT OF HERE.

Glenda waved a hand our way, dismissing us both from consideration, and withdrew, leaving me alone with Harriet.

Those dark pupils tracked over from the computer screen, finding me. Sentient, intelligent eyes, beautiful blue. YOU ARE A FRIEND OF TRIS.

I assumed it was a question. Looking at her, I couldn't bring myself to lie. 'Not a friend, exactly. I'm trying to find her. My name's Nick.'

WHY ARE YOU TRYING TO FIND HER.

I sensed she was angry, but unable to read tone, I felt unmoored. 'My stepfather was killed seventeen years ago. I think she may know something about it.'

I HAVEN'T SEEN TRIS IN YEARS.

A lie, based on what Glenda had told me at the door. It occurred to me that Harriet had only agreed to see me so she could find out what I was up to and notify Tris.

I cleared my throat. 'Do you know where she is? I'd really like to talk to her.'

Her muscle moved in fleeting twitches just beneath the papery skin. WE ARE NOT IN TOUCH.

'It's not just for me,' I said. 'I need to warn her about something.' Those blank eyes stared back at me. 'I think she might want to talk to me, too.'

A long wait as that finger pulsed against the bud. And then, YOU COULD NOT UNDERSTAND THE FIRST THING ABOUT HER.

'I understand more than you realize.'

Harriet's blinks were getting longer. She was having trouble holding her eyes open.

'Can I leave you my phone number to give her if she *does* contact you?'

Beyond her dry lips, her tongue worked, her jaw clicking with agitation. A spider-thread of drool reached down and touched her shirt. YOU CAN DO WHATEVER YOU LIKE.

Her eyes closed and didn't open. Her hand slipped from the keyboard and she shifted slightly, her other arm sliding from the mattress again so the hand and forearm dangled over the edge. I couldn't tell if one of the tubes snaking through the sheets was feeding her air, but the rise and fall of her chest seemed to grow more regular. For a time, I studied that cord running from her computer to the digital telephone, my heart pounding. Then I eased to her bedside.

The computer of course had a massively simplified interface. I touched the tiny bud, nudging the cursor over to the address book icon. Scrolling down, I looked under the Ls. A few Landreth names I didn't recognize. I was disgusted with myself, breathing hard and trying to be quiet. I was terrified that Harriet would rouse and stare up at me with accusing eyes and I would have not a single thing to say for myself. I searched farther down and found a single initial, T. And a phone number. Pulling a pen from the nightstand, I jotted it down on the back of my hand. Using a reverse directory, Induma could generate an address in seconds.

Harriet's breathing took on a slight wheeze. I started for the door, but stopped after a few steps. I walked around to the other side of the bed and lifted her dangling arm. It was unbelievably light, like the wing of a seagull. I laid it gently by her side and tucked the sheet around it.

In the front room, Glenda sat dwarfed in an armchair, watching a dog with its head stuck in a red plastic bucket.

'She doesn't have long now.' Glenda kept her eyes on the TV.

'Maybe Tris'll make it back to see her.'

She scoffed.

Outside, the breeze was hot and smelled sharply of vegetation. I paused on the manicured front lawn, grateful for the openness, the shoved-down horizons, the bobbing palm trees. My chest felt tight and full, like I couldn't get enough air into it.

I stood there a few minutes, just breathing.

44

The phone number sourced to a ground-floor apartment in San Fernando that backed on a French Dip stand and a mechanic's shop with grease puddles and weeds overtaking its cracked-up asphalt. The stale air made my shirt itch, no small feat since I was wearing one of Alejandro's comfortable Dri-FITs, excavated from Induma's coat closet. The heat of the pavement came up through the soles of my sneakers, and a street crew's mess up the block wafted over tar-bitter air.

The numbers had long fallen off the door but their echo remained in the less-faded paint beneath where they'd been nailed. An air conditioner, hung out the window, dripped water and banged away like a jalopy. Competing for dominance, a TV blared – some scripted argument between talk-show participants, their voices fuzzed with static at the edges. I knocked.

A voice, less irritated than run-down, bellowed, 'I'm coming, I'm coming.'

A squat woman in her fifties opened the door, drying her hands on a stained apron, cinched unflatteringly between the bulges of her midsection. She wasn't obese, but thick, spreading with age. Her unwieldy breasts had descended to rest against her stomach. She glanced up at my face and stiffened, her hands freezing in the swirl of fabric.

She flung up a hand to shove ineffectively at her bangs, pasted to her sweaty forehead. Her hair was thinning, so I could see a shine of scalp at her crown. Behind her, a dirty skillet sat on a stovetop, and the place reeked of bacon grease. A rainbow bead curtain, still undulating from her movement, blocked a doorway to her right.

'Oh, sorry,' she said. 'I was expecting someone else.' A patch of eczema had claimed her elbow and made headway up the back of her forearm. She scratched at the white, flaking skin, her nails giving off a sound that made my spine arch.

'Sorry to startle you.'

'I wasn't startled.' She emitted a nervous laugh. There was something familiar in her eyes – not their shape, but the way they creased with her forced, semi-aggressive grin.

'Ms Landreth?'

Her nod reminded me of a squirrel frantically shelling peanuts. 'How did you find me?'

'Through your aunt.'

'Harriet?' Her eyes moistened. 'You saw Harriet?'

'I did. Look, I understand why you're scared—'

'I'm not scared. Why should I be scared?'

'You've moved around a lot. You're hard to find.'

'What are you, the Census Bureau?' She glanced behind me, checking for others. 'What do you want?'

'I want to know about Jane and Gracie Everett. Do you remember them?'

'Of course I remember.' Her hands found a tuft of hair and pulled it around to her temple. She started searching out and breaking off split ends, a repetitive, simian tic. Her hair wasn't long enough for her to see easily, and her pupils were strained so hard to the side it looked painful. The soft flesh of her arms jiggled with the motion. I wondered if she was on speed. 'It was an awful thing. The kind of thing you don't forget.'

I studied the face, looking to recapture that flash of familiarity, but it was gone. One of my friends from night school in Oregon had a baby whom she brought into lecture the next month to show off. I recall how the baby burbled and took on his mother's features for an instant before they vanished back into generic babyness. I found myself straining now to reclaim that same type of satisfying déjà vu.

'You saw the bodies being dumped?' I asked.

'Yeah. I was walking my dog. They pulled over up the street. Didn't see me. It was a dirt lot. I saw two guys. They looked Mexican. Central American, maybe. Anyway, I went home and called the cops.'

It sounded rehearsed – all the requisite beats, well-ordered, as if she'd been running over them in her head for years.

'And you saw Jane over by some trailers several months before?'

But she wasn't biting – 'A *month* or so before.' Her eyes ticked to me, then back to her hair. It was as though she was afraid to look directly at me. 'Look, who *are* you? Why are you asking me questions? Can I see a badge or something?'

'I don't have a badge.'

'Well, then,' she said, and shut the door.

I heard the beads rustle, and a moment later, I sensed a slight swivel of the closed Venetian blinds in the window to my right. I could not afford to wait around and have her call someone. Seeing no other choice, I started back down the walk, the hot breeze lofting the smell of tar into my face. I could feel her stare penetrating my back.

Halfway down the walk, it hit me. Her startled reaction, the creases at the eyes, her high-pitched nervousness and reluctance to look me in the face – she'd recognized me right away. And was terrified I'd recognize her.

Isabel McBride. Bob's Big Boy. Off shift at 1:00 am.

My head bowed, just slightly, and I took a half-step to my right, firming my balance. Seventeen years of assumptions, unraveling. Still, I could feel the eyes behind me, hidden by those Venetian blinds, boring into my back.

I turned. The blinds swiveled again, forming an impenetrable sheet, a child covering his eyes to hide. I rang the bell. There was no answer, just a dread-filled wait, augmented with continued talk-show broiling. I rang again. Waited. Rang again.

Finally the door opened. Jerkily.

'Isabel,' I said.

Despite the deadening heat, she was shaking. 'Nick.'

I said, 'Please talk to me.'

Tears sprang up out of nowhere. Just two, spilling over the brinks of her eyes, sliding in straight tracks down her ruddy face. She jerked her head in a nod.

I followed her into the grease-tinged air, through the chattering rainbow bead curtain. On the squawking TV, Jerry Springer reclaimed his microphone from an overzealous audience member. Across the bottom of the screen, today's caption: ARE YOU MY BABY'S DADDY? Isabel – or Tris – struck the power button as she passed, and we sat on unmatched couches shoved together to form a makeshift sectional. The post-Springer silence seemed so daunting as to be majestic. Through a doorway, I could see a suitcase open on the bedroom floor, the clothes she'd started to throw inside.

I said, 'Are you Isabel or Tris?'

'Tris. I'm Tris. Patricia.' She was back to her hair, eyes crammed to the side, snapping off dry split ends and flicking them to the floor.

I'd rehearsed the tainted fantasy so often in my head since that night. Who knows how many times I'd reinvented Isabel McBride? Added an extra inch or three to her bust, imagined some trick of the tongue, conflated the firm hump of her ass with that of a model, a fling, some woman on the street? Everything possible to make her attractive enough to justify my slipping out that night and leaving Frank open.

She seemed to sense my thoughts. 'Gravity takes over,' she said defensively. 'You lie down, your tits are in your armpits. You'll see. Wait till you hit forty, fifty. Men hide it better but it's no prettier.'

'It's dangerous right now.'

She nodded jerkily. 'I figured it might get that way. The election. I've been careful.' She snorted, nodded at me. 'Not careful enough, I see.'

'Will you tell me what happened?' I asked. 'The real story?'

She looked away, her chin trembling. 'You don't *want* the real story.'

We sat in the silence a moment, then I said, 'You were hired to seduce me? To lure me out of the house?'

'I didn't know that was what it was for. I didn't know why. Money was tight and I had a girl to raise. You weren't half bad-looking, so I said what the hell. Paid better than waitressing. They had me do things. I didn't know.'

'You didn't ask.'

'At first I figured it was some weird rite-of-passage kind of thing. Maybe your dad's friends or something.' A mournful pause. 'No, I didn't ask.'

Every now and then I'd catch glimpses of her old self – the perfect line of teeth, a nuanced movement of her hand, a cord rising in her neck – but they'd vanish almost instantly. It reminded me of those magic childhood stickers that changed images when you tilted them. Now it's Superman, now it's Clark Kent again.

'How'd you know I'd go to Bob's Big Boy that night?' I asked.

'I didn't know anything. They knew you went there every weekend. So they helped get me a job there. You came in my first shift.'

'Who's *they*?'

'I don't know.' She was still shaking. Her nails went back to that patch of dry skin and worked it in a circular motion. White dust fell like dandruff to the carpet. 'I never saw the guy who hired me. He found me through

349

my cousin. My cousin knows people who know people. Everyone has a cousin like that, right? The guy wanted a sexy woman. Experienced, but not a pro. I was. Sexy. Then.'

'You were,' I said, before realizing what a backhanded compliment that was. 'How'd you guys talk?'

'It was all cloak and dagger. I drove to a fire road on Runyon Canyon—'

'At night,' I said. 'You were told to park, turn off the car, the lights, angle the mirrors away, and keep the doors unlocked. He was late. He slid into the backseat. He told you what to do. Where to find me, what I looked like, how to handle me, where to take me. You never saw his face.'

'Yes,' she said, bewildered. 'I guess you've heard the story before.'

'That part.'

'I've been waiting. Seventeen years I've been waiting. For someone to knock on that door. You. Him. And I don't even know who he is.'

'You *never* learned?'

'Do you have any idea what that's like? Never settling in. Keeping an ear to the ground. Waiting for God knows who. Do you have *any idea* what that does to a person?'

'Yeah,' I said. 'I do.'

Her fingers fussed at her shiny scalp, her hair, trembling. She squeezed them hard with her other hand, lowered them into her lap. She spoke again, with a quiet sort of horror. 'I will *never* forgive myself.'

'For what you did to me? To Frank Durant?'

'That was the least of it.' Her voice was hoarse. 'The least of it.'

350

'What else?'

'There were two others. Hired thugs. Tall and dark. Eastern European accents, like bad guys in a movie. Didn't talk much. A week or so after I saw you, they came and said they were sent by him. I was shaken. I saw the thing in the paper about the Secret Service man, and your name. Your mom's. We were just a few years apart, me and your mom.' She leaned forward. 'I swear to God had I known—'

I wanted to keep her on course: 'The hired thugs.'

'They said I had to find someone to take care of my daughter for a few days. They said they'd be back that night, that I'd be paid a lot of money. They said if I wasn't there, they'd find me. I didn't have a choice. I had a little girl to raise.'

Her body continued to shake, almost violently now, as if it were coming apart. But she kept talking. 'They brought me to a house somewhere. I didn't know where I was. Empty, no furniture. The floors were still just poured concrete. There was a woman there, with a newborn. She was still healing. They kept her in a back room, on a bare mattress. I took care of her. Fed her. Washed her. Helped her to the bathroom. She wouldn't let me touch the baby.'

'Grace,' I said. 'Gracie Everett.'

'Right. Gracie.' Her eyes were instantly moist again. A dreadful calm came over her and she stopped trembling and when she spoke again, her voice was even. 'I slept there in the room with them. And early the next morning the men came in and took the baby. The woman screamed and screamed. Hormones on fire. You can't

351

imagine how that is. I thought she'd never stop. She screamed for four hours. I was sobbing, pleading with her. Anything for her to stop. Just to stop.'

Her breathing was shallow, and it made her words breathy. 'They brought the baby back – *Gracie*. They brought Gracie back. And Jane held her and rocked her and said she'd never let them take her away again. Her voice was screamed out. But the men got more and more agitated. I heard them talking on the phone when I came back from getting groceries. They'd taken the baby for another DNA test. I guess there was an earlier one, but they wanted to be sure. They were hyper-paranoid. I guess one of the copies of the first test went missing before. It was a big deal. Something with the Secret Service.'

'How do you know that?'

'I heard one of them say they'd dealt with a leak inside the Service. At first I thought military. But then I remembered the Secret Service guy – sorry, your stepfather – got killed the night I took you out. So you didn't have to be Einstein to do the math.'

I struggled to keep up with it. Frank was the leak. To whom? Or did they mean he was a threat to go public? I wanted to keep her talking. 'And then what happened?'

Tris hugged her stomach and rocked herself a little on the couch. She let out a low wail which sounded weird since she was no longer crying or shaking.

I wanted to loathe her, but I couldn't. She'd signed on for her own fate, sure, but she'd been crushed by the machinery of this thing as much as I had, one compromised choice at a time.

I said, softly, 'What happened next?'

Her voice was quiet, preternaturally calm. 'Those guys were on edge waiting for the DNA results. They took the baby away from her. Kept her in the other room. Jane was too weak to get up, but I tried to plead with them. One of the guys even hit me. They thought she'd be more . . . docile without her baby.' She whispered hoarsely, her face glazed. 'They kept the baby away from her. Two days. I had to go in and feed her, Gracie, hold her when they got tired of her crying. But I couldn't get her to stop. The pressure to get her to stop, it was awful. Then they kept her alone in a crib. I spent most of my time with Jane, listening to her weep. Just *weeping*. We could hear the baby crying through the walls. That baby was crying and crying and Jane's breasts were leaking milk through her shirt. It went *on* and *on*. There was nothing I could do. She pleaded with me, but there was nothing I could do. Her breasts got engorged and they were leaking and they were crying in different rooms, both of them, all the time. It was the most horrible thing I've ever experienced.'

Her eyes grew glassy and she stopped rocking herself.

I was surprised at how weak my voice sounded. 'Go on. Please.'

Tris held herself perfectly still. When she blinked, more tears fell down her cheeks. 'One night the men came in. The DNA test. Whatever it was, it came back bad news. They took Jane. And they helped her up – she was so weak – and they helped her to the door, then outside. I looked through the curtains. I saw them put her in a dark car. They talked to someone, but I couldn't see who

353

because the windows were tinted. The baby was crying in the other room. Then they came back in and I sat across the room, like I hadn't been watching. They went into the other room. And then the baby stopped crying. They went back outside and I saw them put something in the trunk of the dark car, and the dark car drove off. I ran into the other room and the crib was empty. It was empty. I sat down on the floor. I heard them come in behind me. I thought they were going to kill me. But they told me to go home and not to tell anyone. That someone would be in contact with me. And sure enough, my cousin called me the next day. And it was the same meeting, up Runyon Canyon. I was so scared, but I went because they knew who I was and I had a little girl to raise. And that man got in the back of my car and I thought he was going to shoot me, but instead, he said I had to tell the story to the press, about the bodies being dumped. And if I did, and if I stuck to that story with the cops and the press, that nothing would happen to me or my little girl. And I did. I never told anyone otherwise. Until right now.'

'They're coming after you,' I said. 'As we speak.'

Her look held the some comprehensive defeat I saw in Homer's face once he was a few drinks in. But also, a glimmer of something else. Relief, maybe. 'Let 'em catch me. I don't care anymore.'

'How about your daughter?'

'My daughter hasn't talked to me in seven years. Last I heard she was in Costa Rica.'

'Did they pay you?'

She looked at the blank TV screen for a long time,

then she nodded, a jerk of her head that looked like a shudder. Her nails went again to her eczema, that same horrible rasping. 'I don't believe in heaven or hell. But I'm scared of what's waiting for me.'

'Then do something.'

'I've forgotten how. You get touched by something like this, it goes into you. You can never get back to normal. I wouldn't even know where to start.'

She'd spoken my darkest fear. I could barely bring myself to face her. 'Get in touch with the man who hired you.' I needed her to do it not just for me, but for herself, for what it meant about keeping something safe, deep-buried where it couldn't be rooted out and ground into dust. 'He and his men are looking for you. It can't be hard to get the word out to them.'

'No,' she said. 'No way.'

I couldn't find my voice. I just looked at her.

She hugged herself and rocked a bit more. 'I could call my cousin. Maybe he still has a contact who knows someone who has a phone number on the guy. He's good like that, my cousin. But say I reach this guy. What am I supposed to say?'

'Tell him someone contacted you. Someone who already knew the whole story. You need to meet him. To talk, figure out a plan. He's the one who told you to meet me at the pitcher's mound, right?'

'Yeah. He said you were a baseball player and that I should take you there.'

'So tell him to meet you where he told you to take me that night. But don't say it's the pitcher's mound – if it's the right guy, he'll remember. Tonight at midnight.'

'What are you going to do?'

'Watch from a distance. See who he is.'

'Then what?'

'Then I'll know.'

'Will knowing help?'

'Probably not. But I can put the information in the hands of someone who knows how to use it.'

'These are dangerous men.'

'I'll disappear.'

'You won't know how hard that wears on you until it's too late.'

Her eyes filled again, but she blinked her way back from the edge. She grabbed a lock of hair and went back to breaking off split ends, then she threw it aside. '*Okay*. I'll call my cousin, send out the pigeon. Tonight at midnight, meet at the place he told me to bring you. Who knows if the guy'll get the message, but I'll try. That it?'

'It's time to move again. Out of town this time. I'll pay for—'

'*No*. No. I won't have you pay for anything. But with my aunt . . . how long do I have to stay gone?'

'Follow the news. You'll know if it's safe to come back.'

I got up and walked to the door. She followed at my elbow. 'I didn't know. I didn't know what any of it would lead to. You think I'm awful. You think I'm horrible.'

'No,' I said.

She grasped my elbow at the door, gently, as if afraid of setting me off. She was a woman accustomed to men with tempers. She said, 'I just needed to make a little extra money. I had no idea where it would go. And then I didn't have a choice. I was terrified. They threatened me. I had a little girl to raise.'

I thought, *So did Jane Everett.*

I gave her a little nod and she stayed in the doorway, watching me leave.

45

S till raw from Tris's tale, I crossed the parking lot, heading toward the Brentwood Inn. Behind me, midday traffic blasted by on Sunset, a head-numbing rotation of squealing brakes and bleating horns and rap music throbbing from open windows. Alan Lambrose had called with the not-so-covert location for my meet with Caruthers, the glorified motel a few blocks west of the 405. I'd left the Jag around the corner in front of a condo building to keep Induma's plates out of sight.

I found the room toward the back of the humble, single-story sprawl, and knocked. The door opened to reveal Alan, in full bowtie glory, and another aide I didn't recognize but who shared the same debate-team sheen. An athletic man, but he belonged to the political realm, not to the Service. James, the agent I'd first met in Caruthers's conference room, stood at the back of the room. His meaty features fixed on me for a moment, unpleased, then he removed his hand from the stock of his pistol and returned his gaze dutifully to the windows. Caruthers sat in a chair before a narrow stone fireplace, wrapping up a call. He stood, throwing the still-open cell phone to Alan, and greeted me warmly as Alan murmured closing sentiments into the receiver.

Caruthers looked wiped out – I imagined six flights a day could do that to you – and his jaw worked the nicotine gum in a sawing motion, almost side-to-side.

I glanced nervously at James – I didn't like his being here – and Caruthers took the hint. He nodded at the others, 'Give us some privacy?'

The athletic aide went out front and James stepped onto the tiny back patio. A man at each visible exit. The closing sliding glass door seemed to suction the noise of traffic from the room.

Alan was in a scramble in the kitchenette, bringing a cup of coffee to the little table by Caruthers's chair. 'Sorry, Senator. Fred forgot to bring the Sweet'N Low.'

'Oh, for fuck's sake, Alan, any fake sugar'll do.'

Alan set down the coffee and withdrew to the bedroom, already jabbing at his BlackBerry. I remembered Frank telling me that they brought their own food for the principal wherever they went to reduce the risk of poisoning.

Caruthers ran a hand through his renegade hair, and it settled back however it wanted. He muttered, 'Sweet'N Low,' with disgust, then added, 'They like to believe you're more high-maintenance than you are. It makes them feel more important. What kind of sweetener. How many packets. What news channel the TV is tuned to when you check into a hotel. You have to be careful or you'll start believing it.'

'It does get tiring.'

He laughed heartily, and I felt that I'd accomplished

something. Then his green eyes grew serious. 'You're all right?'

'So far.'

'Have you found out anything on Jane Everett's daughter?'

'I have to tell you a story,' I said, 'about your opponent.'

He read my face and knew not to press. Instead, he sat and gestured to the facing chair. I caught him up on everything I'd learned since we'd spoken. When I got to Tris's story, his hand formed a fist, and he pushed the top knuckle against his lips, as if reining in fury. How the baby stopped crying. The trunk of the sedan closing. The empty crib. I told it as Tris had, and the words held the same horror. When I finished, Caruthers shook his head in disbelief, and his brilliant green eyes were filmed with tears.

He sipped his coffee. His cheeks glittered. I stared into the fireplace. Propane flames licking at a cast-concrete log.

He retrieved a handkerchief from a pocket and blew his nose. Then he folded it thoughtfully and returned it. 'I bet Bilton didn't even know any of this. All he knew was that there was this volunteer staffer who he spent some quality time with, maybe she was starting to make a fuss, and that was it. Bilton had people to handle this for him, and they did.'

'So that makes him less responsible?'

His shock had hardened into anger. 'Hardly. But Nick, think about who was working on this for him.'

'Charlie Jackman.'

'And who did Charlie bring this information to?'

I was silent.

'That's right. Frank knew about Jane Everett and the pregnancy, and he didn't come to me. He didn't go to the authorities. He didn't go to the press. And you know damn well why that is.' He let the remark hang for a moment. 'The more you poke at this, the more it all falls into place. You sure you want that?'

'I want to know the whole story.'

'We never get the whole story.'

'Maybe not. But there's something you can help with.'

'Of course. Anything.'

'Tris said she overheard the hired guns saying that there'd been a leak in the Service. But that doesn't really make sense. This whole thing originated with Charlie and the California State Police. Frank caught wind of it, sure, but saying there was a leak in the Secret Service implies it turned into a Service operation.'

Caruthers blinked twice, rapidly. I watched him, watched him closely. The mighty brow furrowed. 'Clearly, the Service was involved more than we'd like to think.' Caruthers took a deep breath. Pinched his eyes closed. The twisting wrinkles made his lids look like little pinwheels. He sighed. 'Goddamnit.' Then he looked up. 'Nick . . .' A quick glance to the door. 'I have to tell you something you're not going to want to hear.'

'There seems to be a lot of that going around.'

His face softened with sympathy. 'I've had my people digging into this. This morning, they found one of the men who held Jane Everett. With the stuff you told me, the picture pretty much resolves. Don't think I like this.'

'Because of Frank?'

361

'Frank's dead, son. I was hoping to shield you. Your stepfather was one of a handful of decent men I've known in a lifetime. I wanted to see if there was some way through this where you didn't have to lose that.'

I stared at him blankly.

'I've seen it before and I've seen it since. Someone gets the right opportunity—'

I said, 'No.'

'—or the right leverage—'

'Not Frank.'

He said, 'Jane Everett was becoming a problem for Bilton. He put Charlie on her to try to control her, keep her off the radar. But Charlie realized there was a payday in it. It looks like he enlisted Frank to see if I'd be interested in buying an ultrasound and paternity test that nailed Bilton. But they decided Bilton would pay more to keep it covered up. Frank pulled in more Service men to make that happen. That's as far as we got before you walked in that door.'

'So what do you think happened from there?'

'From what you've just told me, I think Frank saw where it was headed and couldn't go through with it. He was the leak in the Service the thugs were talking about. Charlie was in a panic, but he was smart. He put the documents somewhere that they'd go wide if anything ever happened to him. And he disappeared to let Bilton's soldiers and the agents clean up what they needed to on their respective ends of the deal. That cleanup started with Frank and ended with Jane and Grace.'

My face felt numb. I did my best to keep drawing him out. 'Frank would *never* have gone along with blackmail, not even for a minute, not even against a politician he despised. And he sure as hell would never have used the Service for an extortion scheme.'

Caruthers leaned forward, grasped my forearm. 'I know that's what you have to believe.' He stood, agitated, paced a tight circle around his chair, the light through the copper-tinged blond hair that, along with his pronounced nose, had landed him the call sign *Firebird*. 'I was going to say I can't imagine how painful this is for you, son. But I can – it's painful as hell for me.' He shook his head, sat down again. After a pause, he reached once again for my forearm. 'It's the only answer that makes sense.'

The shock cleared slowly, by degrees, like a lifting fog, revealing my stone-cold distrust. Caruthers was so close I caught a waft of Nicorette when he breathed. A bead of sweat clung to his hairline. I pulled my arm free.

Caruthers said, 'We're talking about murder, now, Nick. Two murders – hell, *five*. This is no longer about politics and spin. It's about decency. Even if he wasn't involved in the particulars, this happened on Bilton's watch. We can't let a man like that sit in the Oval Office.'

'No,' I said. 'We can't.'

'You've got my word I will make Andrew Bilton pay for what he's done.' He caught James's eye through the glass, gestured him inside. The agent came instantly. Caruthers told him, 'I had to disclose to Nick details from this morning's interview.'

James hesitated a moment, then said, 'That should have remained classified, Senator.'

'It was his *stepfather*. He deserves to know. He's been a

part of this as much as anyone else. And he has some information that we need to get into the right hands.'

James nodded. 'Anything he gives us I'll guard as closely as matters of national security. Even from the Service.'

Caruthers said, 'Thank you, Agent Brown.'

My attention skipped, a rock on the surface of my memory – *James, Agent Brown, James Brown, Godfather of Soul* – and landed on the line Kim Kendall had overheard when she'd called Mr Pager: *Godfather's with Firebird, so all's clear.*

My head roared but my face could show nothing. I'd stumbled into the lion's den, now could I get out alive? A clumsy excuse and a rushed exit would tip my hand. Should I make a break for it? That athletic aide was conveniently out front, guarding the exit. The sliding door was less than five strides away, but the tall fence penning in the patio would take too long to get over with Brown on my heels.

Agitated, I picked at a thumbnail, stopped when I saw Caruthers taking note. If I sat here much longer, they'd read me.

I said, 'I think I have to throw up.'

I rose. James Brown did not step back to allow me more room. A bead of sweat clung to the edge of his sideburn, though his face was as impassive as I hoped mine remained.

Walking down the hall, I could hear a semi barreling by on the freeway, blaring someone out of its lane. Behind me, Caruthers and Brown conferred in hushed, urgent voices. I stepped into the bathroom, locked the door, and slid open the little window, wincing at its squeak. Stepping up onto the toilet, I squirmed out.

I was at the east side of the building – a few feet of concrete and then the fence. Alan was in the bedroom, James back with Caruthers, and the political aide was just out of view around the corner – I could hear him pacing and talking on his cell phone. I scaled the fence as silently as possible and sprinted to the car.

I drove as fast as I dared. If I got pulled over, I'd find myself back in the system, and right now, that wasn't a safe place to be. I didn't have a phone number or I might have called ahead, but part of me needed to hear it in person. I had forty minutes to clear my head.

Still, pulling over in front of the house, I took a moment, closed my eyes. I pictured Frank the first time I ever met him, in our kitchen, too big for the little chair. Hand on my mom's knee. That stupid Garfield clock with its clicking eyes and tail. English Leather and Maxwell House. *There will always be a place for your father in this house.*

I climbed out, my steps heavy up the walk.

No.

I rang the bell.

Not Frank.

A moment later, the door creaked back and Lydia Flores peered out at me. Her face lightened – a break from the crossword puzzles and the cheesy soaps and the porcelain cats and the dead family history depicted in photos on the unused piano and the too-high fence penning it all in, the final insult to a lifetime of injuries.

'Nick,' she said. 'Hello.' She pushed the screen aside

and her expression shifted when she saw my face. 'More questions for your article?'

I blurted, 'Whose campaign?'

'I beg your pardon?'

My words were a jumble. I couldn't figure out how to convey what needed to be conveyed, or what was riding on it. 'The campaign – did Jane work – who was she working for?'

Lydia shook her head, concerned by me, and also taken aback. 'Jasper Caruthers, of course.'

46

Gunning along the freeway, I heard my crappy phone ring. My hand chased it around the passenger seat, then I answered.

Caruthers said, 'Nick.'

The voice caused sweat to tingle across my shoulders. Blood rushed to my face, the cut in my cheek aching again.

'Where to from here?' he asked. I didn't answer, so he said, 'I'd imagine you're not after money.'

'I'm after the truth.'

'And getting it out? Think of the ramifications. You want Andrew Bilton back in office? The world is at stake and he's spent the last four years grabbing his ankles for the special interests.'

'Yeah, but I'm not holding evidence of *his* crimes.'

'Come over. We've got plenty.'

'He didn't kill Jane and Gracie Everett. Charlie and Mack Jackman. Or my stepfather.'

'Baseless claims.'

'Then why are you calling me?'

'I want you to go back to your life, Nick. But with peace this time. Nothing hanging over you. At least give me the opportunity to try to talk some sense into you.'

'You killed your own baby. You want to talk to me about sense?'

'Son, trust me, you're not ready for this game.'

'Don't call me *son*, Senator.'

'Nick, we don't want to do this. I'll erode your credibility so hard your head'll spin. Think about your past. Your suspicious involvement in Frank's death. A conspiracy theorist with an ax to grind with the Secret Service? I'll have you brought in and once you're in the jaws of the system, you'll get chewed up faster than you can say "Scooter Libby", and I'll sail to two terms.'

'I have evidence.'

'We've dealt with forged documents before. This'll get killed before you can blink. Look what happened to Dan Rather, and, Nick, you're a far cry from Dan Rather. My team won't permit me to get sullied by a false story concocted by a man on the run from the law. There's no fax-by-night solution, not in this day and age. It's a long way from a questionable document to the front page, with plenty of interference. I have editors at all the newspapers. I have people who own all the conglomerates. I have disaster-response teams and crisis managers and reputation polishers and flak-catchers. I've got emergency funds with more digits than the inflation in Ecuador. You set this mouse loose in the labyrinth and we'll see who knows this game.'

'Okay,' I said.

'It's not about information. It's about who's *holding* it. No one will believe what you have to say. You're nobody they'll listen to, Nick.'

'So much for a transparent campaign, huh?'

He'd exhausted himself and now just sounded drained. 'Nick, it's complicated. It's all complicated.'

'Not when you're a nobody, it's not.' I rolled down the window and flipped the phone out. In the rear-view, I saw the pieces bouncing at different heights, pursuing the rear bumper like left-behind crickets.

I reached Santa Monica and pulled into a gas station. I paid cash to fill up and found a new brand of prepaid cell phone on the rack behind the counter. The minutes plan sucked, but my cell phones had shorter shelf lives than Hollywood marriages. I added to the counter a convenience-store-priced box of plastic Ziploc bags.

Sitting in the car as the pump ran, I called Callie and asked her to conference in Steve at the office. After some hesitations and an accidental hang-up, all three of us were on the line.

I said, 'It's the other candidate.'

Callie – '*Caruthers?*'

'Jane Everett worked on his campaign. He got her pregnant. He had them killed.'

'Who did the killing?' Steve asked.

'People who worked for him.' What else could I say? Mr Pager? Two Eastern Europeans? The answer was likely whoever was in the dark sedan that drove away with Jane Everett, but I didn't have time to explain all that. If Tris's message got through, I'd find out at midnight. On the Glendale High pitcher's mound.

Steve's voice was muffled. 'They just put out a city-wide BOLO on you. Your face is all over. I guess the public is willing to believe anyone's a terrorist now.'

'What are you going to do?' Callie asked.

I said, 'I'm not sure yet.'

'Will I see you again?'

'I hope so.'

'You're not going to run?'

I could hear her breathing over the line, the click of the gas meter running up cents and dollars, the wax and wane of passing traffic. I said, 'Not this time.'

The pump clicked off. I said goodbye and hung up.

A few minutes later, I eased up that quiet residential slope in Santa Monica Canyon where I'd met Caruthers on his jog. The houses abutted the street – small setbacks, frosted windows, and abbreviated front steps. I parked right beside the spot where Caruthers and I had talked, and grabbed a Ziploc baggie, and a pen from the glove box. When I climbed out, the thud of my closing door echoed off the aloof façades.

I walked over to the gutter and crouched. There it was, preserved as I'd hoped. A beige dot, stuck to the mailbox post. Caruthers's nicotine gum, frozen where he'd thrown it. Using the pen, I pried the piece of gum off into the baggie and sealed it.

Driving back to Induma's, I tried to listen to the radio, but all talk was on politics. A mediocre Senator claimed the moral high ground after his opponent addressed a female reporter as 'honey'. A House Rep pleaded for us to Vote for Change. Someone wanted to tax cigarettes to pay for gasoline, or gasoline to pay for levees. Finally, I opted for silence. Pulling over a few blocks from Induma's house, I wanded down the Jag but found no transmitters. It was the back end of dusk as I scaled the neighbor's fence and hurried through Induma's back yard. I liked coming here, as I liked Callie's kitchen and Homer's tunnel and the other little nooks of warmth I'd carved out of the insanity of the past week. Seven nights ago I'd been dragged off the floor of my condo and hustled onto that Black Hawk. Seven nights, but to me, it felt like a third lifetime.

When she opened the back door, I held up the baggie, letting the chewed ball of gum swing.

She said, 'You know, some guys bring flowers.'

'It's Caruthers's.'

I watched the wheels turn behind her dark, intelligent eyes, and then she blinked once, long, and said, 'DNA sample.'

'You can get one from gum, right?'

'I've heard you can.'

She stepped back and I came in and the house smelled of caramelized onions. We stood just inside, facing each other like nervous prom dates.

'I just got the bone-chip analysis back,' she said. 'The sample in your cheek matched to Charlie Jackman. I have the report upstairs.'

'Can you run one more analysis?'

'Against the person on the paternity report? Unidentified Male?'

'Unidentified Male,' I said.

'You've been busy.'

'Me and him both.'

'Yes, I can get the analysis run. To determine if the same person who chewed that gum fathered that child.'

She walked back to the couch and I followed her. Pillow back in her lap, she took in the update.

When I finished, she ran her hands through her dark hair. She took a deep breath and tilted her head to the ceiling as she exhaled. 'Caruthers is the better candidate for President. You know it and I know it. And you have something sure to stop him.'

We sat with the weight of that for a moment. It seemed like a stupendous choice, but it wasn't much of a choice at all.

Induma's pragmatism finally got the better of her. 'How are you planning to get this out in a way so the public gets onto it?'

'Can you get the DNA results back by Thursday morning?'

'Why Thursday mor—?' Comprehension flickered across her face. 'Oh no, Nick. The *debate*? You can't be . . . ?'

'Town-hall format, remember?'

'The debate's a farce, Nick, like everything else. The questions are all vetted, and the people asking them'll be screened six times over. They're only gonna let VIPs and preselected demographic types even get inside the building. All that on top of the fact that the Secret Service, which'll be *de facto* running the event, will be on the lookout for you.' She shook her head, her dark hair swaying. 'There no way for you to get the ultrasound inside Royce Hall without being seen.'

'Well,' I said, 'there is one way.'

She studied me, an eyebrow arched with curiosity. But she didn't ask. Instead, she said, 'I thought you were going to disappear, mail this in, let someone else handle it.'

I looked over at that sandalwood Buddha, still laughing in the alcove. My throat was dry.

I said, 'There's no one left to handle it.'

The enormity of the challenge sat between us, fearsome and overwhelming. But we started to talk through my plan, one step at a time. Induma brought back the gear I needed from her garage-workshop and rigged it to her satisfaction. Nightfall came shortly, but neither she nor I moved to turn on a lamp. Maybe we were too distracted by what we were contemplating, but more likely, a part of us welcomed the dark. These were unsafe ideas, better murmured in unlit rooms where they were no more than words without owners, where we were faceless shadows on a couch.

Suddenly, Induma's silhouette stiffened. With alarm, I looked over my shoulder, following her gaze, and through the front windows, I saw the band of light that had sprung into existence, illuminating the street end of her walk. Something had tripped the motion sensor down there by the curb. Gnats pinged around in the emptiness between the waist-high bamboo lining the concrete path. We watched, breathless.

A pair of men in suits emerged from the dark of the street, piercing the cold white glow.

Agents. I recognized them from when I'd had that kid run my credit card at Starbucks.

The high-tech lights blinked on in succession, broadcasting their approach.

Induma half stood, one knee on the couch. We were frozen. Their voices came audible as they stepped onto the porch.

The doorbell rang, breaking whatever spell had paralyzed us.

Induma hissed, 'Go.'

'I don't want to leave y—'

'They came up the front walk – they're just here to poke around and harass me. Believe me, I can handle this. But you need to go now or we both run out of options.'

I started for the rear door, hesitated.

Induma said, fiercely, 'If they catch you here, it's over.'

The doorbell rang again.

I scrambled out the back. Someone – another agent – was fussing with the latch, trying to open the side gate. I sprinted across the lawn, vaulted the boxwood hedge, and skidded down the canal enslopement, water seeping through my shoes.

As quietly as possible, I sloshed the length of four houses, ducking footbridges, dodging sleeping ducks with their heads turned to rest on their backs. A flashlight beam played briefly in Induma's backyard, but no one crossed the barrier to check the canal. I misjudged my proximity to a cluster of mallards and they exploded up in a spray of water and pinfeathers, scaring me senseless. I bolted up onto someone's deck and cut through an easement overgrown with foxtails.

Induma's house was no longer visible, but still I crept through front yards to avoid stepping out into the open. The Jag was where I'd left it, in the shadows between streetlights. I drove away, forcing myself not to speed. My hands shook as I called my mom. Steve answered.

I said, 'They're closing the net. I had to warn you they might come—'

He cut me off. 'Yeah, Janice, she can't talk right now. We've got some people here asking about her son.'

He hung up.

I pulled over and sat in the car, breathing hard. Caruthers's men were beating the bushes, cutting down my options, forcing me to keep on the run where I'd be likely to make a mistake. I had to find somewhere to bed down until everything blew open. But I had nowhere left to go.

Except back where it all started.

I blended in with the slip-covered furniture, breathing the familiar air, becoming a part of this house that had become a part of me. The walls echoed with memories. Sitting in the armchair of the otherwise empty living room, sheltered by this structure that had sheltered me as a child, I closed my eyes, and in the sweet musk of dust and rotting wood, past became present and present past. Here Frank had embraced me and called us a family. Here he'd bled to death in my arms. Here I sat, waiting to duplicate my walk of seventeen years ago, from back door to pitcher's mound.

I rose.

It was time to meet Frank's killer.

47

In the dark on the pitcher's mound, I breathed in the smells of my youth. Damp grass, rosin dust, and the vintage blend of infield dirt – silt, sand, and red clay. It seemed inconceivable that I'd played on these grounds, that I'd lost my virginity on this very spot. I hadn't been back to Glendale High, not since that night.

I was waiting in the great wide open. Given that everyone knew what cards I was playing, my strategy had changed. Mr Pager would have been long tipped off that I was the enemy. If he came here expecting Tris Landreth and saw me instead, he'd be unable to resist confronting me, finding out where I'd stashed the evidence, and killing me. Or, he'd just shoot me from a distance. That would render my plan less effective.

In right field, a sprinkler chopped away, going it alone. I couldn't see the streams, just the moist gleam of the darkness over there. I thought about my first glimpse of Isabel McBride on the mound, the breeze plastering her sundress against her contoured form. How different she was now. How different we all were.

My shoes, and pants from the knee down, were still damp from the canal. I was wearing a jacket I'd bought earlier, but it wasn't for comfort alone. Aside from some white-noise traffic and the staccato beat of the sprinkler, the school was quiet. Desolate, even. A few distant streetlights. The buildings, flat blocks against a moonless sky. The glow of my cell phone showed *12:18 am*. Mr Pager, true to form, was fashionably late. Scouting me out this very moment. Crosshairs leveled at my head perhaps, or maybe he was placing a call to two Eastern European gentlemen with a penchant for inquiry. I tried to relax, to let the cool breeze blow through my clothes and cleanse me. I'd been lured to this place, seventeen years ago, to avoid Frank's killer. And now I'd come back to face him.

I sensed movement at the fringe of visibility, shadow against shadow, and then a form resolved. Circling like a shark, head turned watchfully not to me, but to the darkness beyond. I was not a perceived threat. Painstakingly, he drew closer, until I recognized the bearing, and then at last, the pale, lean face.

He stepped forward and stopped, about halfway to home plate. The Boogeyman in a dark suit. His hands were shoved in his pockets, and I noted the bulge in the fabric.

Wydell spread his arms as if to say, *here I am*. Then he put his hands back in his pockets. 'Without evidence, you've got nothing. Which brings us to the question at hand.'

'Or the questions before that,' I said.

'Which are?'

'Sever?'

'Sever doesn't know anything. He's a good soldier.'

'The guys who guarded Jane Everett?'

'Hired hands. Bulgarian operatives, Cold-War discards looking for work.'

'There are Bulgarian operatives?'

'You bet your ass. It's an ugly world.'

'Uglier by the minute. What happened to them?'

'One had an accident. One bought a boat and drifted off. You'll never find him. Least I haven't been able to.'

'You must have had more help inside the Service. Besides the Godfather.'

'Brown?' Wydell smirked. 'Caruthers still has an inner core, sure. Five, six agents. They're loyal. They view you as a threat. They don't need to know anything else.'

I pictured those agents who'd come striding up Induma's walk earlier this evening, how their blank expressions and firm posture conveyed a certain assurance of purpose, a freedom from uncertainty.

'But you still don't get it,' Wydell continued. 'This isn't about Caruthers and some agents. This is the party apparatus. Do you have any idea how many defense contracts and subsidy deals rest on his *not* getting knocked off the ticket? What happened seventeen years ago? No one *cares*. No one even knows the whole story. Not even Caruthers.'

I thought about Caruthers's tears when I'd told him what had happened to Jane and Gracie. Though I believed nothing else about him, his grief in that moment was undeniable. He'd never known precisely how it had gone down. He'd been well-cushioned by plausible deniability, insulated all these years by the people protecting him. Somehow, that made it worse.

Wydell said, 'That's how it gets done. Everyone holds just one piece of the mosaic.'

'Except you.'

He withdrew a pistol from his pocket and held it contemplatively, not aiming at me. 'And now you.'

I constructed a story from the muddle, as I had so many times before. Except this time, it wasn't a story. I said, 'You were on Caruthers's protection detail back then. You found out I was trying to talk to Callie about Frank's death, so you flew two agents in from some shit field office, work-a-day agents who wouldn't mind having a few paid days in Los Angeles. They were willing to take my life away without even knowing why.'

'They *saved* your life, Nick. Think about the alternative.'

'You hired Tris Landreth. And Kim Kendall seventeen years later. You met them up Runyon Canyon. You left the film slip in my locker at the gym tipping me to Mack's address. Then you assigned Sever to sit outside the apartment. He didn't know Mack was already dead inside. You watched from the neighboring roof, the rifle grenade locked and loaded for when I showed up. As soon as you saw that I found the planted Polaroid of Bilton and Jane—'

'You know how many of those things I left lying around that apartment for you to find? You *stepped* on one in the bedroom.'

'I hear doctoring Polaroids is tough.'

'Try getting eighteen-year-old filmpacks, to start with.'

'You planted a bug in my truck, then told me about it so I'd trust you, so I'd ask for you if I got tangled up or taken in. You're the one who sprung me from custody, knowing I'd run to Caruthers.'

'And run you did.'

We stood in the faint mist from the faraway sprinkler.

'You drove the dark sedan that the Bulgarians put Jane Everett into. And Gracie in the trunk.'

He wet his lips and looked at me with those dull, thoughtful eyes. The wind lifted a flap of his neat gray hair into a perfect float over his ear. 'We didn't know about the baby – the father, I mean – until late in the game. If she'd come to Vice President Caruthers earlier, we would've been able to work something out. But she was angry that he'd moved on. What did she expect? You've seen June, for Christ's sake. But Jane Everett' – he shook his head, exasperated, a tourist whose wife won't stop shopping – 'this little girl had delusions. Hormones – you've seen how they get when they're pregnant. She dropped this thing in his lap at the start of her third trimester. There was a scene up at El Encanto – I barely got her out of the lobby before June checked in.'

'Jane got angrier,' I said. 'Made demands. You were trying to work it out with her, but she was getting impatient, unmanageable. Somehow it got back to Bilton's camp that there could be an opportunity there. Everything looked good until Charlie took point on it for Bilton. Dug up the dirt. Jane Everett, scorned lover, was more than happy to give Charlie what she had. Ultrasound. Paternity test. But instead of bringing it to his boss, Charlie brought it to Frank, wanting to make a little coin. But Frank wasn't buying.'

For all my assertiveness, the statement hung in the air like a question.

'No,' Wydell said. 'He wasn't. He came to Caruthers. It

380

never would have occurred to Frank I was already working on containing her.' I didn't confuse it with remorse, but the regret was audible.

I took a moment, the night air stinging my eyes, my breath clean and crisp in my lungs. 'Frank assumed Caruthers would want to handle it decently.' I saw Wydell smirk at my last word, but I continued, 'But since Frank told you guys about the ultrasound and paternity test, you learned that Jane Everett was putting together evidence. And that told you it was a problem that wasn't gonna go away on its own. You needed to shut her down permanently. And once it got to that, Frank made it clear he wasn't willing to play ball. And since he knew the stakes, he refused to give up his source, because he knew you'd kill Charlie too.'

I pictured Frank on his car phone in the garage, talking about the threat to Caruthers. A political threat.

I said, 'So you shot him.'

Wydell looked at me, an odd blend of contempt and respect. 'Frank was no saint. He just wasn't as bad as the rest of us. He wasn't going to the press or riding off to rescue poor Jane Everett. He wanted it to go away. Just like Caruthers did.'

'But Caruthers took steps.'

'I didn't go to the house to kill Frank. I wanted to know who his source was, sure, but I went to get him alone, to have one more chance to convince him he couldn't be neutral on this. Stakes were way too high.'

'Right. When you murdered Jane and the baby, Frank would've gone public. You had to clear the way by getting him out of it.'

381

'He had a choice. Right up to the end. But Frank was the stalwart type, duty, all that. He couldn't see the bigger picture.'

'The bigger picture,' I said.

'That's right. Jane Everett and her baby, they didn't fit into it.'

'No one's life is worth more than anyone else's.' My words sounded familiar, then I realized I was quoting Frank.

'Of course not. But some people's lives take precedence.'

'So that night?' I asked. 'You had Tris lure me out so I'd shut off the alarm.'

He seemed genuinely sympathetic. 'Oh, no. Just to get you out of there. I knocked at the back door. Frank let me in himself. You've been living with *that* all these years?'

A tear obscured my right eye but wouldn't fall. I saw Wydell, warped, through the glassy veil. 'You just didn't want a witness.'

'You were a *kid*, Nick. I couldn't talk with you there. And I didn't want to have to kill you, too, if it came to it.'

'You were there when I got home.'

'Yes. A nice, friendly visit. Once he saw it was me, he even set the gun down on the coffee table. I wanted to resolve it with him. Come to an understanding. But we couldn't.'

'He wouldn't say who had the master docs.'

Wydell shook his head regretfully. 'He was bleeding out, but he wouldn't say. It took much longer than I'd planned.'

'I thought killing him wasn't the plan.'

The reel played in my head, familiar from countless screenings. The bang of the garage's side door against the outside wall. Frank pointing not at the key in the alarm pad as I'd always thought, but at the open door beyond. The dying utterance he'd choked out. *W? W-why?* Not a word, not a question. But the first syllable of the name he'd been trying to tell me: *Wydell*.

I said, 'By the time you got Jane to give up Charlie's name, he'd vanished. And didn't reemerge until a few months ago to make the senator a discreet business proposal.'

The sprinkler stopped abruptly, the relative silence broken by my breathing.

Wydell gestured at me with the gun. 'So you're pretty fucked here, Nick. Every agency's on alert. But I can present a solution to you. Get this mess cleaned up.'

'That's what you're good at, I suppose.'

'Yes, I am. And right now, I'm your only good option.'

'Well,' I said, 'not the *only* good one.' I spread my arms, like a scarecrow, or Jesus Christ in a windbreaker. 'Check me,' I said, 'for a wire.'

'I could rip that thing off you. Torch the recording.'

'It's a live feed. To – as you types like to say – a secure location.'

'How about I hold you down and start breaking things until you give instructions to whoever's on the other end?'

I reached under my shirt and tugged the wire free. Then I broke it in half and threw it toward the outfield. 'Point of no return,' I said.

His lips set with amusement and he scratched that

crooked nose with a single long finger. 'You're still a stupid kid. With all my years in the game, you really think I'd give you a chance to record me?' He tugged a little black box free from the back pocket of his pants and held it up. 'Pink-noise generator.'

I unzipped my jacket, let the flap fall, revealing a device of my own. 'Pink-noise *filter*.'

I wished Induma could have seen the look on his face. Her gadget did look pretty impressive hanging there. I watched Wydell's expression change. His forehead lined, and then his cheeks quivered. His perfect posture didn't alter, but his head canted forward an inch or two.

He came at me fast, fist laced around the gun, swinging to break teeth. Sidestepping him, I grabbed his wrist and snapped his elbow forward until it locked and then bowed the wrong way. It didn't snap. It just yielded with the gentle crackle of a fresh sprig bending. I rode his shoulder down, driving his face onto the pitching rubber.

His breathing was tight and gave off a whistle from his throat. I peeled the gun from his grip, then I stood over him. Wydell didn't move.

'Leave,' I said. 'Forever.'

His breath shoved a furrow into the dirt of the mound. 'You're letting me go?'

'On the run. Yes. If you stop, you know what'll be waiting for you.'

'Why don't you turn me in?'

'By first light, every major law enforcement agency will be looking for you. There won't be a safe place for you anywhere in the country. You won't be able to walk down the street or board an airplane. Who you've been,

384

who you are right now, will cease to exist.' I took a step closer and he cringed a little. I said, 'I'm not gonna turn you in because this is gonna be so much worse.'

My finger had found its way through the trigger guard. His eyes were closed in fearful anticipation, but I pocketed the gun and walked away. When I reached the edge of the field, I paused and looked back. He was still lying there, flat on his face, his arm bent grotesquely out to the side like a broken wing. I could hear his labored breathing. He might have been crying, but I wasn't sure.

48

UCLA was awash in bodies – in lines, at check-points, staggering as one when someone lost their footing – a great human press, filling Dickson Terrace. Flashes popped and signs waved and groups chanted dumb couplets from behind sawhorses. Thousands of people sat on the ground in the quad, concert-style, craning to see the giant video screens suspended from steel cables overhead. The chosen ones funneled to the checkpoints at the broad steps of Royce Hall, where they handed over security passes as if purchasing the right to be patted down, wanded, and walked through metal detectors. Purses and cell phones rode conveyer belts through X-ray machines. Agents with tight, muscular faces peered out over the sawhorses, putting their rope-line skills to work, searching out hands in jacket flaps, the woman who wasn't grinning, the dusky-skinned young man wearing a too-heavy coat, beads of sweat running down temples. Cops wore riot gear, agents wore earpieces, and I wore Charlie's rucksack slung over my shoulder.

Hiding in the crowd, I watched the giant video screens, which showed the C-Span logo and the blank debate stage. Katie Couric's voice rumbled through powerful speakers. The mighty roar of applause compounded as she introduced each candidate.

The picture was surprisingly crisp. Caruthers and Bilton took their places on low-backed stools before acrylic podiums, inadvertently mirroring each other's posture – casual lean to the outside, head cocked with interest and humility, hands laced across a knee. A lush, royal-blue rug bearing the presidential seal stretched beneath the candidates, designating the boundaries should either man decide to pace or roam. Couric perkily continued: *'The debate's town-hall format will permit prospective voters to address their questions directly to the candidates. We ask that you line up in either aisle in front of the microphone, and make sure to introduce yourself and speak clearly when it's your turn.'*

I took a moment to collect myself, to quash the rise of fear in my chest, and then I shoved through the elbow-to-elbow press gaggle and made my way toward the checkpoint.

The speakers conveyed the first question, a woman, shrill with nerves. *'Hello, my name is Cynthia McGinty. My question is for Senator Caruthers. You've said we need a change in our policy in the Middle East. But can we really be blackmailed by the likes of bin Laden into changing our views? Can we really rethink our position because of threats and violence?'*

Jasper Caruthers's smooth voice, a marked contrast with the timidity of his interlocutor's: *'The question in my mind, Cynthia, is whether we can persist with failed policies simply because we fear looking like we're willing to learn from the past.'*

Black Towncars were pulled up onto the walkways and the patio before Royce Hall. Their tinted windows were dark and emotionless, the eyes of predators. The day had gone from Southern California-bright to confused dusk. The buildings that had gleamed just fifteen minutes ago now looked cloaked and grainy.

Caruthers was still going on about reacting to different cultures and updating stances, but finally the next audience member stepped to the microphone: '*Hello, my name is Bill Little, and my question is for President Bilton. As an educator, I've had a hard time understanding the cuts you've advocated while pushing through tax breaks for wealthy corporations . . .*'

My hands swiveled back and forth, tapping my pants on either side. Was I really going to do this? I realized I was holding my breath and I exhaled so hard static tinged my field of vision. I'd gone without oxygen for the past minute. Nice and subtle, Horrigan, teetering red-faced through the crowd.

Adjusting the rucksack, I approached the line of agents, none of whom I recognized. Robotically crossed arms, hair slicked back, asshole-handsome faces murmuring in polite monotones, 'Hands please. Can I see your hands? Hands.' Their eyes swiveled past me. One pressed a finger to the flesh-colored earpiece melded into his head and grinned a sharp grin, a Presidential Detail alpha dog baring his perfect teeth. I recalled Frank's old crack about the Presidential Protective Division guys: two holsters – one for the gun, one for the blowdryer.

Bilton's detail was running the show, of course, but

Caruthers had his faithful crew – five or six agents, according to Wydell – at least one of whom was likely stationed outside, on the lookout for me. Though Caruthers's men didn't know the whole backstory, they'd proven they were all too willing to bend laws to protect their principal.

President Bilton's answer continued, a low-register drone. I sneaked a glance at one of the suspended screens. The bombardment of democracy continued: '*I'm Patsy Ryan and as an elderly person I feel great concern about rising health-care costs. President Bilton, if reelected, would you . . .*'

I walked along the building, glancing at the cordons blocking the side doors. Behind me, the viewers sitting in the quad jeered and clapped, news crews moving among them, bulky with equipment. It was an angry year, an angry election, and the voters weren't afraid to play hardball. '*I'm John Quinn and I'd like to know what the President has to say about the sweetheart deals with war contractors—*'

An overweight college girl stepped aside, leaving behind a wall of her floral perfume and clearing my view to the building. By the last side entrance, his eyes swiveling across the crowd, stood Reid Sever. He was about twenty yards away, behind a line of sawhorses and police officers. I hesitated for a panic-stricken moment that stretched out like warbling piano note.

I rotated away. Caruthers's enormous figure loomed on the screen above me. He had his head bent down, a hand clamped to his cheek, intently focused as Bilton continued to string together catch phrases and slogans. From the corner of my eye, I saw Sever's face lift and freeze with sudden focus. My heart started palpitating.

I turned my head, just barely. Sever was speaking into his wrist. Looking across the quad. There was another Secret Service type – he looked like Brown – touching his earplug. And relaying what he was hearing to the guy next to him. Alan Lambrose.

Then all three looked directly at me. I ran.

Sever hurdled the sawhorses, shouting into his wrist. Rucksack bouncing on my shoulders, I plowed into the heart of the crowd, stepping on legs, tripping over college kids. People scattered, shouting complaints until they saw Sever coming, his Glock clear of the holster. It didn't take long for the news crews to pick up the disruption. Glinting camera lenses swung over to capture me – zooming in from either side, leering from strategically parked news vans, coasting overhead on a crane like Peter Pan in a bad stage production.

I made my way to the heart of the quad and turned, holding my arms wide. The energy of the crowd pulled to me, an electric charge. There were cameras everywhere, people's eyes. Could I actually pull this off? Agent Brown was on Sever's heels, as were several of Caruthers's other agents I recognized from the jogging detail and Induma's walkway. They spread out, closing in at me from all directions, pants whistling as they ran. Innumerable pistols aimed at my head. I waited for the crack of a gunshot, the kiss of jagged lead. People rose, first those nearest me, then in waves, an astonished standing ovation. I thought, at the same time, *this might actually work*, and, *you'll be shot*.

'I'm Nick Horrigan!' I shouted. My voice wasn't thin or

trembling. It was clear as a goddamned bell. 'And I don't have a weapon on me. I have—'

But Sever hammered me, wrapping me up, and then the others were there too, frisking me. Someone ripped the rucksack off my back. There was movement all around us, a wind-up to a stampede. One of the agents shouted, 'He's unarmed! *Unarmed!*'

'What's in the rucksack?'

'Styrofoam peanuts.' The guy was dumping it as he answered.

'*Nothing else?*'

Black shoes stomped near my face, barely missing, as more agents jockeyed for position. I stayed perfectly still, not wanting to give them an excuse to shoot me. An iron bar of a forearm pressed across the back of my neck, grinding my cheek into the ground. Through the ankles and moving bodies, I glimpsed the post supporting the giant horn speakers.

A familiar voice: '*My question is for Senator Caruthers, and it's on behalf of someone who couldn't be here tonight. It's on behalf of Gracie Everett.*'

Despite the lawn smashed to my face, I felt a blast of triumph.

I was hauled roughly to my feet. Cuffs pinched my wrists. I twisted to see the nearest giant video screen, and there Induma was, two stories high, holding the ultrasound aloft so the light streamed through it.

'*Gracie would have been old enough to vote next year. But she was murdered when she was thirteen days old. Along with her mother.*'

A hush passed over the quad, all faces suddenly intent

391

on the screens. The agents around me stiffened and looked at one another, suddenly aware that their crew had been drawn out of the building. A breeze lifted a few of the Styrofoam peanuts from the grass, underscoring my ruse, that Caruthers's men had been diverted out here in pursuit of an empty rucksack, leaving no one inside to shut down the senator's surprise interrogator.

Caruthers sat frozen on the stool – one loafer on the ground, the other touching the footrest as if to keep its bearing. Those brilliant green eyes were lit with alarm. An odd quiet spread through the quad, everyone sensing that something unscripted was taking place. Heads turned, voices hushed, people pointed.

Every set of eyes focused on that black-and-gray film, on the eighteen-week-old curl of Gracie Everett. For a brief moment, she was the center of the universe.

Induma said, '*I have here as well the paternity test revealing that Gracie's father was then-Vice President Caruthers, and a recording implicating him in the murders.*'

Caruthers wilted back into his chair. The lights shined through his green eyes, his unruly hair.

'*You have consistently implored us to question our leaders. To hold them accountable. You said that no man is above the law. You said that every American, no matter his post, no matter his privilege, can be faced down, called to answer. My question for you, from Gracie, is: will you answer?*'

The agents' hands stayed dug into my arms, my neck, but none of us moved. We stood together, frozen, heads tilted back, taking in the spectacle playing out inside and overhead.

Caruthers rose with great dignity, set his microphone on the stool, and walked from the stage.

49

I was held for nearly two weeks on the Mack Jackman murder while the storm brewed, Induma disseminating information from outside, agents and representatives of all stripes poking and prodding at me until it was obvious there was nothing more to get. We turned over the one hundred eighty grand, the ultrasound, the paternity report, Charlie's bone-chip analysis, and the recording of Wydell on the pitcher's mound. I'd done nothing wrong, or at least nothing that the circumstances didn't necessitate. They even opened up Frank's murder file and found nothing to raise an eyebrow at. Having a new ally in the incumbent President probably didn't hurt matters. Charges were dropped and I was released three days before the election.

Returning home, I saw that my place had been ripped apart. The carpets torn up, the plumbing extracted, holes punched in the drywall. It would have been easier just to move, but I decided to stay. Rebuild. It's been a few months, and the place is now functional, but it needs some more cosmetic work. I've been told that these things take time. And, finally, I feel like I have time.

The world, needless to say, is no better for what I have

done. Caruthers lost. I can't say we made him lose, but we sure made him not win. I was his October surprise. Or, more accurately, Gracie Everett was. She only lived thirteen days, but she mattered.

I didn't vote.

The night of his acceptance speech, my old friend Andrew Bilton called to express his gratitude and tell me I was a patriot. But he's still a mediocre human and a worse President. Who would you rather have? A leader who is unthinkingly loyal to opinions you disagree with? Or one who is insincere about opinions you share? A fool or a hypocrite? Too often, it seems, these are our only options. I don't know the answer. Looking at the state of the union, I don't even know that I'd do the same thing over again. All I know is what I did. And I've been told that what you *do* is the measure of a person.

A few weeks after the election, Caruthers was indicted. The connective tissue between him and the murders is thin, but his link can be lab-tested and DNA-analyzed. People were crushed. There were mournful columnists and genuinely dazed talking heads and vehement staffers, holding their devastation beneath an angry veneer of denial. There were even some tears when the news cameras found the right Man or Woman on the Street. I won't say it was like when Bobby Kennedy was shot – neither is it that time, nor is Caruthers such a man – but it was a reminder to everyone that we might be too far gone to have heroes anymore. Maybe that's a good thing.

They made a big show of getting him right when Senate adjourned. Steps of the Capitol Building and all that. The footage has become another tabloid favorite, as overplayed as OJ's Bronco hightailing down the 405 or those Boeing 767s disintegrating into dust and flame. Caruthers being led, handcuffs glinting at the sleeves of his five-thousand-dollar suit. 'This is an outrage,' he says, 'and I look forward to defending against all charges. I'm not concerned in the least.' But in a clip they showed later of him outside the courthouse, he was raising both cuffed wrists to get a trembling cigarette to his lips. Those charges keep proliferating, from murder, to destruction of evidence, to conspiracy, to obstruction of justice, to that new blue-chip favorite: perjury. James Brown took a sweetheart deal to roll, and then two more guys went snitch and the word is the DOJ's putting that mosaic together, piece by piece.

June has stopped showing up for court dates and there are rumors she will file for divorce.

Wydell turned up dead last week in Altamira. In the black-and-white morgue photos, he looked like a homeless person. That neat '50s hairdo grown out into a tangle. Curls of facial hair. Dirt-blackened cheeks. He'd been stabbed in the kidney with a screwdriver for sleeping in a bum's nook on the port, and he'd dragged himself behind a tire-repair shack and bled out.

Given the outstanding arrest warrant and the INTERPOL red notice, they'd done a fine job freezing his money. He had no address or bank account or telephone in his name. His first few weeks, he'd shacked up with his ghosts in a shitty motel in Veracruz, collecting tequila worms and venereal diseases, and burning through what little cash he'd taken. I know how the walls closed in on him at night. I know the bitter taste of panic that greeted him when he woke. I know how he watched people's eyes when he passed them on the street. Waiting for the other shoe to drop. Knowing he could wake up in prison the next morning and every morning after that. Of everything that can grind away at a person, being anonymous is the worst. You give up your power, a bit at a time, until you feel like you're not much of anything at all.

It was shocking to see how poorly a federal agent had fared in just two and a half months on the run, and I must confess a pang of pride at how long I, a nobody kid, had managed. I'd been cracked and damaged, but they hadn't broken me.

I'm inclined to think that Wydell took the easy way out by dying. It's much harder to shoulder the weight of memory, to reconcile with the past, to turn and face your troubles. It's much harder, but I'm finding it worth the struggle.

I am sleeping through the night again. There is an immense power in holding no secrets. I have protection now, in my story being public. If I died, the right people would ask the right questions.

Callie's sketch of Frank hangs boldly in my living room, over a crumbled stretch of drywall. I'd like to think it looks over me, but I know that's not the case. As I recently learned, people are eager to live with stars in their eyes. The problem is, they block out reality. No wonder people want to hide from reality. It's ugly. Brutal. But it can also be graceful, and it offers comforts I'm still acquainting myself with. There are surprises there, not all of them unpleasant.

I thought I had a simple life before. But I didn't.

Simple is going for walks and not checking behind you. Simple is strolling past security cameras and not bothering to turn your head. Entering a restaurant and not scouting the exits. Passing a dark sedan and not having your palms sweat. I'm not saying I'm able to do these things all the time, but I know what they feel like now. It's a start. A fresh one. Day after day.

I pulled into Induma's driveway and sat with the radio on, trying to figure out how I could possibly convey my gratitude to her.

Through the open blinds, I could see her flashing back and forth in the kitchen, cooking herself into a frenzy. I got out, but left the truck running. She was not cooking for me, and I didn't want to intrude.

The Jag rolled in behind me. Alejandro. He jogged over and gave me a hug. He smelled musky, some Rodeo Drive cologne Induma had no doubt selected.

I said, 'I'm glad you guys made up.'

'We have a do-over of our anniversary this weekend. But I give her the gift now because I can't wait.' Proudly, he tugged a Tiffany Blue gift case from his waistband and opened it. A silver charm necklace. He studied my face. 'What?'

I said, 'She can't wear sterling. Gets a rash.'

The case closed with a snap. He turned away, cursed in Spanish.

I said, 'Hold on.'

Back in my glove compartment, the small red jewelry box remained where I'd shoved it weeks ago. The engine hummed; the radio played. I sat and looked at those sapphire-chip earrings. Then I brought the box to Alejandro.

He opened it and whistled. 'The sapphire look *amazing.*'

'Yes,' I said, 'and it's her birthstone.'

'Damn, Nick. You the Casanova.'

I folded his hands over the box. He hopped, excited like a little kid, then hugged me tightly and started for the door.

I said, 'Capra or Howard Hawks.'

He paused.

I said, 'Her favorites. Check out the revival theaters. She loves late matinees. For dinner, take her to Inn of the Seventh Ray, up Topanga. It's all organic and they have plenty of vegetarian stuff. Get a table close to the creek and you can hear the frogs, maybe even see a coyote. Then go to Shutters for hot chocolate. It's the best in town, and they serve it in giant mugs. There are great sofas. The pier's right there. Go for a walk after. It gets cold, so buy her gloves before to surprise her with.'

A few faint lines appeared in that smooth brow. 'But you take her all these places already.'

'No,' I said. 'I never did.'

Relief. That broad smile. Then it faded. An understanding of sorts passed between us. He nodded and headed inside.

I stood on the concrete of the driveway. From my truck's radio, the Stones were telling me I can't always get what I want, though I didn't require the reminder just now.

Alejandro appeared in the kitchen window. Hugged Induma from behind. She spun, surprised at the jewelry box. Opened it. Delight. The flash of those gorgeous white teeth. She kissed him, held up the earrings, put them on. Even from this distance, they looked just as I imagined against her dark skin.

But if you try sometimes, you just might find . . . you just might find . . .

I got into my truck and drove off.

50

I pull up to the big white house and park right in front, in plain view. In the passenger seat, a brown paper bag from Whole Foods, crammed with groceries. I don't get out just yet. It's eight o'clock and dark out. I take a deep breath, tug at the door handle.

Steve answers and we shake hands and make awkward small talk. And then Callie appears, bustling and excited at his shoulder. 'Oh my, and look what you brought.' Her face gleams with almost aggressive pleasure.

Two glasses of red wine wait on the butcher block of the kitchen island, and Steve pours another. Emily sits at the table, reading the dictionary, running her hand, buried in a sleeve, down the rows of words. She glares at us from beneath her hood and stomps upstairs before I can say hello.

Steve curses. Callie starts unpacking the bags, feigning more interest in each item than seems plausible. Steve leans against the refrigerator and sips his wine, staring off at nothing.

Passing, Callie squeezes his arm. 'She's okay.'

Steve says, 'I should go up.'

I say, 'Why don't I?'

Steve looks at me and I cannot read his face. He shrugs. 'Okay.'

I climb the stairs, followed by the sounds of Callie chattering below. She seems happy, giving off that first-date glow. How easy it all seems if you're willing.

Emily has pried some of the Scrabble letters off her door so it just reads *Em*. I can see the hardened globs of glue from the vanquished three letters. I think, *this is good*.

I knock.

'Go a*way*, Dad.'

'It's Nick.'

'What do *you* want?'

'To come in, for starters.'

'Fine.'

She'll allow it, but she'll be unhappy about it.

I enter. She sits on the bed, back to the wall, knees drawn to her chin. She holds an open book down at her shins. I do not know how she can see the book from that angle, but she is intently focused on it. Her hood has fallen away to reveal her face. The maroon and blond streaks are growing out, and her face is so pale it's pasty. She looks much younger than her thirteen years. The TV is on and two joysticks are plugged in, Space Invaders doing their mechanical march across the screen.

Her eyes don't leave the book. She says, slowly, 'The only thing I liked about you was that you didn't like *them*.'

I nod, which is stupid because she's not looking at me.

402

I stand there, lost in the quagmire that is a teenager's mood. The Space Invaders do not seem to pick up on the high-stakes drama.

I wonder how Frank would handle this. I take another step toward the TV, sit heavily, and pick up the remote. Emily watches me from above her knees. I click *Two-Player Game* and do my best, but I always sucked at Space Invaders. The dot-matrix jellyfish chug across the sky, their laser blasts eating away at the bases until my ship fizzles and dies. The second player is up now, but I don't say anything, don't turn my head, don't offer the other remote. It just sits there on the carpet beside me. Emily stares at the screen as the lasers cascade and take out her ship. I play again, wait out her untaken turn, and finish the game, even though she never rises from the bed. When the game is over, I start a new one. I do pretty well this time, clearing a few stages before dying under an alien barrage. The screen flashes *Second Player Ready*.

I think of Frank knocking on my door the night we moved into his house. How he came in and regarded me, his mouth pulled to the side. Before I can think, I am speaking his words: 'What do you want me to not do?'

Her gaze lowers again to the page. The silence stretches out so long that I am certain she won't answer, but I force myself to sit still, to wait, to take it on her time.

Finally, she clears her throat. 'Don't be all weird and brotherly when you're around. No siding with them against me. And don't talk down to me like I'm some kid.' Her eyes are moist. She will not look up.

I turn back to the flashing screen. I say, 'I can manage that.'

Emily puts down her book, crosses the room, and sits next to me.

She picks up the joystick.

Acknowledgements

I have ever-greater gratitude for those who play such a large role behind the scenes, and who make it possible for me to do what I love. Lisa Erbach Vance never ceases to impress and amaze. Aaron Priest remains an invaluable resource, every bit as good as billed. Stephen F. Breimer, Marc H. Glick, Rich Green, and Jess Taylor offered essential input along the way, as did Geoff Baehr, Lucy Childs, Caspian Dennis, Melissa Hurwitz, M.D., Frances Jalet-Miller, Nicole Kenealy, and Chetan Nayak.

I am fortunate enough to have spectacular editors on both sides of the Atlantic, and I pass on a special thanks to Keith Kahla of St Martin's Press, and David Shelley at Little, Brown UK. In fact, the entire team at Sphere was instrumental in establishing me overseas, and I owe much to their hard work and dedication.

Two authors were generous beyond the call with their time: Joe Finder, who provided key guidance at key junctures, and Gerald Petievich, a consummate gentleman, who brought a novelist's sensibility and a

Secret Service agent's knowledge to each question I posed.

Finally, my girls, Rosie and Natalie – our homegrown Laurel and Hardy. And my wife, Delinah, who makes everything that much more meaningful.

I SEE YOU

Gregg Hurwitz

'A performance worthy of applause' *Kirkus* (starred review)

When bestselling thriller writer Andrew Danner wakes up in a hospital bed with no idea how he got there, he is horrified to be told that he is responsible for the murder of his ex-fiancee.

In the resulting celebrity trial, Drew is exonerated on the grounds of temporary insanity caused by a recent brain tumour. But he still has no idea if he did kill Genevieve, and is desperate to find out. Haunted by what appear to be his bizarre night-time actions, Drew is shocked when another woman is discovered dead, murdered in the same way as Genevieve.

Trying to clear his name and understand what's happening to him, Drew enlists the help of a tame forensic scientist, a sympathetic detective, his staunch friend Chic who has helpful underworld connections, and an over-confident teenager. Can Drew discover what really happened that night and unmask the real killer?

'A thrilling, mind-bending journey, it is also deeply humane and beautifully written. You'll turn the final page with profound regret' Dennis Lehane